BUOYANT

THE HEIST OF TITANIC II

Alan Hartwell

Published by Bright Ideas

United Kingdom

Bright Ideas Publishing

www.alanhartwell.com

Book Layout © 2017 BookDesignTemplates.com

Buoyant/Alan Hartwell. -- 1st ed.
ISBN 978-1-0685612-0-7

Dedicated to Eric Hartwell CBE.

Visit me at:
alanhartwell.com

1

Scott Rainey thrust the clutch pedal to the carpet and coaxed the chrome gear-stick into reverse. He slid his 1967 Mustang into the spot with a precision honed by a decade of manoeuvring cars around a tight showroom. It burbled for a moment at a rough idle, and then he killed the ignition.

The following fifteen seconds passed like minutes as he ran through how the coming hours should play out. He reached for the door catch but stopped short, the tremor in his fingers an unwelcome surprise that only confirmed what his chest had been telling him all morning.

'Big day,' he said and closed his eyes. In through the nose, count three, out through the mouth. In through the nose, count three, out through the mouth. After a minute, he again reached for the door catch. The tremor remained, but it had reduced. Or so he told himself.

He got out, locked the door, and ran his fingers along the flawless white paintwork as his polished Oxfords crunched into the gravel of the church car park. A moment later he reached the smoothly worn stone slabs which led to the open doors. But once on the path, the click, click, click of a stone embedded in his heel caused him to stop, raise the shoe to his calf and prise the offending chip from the rubber. With luck, that would be the only unplanned irritation of the day.

Inside, the weight of incense filled the air. This spicy nectar mingled with a lighter bouquet from the floral arrangements and sweetened with each step he took down the aisle. A congregation of around fifty sat patiently, dotted with bright spring dresses and stiff collars. He smiled at those who turned as he passed, and by the time he'd reached the almost vacant front pew, the light organ music had gone a small way to soothing those jangling nerves. He sat and slid along the polished wood to where his cousin Mandy stared ahead.

'Where's Jay? Has he been here yet?'

She shook her head.

'He wasn't in his room when I left hotel, he was supposed to be arriving with me.'

She shrugged, so Scott turned to the row behind.

'Has anyone seen Jay? Did he come with any of you?'

A mixture of shrugs and shaking heads was definitely not the answer he wanted. He pulled out his phone and opened the messages app.

Where are you? Get a move on. She'll be here any minute.

He continued to check his phone every few seconds for the next three minutes. No reply. He decided to call, but it went straight to voicemail.

The most important day in his life and still Jay had to take all of the attention with his absence. If he didn't arrive soon, then Jasmine was going to have to wait outside until he turned up. The embarrassment of it, further compounding her father's opinion of him.

After five more minutes he tried Jasmine's number. Another message, another call, and then repeatedly over the next fifteen minutes, but both his brother and his bride-to-be remained elusive. He turned to his cousin Mandy once again.

'Where the hell are they?' Another shrug. He couldn't take much more of this, he needed to get some air, but checked his messages one more-

'Excuse me,' Scott snapped away from his phone at the pastor's voice, 'but we have another service booked at twelve thirty so it might be wise to consider moving you to another day.'

'Give me a minute will you, Father? I'm sure she's just held up in traffic or something.' But he had no idea what was going on, and where the hell was Jay? Up to no good with a bridesmaid more like.

'Sorry I'm late, had a bit of… well, an issue going on,' Jay said, and then looked away.

'Jay, where have you been?'

'I've got this,' he slid into the pew and held something out for Scott to take. 'Think you should read it.'

Scott unfolded the heavily embossed sheet of hotel notepaper to reveal Jasmine's handwritten note.

I'm so, so sorry, but there's no easy way to say this. I just can't go through with it today or any other day, as I've now realised. I know this is hard to read, but there's someone else, and it'd be a lie to say it meant nothing. It did. I don't know if this makes any sense, maybe I'm rambling, but all I can say is goodbye. We had fun, but now things are different. I hope you understand, sorry. X

Understand, how could he possibly understand? This was their day, their special day. What did she mean by someone else? He reread the note and then once more. Finally, he screwed it up and shoved it into his jacket pocket. He rose, barged past Jay into the aisle, and stormed towards the doors. He needed air.

Outside, the early spring sunshine glinted off the Mustang, and he made straight for it, pausing only to jam the key into the lock. He missed at the first attempt and left an ugly gouge across the paintwork.

'Arrggh.'

The second attempt succeeded and he slumped into the driver's seat.

Today should have been perfect. Everything planned, everything practised, everything checked. But the plan had gone to hell, dragged there by some unknown demon. He started the engine and spat gravel at the church as he spun across the car park and out onto the road.

Six minutes later the tyres screeched in anger as he careered down a country lane just outside the drowsy village of Wescott. He endured a further minute of branches and foliage whipping along the immaculate paintwork and then entered the quarter-mile driveway which led to The Buckingham Crescent Hotel.

A moment later the Georgian mansion came into view. He raced towards it and slammed the brake pedal into the floor as the car slid to a halt beneath its vast portico. He jumped out, engine still running, and ignored the valet's outstretched hand as he sprinted up the steps. The doorman had only a second to react and get the door open before he burst through it.

'Good morning, sir.'

'Jasmine Bailey,' he barked at the receptionist. 'What room is she in?'

'I'm sorry sir, that's not information I can divulge without her permission. If you want, I could leave a note for-'

'I'm her fiancé, damn it, and if you check the booking, I paid for the room.'

'Let me just check for you, your name please sir?'

'Scott Rainey. Please hurry, this is urgent.'

'One moment, sorry the system's running a bit slow today…' It felt like someone was walloping his chest with a mallet.

'Ahh, here we are.' Another pause, 'she checked out at seven twenty-three this morning.'

'What? That can't be right.'

'It is what the system's telling me sir, and her room has already been prepared for…'

He was no longer listening. Home, she must have gone home. It was cold feet, nothing more. He ran back towards the entrance, the doorman prepared for him this time, and down the stone steps two at a time. But now his Mustang had vanished.

'Where's my bloody car?' he shouted to the doorman, who casually tipped his head to the right. Scott followed his prompt to see the valet walking back towards them from the far side of the building. He sprinted towards the lad, snatched the key, and was charging back down the twisty lane moments later.

Someone else. What could she have meant by that? Surely there couldn't be another man involved? Cold feet, that was definitely it, must be. She'd just needed a plausible excuse. He'd reassure her, talk some sense into her. She always was a bit flaky.

Phone, where was his damned phone? Must call her and stop this madness. He patted his pockets, not there. He glanced to the passenger seat, also not there. But a momentary flash of reflected light from the passenger footwell, and there it was. A second look confirmed it, but proved to be just enough of a distraction to misjudge the upcoming corner. The rear wheel clipped the muddy bank and sent the car into a tailspin. An ungodly scream and a loud crunch as his nose walloped the steering wheel. Dazed, he pushed away from it, but caught his thumb in the spinning spokes, snapping it with such violence that a bone burst through the skin. A slam as his head hit the side window, the uncontrollable sequence of events drawing him further into the depths of hell. Tarmac, sky, tarmac as the car spiralled onto its roof and then back again. Roaring, shrieking metal, tarmac, sky, tarmac as it went over again. Finally, a massive, jarring impact as the car walloped into a cherry tree and brought his ordeal to a sudden, violent end.

Woozy and confused, he looked down at his legs. One was broken for sure, the other trapped by a jagged piece of metal under the dashboard. His right arm also had one too many joints. The sight of pink cherry blossom falling all around him like confetti was the last thing he registered before consciousness bled away.

2

Six weeks later, Scott sat in a plastic-coated armchair next to the bed which had been his home since the accident. The turnover of patients in the orthopedic ward had been endless. All of them arrived broken, were then patched up, and finally sent on their way before more broken people replaced them. He had to admire the staff for putting up with the endless loop of complaints, groans, pills and plasters. It was a thankless job.

'Nice holiday?' Jay said as he walked down the row of beds. Scott struggled to his feet without acknowledging the comment.

'Make yourself useful and pass me that walking stick.'

'Calm down, Granddad, I'm getting it.'

Scott took it in his left hand, as his right still wore the bandages from his many surgeries. The surgeon had installed several plates and screws to return both his hand and his arm to their rightful positions, but it was going to be sore for a long time to come. He'd been lucky, and ninety per cent of his functionality should return once he'd healed.

'Get me out of here. And don't forget my party bag.'

He nodded to the paper pharmacy bag on the bedside cabinet.

'Don't mind if I do. It's a shame that might go missing between here and your place.'

'Just get me home, will you?'

Once downstairs, Scott waited on the steps. An ancient silver Audi estate pulled up and Jay flung the passenger door open. Moments later, they were on the main road.

'I'll need to stop, grab some milk and stuff. I could do with some lunch too as the food in there wasn't exactly Michelin star.'

'Gotcha. How about stopping in Shere? I've got something to drop off thereabouts so we could combine it.'

'So long as it's not my painkillers that you've sold while you were getting the car, that'll be fine.'

'Would I do such a devilish thing?'

'Yes, Jay, you would.'

'I'm so hurt,' he stuck out his bottom lip.

'You will be if you have.'

'Trust me.'

'Like that's turned out so well in the past.'

After fifteen minutes, Jay pulled the car up outside The White Horse, a pub central to the country village. Scott wrestled with getting out and eventually managed to stand, balancing on one leg until he could retrieve his stick from the footwell. But Jay accelerated away before he'd even closed the door, the momentum of the car slamming it shut.

He shook his head and hobbled across the road to an outside table. Once he had managed to sit, lifting his bad leg over the bench seat with his good arm, he looked up to the sky. The lightly broken cloud had given way to a weak burst of spring sunshine. It wasn't that warm, but the fresh air tasted good after a month and a half of the antiseptic and vomit which had filled his nostrils during his incarceration. Jay reappeared, swinging his car keys around on a tether like a cowboy about to rope a steer.

'What 'ya having, bruv?'

'Orange juice and a jacket potato, cheese and bacon please,' he threw his debit card onto the table. 'On me.'

'Nice one, back in a jiffy.'

Some minutes passed before a maroon Bentley convertible drew up in the small square that the pub bordered. A woman on the passenger side got out and ran into the convenience store. Scott shook his head. Sure, these drugs he'd been given were potent, but strong enough to give him hallucinations? He doubted it, but then again...

She came out of the shop a moment later, so he squinted to get a better look. Could it really be her?

'Jasmine,' he shouted as she reached the car. She looked up, paused a second, and then slid back into the passenger seat. The driver quickly turned the car in a tight circle to return in the direction from which they had come. It afforded Scott a much closer look. It was her, no doubt whatsoever.

'Jasmine,' he called again as he struggled to stand. But as he rose, he plunged his injured hand onto the table to lever himself up. The bolt of pain was immediate and vicious. He stumbled back, caught his bad ankle, and it twisted beneath him. The awkward fall had him wallop his head on the cobbles and fire another bolt of pain, this time throughout his entire body. He lay helpless and overwhelmed at what had just happened.

'Bloody Hell, I can't leave you for five minutes without self-harming.'

'Shut up, Jay, just help me up.' Jay stooped to grab his bandaged arm. 'Not that one, you idiot.'

'I'm not the idiot rolling around on the floor.'

'Just help me, will you?' When he was back on the bench, he took a second to gather his thoughts. 'That was her, Jasmine, in the Bentley with some bloke.'

'Oh yeah, I meant to say. She was in one of those gossip mags a couple of weeks ago, met him in a coffee shop near the film studios in Shepperton apparently.'

'Met who?'

'That bloke, what's his name, you know…'

'No, Jay, obviously I don't.'

'That actor, Jacob something, Jacob Delta, something like that maybe.'

'Jacob Del Toro?'

'Yeah, that's him, does those action films.'

'The wedding was six weeks ago, so she can't have met him just two weeks ago.'

'Don't shoot the messenger.'

'That's a major problem.'

'For who?'

'Me. How am I going to get her back when I'm up against him?'

Jay laughed for a moment before answering.

'Mate, you're a failed second-hand car dealer who supports his income with small-time jewellery shop heists.'

'Keep your voice down.'

'You've got no chance with a megastar like Del Toro, so just forget it, move on.'

'We need to step things up, go a bit more bigtime. Bigger heists have bigger rewards. That's the only way. And get me a very large vodka to go with that orange, will you?'

'Is that a good idea? You know how you get with–'

'Just do it. I don't want to have to struggle up there myself.'

'Okay, okay, consider it done.' Jay stood, leaving his pint on the table. 'Are you sure about this?'

Scott grabbed Jay's pint with a trembling hand and downed it in one.

3

Eighteen months later

Scott shoved the door to the high-end jewellery shop open and held it for his partner. His jaw clenched and his shoulders were tight, but there was no going back now.

Inside, a multitude of downlights reflected off the glass and chrome cabinets to create swirls of light on the tinted lens through which he peered. His eyes adjusted as he took in his surroundings. The shop was modern, big enough to park six cars, and each glittering square metre held enough stock to set him on the road of winning Jasmine back. Was that why he felt so buzzed? Or was it the danger? The chance of getting caught?

Three people stood by the sales counter at the far end. Scott and his partner, Pascal, drew sawn-off shotguns from their chest holsters.

'On the floor, now.'

His demand sounded slightly muffled behind the dark visor of his motorcycle helmet, but his intention was clear to the people ahead of him. He waved his gun in their direction before pointing the muzzle to the floor.

The fifty-something woman lay down on her front, hands behind her head. The sapling of an assistant in an inexpensive suit followed. But the elderly customer in golfing attire lowered himself with more care, his white-moustached upper lip flinching with each creak of his knees.

'Come on, we don't have all day.' Scott's grip tightened around his weapon. He had to assume that the police were already on their way. There was no time to waste. Gems and watches sparkled in their sleek cabinets, but he stuck to his hierarchy. Start with the highest value items first, and work down.

'Is anybody else in the building?' He asked. The woman shook her head so he continued towards her. He tapped his boot on her ankle. 'On your feet and open the safe.'

She hesitated a moment, looking at the elderly customer spread out on the floor nearby.

'This is an outrage. My family has owned–'

His boot struck her again, but this time with slightly more force.

'I'm in charge here, do as I say, or I'll blow your face into that carpet.'

She drew herself up, teeth chattering, and grasped the countertop for support. Scott gestured to the rear of the shop with the gun. After a second, she started towards the office.

Come on, come on, get a move on. She fumbled at the safe's dial, fingers shaking, and then paused to compose herself. A moment later the heavy door swung open with a shudder.

The woman stepped back and glowered at him. Her face turned red as tears traced down her cheeks.

'You disgust me.'

'Don't give me a reason,' he raised the gun. 'Back in there, on the floor,' he motioned with the weapon.

She responded after a pause, long enough to show defiance but not so long as to prompt reprisal. He watched her walk back into the shop, and then his eyes glanced to the front door. His partner Pascal remained vigilant.

Then his attention returned to the woman. She was obediently lowering herself to the carpet. He then slipped back into the office. Once inside, he put the shortened shotgun on top of the safe and slid the rucksack from his back. The safe was a decent size, about one metre cubed. He saw every shelf crammed with antique necklace boxes and modern display cases. He smiled at the potential value of the haul and snatched them out in turn, opening each box and dumping their contents into his rucksack, filling it quickly. Next, he opened the ring boxes. Gold and platinum bands set with every stone imaginable, all emptied into his bag. But he froze at the sight of one in particular. He took a closer look as his gloved hand began to shake.

It was a white-gold De Carlo Pavé engagement ring with a heavy Princess-cut diamond in the centre. The band was set with alternating sapphires and smaller diamonds, a tiny ruby opposite the princess on the palm side. It was Jasmine's. She had never given it back to him after... It had been almost two years, a coincidence? It couldn't be, could it? His shoulders drew tight again as his head swam with thoughts of her, of that cheeky smile, of their wedding that didn't...

'Snap out of it.'

He slipped the ring into an external side pocket of his rucksack, away from the rest of the haul. Take a proper look later.

Once the safe was empty, he rushed back into the shop but paused at the counter.

'Concentrate, keep focussed.'

His tinted visor fogged momentarily. He shot back into the office and slid his gun from the top of the safe. Back in the shop, he began on the cabinets behind the counter. His thoughts went briefly to his second crew, raiding Mrs Braithwaite's competitors sixty metres away. Both jewellery shops were being hit simultaneously. A pair of two-man teams working in tandem, but how were the others doing? He'd find out soon enough.

The shop was eerily quiet, the laboured ticking of a grandfather clock a metronome to the choreographed robbery. He looked at Pascal, who glanced down to the stopwatch on a cord around his neck and nodded. They had time for the window.

Each glass divider drew back smoothly, so he reached in and stuffed handfuls of watches and diamond-encrusted gold into the second rucksack he wore on his front. A moment later he heard a tap, tap, tap. The sound of well-oiled steel on glass was Pascal's signal. Time was up. Scott pulled the front rucksack from his body, made his way to the entrance and handed it to his partner before they burst out of the front door.

Each mounted a large superbike, and they both slid their guns into chest-mounted holsters. They fired the engines into life and took off down the incline of the cobbled High Street.

They made good time around the one-way system and then went south towards Godalming. Two minutes later, Scott saw the bikes of Jay and Ramirez, fresh from holding up the other jewellery shop, and they joined them on the twin lanes of the A3 south towards Portsmouth.

He led as they weaved between the occasional cars and leaned into the winding bends of the road, confirming his research that it would be virtually empty at this time of day. He kept a watchful eye in his mirrors for the inevitable chase all the same.

A bridge in the distance signalled the start of it. A squad car screamed across, with blue lights pulsing. It took the slip road and joined the A3 fifty yards ahead but stood little chance. Scott pulled back the throttle and had the bike up past one hundred miles per hour in a blink. His crew did likewise. The buffeting of the wind became so violent that he tucked in as tight as he could behind the fairing to ease the strain. Sweat traced down his forehead, but only a fool would release the handlebars at this speed to flick the visor open and wipe it away.

They reached one-fifty in seconds, and any police cars were relegated to tiny spots in the rear-view mirrors.

He knew it couldn't be that easy, and tensed when he saw the next junction in the distance. Five more patrol cars had joined in the chase. As they closed in on the string of marked and unmarked cars, he quickly anticipated what might come next.

The cars snaked left and right in formation across the width of the road in a gradually decelerating roadblock. He slowed to the speed of the police cars and they had clearly fallen into a trap. They were down to what felt like a walking pace, forty miles per hour and still slowing. His rear-view mirror showed the officers that had disappeared a few junctions earlier were also closing in behind them. They needed to do something, and fast.

The cars ahead swerved from side to side, and after a moment, his opportunity came. A small gap had appeared between two marked cars, so he pinned the throttle and shot through.

A glance in his mirror saw Pascal also make it through, and then Jay. But the gap disappeared once the vehicles closed ranks to trap the last rider. A puff of smoke from a locked brake, a shower of sparks, and Ramirez tumbled end over end on the tarmac, his bike sliding to a halt on its side.

The patrol cars screeched to a stop, blocking the road. Uniformed and plain-clothed officers were out and running towards the felled rider.

Scott watched in his mirror. He braked hard, spun the bike around, and headed back to help his accomplice.

Ramirez was pinned to the ground by two uniforms, and the number of officers around him increased by the second. Scott screeched to a stop six metres away, drew the shotgun from his chest holster and fired a thundering shot into the air. He levelled the barrels at the officers. One by one, they retreated. Ramirez rose to his feet and ran to Scott in a half-hop, half-limping jog. He then climbed aboard the pillion seat. Scott holstered the shotgun, stamped the bike back into gear and charged off in pursuit of the others. With the police cars blocking the road further back and the delay it had caused, the road ahead was now empty.

The reprieve was short-lived, though. Two miles later, Scott's ears were invaded by the loud thud of a low-flying helicopter. Outrunning it would not be an option.

He pushed the limit, but one fifty-five was as fast as he dared. Keep it steady, they were almost there.

The buffeting and drag of his rucksack, plus the unexpected passenger, made it difficult for his tensed arms to keep control.

The bike was unstable, and his recently healed hand throbbed with pain. Then his visor began to fog.

Arms, legs, everything ached with the effort to hold on so damned tight, but there had to be an element of danger, or just anybody could do this. His temples throbbed against the helmet lining, his pulse high and his focus absolute.

With vision blurred, he glanced to the mirrors: still clear. The few cars he'd caught up to were now becoming a hindrance, prompting horn blasts, but the traffic was manageable and well spread out.

The Hindhead tunnel came into view as the road straightened, and his pace picked up again. He was closing in rapidly on the others. A glance overhead confirmed the helicopter was still close, maybe too close. He took the lead once more, hopefully, they'd make it in time.

A black pickup truck entered the tunnel ahead, sitting in the fast lane but holding a sedate pace. A parcel delivery van came up fast behind it. The van flashed its lights, but the pickup didn't pull across. After a moment and a few more flashes, the van overtook on the inside with the driver gesticulating.

The helicopter was still low but now forced to pull up rapidly to avoid colliding with the hillside. There was a burst of fumes from the exhaust as the pilot reached his altitude and dipped the nose, throttles pinned, in an effort to make it to the tunnel's exit before the bikes. It would land on the carriageway to block their exit, Scott was sure of that.

He stole a glance over his shoulder, the wind incredibly turbulent as he pulled out of the protective bubble of the bike's screen. The police pursuit was still a fair way off. They entered the tunnel and cut their speed to that of the black pickup. He and Jay pulled slightly ahead of it.

Scott watched in his mirror as Pascal drew alongside the bed, matching the truck's pace, before hopping first up onto the seat of his motorcycle and then releasing the handlebars to leap from it into the back of the pickup.

The bike shook violently, the front wheel losing control. It smashed into the side of the tunnel once, twice, and then slid along the floor in a burst of sparks and cartwheeling plastic.

Jay was next. Same process, same result. His bike slid but was engulfed in flaming vapour as the sparks ignited the fuel tank and billowed black smoke.

Ramirez was third, Scott lining up with the rear, like the others, to allow the bulky Marine Commando to step from the pillion seat into the truck.

Finally, Scott. He drew alongside the bed once more in preparation for his jump. Up onto the seat, but as he let go of the handlebar, it caught the side of the truck. The bike lurched sideways, away from the vehicle.

His leap wasn't enough to make it into the bed. Both arms and half of his torso were in, but his lower half dangled over the side. Timberlands kicked and bucked with each momentary strike on the fast-moving tarmac below. He twisted and fought to climb up through jolts of pain.

There was no time to think as the end of the tunnel approached, and it would definitely give their game away. Jay grabbed one arm, Ramirez the other. They tugged, but his rucksack had caught on something, keeping his body twisted. Another more aggressive pull From Ramirez, a rip, and they hauled him up, legs fighting for traction on the bodywork. He scrabbled frantically over the side and into the truck.

Pascal yanked the tarpaulin over them a second before daylight burst onto the truck's bed as it exited the tunnel. The thudding helicopter was only a few feet above them, waiting for the bikes that would never appear.

'Merde, that was close,' Pascal said, his accent Parisian.

'Timed to perfection,' Scott said, still shaking with adrenalin.

Wesley drove the pickup truck south, singing badly to Blur's "Parklife". The windows open, and not a care in the world, or so an observer might think.

They continued for two junctions before taking a slip road into the small village of Liphook. Three minutes later, they were on the Rake Road, and a mile after that, the houses thinned to a landscape of mostly fields.

The pickup slowed near a For Sale board and turned left down a narrow, wooded track towards a smallholding. It pulled to a stop in a clearing just before they reached the property.

Alone, partly obscured by trees, sat a light bronze Audi Q8 with two Disney stickers on the tinted rear window. They climbed from the back of the stolen truck and transferred the haul into the Audi, stowing the rucksacks in the rear but leaving the helmets and leather jackets behind.

Scott slid into the driver's seat of the Audi and started the engine with an iPad. Jay climbed into the passenger seat. The faint smell of baby vomit hung in the air, but dissipated once the air conditioning came to life.

Wesley popped open the fuel flap before leaving the cab of the pickup. Pascal removed a rag damp with petrol from a sealed bag in the truck's bed, stuffed it into the fuel tank's filler neck, and lit it with the flame of his Zippo. They ran to the Audi, hopped into the rear, and Scott pulled away.

Once at the end of the track, he waited for the boom and then turned right, back towards the village of Liphook.

'Everybody good?' A mix of cheers, whoops and a 'Right on,' from Ramirez filled the interior.

'Ramirez, you hurt after that tumble?'

'Couple of bruises maybe. Man, I love Kevlar padding.'

Scott smiled, ran his fingers through his hair a couple of times to untangle it, and then turned to the passenger seat once the noise had calmed. His brother Jay finished lighting a cigarette and then turned to stare out of the window.

'Ours went well,' Scott said. 'The owner was a little prickly, but the safe was brimmed. I think it's been a good haul my end, how about you two?'

Jay turned back to him, exhaled a cloud of smoke and then paused.

'Well, obviously I did better than you, like always.'

Scott reached for his door panel, and his finger found the window switches. He lowered both his and the passenger's side a couple of inches. Jay smiled sarcastically and then returned to the view outside. He then pressed the switch to close his window.

It always had to be a competition.

Scott pulled a pair of sunglasses from his top pocket and slid them on, his attention back on the road as they sped along under a vivid sapphire sky.

4

Detective Inspector John Sharpe stopped at the tunnel entrance. He tossed the stub of his cigarette to the ground and crushed it under a well-worn brogue. He was the first man of rank on the scene.

'It's a bit of a mess in there, sir.'

'Thank you for that accurate report, constable. Do you have anything more constructive to add, or is that the sum of your appraisal?

'Actually, don't worry. I'm sure I can draw my own conclusions, but if any earth-shattering insight hits you before I've concluded my inspection, then please feel free to share it.'

'Very good sir, will do.'

'And let me know when the Scene of Crime officers get here. The quicker we get this tunnel re-opened to the public, the better.'

Sharpe walked with his partner, Detective Sergeant Lorenzo Rossi, into the mouth of the tunnel, and both coughed involuntarily on the acrid smell of burnt plastic and spilt fuel.

After a moment to recover, they continued. It took them several minutes to get far enough into the tunnel to round the first bend and get a clear line of sight to the mess the first riderless bike had made.

'Pay attention, Rossi. I'd conclude that the motorcycle initially bounced off the curved tunnel wall here,' he pointed to the fresh scrapes with his pen whilst they walked.

'Then continued on its wheels for a few more yards before impacting the side once more,' again gesturing with his pen, 'this time probably with enough force to lose stability and dump the bike onto its side.'

He drew a small tape measure from his pocket and measured the marks in the wall. He wrote his findings in a notebook before continuing to where the bike had come to rest several yards later.

'The scene seems fairly tame by all accounts,' he continued, Rossi nodding along, 'but the heavy soot in the air gives me a clue that not all the bikes ended their journeys quite so sedately.'

'No, Boss, that's for sure.'

Lumps of broken plastic bodywork and headlights littered the road. Sharpe paced the length of the gouges in the tarmac to calculate the speed of impact and wrote the estimation in his notebook along with a quick sketch of the trajectory.

He re-paced the length to be sure, but the spilt oil from the bike proved too much of a challenge for the worn soles of his shoes, and he slipped over backwards, landing awkwardly on the tarmac.

'Boss!' Rossi said, rushing towards him.

'I'm fine,' Sharpe replied as he struggled to his feet. He chucked the tape measure to his colleague.

'Go and measure something, will you?'

Rossi caught the tape easily before retracing his steps to the initial impact point. Sharpe continued into the tunnel, the stench of petrol getting stronger. Then he realised it was his jacket, soaked in it from the floor.

'Bloody marvellous.'

After he'd removed the offending item and dropped it to the ground, the smell persisted. A quick sniff confirmed that his shirt was equally as sodden with the acrid fuel. He paused, rubbed his temples for a moment, berated himself for having the foolish urge to light a cigarette, and continued.

Only when he rounded the next bend was the extent of the destruction evident. He observed two further bikes in the long, straight section of the tunnel that followed. Both lay on their sides, but only one recognisable as the motorcycle it once was. The other looked to have impacted the wall in the recess that housed a fire exit.

He cast his eyes over the now extinguished mess of molten plastic, aluminium and steel, wondering how it could lead him to the identity of the thieves. He paused to think for some moments and made further notes. Then, with a renewed lust for nicotine, he turned to walk back to the entrance. But he stopped almost immediately as a glint caught his eye.

He crouched to investigate, and saw something which surprised him. Extremely rare for someone who had been in the force as long as he had.

'Well, well, what have we got here?'

*****

Scott eased the front of the Audi up to the rear bumper of a small Winnebago. He pulled the handbrake up and left it in gear. They climbed out, stretched, and retrieved their rucksacks from the boot. He then led them to the closest exit and up the stairs. His thoughts were totally dominated by the ring and his need to check if it really was Jasmine's.

Once they reached the main passenger deck, he made straight for the toilet. Once inside a cubicle, he swung the rucksack from his shoulder but froze in disbelief. The walls closed in, his head spun and a deep sense of dread overcame him.

'No, it can't be gone.' He pulled at the rucksack where the side pocket had been ripped open, and just a flap of fabric remained.

5

Candy Jones climbed onto the bus just outside Kingston University. The familiar filthy parade of charity shops and fried food establishments slid by the window as the bus set off, and she made her way down the aisle. There were only three seats left, so she took one halfway down, next to a woman who looked to be in her late seventies.

Candy slid her bag between her ankles and took out a heavy folder. She fanned the pages and stopped at the page titled 'The Crown Vs Shilling, Robert'. The trial date was the fourteenth of May, 2012. Over ten years ago now, but it had been a landmark case. She struggled to see why, but maybe that was just the fatigue setting in again.

She looked through the transcript, a good two inches thick, and settled in to absorb as much of it as she could before she got home.

'Are you a solicitor, dear?'

Trust her to get some nutter when she was trying to concentrate. She ignored the woman, but then a nudge came.

'No,' Candy said and went back to her legal documents.

'Only I can't seem to get anywhere with the Citizen's Advice lot, so you can probably help me. Only it's my neighbours, see, makes an awful din, they do.'

Candy continued to ignore her, hoping she'd get the hint.

'Especially when it's Countdown on. My favourite, see, and they ruin it with all that din they make. Shouting and banging, it's like they're in one of those wrestling shows. You know the ones, on late at night they are.'

It was a challenge to grasp even the gist of the case, what with so much jargon and 'legal speak' to get her head around.

'Do you watch it?' another nudge, 'Countdown, that is, not the wrestling.' She giggled. 'Mind you, I can't see a girl like you watch–'

'I'm trying to concentrate,' Candy snapped. 'So, if you don't mind,' but heat filled her cheeks when she saw how hurt the old woman looked. 'Sorry, I meant can I just get on with my reading, please? It's very important.'

'Charming, just trying to be friendly. People these days have no…'

She gave up, slammed the file and closed her eyes for the rest of the journey, fighting off the sleep that would be so easy to give in to.

Once they'd passed Feltham Young Offender's Institution she gathered her stuff, stood, and made her way to the front. It was a three-minute walk, down an alley and across a footbridge, before she reached the top of her road. She knew something was wrong, even from fifty yards away.

The front door wasn't just open, it hung crookedly from one hinge. There was also someone on the floor, just inside, unmoving.

'Christian!' she shouted as she began to run, but the closer she got, the clearer it became that it wasn't her boyfriend, but a woman. A woman with long blonde hair, just like hers. Just like her sister's. She dropped her bag and sprinted.

'Becky!'

6

Jay took the wheel for the final part of their journey to Paris. They arrived well into the night and dumped the Audi in a car park on the outskirts, then split into two groups to head into the centre.

Scott, Jay and Pascal took the Metro, Wesley and Ramirez a mix of busses and taxis, the gems and watches split between them along with the hauls from two previous London robberies. Scott peered into his rucksack, it was almost brimmed with jewels, but he'd pushed them down to make a little space at the top for a few toiletries and a change of clothes. Had Jasmine's ring just been a fantasy? A defective memory? Had it really happened?

After a day in the beautiful city's cafés and tourist spots, they arrived at Gare-de-Lyon by early evening to join the meandering overnight train to Marseilles. His brief had been simple. Pretend not to know each other whilst in public, then all meet back at their six-sleeper carriage at ten to bed down early. No alcohol until the other end when they were in relative safety and the gems had been unloaded to Terry the Fence.

The train was due to depart at ten to seven, so he glanced at his battered stainless-steel Rolex to confirm he had enough time for a quick purchase. A survey of the area confirmed the ex-Marine Ramirez was in the station, trying to hide his limp as he walked along eating a sandwich. It looked the size of a kiddie's party triangle in his hands. Pascal, the slimly built Frenchman, sat reading Le Monde on a nearby bench. Wesley and Jay were nowhere in sight. He pushed on and spotted Wesley, the driver, exiting a hamburger joint.

Scott noticed a high number of armed soldiers patrolling the station, and more gendarmes than he'd have thought normal for a regular day. Could they be for a gang of jewel thieves to show themselves? His jaw tightened. A line of retail shops ran along two sides of the concourse and he scoured the windows, then spotted what he was looking for.

'Bonjour,' the salesman greeted as he entered the designer luggage shop.

'Hi, err, bonjour, I'm looking for a small suitcase.' He mimed the size of a carry-on bag, 'with wheels.'

'Ahh yes, monsieur, we have just what you are looking for.' The slim man hurried across the shop in small, brisk steps to a window display. He showed Scott some leather cases offering not just the convenience of wheels but a telescopic handle with which to pull it along.

'Perfect, I'll…' Scott's eyes focussed beyond the glass to the other side of the concourse where Jay was talking animatedly. He had a gendarme on either side of him.

'Monsieur… Monsieur?'

'Yes, fine, I'll take it.'

'As you wish, would sir like it boxed?'

'No, it's fine.'

The man returned to the counter, produced a card machine and punched in some numbers before sliding it towards him.

Scott waved his card at the contactless icon, but it bleeped disapprovingly.

'Apologies sir, it is a limit of fifty Euro contactless.'

Only then did Scott see he was being charged just under four hundred for the small case. Eager to find out what trouble Jay had found, he stabbed his card into the slot too soon, prompting another beep.

'Une moment.'

The salesman painstakingly re-entered the information. Scott sneaked another look through the window, but Jay and the gendarmes were gone. The tension increased between his temples, and he ran his hand through his hair.

The shopkeeper held out the machine. Four digits and a green button confirmed the sale. Scott stuffed his torn rucksack inside the case, not wanting to lose anything else from it.

He went back out to the departures area, where the rows of trains sat at rest with their two red taillights glaring at him disapprovingly. Like demons coming for him.

Ramirez and Pascal were no longer there; already aboard? Wesley was through the platform barriers and walking along the carriages. Scott checked his watch once more, twelve minutes to seven, two minutes to go. He walked towards the platform, scanning as best he could for police, but it was difficult to be subtle without sunglasses. Where was Jay?

'Carriage neuf, monsieur,' the guard advised after he'd got through the automatic barrier.

'Merci.'

Scott continued down the platform, but became acutely aware of sirens in the distance that were definitely getting louder. What to do? Get on the train and hope it disembarked before the police arrived? Run down the tracks? Head back to the Metro and try to blend in? The second two would abandon his plan, which was not something he relished, but was the first option viable? It was a tough call, so he kept his options open by sitting on a bench. He checked his watch, one minute to go.

He checked it once more. Fifty seconds. But was it right? He pulled out his phone for confirmation.

At thirty seconds and the bleep of the doors, he rose, strode towards the train and got on.

Six Police officers burst through the gates and sprinted down the platform. He watched from the open doors, willing them to close, but they remained stubbornly open.

The first two officers changed tack and headed to the adjoining platform, accosting a young lad in a football shirt and his companion, wrestling them to the ground. As the other four officers surrounded the youths in a flurry of handcuffs, Scott allowed himself to breathe once again.

The carriage lurched into life and they were away. Isolated from the rest of the world, there was little risk of bumping into a gendarme with prying questions. Their odds of being caught had now dropped considerably.

Where was Jay? Had they all got on?

The grime of trackside Paris slid past the dirty windows as the light disappeared, and the low cloud cover increased the oppressive feel of the view. Sporadic French graffiti brought indecipherable bursts of colour to the passing grey concrete and certainly added life to this otherwise depressing part of the city.

He headed to their pre-booked sleeper carriage and found Jay entrenched in the top bunk with a French adult magazine.

'Seriously?'

'Mate, it's only natural.'

'No, what you're looking at really isn't. Anyway, what was it with you and those two gendarmes?'

'Oh, them coppers, they just found it amusing because apparently, only the English still buy their awful seventies porno mags from the street vendors. They had a bet on if I was English or not, that's all.'

'Great job on being inconspicuous, I'm going to get a coffee. Want anything?'

'Naah.'

Scott rolled his neck and stretched before leaving the compartment, and then swayed his way to the buffet car. Pascal sat at a small table with a flimsy plastic cup in his hand and a crushed tin of Coke rolling back and forth lightly in front of him on the surface. He gazed blankly out of the window, his Iron Maiden 2007 tour t-shirt reflected in the glass and his limp blonde hair just touching his shoulders.

A slim bar ran along one wall of the carriage, just a twelve-inch plastic surface jutting out of the wall. Ramirez, a six-foot-six half-Mexican, half-Texan bulldog of a man, sat facing it on a stool, nursing a bowl of tomato soup. He seemed captivated by an old paperback. Wesley sat a few stools further along, holding a can of beer and reading the paper.

Anger flared inside Scott as the most minor player was the only one breaking the rules. The rules that he had gone to great lengths to ensure everyone knew like a mantra. He turned and left the carriage before his rage had him break his own first rule of no communication in public, by pulling him to his feet and berating him on the spot.

Back in the sleeper carriage, he found Jay still entranced by his lurid magazine.

'Unbelievable, I've just caught Wesley downing a beer. What's up with the bloke? All he had to do was drive a truck at fifty miles per hour, yet he's the only one acting as if he took a big risk and needs a chill-out. He's off any further jobs.'

'Chill mate, I'm sure he'll only have the one.'

'Rules are what keep us out of prison. Break them, and we all end up being gang-raped for twenty years in some three-by-three cell. I make them for everyone's safety, and if you can't see that breaking them puts us all at risk, you're no better than he is.'

'Okay, okay, he's a tosser,' Jay mumbled apathetically before returning his attention to his magazine. Scott sat on the edge of his bunk and tried to stop his leg from jigging up and down.

7

D.I. Sharpe cradled the telephone between his shoulder and chin, his desk way more cluttered than usual so papers and memos went floating to the floor as he struggled to find his notebook.

'Six miles from the tunnel, you say,'

He scribbled the details of the torched pickup discovered shortly after the helicopter chase.

'So, nobody thought it relevant to mention this to the chief investigating officer for over twenty-four hours?' Sharpe raised his eyes to the ceiling.

'Chassis number returned as stolen—what a surprise. Keep me in the loop, and let me know if anything else crops up down there.

'This lot have made complete idiots of us already, so I don't want some journalist printing a front-page scoop on the whereabouts of their hideout before we know anything about it.'

Sharpe slid his copy of the Daily Mail into the wastepaper basket. The front page told of how Surrey's finest let a team of thieves' raid two high-end jewellers in broad daylight and then escape across the open English countryside, evading a dozen police cars and a helicopter.

He picked the clear evidence bag up off his desk and held it to the light. An engagement ring inside sparkled with glints of white and blue. Of course, there hadn't been any decipherable fingerprints on it, but a nagging feeling persisted that this could be more of a clue than it first appeared.

There was a ping from his computer, then another a second later. He wiggled the mouse to wake his email window. The first was the footage from the Hindhead Tunnel authorities he'd requested. He clicked the link to watch the short clip.

'Clever buggers.'

He then opened the second email, this one from one of the Guildford jewellers. He immediately grabbed his phone and dialled the number within the message.

'Hello, is this Mrs Braithwaite? Detective John Sharpe here.'

As they spoke, he tutted and lifted one of Rossi's half-empty Starbucks cups from his desk. He tossed it at the wastepaper basket, but it jettisoned its lid upon impact with the rim and sent a splash of cold coffee across the right leg of his suit trousers.

'Bugger.'

'Excuse me?'

'Oh, sorry Mrs Braithwaite, not you…'

8

Over the next hour, the city and suburbs gave way to the slopes of the French countryside, the light fading as the glass slowly morphed from windows to mirrors. Ramirez entered the sleeper to join Scott and Jay.

'So, is he still drinking?' Scott asked.

'That's not for me to say,' Ramirez slid the carriage door closed.

'Is he or not?'

'You'd best take a look yourself.'

'What the hell does that mean?'

Ramirez shrugged, balled up his faded combat jacket, and made himself comfortable with his paperback on a lower bunk. Scott stood.

'Neither of you leave this carriage till I get back.'

After slamming the sliding door, Scott swayed his way to the rear of the train. When he reached the buffet car, his blood climbed to near boiling point. Wesley and Pascal sat at a table with two girls, and they all appeared quite drunk. Wesley had a bottle in his hand and poured tequila into four plastic cups. A carrier bag sat between the two girls, and poking from it were bottles of gin and vodka.

'Party's over. Both your wives are asking where you've got to.'

The girls looked at each other quizzically.

'Nice meeting you, but maybe we should go,' the blonde girl said before sliding from her chair. Her brunette friend followed.

'What did you have to ruin that for, genius?' Wesley said.

'Get back to the sleeper carriage,' Scott said before turning to leave.

'Cocksucker.'

Scott ignored the insu blt as he made his way towards the exit.

'I said–'

Scott spun around and glared at the two, his eyes doing all the talking. Pascal slid from his perch and moped back towards the sleeper compartment. Scott held Wesley's glare a moment longer and followed the Frenchman out.

After several minutes, Wesley entered the carriage looking furious. Scott began the short but much-needed lecture.

'You are all under my employment until we get our split from Terry the Fence in Marseilles. That means we are all accountable for each other and need to rely on everybody doing what they've been told. Am I clear?'

A mumble filled the dead air of the crowded railway compartment.

'More importantly,' he continued, 'we all need to follow the rules for everybody's safety. Pascal, I'm surprised at you. We've worked together before without a problem, so why now?'

He shrugged.

'Wesley, you're a liability. You have put everybody at risk today, and for that, there is absolutely no excuse. You and I will never work together again. And if you think that gives you carte blanche to act as you like for the rest of our time together, then think again. I'll put a bullet in your skull rather than worry if you'll keep your mouth shut, so don't give me another reason to doubt you or I will.'

'It was just a drink. Stop being so–'

Scott instantly lashed out. A brutal punch dropped him to his knees. Wesley's hands immediately went to his bloody nose, his shoulders rising as he took several rapid breaths through his mouth.

'Anybody else fancy a tequila slammer?'

9

Scott was first to rise, the splitting headache so violent it had him off balance at the first attempt. He shook his head to clear it, but the dizziness had him grasping one of the higher bunks to steady himself, stirring the others.

'Jesus, what's happened to my head?' Jay said.

'Yours too? Christ, who left such a mess in here last night? I thought I was last to bed?'

Then it struck him. The stash. Scott dropped to his knees, hurriedly sifting through the mess beneath the lower bunk to where he had stowed the rucksacks. The more he searched, the tighter the lead fist in his stomach clenched. Their bags were gone.

'Aaagghh,' he slammed his fist into the wall, his rant loud enough to wake everyone.

'Gas. We've been gassed and bloody well robbed.'

'You're kidding me, right?' Ramirez said.

'Jeez, I thought this hangover was bad,' Pascal said. Scott's right arm muscles tensed for the blow, but punching him wouldn't help. Instead, the wall got it a second time.

'Wesley, you piece of shit, what did you tell those girls last night?' he grabbed him by the neck of his t-shirt and twisted it tightly.

'Nothing, honest, we were just goofing.'

'Pascal?'

'Yeah, we didn't say anything.'

'So, tell me how on earth somebody knew to break into our compartment?' Silence.

'Jay, Ramirez, could you have been followed?'

A murmur of denials and shrugs followed before the news sank in.

'Holy shit,' Jay shouted as he threw a water bottle at the train window, 'this just can't be happening.' And a barrage of everyone's voices filled the room. Scott raised his voice above them.

'I know it's going to be largely a waste of time, but we need to split up and search the train.'

The others began to quieten as he continued.

'Any likely looking people, just bust into their carriage and search it. There's no harm in drawing attention now, as they've got nothing on us with the evidence gone. I'll go and talk to the guard and see how many stops there were during the night.'

Scott pulled on his jeans, slid his feet into his boots and drew back the sliding door. Outside, the carriage was in mayhem.

'It wasn't just us. Looks like they did the whole train.'

10

Terry the Fence pulled his sixteen-stone bulk from the crisp white sheets with a heavy awkwardness and padded to the en-suite. A quick shower and a line of coke had him feeling human again, just. Soft slippers comforted his sand-sore feet, and the towelling dressing gown felt prickly against his sunburnt shoulders.

'Zara, get up you lazy cow. He'll be here in a minute.'

The mop of bleached hair moved slowly on the bright white pillow, sunlight from the louvred shutters causing the film of sweat to glisten on her bronzed back.

'Leave it out Terry,' her voice a raspy Essex croak, 'I'm zonked.'

'Well, un-zonk yourself, darling, I'm putting the kettle on and expect to see your sexy little smile all pinky and perky when I get back with your coffee.'

'Yeah, yeah, give me an hour.'

He chuckled to himself as he padded out of the room, down the stairs, and into the kitchen in search of breakfast. One hour later, the villa's doorbell sounded.

'You two are travelling a bit light,' Terry said as he swung the front door open to see Scott and Jay.

'We need to talk.'

'Come through, take a seat outside, and I'll be with you in a moment.'

Heading to the kitchen, he paused at the bottom of the staircase. 'Zara, get down here you lazy cow.'

He made his way onto the patio a few minutes later, holding a tray of coffees. Scott had sunk into one of the wicker seats, but Jay stood looking over the balcony.

'Nice view you've got here,' Jay said. 'But of all the places in the world to call home, why'd you choose one that looks out over an old prison?'

'That, old son, is Château D'If. It was the inspiration for the book The Count of Monte Cristo.'

'Count of what?'

'Monte Cristo. It's a tale of subterfuge and revenge. A man was double-crossed and wrongly imprisoned, so he escaped and came back to take his revenge on the man who betrayed him. It sits out there in the Med and reminds me of a couple of things you'd do well to keep in mind, son.'

'Oh yeah, like what?'

'Firstly, never double cross anyone. Or if you have to, make damned sure they're very, very dead. I for one don't want to be looking over my shoulder for the rest of my life, waiting for the inevitable payback to come knocking when I least expect it. And second, every day I'm up here on the outside looking into a prison, I'm not on the inside of one looking out. It keeps me focussed on what happens when you get sloppy. Talking of which,' he turned to Scott and raised his eyebrows. 'Do enlighten me.'

'What?' Terry growled in tones as calm as he could manage after Scott had filled him in. 'You mean to say you've got absolutely nothing?'

'Yes, and for your information, I can assure you it's not exactly good news for any of us. Months of planning, multiple set-up jobs to get the equipment to rob this lot, all gone in one hit. So, if you get offered any of it, you'd better let me know so I can personally break their necks.'

Terry's brow furrowed and his eyes reduced to slits.

'You know there's going to be some pretty disappointed people down here, and I'm going to be the one to cop the brunt of it.'

'Well, you know what, Terry? That's little concern of mine as we've done all the work.'

'Either of you for more coffee?' Zara asked as she wandered onto the villa's patio.

'Yes, black, no sugar.' Scott answered, not breaking his eye contact with Terry.

'Mint, ain't she?' Terry said once Zara was out of earshot.

'Bit cute for a fat git like you, Terry. What d'ya pay for her?' Jay asked.

His answer was just a chuckle as he sat back in his chair. When Zara returned, he continued.

'Scott and the boys here have misplaced all their loot, love.'

'Seriously?'

'Yeah, had it nicked off them last night apparently.'

'But Terry–'

'I know,' he turned to Scott, 'Zara had quite a few of your little trinkets lined up with buyers. And she's got some great connections for diamonds, but I guess that deal's going nowhere now.'

'Like I said,' Scott placed his palms face down on the table and leaned forward, 'we're not exactly chuffed either.'

'So you did. Now what are we to do with all your boys who need to get home?'

'Their problem, they've got credit cards, as thankfully the thieves bailed without taking our wallets or passports once they found what was in the rucksacks. After all, greed will always get you caught in the long run.'

'Just the point I was making earlier. Why don't we all get together for a consolatory drink and slap-up meal down the Old Port this evening? On me, of course, as you've all taken the trouble to come and visit your uncle Terry.'

'I'll put it to the boys. I'm sure we'll take you up on it. In the meantime, there was a particular ring in the haul I'd like you to keep a lookout for. That engagement ring you had made for me. Let me know if it crops up anywhere.'

Terry shook his head and smiled broadly. 'That ring doesn't seem to be bringing you much luck, does it? Are you sure you want it back if I find it?'

*****

Terry walked arm in arm with Zara along the waterfront, yachts bobbing in unison to the gentle lap of the Med. The cockroaches offering neon necklaces and counterfeit Gucci scuttled back into the shadows as he approached, many having sampled the sharp end of his growl. Word had finally got around.

Fuzio's was lively but not overly loud, and the crew occupied a table outside. Terry sank into the middle of the three unoccupied chairs, and despite Zara sitting next to him, she immediately turned her attention to Jay, who sat on her far side. A certain amount of bragging was in force, escalating with each round of drinks until their plates of food arrived.

Although relaxed, Terry kept an eye on the level of attention his girlfriend was receiving from Jay.

'So Wesley,' he said as he finished off a lamb cutlet, 'by the bruise on your neck, I'd say you probably upset my friend Scotty here.'

Wesley stared down, refusing to rise to the comment.

'My Zara could probably tan your hide a good'n an-all.'

She flashed a sarcastic grin and then leaned over to kiss Jay on the lips. Terry's sense of humour vanished.

'I know what you're up to, so cut it out,' he warned Jay when Zara went to the ladies. 'Continue trying it on with my missus, and I'll smack you up proper, you hear me?'

'Chill, Terry, I'm just having a laugh. Anyway, it's fun keeping you on your toes.'

'I'll cut your sodding toes off if it continues.'

'Okay, you've made your point, and I've lost my appetite. I'll see you around.' He stood just as Zara arrived back.

'Casanova's leaving,' Terry said before smiling at her. 'It seems you were boring him.'

Jay tossed his napkin onto the table.

'Right, who's up for a nightclub?'

'I'm done, just shower and bed for me,' Scott said.

'I'm with Scott on that one,' Ramirez said. 'Figure I'll take the early train home tomorrow. Guys?'

Ramirez looked to Wesley and Pascal

'Nightclub sounds sweet to me,' Wesley said.

'The hotel's already paid for a couple of nights. So we make the most of it, yes?' Pascal shrugged.

'Get your clobber together, love,' Terry said to Zara before he gestured for the bill, 'we're heading back to the villa.'

'But Terry–' his look silenced her immediately.

11

The following morning Scott was woken by a text from Terry.

WTF have you been up to? Meet at Monty's bar on Rue des Catalans, midday. Trouble.

Should he meet or just get the hell out on the next train? He slid out of bed and went to the bathroom, but as he emptied his bladder, the face in the bathroom mirror was also out of answers. He grabbed a towel, pulled on some trunks and headed to the hotel's basement spa to pull a few lengths. With luck, the cold water might clear his head.

By ten-thirty, he'd made his decision. He left a note for the still sleeping Jay and stopped by the hotel dining room to pocket a steak knife on his way out.

*****

Terry sat outside Monty's at a table for four, halfway through a plate of sausage, egg and chips. He eyed Scott's approach carefully. Could he still be trusted?

'This had better not be anything to do with you or one of your boys.'

'What do you mean?' Scott said, taking the seat opposite.

'Four yachts got turned over in the Old Port last night.'

'I'm not following. What's that got to do with you?' Scott ran his fingers through his hair, and then a waitress appeared.

'Bonjour, may I get you anything?'

'Coffee please, black.'

Terry shook his head and waved her away.

'The code, that's what it's got to do with me, the code of honour amongst thieves. One yacht was Harry's, my mate from Parkhurst when we both did a stretch eight years ago. Another was Jim's, the geezer that was fronting the money for the stash you carelessly misplaced. And don't let me even start on the Russians. I'm telling you this is red hot and I don't want to be anywhere near it.'

'After I left you yesterday, I went to the beach for some air, then watched the football in the hotel bar. I think I was in bed by midnight.'

Terry turned his attention to the plate in front of him, stabbing chips with his fork more aggressively than the task warranted.

'You have my word, honest, I know nothing about this.'

Terry stuffed the chips into his mouth and held Scott's stare in search of any hint of deceit. But the exercise was futile as the answer came up the road with a beach bag over his shoulder just five seconds later.

'Cool, knew I'd find you two together.'

'Wesley, what the hell? How did you know we'd be here?'

'I didn't know Terry's number so I followed you out of the hotel. Thought you might be meeting him but didn't want you trying to catch a cut of the stash I earned last night.' He opened his bag. 'Will you just look at all these beauties?'

Terry and Scott glanced inside, and then looked at each other in resignation. Wesley might have solved mystery, but now they had a bigger problem on their hands.

'Meet me up at my villa around ten tonight. I'll let the Russians know they can buy their gear back, and I'll have a large suitcase of cash ready for you.'

'Seriously, you can arrange it that quick for me?' the smile radiant on his face.

'Well, I am a fence, aren't I? It'd be pretty shit if I couldn't shift some hooky gear a bit sharpish now, wouldn't it?'

'Suppose.'

'Tell me, the cash you also swiped, was it Euros or Rubles?' Terry asked.

'A mix but mostly Rubles.'

'Good, well bring them along and I'll change it into Sterling, the Euros as well. Everybody wants to get rid of their Sterling down here what with that Brexit mess, so bring it all and I'll guarantee to beat the exchange rate you'll get anywhere else.'

'Sounds cool, do either of you want a beer?'

'No, now piss off until tonight. Me and Scott have some private business to discuss.'

Wesley rose, bowed theatrically, and wandered off towards the shops, no doubt lining up some of tomorrow's purchases.

'Christ, I don't believe it.' Scott said. 'But you slipped up.'

'What do you mean? He's your boy, not mine.'

'When you were talking to him, you asked about the Rubles.'

'So?'

'He never mentioned that it came from the Russians, so how would you know?'

'It's a good job he's a bit thick then, ain't it?' Terry chuckled for a few seconds, and stabbed another chip with more force than necessary.

12

Wesley reached behind and pulled the shirt away from his sweat-soaked back. It flopped back down immediately and stuck once more.

'Damn this heat,'

The hill he steadily climbed made the beach bag seem heavier with every step. He had to get fitter, maybe get back to that gym he quit two years ago, or was it three? It could even be four. He was past caring.

Halfway up the unmade road, he paused to rest and looked out over the Med. The moon was full, and he could see to the horizon, the weak light reflecting off several of the islands a kilometre or two out. He lifted his L.A. Dodgers baseball cap and wiped his brow. Then a car passed at speed, leaving a thick cloud of dust in its wake, causing him to cough and then curse as he fanned his face.

A moment later, only the cicadas' incessant rasping invaded the tranquillity of a beautiful evening. He arrived at the gates of Casa Boa Vista, double-checked the scrap of paper Scott had given, and pressed the intercom.

With a buzz, the wide gates swung open to reveal a cobbled courtyard housing a Range Rover Sport and an Audi R8, both gloss white and on English plates. He was in the right place.

He crossed the dimly lit courtyard and arrived at the front door. It was already open. He paused to knock and call out Terry's name and then followed with the customary 'Hello?'

Over the threshold and a few paces in, it occurred to him that if the front door was open, surely the hallway light should have been on? Something didn't feel right—no television noise, no cooking, not even a lamp on in the living room.

He clutched the beach bag tight to his chest and inched further inside. It would probably be unwise to announce his arrival any more clearly by flicking a light switch. Then something caught his eye on the patio.

Could it be just a reflection? Or was that somebody outside on a wicker chair? His eyes seemed like they were playing tricks. He moved into the central part of the lounge. Then cursed quietly as his foot caught a copper urn and knocked it over with a hollow 'dunk', followed by the sound of it rolling forward and the 'dunk, dunk, dunk' of it dropping down several steps into the dining area. If anyone had been waiting for him, Wesley was sure that now was when they'd make themselves known.

Maybe it was someone he really didn't want to meet. He ought to go, come back in daylight. The thought came a moment too late as he realised, he was standing on a plastic sheet.

A figure came at him from behind. Before he could react, a thin wire was around his neck and pulled just hard enough to bite into the skin. Enough to let him know this might be his last breath.

He dropped the bag, and an involuntary shaking overcame him. His legs almost gave way and suddenly felt warm. The sound of liquid hitting the plastic-covered tiles filled the room. But the only thing he cared about was that wire biting deeper.

'Terry's not very pleased with you,' Scott whispered. 'In fact, a lot of people would be quite appreciative if I put your head on a spike and delivered it to them right now.'

What could he do? There was no way he could fight. One slight movement and his throat would open in a crescent, and that would be it.

'So what you're going to do, is leave here. You're going to get on the first train you can, and if I ever come across your pathetic face again, I'll cut your head clean off your body. Am I clear?'

What could he do? He daren't nod, the wire would go deeper, possibly too deep. He raised a shaking hand and gave a thumbs-up. After a long few seconds, the pressure eased, and then the wire was over his head and gone. He gulped in air and dropped to his knees.

Scott held the cheese wire in one hand, a few drops of blood falling from it. Wesley looked to his own shirt, a few lines of crimson but not as much as he'd feared. His hand went to his throat.

Terry slid the patio door open.

'What's that runt still doing here? Please tell me he hasn't pissed on my floor?' he boomed.

Wesley was running, out of the house and into the night air as fast as his legs could pump. Thanking a long-forgotten God that he was still alive.

13

The car showroom sat slightly back from the Esher to Cobham A-road. It was a glass-fronted building which had probably looked quite modern in the eighties, but the Austin Allegro might also have been considered quite modern back then. Now, it was nothing more than what an estate agent would call 'An ideal development opportunity'. The flat above hadn't weathered the years any better and now sported cracks in the brickwork around the windows, like laughter lines that aren't funny.

A yard with eight cars sat out front, the showroom being home to a further three. The stock of Rainey's Quality Used Cars certainly belied the faded signage's claim.

Scott rifled through the paperwork in his filing cabinet, hunting for the purchase invoice he knew was in there somewhere, relating to the Subaru he'd just sold at a loss.

'Where the hell is it?'

His phone buzzed somewhere on the desk. He pushed aside a few red reminders to uncover it and hastily swiped the screen to answer the withheld number. He immediately regretted it. The voice on the other end belonged to the Bulgarian he'd been avoiding. After a minute, he managed to get a word in.

'Obviously I've got something in the pipeline that'll cover it, I've just–''

He was interrupted, and despite several attempts to cut in, he had to wait for a lull in the Bulgarian's calmly delivered threats.

'Well if you do break my legs, it's going to make it pretty difficult to get you your money–''

He was interrupted again.

'What do you mean, look outside?' Scott walked through the showroom to the front of the building, and saw two of the cars on his forecourt had heavyset thugs standing next to them.

'I would advise you not to go outside,' the man on the other end said. 'I wouldn't want you to upset my boys. They can get,' he paused, 'emotional.'

The thugs drew hammers out from behind their backs and began smashing the windows of the cars they were standing next to. Scott ended the call and went back inside his office.

Above him came the clomp, clomp of heels on bare wood as Sophia descended the stairs.

'What's going on?' she said as she entered his office. Her appearance was professional in a black knee-length skirt, cream blouse open at the collar and a pair of moderately high but polished heels.

'I would have thought that was obvious.'

'Have you called the police?'

'They wouldn't stand a chance.'

'What do you mean? You can't let hooligans vandalise your property like that. In broad daylight as well.'

'Whatever. Where are you off to?'

'We, you mean where are we off to? Or have you forgotten about the viewing?'

'The viewing? Viewing what exactly?'

'Our house Scott, Christ, don't you dare make excuses. We've been talking about getting out of the flat above here for months.'

His shoulders dropped.

'You mean you've been talking about it for months. Anyway, this isn't a good time,' he returned his attention to the filing cabinet.

'It's never a good time with you. You said once you got back from your lad's trip in France, we'd take it seriously and find a new place.'

Jasmine would never have nagged him like this. She always gave him space. Maybe too much.

'Things happened there. I can't go into it.'

'What? You met someone else?'

'No, nothing like that, I was counting on a deal and–'

'Scott, seriously, one hiccup on a long weekend break does not mean our future has to be put on hold. Unless there's something else going on you'd like to talk to me about? You've been utterly miserable since you got back, so maybe you'd better start explaining.'

'I can't,' he slammed the filing cabinet. 'It isn't what you think.'

'Oh, I know exactly what this is about,' her hands went to her hips.

'Do enlighten me because I can guarantee you haven't the faintest idea.'

'This is about *her*, isn't it?'

'What are you talking about?'

'Jasmine,' the aggression rising in her voice. 'That one you have up there on a golden pedestal.' She jabbed a finger towards his head.

'Sophia, seriously, what are you talking about?'

'You're chasing a ghost. She's never coming back.'

His jaw began to ache.

'You don't know the first thing about her.'

Her arms crossed over her chest but the frown on her face conveyed more disappointment than anger. 'You run from making the slightest commitment in business, our relationship or even a phone contract. I've never known anyone to change their mobile number as often as you do. All my friends are married or engaged or pregnant, and you can't even commit to a house viewing. What are you running away from?'

'This conversation is over, get out. I've got paperwork to finish and broken glass to sweep up.'

'Broken glass, I'm so glad that's your number one priority. What about our broken relationship? You can't just sweep that up, can you?'

'Look,' his voice raised, 'get out of my office and leave me alone.'

'Alone? But you're never alone, are you Scott?'

'What's that supposed to mean?'

'Don't think I haven't noticed you still keep a picture of Jasmine hidden in your wallet.'

He ran his fingers through his hair several times.

'Well, you can keep her, and her precious pedestal, because I've had it with playing second best to a woman who dumped you two years ago. Get over it and grow up.'

'How dare you.'

'I'm leaving,' she scrabbled in her bag for her keys, rotated a chrome Yale around the ring, and then threw it onto his desk. 'Keep your bloody fantasies. I need a real man in my life.'

'But Sophia–'

She slammed the office door and stormed back upstairs. Scott slumped into his office chair and lowered his forehead to the desk littered with red payment demands. Then let out a long groan. After five minutes, he sat up and slid his phone from his pocket.

'Jay, fancy some lunch at The Cricketers? I've had a great morning, so I'll treat you.'

'Cool, meet you there at half one.'

He ended the call. Then, after another brief look for the Subaru's purchase invoice, he left the office and called upstairs.

'Remember to take Chester.'

Silence.

'I said–''

'Keep the bloody cat. Maybe he'll teach you how to commit to something other than the past.'

'I can't look after your cat.'

'That's exactly my point.'

'Seriously?' He closed his eyes, and his shoulders dropped a couple of inches.

His footsteps echoed off the tiled floor of the showroom as he made his way to the glass frontage. He locked the door and then flipped the sign around to 'closed'.

Back in the office, he grabbed a set of car keys from the safe box and then headed through the workshop to the yard at the rear of the building.

A pair of indicators flashed on a yellow Porsche 911 cabriolet, and he paused to admire it, even though the valeter was yet to work his magic on the slightly iffy bodywork. He pulled the driver's door open, but paused, forgetting that he'd got it on the cheap as it was left-hand-drive. He slammed the door and walked around to the side which had the steering wheel on it.

By the time Scott had driven it out onto the wrecked forecourt, Sophia was there with her bags, presumably waiting for a cab to arrive. The place looked like a bomb had hit it. He pulled onto the road, passed her without acknowledgement, but did catch her arm gesture in the rear-view mirror as he sped away.

14

He wound his way through the beautiful Surrey countryside towards The Cricketers in Cobham. It was just a five-minute drive and, as the name would suggest, sat on a picturesque village cricket green.

What he really needed was a distraction from the whole Sophia thing and some distance from all the other frustrations in his life. Get some perspective, and then hit restart. But it always came back to Jasmine, and how to get her out of his head and back in his life.

He found a space at the far end of the pub car park and squeezed the Porsche into it. The engine gave an extended rattle as he killed the ignition.

'Great, another bill.'

Inside the pub, he ducked under a succession of low beams and stood at the bar alongside a lad of around twenty. He'd ordered a pint of lager, but no matter how many times he waved his phone at the card reader, it remained unable to pay for his drink. Embarrassed, the lad slunk away and left Scott standing in front of a brimmed pint. He tried not to look at it and opened his mouth to order an orange juice.

'He's probably not even old enough,' the barmaid said as she collected several empty plates from the bar. 'Have that one on the house to save me pouring another.'

'But I don't–'

She turned and strode into the kitchen before Scott could finish. He knew he shouldn't take it, but after a battle of conscience and the morning he'd had, no, make that week he'd had.

'Damn it.'

He slid it from the bar. The war had begun, but he'd waved the white flag before the first shot had even been fired. A glance at his watch told him it was quarter past, and still no sign of Jay, so he grabbed the paper on a nearby table and took a seat. The spring sunshine felt warmer than expected in this claustrophobic pub, the beamed ceilings low, the windows small. It wasn't long before the alcohol numbed his senses into that deep fuzz of relaxation that drinking on an empty stomach brings.

'That finished, yeah?' The barmaid said, snapping his attention away from the view outside the diamond-leaded window.

'Err, yes take it please.'

The temperature felt like it had risen. Maybe the small beer garden at the front would be a better option. The view would be better too, as it overlooked the green. He surrendered to a second pint en route.

Here it came, the draw of the encroaching blackness as the alcohol filled his veins. It gave his temples a throb, no, a purr. From the first sip of his second pint he knew that the euphoria was close. Like the roller coaster clawing its way up the first incline, click by dreaded click, the peak ahead, closer, closer, then the weightlessness, the rush, oh the rush. It was coming, but not quite yet. Not until he was at least three pints in.

But once he'd tipped over that edge the pain of coming down the far side of that peak brought way more consequences than a mere amusement park ride. Sod it, he'd no plans for tomorrow so resigned himself to being its slave for at least the next twenty-four hours. It would probably be more, much more.

He sank into a chair at the only vacant table outside. It was near an open window, and through it, the drone of a news channel leaked, tarnishing this idyllic setting.

He tried to block the sound out, but it wasn't working. The alcohol already slowing him down, and he felt too lethargic to go inside and ask somebody to turn the volume down, or better still, off altogether.

Jay arrived twenty-five minutes later to find him halfway through his third pint and a little more philosophical.

'I'll have a vodka and lemonade please old boy, slice of lime.'

'Great, you can get me another pint whilst you're there.'

'Thought this was on you?'

'Lunch is, not the aperitifs.'

'Tightwad. Back in a min.'

Jay made his way inside and returned several minutes later with a barmaid's phone number and a couple of supposedly free drinks.

'So, what's made your day so sweet that you're buying your brother lunch?'

'You're so late I think they've stopped serving.'

'She'd do anything for me now, that little beauty, you mark my words.'

'Go on then, get us two bowls of chilli on the house.'

'Consider it done, you doubting Thomas. You wait 'till you see the sparkle she has in her eye for me.'

'Go on then.'

'What?'

'Use that silver tongue of yours to sort our lunch.'

'Timing mate, it's all in the timing.'

'Right.'

The brothers sat in silence as the report of another Middle Eastern bombing came from the open window.

'Hate that, all the depressing crap they put on the news.'

'Don't know why people watch it, to be honest,' Scott said.

'Nor me, shall we ask them to turn it off?'

'What, and ruin the depressing soundtrack to our quiet lunchtime pint?'

'You told me it was past lunchtime.'

'Maybe you're right, but I'll get that barmaid with questionable taste to turn it off anyway.'

'Questionable taste? How's your love life going then, Romeo?'

'Left an hour ago in a cab, as it happens.' Scott took a sip of his pint.

'Another one ditch you 'cos you're not rich and famous like me?'

'Jay, you're not rich and the only way you're getting famous is on Crimewatch, so I seriously hope you aren't.'

'Talking of Crimewatch, I was sort-of relying on that last job we pulled. You know, to get some cash in.'

'You mean to pay me back the ten grand you already owe me?'

'Well yeah, that as well obviously, but as things didn't quite–'

'No.'

'What do you mean, no? I haven't even–'

'I'm not a bank, and I've carried you more times than I can remember. The last ten grand was on the back of my writing off the debt you already owed me, so no, I'm not lending you any more.'

'An early birthday present then?'

Scott ignored the question and they sat in silence once more, but this time it was broken by some intriguing news.

'British Billionaire Lucien Croft is reportedly well underway with an ambitious project. He has commissioned a replica of the ill-fated liner Titanic to be constructed by the Jau-Tu shipyard in China. But this isn't a one-hundredth scale model. It's a full-sized, ocean-going liner that will sail the Atlantic with over one thousand crew and almost two thousand passengers.

'The ship is to be almost identical to the original, but with some important exceptions. It remains the same in spirit, but the enhanced level of luxury and modern splendour will satisfy even the pickiest of billionaires.'

'Sounds a bit flash,' Jay said.

'Gone are the third class dormitories and steel shutters, replacing them are more second class cabins and enhanced luxury facilities which not even the first class passengers enjoyed on the original. Finally, the steerage promenade deck found at the rear of the ship will now be home to an outdoor swimming pool for all to enjoy.'

'Haven't they seen the film? It doesn't end well for that ship,' Scott said.

'The ship is due to be finished in just over two years and its maiden voyage will mimic that of the original's planned route of Southampton to New York, hopefully without meeting any icebergs on the way.'

'Let's hope they don't run into any pirates either,' Jay said after trying to swat a persistent fly.

'Ticket prices are yet to be announced, but it's thought that a first class suite will start at one hundred thousand pounds. However, a second class single cabin should be considerably less. Derek O'Halloran, BBC news, London.'

'Some people just have too much money. Talking of which, when are we going to look at lining another job up? I could do with a new car.'

'I'd offer you finance on the Porsche I arrived in but I'm sure the finance company would just laugh at you, so I'll save you the embarrassment.'

'Got rid of that ropey old Subaru yet?'

'Went this morning as a matter of fact. Where's my lasagne?' Scott lifted the glass of rapidly vanishing beer to his lips.

'Thought you wanted chilli? Anyway, what about doing another job?' Jay stirred his vodka with a straw, the fly having now buzzed off.

'Not much I've heard of. And those Bulgarians came looking for their loan repayment earlier, so I've got to do something about it before they get really serious. We'd better start planning something, and soon. Got any ideas?'

'We could rob that new Titanic.'

'Shut up Jay, it's not even built yet. We need to think bigger, ideally a job worth several million. I'm done with this small-time stuff and each job we do just increases the chances of getting caught. We need to make the next one count.'

'You mean you want enough to buy a big house and a maroon Bentley.' Jay put a cocktail stick between his teeth and smiled. 'What, so you can impress someone in particular?'

Scott's knuckles whitened around his pint glass.

'Oh, and pay back your nice Bulgarian friends, obviously,' Jay continued. 'But before you do that, I really could do with that loan, just until the next job.'

'Don't you think I've got enough on my plate with Sofia walking out and those friendly Bulgarians smashing my place up?'

'It's just a couple of grand. I'll pay it back with interest, honest.'

'Just like all your other loans?'

'Marseilles weren't my fault. You know that, and I would have sorted you out first thing after I got my share.'

'No, I'd have deducted what you owe me long before you got anywhere near it.'

'There's no need to be like that.' He stuck out his bottom lip.

'Ten grand Jay, that's not insignificant.'

'So, round it up to twelve then. Nice even number.'

'I prefer the number zero where your debts are concerned.'

Jay dropped his head and his shoulders slumped. The lip even came out again. Scott knew it was all just an act, but he acquiesced anyway.

'Okay, two grand, not a penny more. Come by the showroom tomorrow afternoon.'

Jay brightened immediately.

'Oh, and back on the subject of Marseilles, I was going to have a word with you about that.'

'What do you mean?' That'd caught his attention.

'Apparently Pascal was in on that yacht job in the marina as well.'

'That's history as far as I'm concerned,' Scott sat back in his chair. 'And now Wesley's off the scene Pascal should fall back into line, so I'm not overly fussed about taking him to task over it.'

'Let's do Richard Branson's Necker Island.'

'I'm not even going to justify that with a response. Finish your vodka, I'm heading back to the showroom. I've got some sweeping up to do.' Scott downed the last of his pint.

'What about the lunch you promised?'

Scott reached into his pocket and tossed a pound coin onto the table.

'Kitchen's closed. Treat yourself to a bag of crisps.'

He went to the car, blipped the remote, and once again got into the wrong side. This he took as a sign, and pulled his phone out to call a cab before attempting to switch to the driver's seat.

Down the narrow lane and onto the country roads, the cab driver put his foot down a little more aggressively than felt safe. Even after several pints, Scott found himself gripping the door handle and pressing his feet into the floor with every twist of the road. But once clear of the lanes and onto the straighter A-road, his mind felt the darkness creeping back inside. His next hit, the rush of more alcohol, and the oblivion that it offered. His mouth was dry, his head swam, and his body ached with a visceral longing for Jasmine. Two years gone, yet still there every day, in his head, her absence torturing him.

'Can you pull over please mate?'

'You going to be sick?'

'No, just stop here please.'

The driver drew to a halt outside Sanjay's Wines and he climbed out. A couple of minutes later he slid back into the rear seat with two bottles of vodka, one tequila, six beers and a lamb samosa which wouldn't get eaten.

On the drive back to the showroom, and his flat above, he reflected that maybe his brother wasn't being so ridiculous. What if there was a way to rob the new Titanic once it was ocean-bound? He decided it warranted some deeper thought, but this really wasn't the time. For now, all he wanted to do was open a bottle and put as much distance as possible between his brain and reality.

15

The rasping of a cat's tongue drawn repeatedly up the side of Scott's nose brought him back to consciousness. A swipe of his arm catapulted the feline away with a yowl of protest, but he stalked back, just out of range and mewing incessantly.

It was twilight, but morning or evening was anybody's guess. He certainly had no idea.

He peeled his face from the foul-smelling rug in his upstairs lounge and saw a crust of dried vomit less than six inches from his face. It explained the smell.

'What day is it?'

He rolled onto his back and took a couple of slow breaths before sitting up. A dizzy, nauseous rush to his head had him pause a moment before noticing he was wearing only a t-shirt and his boxers around one ankle.

'Oh Christ.'

The place was a mess, spilt drinks, a half-eaten pizza and a grouchy feline. Not that that was unusual. But there was a sketch in biro on the inside of the pizza box. He couldn't recall doing it, but it was of a very familiar Princess-cut diamond ring only he would have recognised.

He eyed the vomit, and in it was a photograph. The one of him and Jasmine they'd taken on Brighton Pier all those years ago, the one from his wallet.

'Please, no.'

He lifted the corner, but it was bonded to the rug, soaked through with the liquid from his stomach to melt it into the cheap nylon weave of the only carpet in his flat. Carefully he teased the paper from the fibres, but it was no use. It had become one, threatening to tear with even the slightest persuasion. He wept.

The rasp of licking returned to his cheek sometime later, with a shushing noise like gravel being thrown onto glass. In resignation, he opened his eyes to see rain hammering on the skylight. It was still twilight, but probably twelve hours later.

'Come on Chester, let's get you some breakfast. Or is it dinner?'

16

Lady Astbury looked through the tall window of her first-floor apartment at the bright flashes of white reflecting off the car windscreens as they turned left out of Bruton Street and into the one-way traffic. The dark blue Maserati she had been waiting for appeared a few minutes before their agreed time and nosed into a parking space on the south side of London's Berkley Square.

She turned from the window, retrieved her walking stick from the side of her armchair and carefully made her way towards the front door. It took such a long time for her body to warm up into anything remotely like fluid motion these days, she found it infuriating.

'Maria, you may as well take the next few hours off, I'm lunching with Alistair at Polo's and he can see that I get back okay. Just be a darling and summon the lift for me, would you?'

The maid appeared from the kitchen in traditional light grey attire with a white apron. She propped open the front door with a twelve-inch art-deco bronze and pushed the lift call.

Outside, Lady Astbury was met by a tall, slim gentleman in his seventies wearing a blue blazer fastened by a single, crested brass button. They embraced, air-kissed and held one another's gaze for a moment.

'Still got that little sports car, I see.'

'Some habits die hard. You're looking wonderful as always.'

'Forever a charmer, aren't you Alistair? I see Luigi is still keeping your hair a shade or two darker than nature would have intended. Am I to take it you're still single?'

*****

Two hours later D.I. John Sharpe sat on Bruton Street behind the wheel of his unmarked five series. Berkley Square was just fifty yards ahead whilst his phone was pressed tightly to his ear.

'You're sure that's all? Just a few nylon fibres and a trace of leather polish.'

He listened for a moment as the other person spoke.

'Okay, I agree, probably from the rider's glove. Look, send the ring back and I'll see if the owner can shed any more light on it. Thanks again.'

He ended the call and frowned into the distance. Now with his knowledge of how they had disappeared into a puff of thick black smoke, thanks to the CCTV footage, he had half a chance of catching them next time. Provided there was a next time, of course. Not only that, but a very similar heist had happened a week prior to it in central London. But of course, nobody had put two and two together until he'd seen the link.

'Time to move on, I'm utterly sick of this. Cops and robbers is a waste of bloody time.'

Aware that he'd spoken it out loud, he confirmed that it was definitely time to move on.

The thump of an elbow on the passenger side window startled him as his partner Lorenzo Rossi juggled with drinks and a bulging brown bag. The man struggled to open the car door with just an outstretched index finger.

'God give me strength,' Sharpe muttered before leaning across to open the door from the inside. 'What on earth have you got me now, some iced mocha java tossachini?'

'It's just an iced coffee, Boss, nothing your delicate English constitution will object to.'

'I've told you not to call me Boss, please use my correct title.'

'Sorry Boss.'

Sharpe exhaled heavily before Rossi continued.

'You want the grilled vegetable panini with pesto or the Iberian ham focaccia with goat's cheese?'

'Well, I asked for an egg mayonnaise sandwich and a cup of tea, so I really don't care.'

'I think you need to broaden your culinary horizons. Why don't we go half and half, Boss? It all smells absolutely wonderful.'

'It stinks like a goat herder's damp sandal. Just get on with it, will you? I'm famished.'

Rossi set about dividing the food and handed Sharpe his lunch. After taking the first bite, he had to admit that Rossi might have a point, although he'd be damned if he would let the Italian know.

'Forensics didn't come back with much, although they did get some nylon fibres which could be from the rucksack. So, if we ever do catch this lot, at least we have a chain of evidence to bolster our case for the prosecution. But it's pretty weak.

'After today we should know if there's a real connection between the Chelsea heist and the Guildford one,' Sharpe continued between chews. 'They revolve around the main road south, the A3, as both locations have easy access to it. And we obviously know that was the Guildford exit strategy.'

'Uh huh,' mumbled Rossi, cramming food into his mouth.

'Therefore, the mid-point between the two is the M25 intersection with the A3. So I'd say somewhere around the Cobham, Ripley area.'

Rossi nodded as Sharpe continued.

'It makes sense to focus our investigation there, say a six-mile radius from that junction. Get on to the office and have them pull up every likely suspect within that area. I'll bet we have at least one of them on the list, possibly more. And highlight any with prior motorbike or jewellery related convictions whilst you're at it.'

'Okay Boss,' he said and scrunched the paper wrapper from the first half of his lunch before tossing it into the bag. 'Now look at that elderly couple walking towards us,' Rossi gestured towards the windscreen. 'He's what you'd call an old pro. He's definitely on the shakedown for that wealthy older woman. I can smell his cologne from here.'

'I think you'll find that reek is coming from the pesto oozing from your focca-bread-thing. And as she's walking with a cane, I doubt he's doing anything other than being a gentleman. We English don't have an ulterior motive you know, unlike some of your friends, no doubt.'

'Yeah, but look,' he gestured again, 'he's being way too attentive, laughing at every word. And the body language, don't even start me on that.'

'Yes, please don't start.'

'I'm telling you–'

'Okay, you've told me, now can I get on with my lunch please? We need to be in Chelsea to interview the staff of the two jewellery shops by four.'

'Just saying, Boss.'

Sharpe huffed and returned to his food, only noticing that the pesto had dripped down his Marks and Spencer tie after it was too late.

'Bugger.'

*****

Lady Astbury and her luncheon partner continued at a sedate pace along Conduit Street as it crossed into Bruton Street. They were deep in conversation and comfortable with both the fuzz of a boozy lunch and their familiar surroundings.

'Oh Alistair, you're such a darling. So how is Janet getting on down in Monaco? I must go and see them again it's been over a year since I've been down and her lovely husband is always so kind to me.'

'I'm sure they'd love to have you, especially now they've both given up on the golf. There's only so much gip a knee replacement will take you know, and the longer par fives were playing merry hell with Janet's sciatica….'

*****

'Boss, Boss,' Rossi threw the remains of his food onto the dashboard. He banged elbows with Sharpe which caused the D.I. to slop some iced coffee into his lap.

'Oh, for Christ's sake, you idiot.'

'Quick Boss, the bike.'

Rossi was up and out of the car. He sprinted down the middle of the road towards the elderly couple. They were oblivious to the scooter that had mounted the pavement behind them and was rapidly closing in. Within seconds, the helmeted rider had skidded to a stop and knocked the gent to the floor. The shocked woman fell back against a shop window and her walking stick clattered to the ground. After grabbing the handbag from the woman, the attacker produced a knife, gesturing for the fallen man to put his phone and wallet into the bag. This gave Lady Astbury a moment to recover. She retrieved her stick from the floor with surprising agility and stabbed their attacker in the torso before walloping him on the shoulder.

Rossi was close now, just a few metres away, so the attacker made his escape, careering along the pavement past him at high speed towards Berkley Square.

Engine running and steering wheel cranked all the way to the right, D.I. Sharpe knew it was all just a matter of timing. The scooter had left the two victims behind, and despite Rossi's efforts, he was still far from catching his quarry.

'Three.'

Sharpe put down his sandwich as the scooter buzzed along the pavement in search of a gap in the line of parked cars.

'Two.'

A final slurp of his iced coffee, and he slid the car into gear.

'One.'

Sharpe punched the accelerator, and the vehicle leapt up the curb into the path of the approaching scooter. The rider swerved to avoid a collision but not quickly enough, and the bike took a glancing blow with the car's front bumper. There was a screech of tyres, metal and plastic as they impacted first the pavement and then the wall of an art gallery. Sharpe was out of the car immediately and pinned the offender to the ground. Rossi arrived a moment later, wheezing. He handcuffed the youth with little sympathy and then pulled him to his feet before shoving him into the back of the car.

Over the next two hours, the scene was extensively photographed and skid marks measured. Then vehicle positions were recorded, and statements were taken. The incident tape was finally pulled down by one of the uniforms as the shadows began to lengthen. D.I. Sharpe turned to his partner.

'I think we should check on Lady Astbury and her lunch partner back at her residence. A couple of things have occurred to me since they left. It's only a short walk.'

They arrived at the imposing building a few minutes later.

'A private lift boss, that's pretty swish,' Rossi said, gawking at the oak panelling and polished brass. 'I'll bet these places are worth a few quid. Our combined annual wages wouldn't even cover one mortgage payment.'

'I seriously doubt the sort of people who live here have ever even heard the term mortgage, Rossi. Now do me a favour and don't embarrass us.'

The ancient lift jerked to a stop, and the detectives stepped out. After a brief inspection, Sharpe noted there was only a single operational door on the entire floor. The others were sealed and painted in the same light blue eggshell as the landing walls.

As if on cue, the large mahogany door swung open. From behind it appeared a maid.

'Good afternoon, you must be the police officers,' she said in a Sicilian accent.

'Si signora,' replied Rossi, drawing a scowl from Sharpe.

'Come in, please, Lady Astbury is in the lounge but Mr Landridge has left. May I offer you some refreshment?'

'I could murder a cup of tea. Earl Grey would be fabulous.' Sharpe said before Rossi could continue in his native tongue.

'Of course, I'll bring it through,' she said and led them in. She gestured towards the sofa and they sank into its plush cushions. Lady Astbury sat adjacent to them in an armchair so large she resembled a child.

'I'm so fortunate you were on hand to help us, inspector,' Lady Astbury said, her voice muffled under a clear oxygen mask. 'Please forgive me,' she continued as she pulled the face-covering away, unhooking the elastic from her ears.

'We didn't stand a chance with the shock of it all and it makes me wonder about my safety all the more these days.'

'I wouldn't worry, Lady Astbury, this sort of thing is fairly rare in this part of the city and it would be very unlikely that you will experience anything like this again,' assured Sharpe.

'Even so, detective, I may think about some sort of personal security just for my own peace of mind. Here's my card. Would you be so kind as to let me know if anyone comes to mind? It'll be well paid and well-travelled so you would certainly be doing them as much a favour as you would me.'

'Thank you, Lady Astbury, I–'

'Sounds perfect Boss, would save me spending every day with a grumpy sod like you.'

'Go and get the car, Rossi,' he chucked the keys to the Italian with far more gusto than required. 'We need to get to Chelsea before they all go home,'

17

Scott tickled the accelerator of his 1967 Mustang. He couldn't have counted the number of hours he'd spent over the past two years restoring every nut, every bolt and every panel to its former glory. Well, eighteen months to be more accurate, as his body had needed restoration from his multiple broken bones before he could start restoring the car.

It burbled, coughed, and then burst into life. Unable to keep the smile from his face, he gently slid the car into gear, edged it out of the workshop and into the yard.

He got out, locked up, and admired his work once again. He ran a finger along the white paintwork and the green pinstripe which ended in a graphic of a small flower. Not just any flower, the five bow-shaped petals of a jasmine. He slid back into the driver's seat, and pulled his wedding ring from his jeans' pocket. He then twisted it around the keyring so it sat next to the ignition key. After warming the engine, he headed out onto the main road.

Within minutes he tingled like a six-year-old birthday boy. He told himself it was the achievement of rebuilding such a classic and driving it again for the first time. However, the small voice inside his head had something else to say on the matter.

Traffic was light and he pulled into the village square just as a parking space was being vacated directly outside The White Horse, the only pub in Shere to boast Cameron Diaz and Jude Law as former patrons.

'Usual sir?'

'Please. I'll be by the window.'

The barman slid his coffee onto the table a few moments later.

'Well would you look at that. Beautiful.'

Scott immediately looked out of the window. He half expected to see Jasmine stepping elegantly from a Bentley and coming to find him because she recognised the car. But all he saw was a rainbow bursting over the graveyard opposite.

Two coffees, a jacket potato and thirty pages of his current paperback later, he stood to leave. The barman was outside clearing glasses.

'Same time tomorrow, sir?'

That shook him. This was becoming an obsession, and even the staff had noticed.

'No, busy tomorrow, but see you soon,' he said just a little too abruptly.

He bumped up the rise into the car park just off Queen's Road in Weybridge thirty-five minutes later. He crossed the road and threaded his way along the maze of back alleys that ran behind the shops and restaurants that fronted the main road. It was like an assault course dodging the bins, bicycles and a heavily stained mattress. Finally, he reached an open door from which a jet of steam billowed.

'Hey, Pascal, got a minute?'

'Merde, your timing is crap,' the Frenchman exclaimed as he drained a pan of six poached eggs. Scott waited whilst he placed each one onto a diagonally sliced piece of toasted French bread, then slid them in turn onto plates with a range of accompaniments from avocado and lettuce to bacon and sliced sausage. He rapped his knuckle twice on the serving hatch, and then turned.

'Okay, what do you want?'

'I've been thinking.'

'Please don't tell me that.' Pascal picked up the spatula.

'Table two, one sausage, egg and chips, one Cesar salad,' a female voice shouted from the serving hatch.

'Quick, I'm busy,' Pascal said to Scott.

'I've got a job that will set us up for life, no more running a café.'

'I like running a café.'

'Okay, no more taking shit from your missus. Because your café isn't making any money.'

'Ahh, now you're talking,' he smiled.

'Where's table seven's vegan breakfast?' the voice demanded through the hatch.

'You could so leave all this behind.' Scott said.

'Pascal, vegan breakfast, where is it?' She sounded angry.

'I'm beginning to see your point.' Pascal said. Then a woman of around thirty appeared through the doorway to the café.

'Hi, my name's Candy, Candice Jones actually, I'm here about the job.'

'Merde, sorry I forgot you were coming. Just one moment.'

'Be at mine tomorrow afternoon, four o'clock.' Scott said.

'I think I just might.'

Walton-Upon-Thames was next on Scott's list. Not the High Street but a backroad that provided office space for several small manufacturing and repair companies. The courtyard had scruffy two-storey workshops on three of the sides and looked to have been built on a tight budget sometime in the seventies.

He pressed the buzzer for Tech-Ops and smiled into the tiny camera above it. There was a clicking sound from the front door latch, so he gave it a shove and walked into a small hallway. A door opened at the end.

'Mr Ramirez.'

'Cool to see you too, bro.' The South American former Marine filled the opening and offered a fist-bump. Scott guessed he'd been elbow-deep in soldering electronics by the look of his bench and the surrounding detritus of wires and circuit boards.

'Welcome to paradise. Take a seat.' Ramirez gestured to a worn sofa next to a tiny kitchenette. 'What brings you here in that sleek pimpmobile you've finally resurrected?'

'What do you mean finally? It's only been a couple of years.' Scott smiled, 'I've come to offer you the job of a lifetime.'

'Oh man, don't lay that on me after the mess in Marseilles.'

'It wasn't our fault, and you know it.'

'I've got a good thing going here, growing every week.' He gestured to a rack neatly stacked with mobile phones, laptops and even a toaster.

'What, you're clearing five hundred a week, a grand at most, what with overheads and narky customers who don't pay?'

'It's all legit. I come to work, I pay my bills, I don't go to prison. It's simple, and it's where I'm at.'

'This really is the job of a lifetime.'

'No.'

'Be at mine tomorrow afternoon, four o'clock.'

'No.'

'I reckon its worth between one-fifty and two hundred million.'

'Definitely no then, risks must be huge for that kind of gig.'

'Nope, and it's aboard a ship so just your kind of job. Be at mine, four o'clock.'

'No. Are we done?'

'No, think about it. One more job, then retire in style.'

'Get out. I'm not doing it.'

'See you tomorrow then.'

Ramirez laughed, 'Go on, go. I've got paying customers waiting on stuff.'

Outside Scott dropped into the seat of the Mustang and banged the steering wheel. But driving out, an idea came to him, and his focus returned to luxuriating in the beautiful scent of freshly trimmed leather. He reached into his jacket, pulled out his phone, and rang Jay.

'Wassup? You sound like you're parachuting.'

'In the car, don't have hands free.'

'That's illegal, you could get told off by a twit in a uniform half your age.'

'Shut up Jay, I have an idea but it needs some development. Could be a decent retirement plan if all goes well but I think Ramirez needs some convincing.'

'Bullshit him, tell him it's worth two hundred grand.'

'It's worth over one hundred and fifty million.'

'That hands free you're not using must be playing up, what's it really worth?'

'I just told you.'

'Seriously?'

'Seriously, are you in?'

'I'd need a psychiatrist not to be.'

'You've needed one of them for as long as I can remember. Just be at mine tomorrow afternoon at four o'clock. I'll also need you to work some magic in convincing Ramirez.'

Scott ended the call and tossed his phone onto the passenger seat.

18

Scott cleared some space on the bench in his workshop before the others arrived. He assembled his notes and made a quick mug of peppermint tea. Jay entered first, shortly followed by Pascal.

'No luck with Ramirez?'

'Naah, he's apparently happy soldering crap back together for a fiver,' Jay said.

'Damn, we really do need him on this. I've only outlined a few ideas but without a tech I can't see that any idea will work.'

'What won't work?' Pascal said.

'Jeez where do I start?' Scott ran his fingers through his hair, and then gestured to the bench. 'Pull up a seat, gentlemen, because there's one fifty, maybe two hundred million pounds worth of gems and jewellery here for the taking,' he tapped his notebook. 'All we need is a little smart thinking. Oh, and it'll take a couple of years to pull it off.'

'I'm lost, what are you talking about?'

'Titanic, Titanic II to be more precise, is a ship being built in the far-east right now. The original was so hyped that it attracted the highest concentration of millionaires anywhere on the planet for its maiden and only voyage.

'Yeah, so?' Jay said.

'So Titanic II isn't just going to mimic the shape and design of its predecessor. It's also going to mimic the prestige. Everyone who's anyone will be clamouring for a ticket.'

'Come on,' Pascal shrugged. 'Where are you going with this?'

'The type of person who was a millionaire one hundred years ago is now a billionaire, and this little party boat should have the likes of Elon Musk, Bill Gates, Brad Pitt, Warren Buffett and Coco Chanel on board when it sets sail for its maiden voyage.'

'I think you'll find Coco Chanel died a long time ago,' Pascal said.

'Okay, whatever, you get the idea.'

'But everything is digital now,' objected Jay. 'Gone are the days when a shotgun and a ski mask at your local Barclays could set you up for life, now it's all nerds and laptops, so how are we going to rob them?'

'One hundred grand is all I need to say to you guys. One hundred grand is not how much this job is worth. It's not even how much you'll earn. It's how much the first tickets have sold for to be a passenger on this thing.

'Imagine if they are dropping a hundred Gs on a ticket for a six day trip what their jewellery collection is going to look like. It has been estimated that over one hundred million dollars of jewellery, diamonds and bonds were lost on the original ship, and that was over one hundred years ago. I'm talking fifty million each, probably more.'

'I'm not convinced,' Jay said. 'Nobody carries that kind of dosh around.'

'Remember Tamara Ecclestone?' Scott said. 'She was robbed just a few years ago and the thieves got away with twenty-five million. And she's just the sort of person who's going to be on this ship. Twenty-five million, one person, so if anything, I've massively underestimated the potential haul. Do the maths, two hundred million pounds only represents eight Tamara Ecclestones, and there's going to be nearly two thousand passengers on board.'

Pascal and Jay both straightened up, and their eyes looked to have brightened by a couple of shades.

'With a pay-out like this,' Pascal said. 'Maybe a two-year project doesn't seem so, how you say, intolerable? How do we do it?'

'I'm not quite sure, that's why we're all here. Try and pull some ideas together, agree on a rough direction.'

'Well first-off,' Jay said, 'we're going to need some cash to keep us afloat until pay day.'

'Granted,' Scott said. 'I've already sorted that part of the plan, so don't worry about working capital or your hooker tokens.' Jay didn't bite.

'Most insurance companies settle theft claims in two to three months, provided all the paperwork's done on time. And a shop can't survive on zero stock after a robbery, so it'll probably plead an extension of credit with its suppliers to bridge the gap between re-stocking and the insurance company paying out.'

'What's your point?' Jay said.

'Not only did we hit the two Guildford jewellery shops six weeks ago, we also would have taken a great deal of their dead stock. Therefore, of a lower value than what they've replaced it with. I say we hit them again in a further three weeks to make sure they're all re-stocked and just repeat the raid exactly as before.'

'One problem,' Pascal said. 'You ditched Wesley, so we don't have a driver.'

'He was out of control and would have got us all caught. It had to be done. We don't need his type and if you think otherwise then walk out now, no hard feelings. But if you stay then abide by my rules or you'll be out too. Am I clear?'

He mumbled an insincere agreement.

'Right,' Scott continued. 'Another driver shouldn't be too difficult to source but I don't have anyone in mind so open to suggestions.

'We also need to think of a viable plan for the raid on Titanic II. First question is how do we get the loot off the ship, provided we even come up with a plan to get a hold of it in the first place?'

An hour of ideas and discussion followed, but nothing workable came from it.

'One thing seems clear to me from the outset,' Scott said. 'We need an inside man to get a copy of the blueprints for the new ship. Information on where every air duct leads, every wire goes and every crawl-space is. We may need to disappear quickly or travel the length of the ship unseen.'

Both Jay and Pascal remained silent.

'Okay, find somebody working on the build and let your imagination run free for ways the job might be achieved. And Jay, I've had an idea but I need your silver tongue to work a little magic. Oh, and watch the James Cameron Titanic film at least twenty times just to get a feel for what we're getting ourselves into.'

'Lifejackets by the look of it then,' Pascal said.

19

Candy heaved the bag containing her college folders up onto her shoulder. It weighed just a few grams less than the bus she'd stepped off five minutes earlier, and she'd been walking with it ever since. Why couldn't there be a closer bus stop? Finally, she reached the café and pushed the door open. There were no customers inside, but she could hear voices from through the serving hatch, so she moved closer. But before she called out, one of them said something which piqued her interest.

'Two hundred million seems an awful lot of money to turn down. What's with him?'

The accent was clearly French, but she'd forgotten his name already.

'Dunno, needs a slap around the face if you ask me,' the other man said.

'Ha, Jay you're such a fool. He'd splat you with his little pinkie if he wanted to.'

'Shut up you–'

The clatter of a fallen chair echoed around quiet café. Candy's bag had caught the back of it and she hadn't noticed it toppling.

'We're closed,' the Frenchman called from the kitchen.

'You forget to lock the front door?' The other one said quietly.

'No kidding, Clouseau.'

The Frenchman opened the door which led to the kitchen.

'You're still here? Can I help you?'

'I'm here about the job. You told me to come back at four today, remember? You were too busy last time.'

'Merde, yes, sorry I forgot. Do you have any experience waiting tables?'

'Well, I've done pub jobs and the like between studying, so I know the ropes.'

'Ropes?'

'Sorry, I'll be fine. Just give me a notepad and your life will get infinitely better, I promise.' She gave him her best smile, and hoped it had reached her eyes. Because that's what they always said, wasn't it? If it doesn't reach up there then they'll know you're having them on.

'Okay, we will give it a go. Start Monday morning at six. Not a second later or you're fired before you start.'

'Oh wow, thank you. It means so much to me. I won't let you down.'

'See you Monday. Now, I need to get back to the kitchen, so if you don't mind,' he gestured towards the door, but then paused.

'Oh, what was your name again?'

'Candy.'

'Okay, I'm Pascal. See you Monday.'

She left to the clunk of a lock being turned in the door behind her. At last, something stable to tide her over until she finished college and could embark on her new career. Her shoulders were so light that she barely noticed the weight of her bag on the way back to the bus stop. She almost felt like skipping there. Halfway along the road a silver Audi pulled up beside her and kept pace with her steps. The window slid down but she kept looking dead ahead. She really didn't need this, some kerb-crawling creep.

'Give you a lift love?'

She squinted, but couldn't even see the bus stop in the distance.

'It's alright, I was in the café with Pascal just now.' She upped her pace. 'Congratulations on the job, Candy.'

That stopped her, but the car overshot so had to reverse back a few feet. The sudden blare of a car horn jarred her as a second car swerved past. The passenger door of the Audi swung open and the man inside leaned over.

'Come on, get in. I'll give you a lift.'

The bag was digging into her shoulder now and the sharp sting of a blister had begun to make itself known on her right heel.

'Sod it. But I'm warning you, any funny business and I'll claw your eyes out.'

Five minutes later they crossed Walton Bridge on their way to her flat in Feltham. She'd warmed to him already. So confident, so witty, she struggled to keep her eyes off him.

'So Candy, you seem the adventurous type, how would you like to go screaming down the open roads this weekend on the back of my motorcycle? What would you say to that?'

'I'd say move over, I'm riding,' she then laughed. 'Anyway, was that an invitation?'

'Not yet, we're just getting to know each other. Tell me something interesting about yourself.'

'I learned to ride a motorcycle when I was seven, and was driving a car by ten.'

'Yeah right, maybe something I might believe?'

'It's true. My dad owned a farm and taught us in the fields. He thought I might grow up to be a race car driver.'

'And then your career landed you waiting tables in a café, how sweet.'

'It's not by choice,' she said, and turned her head away. But a moment later, she softened and looked back in his direction.

'So,' he said. 'Tell me a bit more about being a race car driver.'

'To raise some money my dad rented one of the fields out to the local stock-car racing club. I even sweet talked myself into the driving seat for a few races.'

'And did crap I'll bet.'

'Finished second in one race, actually.'

'Well, what are the chances? I'm looking for a decent driver as it goes. Do you think you're up for something a little over the line?'

'Illegal you mean?'

'Could be.'

'Is that what I heard you talking about in the kitchen?'

Jay was silent for a minute.

'Can I trust you?'

She thought of her law degree and the potential it held for a better life, and the slightest hint of a criminal conviction would have her barred from a criminal court before she'd even qualified.

'Sorry, I can't. It's just not worth it.'

'I haven't told you what it's worth yet.'

'No, it could compromise everything. I'm sorry.'

'Suit yourself. If you want to miss out on the biggest opportunity of your life, who am I to judge?'

They drove in silence for six long minutes.

'We're almost there, left here please.'

'Feltham Young Offenders Prison,' he read.

'Yes, I'm in the road opposite the entrance, just along here on the right.'

But as they turned into the road, Candy could see her front door in the distance. An image of her sister Becky flooded her mind, lying in the open doorway, covered in blood, her spine twisted like a knotted old branch.

'How much?' she said.

'This isn't a taxi love, don't worry about it.'

'The driving job, how much would I get? It is what you were talking about with Pascal, isn't it?'

20

Scott looked from the sea-sprayed porthole to the foam below as it danced on the peak of each foreboding wave. He imagined the deep black pits between them all had the potential to swallow him whole, draw him down, down into the freezing depths below. God, he hated boats, and he'd been aboard this one for far too long. Two hours down and a tortuous six to go. Each time the cabin dropped his stomach followed, but only in time for it to compress once the room began to rise once again. Over and over, knowing that the watery bile was on its way up, but not yet, just a little more torture before it does.

The swell had incessantly grown since they left Liverpool, and showed no signs of calming. Maybe food was the answer. He drew himself up from the bunk and dropped his Timberlands heavily to the floor. He stood, pulled on his jacket and then left the cabin.

In the featureless corridor, he bounced from one Formica wall to the other until he reached a stairway towards the centre of the ferry. He grabbed the handrail and ascended the narrow treads as they wound their way from the cabin decks up to a tastelessly decorated public lounge. As he crossed it, the aroma of fried food grew stronger so he followed his nose to the restaurant.

'Egg and chips please.'

The woman behind the counter looked to be in her sixties. She eyed him with what appeared to be pity.

'You look a bit green, not taking the waves well are we, pet?'

He raised an eyebrow.

'Could I get an orange juice with that as well please?'

'You could love, but orange is high in acid so I wouldn't recommend it. What you need is a dose of ginger beer.'

'I really don't want beer, of any description.'

'Well ginger tightens your oesophagus. Helps keep what's in your stomach, in your stomach if you know what I mean. And it's not alcoholic if you're worried about driving the other end.'

'Okay, whatever. Don't make those eggs too greasy either, could you poach them please?'

'Okay love, I'll bring them over if you want to go and see Marge on the till. Remember to take your ginger beer from the fridge.'

'Thanks,' he replied without enthusiasm. After paying he took a seat, ran his eyes over the bill, and mused that it wasn't just him who stole for a living.

The food arrived and along with the ginger it worked a certain amount of magic. Once finished, the churning in his stomach remained, albeit to a lesser degree. But a niggling sensitivity in his gullet drove him to see what solutions the shop might have to offer.

He found a small packet of green and yellow boxed pills, apt he thought given his pallor, and pulled the plastic strip from the box. He pressed four white discs from their foil nests into the palm of his hand and swayed with the others in line for the till.

In addition to his pills, he held another bottle of ginger beer which he opened in preparation. He swung the palm of his hand containing the four tablets up to his mouth. As he did so, the man in front of him waved his card at the reader, and after a bleep, he moved aside.

Jasmine's face looked back at him from behind the till. As this recognition hit home, so did the pills, squarely in the back of his throat. But without a wash of ginger beer, they got no further. He choked and gagged, struggling for air. His head swam, his diaphragm lurched, and his legs gave way as he dropped to all fours, desperate to take a breath.

A wave of vomit carrying his partially digested lunch gushed in stringy chunks from his mouth and nose, splashing onto the vinyl floor. A woman behind him screamed.

Eventually, his airway cleared enough for him to take a deep, acidic breath and his focus returned to his surroundings. But this awareness also brought the realisation that it was just a life-size cardboard cut-out of his former fiancé advertising a mineral water. Evidently, her modelling career had taken off.

Feeling foolish, he recovered after a couple of slugs of the drink he'd yet to pay for. He decided it was probably best to return below and close his eyes until the ferry docked.

*****

Scott looked over the ship's railing as they nudged up to their berth. Belfast had an oppressive cloud of dank mist smothering it. The time was just past six in the morning and there were a few hours to kill before he could get to work. Before he disembarked, he returned to the shop, pulled out his phone, and snapped a picture of Jasmine's smiling cardboard face. With modelling gigs like that, Del Toro's influence must be helping her career along very nicely. He had a long way to go to win her back, but win her back he would.

After a short walk he found an open café near the water's edge. He took a seat next to a plate glass window and could just make out the silhouette of the Titanic Museum on the opposite dock. He made a phone call.

'Jay it's me. Just wondering how your silver tongue worked on that landlord.'

'Smoothly, as I predicted.'

'Did he agree to it?'

'Yup.'

'What's it costing us?'

'Six grand.'

'You're kidding? Just for five minutes of acting.'

'Says he doesn't want to lose the rent.'

'Offer him five, but if he doesn't play ball just give him the six.'

'I'll pass by on my way out later.'

'Just don't get caught.'

Scott ended the call and stared across the water. Even in the mist, the museum stood out from the surrounding buildings with its striking architecture. Although square in central design, the modern structure also had four diagonally ascending wings, one from each corner. Supposedly they mimicked the bough shape of the original Titanic and gave the cube-like building an Oriental look.

Curious, he thought, the Orient is precisely where the ship's replacement is being born and where he too would be heading soon.

21

Sharpe waited as the pair of scrolled iron gates swung open. They had to be at least twelve-feet high. He eased the BMW forward and it crunched down the white gravel driveway towards a glass-fronted house. It might have cost slightly less to illuminate than the Guggenheim, but he doubted there would be much in it.

'They'd need a giraffe just to clean the windows on the ground floor,' Rossi said. Sharpe ignored him.

'Stay in the car, I think this might require some tact and I doubt you've heard of such a thing.'

'Okay, Boss.' Rossi's attention returned to a football match on his phone. Sharpe got out. He exhaled a light fog and his index finger pressed the surprisingly cold doorbell. He waited, admiring the modern door which could easily accommodate his office desk being carried through it, sideways.

'Be out in a tic,' a female voice came from a hidden speaker. Thirty seconds later, the door glided open and Sharpe stumbled back as a woman shoved a carry-on suitcase at him before returning inside.

'Just got to get a couple more bits, so you may as well sling the case in the boot whilst you're waiting.'

Sharpe frowned, and she returned a moment later with an overflowing Louis Vuitton bag in one hand, and a tiny dog in the other. She thrust the bag at him even though he was still holding the case.

'Come on, don't just stand there like a lemon. I'm meant to be on set by eight.'

'Sorry, Miss…'

She looked at him with more scrutiny now.

'You're not their usual. Has Bob pulled a sickie?'

'I'm Detective Inspector John Sharpe. Might I have a word?'

That certainly slowed her down.

'What's happened? Who's died?'

'Don't worry, I can assure you it's nothing so grave. But I would like a moment of your time and it is very important.'

She pulled a phone out of her spray-on jeggings and checked the time.

'The driver's due in two minutes, so you'd better talk fast.'

Sharpe lowered her bags to the ground, reached into his pocket, and drew the clear plastic evidence bag up so she could see the sparkling engagement ring inside.

'Mrs Braithwaite, owner of the jewellers, gave me your address. I was hoping you could tell me what relevance this might have to someone other than yourself, Jasmine. Own a motorcycle, does he?'

'Oh no, what's he gone and done now?'

22.

The pedals on Ramirez's carbon-fibre triathlon bike spun in a blur as he shot along the paved section next to the river. Insects occasionally bounced off his clear lenses, with the odd one landing in his mouth. There was a chill in the air, but the sun was up and the sky showed promise for the day ahead. Yes, it was probably going to be a good day, he thought to himself as he powered the cranks around and picked up speed along a straight stretch of concrete.

He checked his watch, twenty-four minutes and twenty-six seconds, not bad. He cranked, and then stood on the pedals to roll over the speed bump at the entrance to the industrial park. He could see his building ahead, but something new had caught his eye on a lamppost near the entrance. It was a yellow poster, a planning permission poster.

He looped around and pedalled back to read it.

Seconds later, he threw his helmet against the nearby wall and kicked a rubbish bin with enough force to dent the steel.

23

Scott sat at the head of his workbench with Jay on one side and Pascal on the other.

'Okay guys, I want to hear your ideas before I tell you what I've come up with. Jay?'

'Dunno really, it's all a bit outside my line of expertise, all this, boats and stuff.'

The door behind them gave a light groan as it opened. Must oil that, thought Scott as he turned to see Ramirez enter, rucksack over one shoulder.

'The wanderer returns,' Jay said.

'Right,' replied the Marine as he thundered across the workshop.

'Good to see you,' Scott said. 'Is this a social visit?'

'They're turning my workshop into a McDonalds. Landlord has given me three weeks to be out, so I'm fresh out of options.

'Seems it's not so easy to make an honest buck, so looks like I'm back to the dishonest ones.'

'What I like to hear.' Jay offered a palm for a high five, but the sombre Ramirez ignored it.

'I took an educated guess and did some online research. I came to the conclusion that the only job that you could be planning, given the kind of dough you mentioned, is this new Titanic.'

'Well deduced,' Scott said.

'I looked into it further and it turns out that an ex-marine buddy of mine is already on the job, in China that is,' Ramirez continued.

'What, he's a male prostitute?' Jay said. But the look Ramirez gave him rapidly melted the smug grin from his face.

'So, I emailed him.' Ramirez continued as he placed his rucksack on the bench. From it he pulled a ream of papers. 'I got him to send me some pictures of the ship, but access is limited apparently. These are all internals of the area he's working in.' He laid the pictures out into rows and columns. 'He's there as an independent contractor for CFX Welding and should be for at least the next year.'

'It looks pretty basic,' Scott said. 'But it's early in the build process I suppose so that's to be expected. Amazing work though, Ramirez, and great initiative. Thanks. Is there any way he could get us work there, on the ship, during the build?'

'Yeah, should be cool, he's solid.'

'How come he's working at a Chinese shipyard in the first place?' Pascal said.

'He's a really talented welder, probably headhunted as he's renowned for his work with marine grade steel. Got years of experience welding submarines back together. After years in high pressure hostile environments, they certainly take a beating.'

'I had a bird like that recently, high pressure and hostile, but could certainly take a beating, if you know what you mean.' Jay said with a smile, but no one acknowledged the comment.

'Well, I'm a coded welder,' Scott said. 'And so is Jay, so see if your man can get us on his crew. If this little job goes to plan I'll make it well worth his while.'

'Will do,' Ramirez said. 'I'm coded as well, but think I need to renew.'

'What is this code thing?' Pascal said.

'It's just a qualification, like a driving licence for sticking shit together,' Jay said.

'Any thoughts from you Pascal?' Scott said. 'Another way to get in on the build maybe?'

'No, no ideas,' he shrugged. 'Not great with planning stuff, you know? Well, carpentry's a passion. I'm very creative with wood in my spare time.'

'That's music to my ears. The original ship had plenty of woodwork. In fact the whole interior was wood of some description, if the film was accurate. We need to get you work as a carpenter. Jay, you had some thoughts on securing a cabin, didn't you?'

'Yeah, basically I can have a chat with the bird who does the bookings. I'll probably be able to sweet talk her into getting us a specific room once we've seen the plans of the ship and know what the layout is.'

'They aren't rooms, Jay, they're cabins.' Chester leapt up onto the bench and caused Pascal to jump. Scott gave the cat a few strokes before carrying him to the door and throwing him into the yard.

'Okay, good work so far. But pay attention because here's how we're going to lift a couple of hundred million pounds worth of loot from the doomed liner's replacement.'

Ramirez and Pascal nodded but Jay fiddled distractedly with a dating app on his phone.

'The job is straightforward in theory but undoubtedly more complex in execution. The first thing we need to achieve will hopefully be sorted by Ramirez inasmuch as we need to get aboard the ship during its construction. The reason for this will be clear in a moment. Losing all of that jewellery on the Marseilles train was a painful lesson, but it's given me an idea.'

Scott opened an A4 note-pad. The page was neatly ordered with numbered bullet points and some sketched diagrams.

'You see the thieves took our stash whilst we were asleep. Not the easiest thing to do to a light sleeper like me, but with the aid of a little anaesthetic gas they could have ridden an elephant around the room and nobody would have been any the wiser.'

'Except all the shit,' Jay said. 'Elephants shit everywhere. Leave a right mess they do.'

'Thank you, Doctor Doolittle, now can you shut up before I get distracted and leave an important detail out?'

'Righto.'

'We were rendered unconscious for probably a couple of hours and that's exactly what we're going to do to all aboard the Titanic II.'

'But how are we—'

'Jesus Jay, would you just shut up. I'll explain everything if you just close that mouth of yours and listen for once.'

'I was going to ask if anyone fancied ordering a delivery pizza, but I won't now.'

Scott was about to respond, but heard a knock on the showroom window next-door. He let it go.

'The first task is to research what gas we can use to achieve anaesthesia for the passengers and crew. Three thousand people in all, believe it or not.'

Pascal and Ramirez let out low whistles simultaneously before Scott continued.

'We'll be wearing gas masks that we've hidden in advance aboard the ship. Ramirez, can I task you with this research along with sourcing half a dozen masks that will be suitable for the type of gas we need?'

'I've some military contacts who owe me.'

'Good, I take it the usual carbon filters for some gasses won't work, but I really don't have any knowledge in this area. We need to be confident in the amount of gas we need, the type that will knock a ship-load of people unconscious, and a reliable system to ensure we aren't included.'

'Cool.'

Scott took a second to write notes next to his bullet points and then turned the page of his notebook.

'Pascal, your knowledge of carpentry is actually fortuitous. We'll now need you on the crew that's going to China.' Scott held up a finger. 'Before you ask, I'll elaborate.'

There was another knock on the showroom window, this time louder.

'Come on Sherlock, when are you getting to the juicy bit?'

'Shut up and listen Jay. All of this is important.'

Jay mimed slapping the back of his own hand, then sat back and crossed his arms.

'Where was I? Oh yes, before I get too far into Pascal's role, I want everyone to go to their doctor claiming chronic insomnia and get the strongest sleeping pills available on a repeat prescription. If your doctor won't play ball then there's plenty of over-the-counter pills that are pretty potent, just get as many as you can. We'll need around two thousand tablets, so get busy with that insomnia routine.'

Jay yawned deeply.

'Our first goal is to take control of the bridge. This will have an independent air conditioning unit through which we will pump our initial burst of gas. Once the crew are out cold, we can then use the automatic locking device to seal the outside deck doors if it hasn't already been done due to weather conditions. The Atlantic can cut up pretty rough in the spring, and that's when the ship's due to sail.

'As you might expect, we'll be doing this late at night, so there won't be many people on deck, if any, but we need to ensure that the ship is as gas-tight as possible. Phase-two is where the anaesthetic will be routed into the public air conditioning system and effectively knock everybody else unconscious.

'We then have a limited amount of time to clean out every cabin of its valuables, starting on the upper deck with the first class suites and working our way down until we either finish the last cabin in second or the passengers start to show signs of reanimation.'

'How we going to get all that loot off the ship and away in the middle of The Atlantic?' asked Ramirez. 'It's not as if we can air-lift it by helicopter as they wouldn't have the range. And a drop and dash ship would not only have to be large enough to pull a trans-Atlantic crossing but also easily picked up by the authorities within twenty-four hours. I can't see a viable solution.'

'The simple answer is the loot never leaves the ship. It just vanishes into thin air as the passengers enjoy a deep night's sleep.'

'Okay,' Pascal said with a shrug, 'you really lost me now.'

'This is where the China part comes in. We need to get ourselves out there in order to perform a little magic.

'If you can get yourself, Jay and me on as specialist welders,' he said to Ramirez. 'And Pascal as a chippie, then you have actually eliminated some of the obstacles I had anticipated. So now my plan should work even more efficiently. Instead of me going into greater detail let me show you what I've been working on.'

Scott pulled a rolled poster from under the workbench.

'You can get anything off eBay these days. Take a look at this blueprint of the original Titanic,' he smiled and then unrolled the large print on the worktop, using a coffee mug and a couple of large spanners to prevent it from rolling back up.

'Okay,' using a pen to mark the print. 'All of the upper decks seem to have a mix of cabins, being first and second. The lower you go, the less first and the more second, eventually mixing with third class on E Deck and solely third on F Deck. Obviously the higher the class of ticket you buy, the slightly more living space you will have, but space is certainly at a premium on a vessel like this. The new ship only has first and second class but I think the layout will be roughly the same.'

'I thought the whole idea of the Titanic was that, as the name would suggest, it is enormous.' Pascal said.

'You're partly right, but this was built in the early 1900s and compared to the cruise ships bobbing around the Bahamas today, it's a lot smaller.

'When the original ship was built, there were big old heavy-duty cables, and the pipe-work for the sanitary-ware was iron and therefore bulky. Naturally, the design had to incorporate large cavities in the walls for all the service items to reach each cabin.

'But now, think about the technology of something as ordinary as your mobile phone. It's incredibly compact with the power of a computer that would have taken up two large buildings as recently as the seventies.

'Now we've got materials like carbon-fibre or Kevlar for ducting, titanium instead of iron, and flexible plastic replacing heavy earthenware toilet wastes. The space-saving inside the walls will be dramatic, but the whole brief with Titanic II is that it is to be as near to the original specifications as possible. So, the more compact everything is inside the walls, the more space there will be for us to conceal the gas cylinders and then later the loot inside of them. Scott changed his focus. The two figures walking past the obscured glass window on the left-hand side of the workshop concerned him.

'From this blueprint,' he circled an area with his pen, 'you will see that all of the ducting for the upper levels travels under the floor of E Deck, then branches off to its respective destinations. We need two cabins on E Deck to tap into this, so it's vital we get on the construction team in order to create hideaway cavities inside the walls of two adjoining cabins in this area here.'

He highlighted a short line of cabins on the starboard side forward of amidships from E20 to E40.

'It should be possible with the reduced bulk of the wires and service pipes to make some decent space. Once these cavities have been created, we slide the gas cylinders holding the anaesthetic inside. These will then be sealed so our work remains undetectable to the casual observer. This will be achieved by fixing the furnishings to one wall and the bed to the other, effectively hiding the access panels as per the original ship.

'We then finish our contract work for the shipbuilders and head back home in preparation for her maiden voyage, ensuring we have booked the two cabins in which the storage hides have been created.

'As I said, we then board the ship for the maiden voyage, gas the passengers and crew mid-Atlantic, and rob them of anything valuable. We put the loot in the hides which previously held the gas, and Pascal then re-seals them.

'Jay, Ramirez and I will then take the empty gas cylinders-' there was a series of bangs on the workshop's roller-shutter.

'Shit, must be the Bulgarians, grab a weapon.'

Scott grabbed a tyre iron as the others grabbed hammers and spanners. Another burst of bangs at the roller-shutter, this time more insistent.

'Police, open up.'

'Change of plan,' Scott said, dropping the weapon and thrusting his notebook and some loose sheets into Ramirez's hands.

'Get upstairs and shove this lot in the wood burner, now.'

'Roger that,' he jogged to the stairs.

'You two get upstairs as well, stay out of sight.'

A louder bang came. This time, they were serious.

'Be there in a minute, just washing the oil off.'

*****

Sharpe stood back as the roller-shutter rattled up.

'Ahh, you, I thought the name was familiar,' he said holding his I.D. at arm's length for Scott to see.

'I'm busy, what do you want?'

'We've met, but this is Detective Sergeant Lorenzo Rossi. Could we come in?'

'Like I said, I'm busy.'

'Okay, I'm wondering if you could tell me your whereabouts on Thursday 7th of March?'

'If you hadn't noticed, this is a car showroom, so I'd have been here all day. Is this going to take long?'

'Just a few questions,' Sharpe made a show of looking around the workshop from the entrance. 'I see you've rebuilt that American car.'

'What does that have to do with anything?'

'Curious that it was damaged right where the chassis number was supposed to be, but I guess you got away with that one.'

'We went through that when I was in hospital. You came up with nothing then, and unless you've got something better this time, I really must ask you to leave.'

'Drop this did you?' he pulled the evidence bag containing the ring from his jacket pocket and held it in front of Scott's nose. He'd rarely seen a man look so taken aback.

'Only we found it a couple of weeks ago in a tunnel just south of Guildford. Jasmine thought you might have mislaid it whilst jumping off a stolen motorcycle.'

'This has nothing to do with her.'

'What, precisely, has nothing to do with her?'

'I think this conversation is over.'

'Son of a bitch!' a yell rang out from upstairs, followed by a bang.

'Got company? Maybe we should come inside and see if we can be of assistance?'

'If that's all, I've got to go.' Scott stepped back and pressed a button. The shutter rattled its way steadily down. When it reached the floor, they turned to leave.

'What do you think, Boss?'

'I'm not quite sure.' They began walking back around to the front of the building.

'He certainly looked surprised at that ring,' Rossi said.

'Yes, but I don't know if that was just because he hadn't seen it for a couple of years, or he recognised it from the robbery. It's difficult to tell.'

'And the car?'

'Arrested him for it at the time, suspected it was stolen but couldn't prove it. He got off with a smart talking solicitor.'

'So where do we go from here, Boss?'

'Keep searching this area. I don't like Mr Rainey but I don't think he's got the resources to pull off a job like this. Still, best not remove him from our enquiries just yet.'

They got in the unmarked five series, and Rossi started the engine.

'Back to base?'

'No, drive around the block, and then find a parking space with a clear line of sight to the showroom. I want to see who that was upstairs.'

*****

Ramirez thundered down the stairs clutching a sheet of fluorescent yellow paper.

'What the fuck is this?'

'Paper. What's got into you?' Scott said.

'Paper, like the council use for planning permission notices. You'd better not be yankin' my chain or I'll rip your head off.' He was up in Scott's face now.

'Cool it, Chester went missing for a couple of days so I made some posters to stick on lampposts, see if anyone had found him.'

'As I said, if I find out you're pulling something to get me on this, you'll regret it.'

'Okay, now if you're finished can we get on please?'

Tension in the room slowly ebbed and they eventually gathered around the bench.

'With my notes gone, I'll finish off by memory, so forgive me if I repeat a couple of things.'

24

Streetlights cast a ghostly glow over the nearby Richmond Bridge, exaggerated by the hanging fog which crept along the river below. On the south side of the bridge, a small cobbled courtyard lay in shadow. Pascal stood at the corner as a lookout, blowing into his hands to keep some life in them.

'Hurry up for Christ's sake,' he said, the anxiety deepening his accent. 'Somebody will be here in any second.'

'Chill out, will you. Nobody's around at this time of night, and unless they're Old Bill, they won't give a toss anyway,' Jay said. He resumed pumping his arm back and forth, the hacksaw blade slowly making its way through the tubular steel loop embedded into the pavement like an oversized frown. Finally, after an agonising six minutes, the steel sheared half an inch across, and their job was almost done.

'Gimmie a hand then, you slack French twat.'

Pascal hurried over and crouched next to Jay. They both grabbed the steel tube and heaved. A groan sounded as the severed ends slowly parted, and finally, there was enough of a gap to thread the length of the hardened-steel chain attached to the thousand cc sports bike through.

'Oi, what are you up to?' came a deep voice that broke the still night air, followed by the scuffle of leather-soled shoes on gritted pavement. A broad man in a rugby shirt appeared at the street corner and sprinted towards them.

What to do? Pascal shuffled back to prepare for a confrontation. But Jay stood his ground, grabbed the crowbar, and walloped the man in the side of his head before he could even get a punch in.

'Don't you hate these busybodies that haven't anything better to do?' Jay said.

Pascal looked at the unconscious man lying awkwardly on the cobbles and shook his head.

'You're totally mental. He needs an ambulance.'

'He's fine. Don't just stand there, we've got a bike to nick and it won't get in the van by itself. Gimmie a push at least.'

They heaved the bike into a waiting van and then headed back across Richmond Bridge towards Kingston, and eventually home.

25

It was the first time Scott had set foot in Brighton since that weekend with Jasmine. He stepped off the train and walked along the platform, through the station, and admired the ornate ironwork which supported the glass roof. It looked to be Georgian, so probably built around the time of the original Titanic. An omen maybe? He'd arrived forty minutes early so had some time to kill before the real reason he was here.

He exited the station and the first thing he noticed was the road name opposite. Guildford Road. His reason for being here was directly connected to the next Guilford job. Another omen? He turned south, down Surrey Street, and shook his head gently smiling. These omens were piling up by the second, what with Guildford being in Surrey. But when it turned into Queens Road, he got his first glimpse of the sea and it took his breath away. Not because it was spectacular, but because so many memories came flooding back to hit him like a tsunami had risen from the sea and knocked him flat.

It took him a moment to return to the present and continue walking. Now with a renewed urgency to get down to the seafront and taste the salty air without the reek of traffic and fast food.

In five minutes, he was past the clock tower and getting closer. Three minutes later he was there, out on the promenade with the screeching seagulls and the old fire-damaged pier to his right. Then, to his left, in the distance was its replacement. Magnetised by its draw he hurried along the seafront, almost breaking into a jog but controlling it, just. Past The Lanes where they'd flirted and joked, and then had lunch in a small café; was it even still there? And then they'd gone on, to the place he was closing in on.

Finally, the tarmac turned to block paving and he'd arrived, breathless from the anticipation rather than the exertion. The gabled entrance to the Brighton Palace Pier was before him. He hurried under the clock tower, past the tacky stalls selling ice cream and candy floss, hot dogs and chips. The smell assaulted his senses with a sickly-sweet craving for junk, but he ignored it. Further along he entered the arcade where he'd beaten her at some of the games, whilst she'd had the better of him in others. The cacophony of pings and electronic effects was jarring, but he could sense Jasmine's echo everywhere. Back outside, into the fresh air, and onwards. He took the right-hand side of the divide along the covered benches that were dotted with pensioners and teenagers. Again, the ornate ironwork mimicked the railway station as well as the original Titanic, bringing the past into the present. When he glanced at the wooden deck, and then beyond the railing and out to sea, he could almost be on a ship heading out of port. The omens were whispering in his ear.

There, just a short way ahead he could see it. Finally, he'd reached his destination, Victoria's Bar. He dropped into a seat at one of the outside tables and took in the view. To his left were the helter-skelter and the other rides which marked the end of the journey. Over the side, the view was back to The Grand, The

Lanes, and the hotel they had stayed in which sat somewhere in between. They'd even looked at engagement rings that weekend, down The Lanes, playing hunt the bargain. Not that he'd have been so stupid to pay their prices with Terry in his contacts list, but it'd been fun, and a glimpse of his future. Or so he'd believed at the time.

He sat for a moment swimming in nostalgia. Then, on an impulse he decided to recreate the selfie that she had taken of them that day. The only picture he possessed of them together, until it had become one with the rug in his flat, glued there by decomposing bile. He hadn't had the heart to throw it out yet.

Once he'd caught his breath, he stood, and walked over to the lamppost they'd been leaning against in the picture. The five opaque spheres which held the bulbs had been like mistletoe above them. He pulled out his phone and opened the photo app, and flicked the camera around to face him. Click, wrong angle. Someone's phone started ringing. Click. Better, but not quite right. Why didn't they answer it, it was really spoiling his moment. Click, almost there. Answer the bloody phone will you. Click, that's it.

Then he realised it was his burner phone ringing inside his suit jacket. He pocketed his regular phone and pulled out the burner.

'Hello.'

'Oh hi, just checking we're still on for midday,' a public-school accent, slightly condescending. Scott almost didn't feel so bad about what he had coming.

'Of course, that's what we'd arranged.'

'Great, although there has been a slight deviation, my partner called in sick this morning so it's just me here today. You might need to wait a few moments if I get a customer come in off the street just prior to your allotted time.' Another good omen, he could get used to this.

'No problem.'

'Great, see you when you get here.'

He ended the call, crushed the sim under his heel and tossed the phone into a nearby bin. Then he returned to Victoria's Bar but took a seat at a different table. This slight change of perspective brought with it a flash of recognition. This was the table they'd actually been sitting at after that selfie she'd taken of them. There had been an argument, both of them shouting. One of them had drunk too much, could it have been her? It felt like it but he couldn't be certain. Why hadn't he remembered this before? A glass got smashed and they were asked to leave. Had they both been drunk? It perplexed him to have this sudden recall. He drew out his regular phone and looked at the screen, to the pictures he'd just taken. They were all wrong. The sky was wrong, the light was wrong, he was wrong. In the picture with Jasmine it'd been sunny, they were laughing, they were wearing t shirts and sunglasses on the tops of their heads. But now he wore a three-piece suit, there were dark clouds overhead and he looked like he wanted to kill someone.

26

Scott walked into the showroom which wasn't so dissimilar to his, only to see a valeter detailing the interior of a Jaguar. After the salesman's call an hour earlier, he'd decided on plan B, meaning that he'd do what he needed to here, in the building. But now with another witness it was back to plan A, and out on the open road.

A thin, henpecked looking man appeared from the small office to the rear of the showroom.

'Good afternoon, it's the Cayenne you're interested in isn't it, sir?'

'Definitely, the v8.'

'As it happens, I'm glad to say we have two of those in stock.'

'That's why I'm here,' Scott said. 'So, let's get straight to the point of my visit as I see you've got the black one waiting outside. I want to take a quick ride around the block to check it's just what I'm after and then we can sort out the details and finance options.'

'That sounds perfect to me, sir. Now if I can just take a copy of your licence for our records, mister....'

'Stanton, Geoffrey Stanton,' Scott said as he handed over the stolen driving licence. The man headed for the photocopier and Scott scanned the room for cameras. Five minutes later, they sat in the tedious Brighton traffic.

The salesman assured Scott that the leather was naturally sourced. The engine was wild but at the same time eco-friendly, and the instrumentation so intuitive a ten-year-old could master it. He didn't care.

They wound through the narrow roads north of the coast before finding a decent stretch to open the car up properly. Scott gazed through the passenger-side window and waited patiently for the swap-over point.

Shortly after passing the racecourse, the salesman slowed the car to a crawl and flicked the silent indicator. He pulled into a small, bumpy layby on an open stretch of road surrounded by fields and thankfully no human witnesses. Perfect.

The salesman drew to a stop and killed the engine, then took the key fob with him as he stepped from the car and made his way around the front of the vehicle. Scott reached into the inside pocket of his jacket and drew out a clear plastic Ziploc bag. From it he withdrew a pump-action bottle around twice the size of a lighter. He then slid a pair of clear-lensed glasses on and pulled himself from the comfort of the oxblood leather.

At the midway point, he raised the pump-action bottle and sprayed its contents into the salesman's eyes. The blend of surgical spirit and extra hot chilli powder had the man screaming and scrabbling for something solid to grab onto. A kick to the back of his knees put him straight to the floor. Scott then pressed the tip of a syringe through the man's shirt and into his arm, administering his own mix of tequila and finely powdered sleeping pills directly into the salesman's veins. The time he'd spent in hospital had given him plenty of opportunities to swipe the tools of their trade.

He removed the needle, threw it down a drain, and then returned the empty syringe to his jacket pocket. Then he bent to retrieve the Porsche key fob from the muddy ground next to the salesman's body. He pocketed the key and then grabbed the legs of the inanimate man to drag him into a nearby ditch.

A moment later, Scott appreciated the security of German engineering as he felt the seatbelt buckle glide home with a reassuring clunk.

Back at his workshop, he found a suitable screwdriver and crouched to remove the front number plate. The squeal of the side-door announced someone entering. He stopped what he was doing, reversed his grip on the screwdriver so the blade faced down, and stood. Once he saw it was only Jay, he crouched back down to continue.

'You think she's up to the task then?' Scott asked after a moment's conversation. 'This woman, Candy, you're seeing at the moment?'

'Yes mate, she's mint. Done some banger racing and she's certainly no angel.'

'There's a big difference between driving around a field and being a key role in a double armed robbery.' Scott stood and placed the screwdriver on the bonnet. 'I'll have to see what she's like under pressure behind the wheel. If she's going to be our getaway driver, I don't want to be giving instructions on parallel parking with her in tears and twenty police cars bearing down on us.'

'Don't worry, like I said, she's mint.'

'In your language it usually means she looks like a stripper and has a brain the size of a gerbil. Please tell me she's not a stripper.'

'Honest. She's doing law.'

'Jay, the whole idea is that she's keeping us away from the law.'

'Well at least she'll get us off if we do get caught.'

He punched Jay in the chest a little too hard to be playful.

'Bastard, what was that for?'

'I can't believe that of all the people we know in the game, we have to resort to a complete unknown as our driver. Are you absolutely sure there's nobody else we can use?'

'Trust me, it'll be just like the Dukes of Hazard.'

'No Jay, I seriously hope not. Go out tonight and nick something big and fast. An X5 would be good, or better still, another Cayenne. I need her to get a feel for how a car like that handles when she's smashing it around.'

'Will do, should I paint a confederate flag on the roof?'

27

Clouds made their promised appearance whilst Scott waited in a potholed car park at the rear entrance of Kingston University. After a couple of minutes, they opened to bring a light pattering of rain onto the BMW X5's glass sunroof. The sound may have been therapeutic, but he was far from chilled at the prospect of a wasted afternoon with one of Jay's temporary girlfriends.

An emergency exit swung open and banged when it thumped the fire escape. A pair of girls emerged wearing velour tracksuits over anorexic frames and tans the colour of rust. They pulled on cigarettes as if they alone were providing their much-needed oxygen.

'Christ, please don't let it be either of those two trolls.'

They crossed the yard and got into a small white Mazda which had one door coloured in grey primer. The car pulled away with plumes of blue smoke billowing from the opening windows mixed with the distinct sound of rap music. Scott's attention returned to the building, and he was surprised to see a girl almost upon him, having crossed the car park at a jog before she bounced into the passenger seat.

'Hey, you must be Scott,' she said, wearing a narrow, almost shy smile, 'I'm Candy.'

'Seatbelt,' he said, starting the car.

They drove in relative silence, the awkwardness of first date hanging like the smog of a Havana in the closed environment. But his interest was now piqued by her seemingly humble, quiet character. Not at all how his somewhat low expectations had pictured her. She was pretty, but far more subtle than one of Jay's typical conquests. She had good taste in clothes. Stylish, if a little on the conservative side, and wore blue stretch jeans with a clean white sweater. He was impressed.

Her voice, what little he'd heard of it, sounded like she'd been to one of those private schools, Surrey or Sussex maybe. No fake boobs or Botox, just a naturally beautiful woman, keen to become a professional criminal.

Through Surbiton and out towards Esher, now up to forty miles per hour but just off idle for the powerful engine of the X5.

'Those will have to go.' He motioned to her grey, but not overly high, heels.

'Don't worry, I drive barefoot.'

'Not any more you don't. Running shoes are compulsory. If you have to dump the car and make a run for it you need to be prepared. This isn't something to be taken lightly, as all of our lives are at risk. Rule one is you always do as I say, no exceptions.'

'But what if I don't think you're right?'

He pulled to the side of the road and leaned over Candy's lap to release the door catch and push it open.

'Sorry, this has been a waste of my time. Out.'

'No, it was a serious question. If you expect me to trust you then I need to know why I should.'

He looked at her for a long moment, considering his response. She leaned out to grab the rain splattered door and pulled it shut.

'I said get out. Open the door and get on the other side of it.'

She sat where she was, holding Scott's gaze for several seconds before replying.

'At least drop me at the bus stop, or are you not considerate enough to even do that?'

He waited for a beat, threw the car back into gear and released the brake, turning the wheel just as a juggernaut hurtled past at speed, the horn's blast filling the interior.

'Jesus!' his heart jumped two beats in one. Then, after waiting another beat, he eased the brake off once more. This time he took a long look in the mirror before pulling away.

'Like I said, if you expect me to act on your command without question, how can you reassure me that it really is in our best interest as a team?'

He paused, ran his fingers through his hair, and then answered.

'Because of my experience, because I've been doing this for more than ten years, because after all of those jobs and all of those years I've developed a feel for what's the right thing to do in a certain situation, and I get a sixth sense of what's likely to happen a few moments before it does.'

'Your sixth sense didn't anticipate that truck a second ago.'

He ignored her comment.

'For a job to go smoothly, it takes months and months of rigorous planning, group discussions about every unlikely scenario, unforeseen problem, and eventuality. What if a car won't start? What if there's a police car at the end of the road? What if it's raining? Then the more serious issues like what if there's a helicopter above us or we end up in a hostage situation? All of these questions need to have answers before we even begin to draw up the plan. So, when the job is underway, and I tell you to turn left, not right, I've done it because I already know what would happen if you'd have turned right, understand?'

'Thank you. Couldn't we have had that answer instead of all the dramatics a moment ago? After all, I'm serious about working for you and need to make sure I'm not going to be spending the next twenty years scrubbing floors and being forced to suck some prison guard's unwashed...' she shuddered.

Silence fell and he continued to drive, ignoring the three bus stops they passed before joining the dual carriageway which led to the southbound A3.

Forty minutes later, he pulled into a disused military base just outside of Aldershot. Several buildings, a perimeter road and a small airstrip were the only evidence of the former military base. A wrecking ball had levelled the rest.

He surveyed the area to find two aircraft hangars stood empty with their doors open to the side of the strip. A dilapidated plane sat outside one of them, missing about a third of the parts it would need to fly again. He drew to a stop in the hangar and got out.

'Get behind the wheel and get used to the feel of it, then come back here in five minutes, no longer.'

Candy slid across into the driver's seat and roared off, wheel-spinning away in a plume of smoke as she raced onto the runway. Thankfully the rain hadn't followed them this far south. He set about creating a makeshift course using a selection of things he found in the hangars, traffic cones and empty oil drums for the most part.

He kept an eye on what she was up to as he laid out a course, and was impressed with her fluid control from slides to hard power acceleration on the runway. It was a good start, but her accuracy and stress control were what mattered, and that was what the next stage was all about. He checked his watch as Candy pulled back into the hangar, four minutes and fifty-six seconds later.

'You seem to have got to grips with it, let's see if you can park without bleepers.'

That earned him a narrow-eyed glare. He climbed in and drew the seatbelt across his chest.

'No offence, but women drivers make me nervous.'

Candy floored the car in response, causing the passenger door to swing shut with a slam.

'Stop,' he shouted, 'you have no idea what I want you to do yet, Miss Antsy.'

'Do not call me that.'

'C'mon Miss Antsy, drive out of the hangar nicely then reverse through those two cones to the left of us. Then spin the car clockwise one hundred and eighty degrees.'

'Don't call me that,' Candy yelled over the sound of squealing tyres, flawlessly executing the move Scott had requested.

'Too slow, Miss Antsy and I said clockwise.'

'That was clockwise. It's as fast as this heavy old bus will go.'

'Again,' Scott demanded. 'But correctly this time, please, Miss Antsy.'

Candy repeated the move but now span the car anti-clockwise.

'Jeez, don't you listen? I said clockwise. Get it right this time will you or you're out.'

He continued to taunt her, but she kept her cool and followed his instructions. The next test was a high-speed pass between two narrowly spaced cones and then a sharp handbrake turn to line up for another pair of narrow cones.

Following that, a lap of the perimeter road without her dipping under eighty miles per hour, before slamming back onto the runway to repeat the handbrake manoeuvre.

He doubted that she could follow the order. In fact, he doubted that anyone would have the skill and precision to do as he'd asked, but Candy threw the car into gear and floored it once more, performing the first handbrake slide with precision. She then went through the second set of cones, around an oil drum and onto the perimeter road. Scott looked over at her.

'Are you chicken? Don't tell me you're too scared to keep the accelerator flat to the floor through this first turn.'

She eased off slightly but still had him secretly gripping the side of the seat. She rotated the steering wheel enough to get the rear of the car moving sideways to send a stream of white tyre smoke into the air behind them. She kept her cool and ignored his comments.

'Did you even pass your test, Miss Antsy?'

She looked to be constantly feeling for grip through the steering wheel and easing the power in as smoothly as the adhesion would allow, impressive. Off the perimeter and back onto the runway, she had the BMW up to one hundred and fifteen.

Scott yawned and mimed a stretch, his arm obscuring her vision, so she swatted it away.

'Careful Miss Antsy, I could have you for assault.'

Thirty metres from the cones, she shut off the accelerator and stamped on the brakes, slowing the car to fifty-seven. It was the perfect speed to negotiate the gap and handbrake into the direction of the second set. He grabbed the steering wheel without warning and yanked it around. She jumped, as he had predicted, and it caused the car to lurch violently to one side, upsetting their trajectory.

They ploughed over one of the cones, but she spun the wheel to adjust the angle and managed to get it almost right for the following set of cones, just clipping one to send it flying. They screeched to a halt, and Candy looked calmly ahead through the windscreen.

'Shall we do that again properly this time?'

'I think you've got an idea of my skill, so mightn't be a good idea to make any more noise than necessary and draw attention to this car, which I'm presuming is stolen, don't you think?'

'Good answer. I'm glad to inform you that you've passed your test and may proceed to the exit.'

She pulled away, this time more sedately, towards the exit road. Scott saw she was smiling, her performance had been exceptional, and she knew it.

He caught her looking at him in the reflection of the glass several times on their journey back but didn't comment. There would be plenty of opportunities to get to know her more intimately in the immediate future.

28

D.I. Sharpe stood at his office window and looked out onto the rows of desks, all occupied by officers endeavouring to make the world a safer place. He lowered the Venetian blind, rotated the stick to obscure their view and began his eleven o'clock ritual.

Teapot filled, bone china cup warmed and two pieces of shortbread waited patiently on the saucer. He lifted the teapot and gently poured the Earl Grey into the cup. Salivating, he watched it swirl and mix with the fresh milk until it crept ever nearer the brim. Perfect.

He carried the cup from his filing cabinet, these days nothing more than somewhere to hide office junk, and eased himself down into the chair behind his desk. He reclined it to just the right angle before lifting his left foot, then his right onto the desk and crossed them at the ankles.

'A moment of peace in a world of madness.'

He drew the cup to his lips by the saucer and blew gently on the steaming tea before taking a tentative sip.

'Glorious.'

Next was one of the slices of Highland shortbread, Waitrose, of course. He bit into it and appreciated the crunch of a freshly opened packet, then sipped a tiny amount of tea to help soften the biscuit as it melted onto his tongue. With the cup and saucer resting lightly on his chest, he closed his eyes and savoured the world of delights circling his mouth as he slowly began to chew.

'Boss, Boss,' Detective Rossi shouted as he burst in, jolting Sharpe from his relaxed state and catapulting the reclined chair to its upright position. The cup of tea launched itself down Sharpe's M&S shirt and tie, quickly soaking through to scald his skin.

'Christ almighty, you buffoon.' he shouted, holding the hot, soaked fabric away from his chest and burning his fingers in the process.

'Boss, it's happening again, just like last time.'

'Speak sense man, what are you saying?'

'The jewellers on the High Street, two crews on bikes. We got an alarm.'

'Bugger.' Sharpe stood and grabbed his jacket from the back of his chair. 'Get all units to respond, and I mean everything from cars and helicopters to horses and bikes.'

'We don't have any horses.'

'Just do it.' He snatched his keys off the desk and charged towards the door, thrusting his arm down a jacket sleeve.

*****

Scott felt a flash of anger. The owner of Braithwaite Jewellers had seen them pull up on their bikes, so she'd rushed around the counter and locked the front door before they'd even dismounted.

He tried the door just in case the catch hadn't clicked home but it was solid. He withdrew his sawn-off shotgun from the shoulder holster and rammed its stock into the glass part of the door. It fractured, but the security film prevented it from being smashed.

He tried again, then again, but still no luck. As a last resort he spun the shotgun around and fired.

*****

Sharpe jumped into the five series and screeched the tyres across the smooth concrete car park floor as he hurtled up the ramp to ground level. Rossi emerged from the building just as Sharpe reached the barrier and jumped into the passenger side.

Sharpe waved his I.D. card frantically at the scanner, but the barrier remained motionless.

'Oh, give me yours.'

He reached over to grab Rossi's card, yanking it towards the machine, but it stopped short. Rossi had lurched sideways as it was still attached to the lanyard around his neck.

'Take it off will you man? This is urgent.'

Rossi quickly did as asked, and they rushed out of the car park moments later. At the road they turned right.

'But Boss, it's that way.' Rossi said pointing left with his thumb.

'I know.'

*****

Scott reached through the broken window and unlatched the door as a heavy crack of thunder filled the air. It was so loud it could have been another gunshot. Once inside, he went around the counter and straight to the office door. He tried the handle, but it was also locked. He turned to Pascal.

'Start doing the windows, we're running out of time.'

He drew the butt of the shotgun up and banged the door.

'Open it now, we won't hurt you.'

'Go to hell,' came her muffled reply.

'Last chance, if I have to blow the door off its hinges your head will be next. Open it now and we won't hurt you. Three, two…'

The door clicked and swung open. The owner stood on the threshold, glaring, with the assistant just behind her.

'Open the safe, now.'

She stood there defiantly.

'Fine.' He pointed the barrel of the shotgun at her knees and slid his finger inside the trigger guard.

'Okay, okay, you win.' She backed away towards the safe. The assistant dropped to one knee and then the other, hands raised.

*****

The interior of the five series was filled with sporadic blue light and the staccato screech of the siren.

'Get on the radio, have dispatch put a call into the Hindhead tunnel staff. I want it closed to all southbound traffic in exactly five minutes.' Sharpe braked suddenly ahead of a tight bend, causing Rossi to lurch forward. His seat belt strained and, his arm suddenly outstretched, he lost grip of his phone. It flew onto the dashboard, bounced off of the windscreen then disappeared through the open window as Sharpe threw the car into the bend.

'Nooo!'

Rossi craned his neck to see if his beloved new iPhone had, by some miracle, landed somewhere soft. But it was far too late as Sharpe was already negotiating the next bend.

'Boss, where are we going?'

'Watch and learn, Rossi, but get on to dispatch first.'

Sharpe ducked down a lane, narrowly avoiding a flying cat, and bounced onto a slip road that merged with the A3. He joined the main carriageway, drove at a steady fifty, and flicked off the concealed blue lights. He cruised along, repeatedly glancing in the mirror.

'I'm still not getting this, Boss. They're back there in Guildford.'

'You've got a lot to learn, it's all in the timing.'

Two minutes later, four motorcycles fired past in the outside lane. Sharpe floored it and hit the switch for the blue lights once more.

'Update dispatch on our whereabouts, Milford junction southbound in excess of one hundred miles per hour.'

*****

With every junction Scott and the crew passed, police vehicles poured onto the road like ants. He'd not seen so many outside of a cinema screen. And as their altitude slowly climbed, the sky's bruised clouds seemed to drop ever lower. Then the raindrops began to wallop his visor.

Just as before, the distant thud of helicopter blades had steadily increased until the boom now filled his ears. In seconds it was above them, but this time it didn't just keep pace, it raced towards the tunnel which had finally come into view. But it seemed an impossible distance to cover, especially as they'd been forced to ease off now the grip had dropped by almost half on the slick, wet road.

Red X signs then flickered into life on a gantry above the tunnel, indicating it was closed to all traffic. A burst of brake lights filled the road ahead as each car slowed to a stop, clogging not only all lanes, but also the hard shoulder as some vehicles veered left. The red became just blurry splodges on his fogged visor as the tailback grew to one hundred metres in seconds. He rolled off the throttle even more and the others followed his lead.

*****

Candy chewed on a cuticle as she watched the livestream on her phone. The camera sat fifty metres from the tunnel and was set to show the crew passing that waypoint. The anticipation had become intolerable.

A tap on the window caused her to jump. She pressed the switch to lower it.

'Is everything alright madam?'

'Yes officer, I'm fine.'

'Might I ask then why–'

Ping. The app signalled the crew were nearing the tunnel. She needed to get going.

Her cheeks burned. Words, even simple ones, were out of reach. What could she do to get rid of him? What could she say?

'Only, stopping on the hard shoulder without a valid reason is an offence liable for prosecution in breach of the–'

'Oh, okay officer I'll be on my way then, terribly sorry.'

There was a moment's silence, it stretched for far too long. Just when she thought it couldn't get any more painful, a squawk came from the radio attached to the officer's stab vest. 'All available units to the Hindhead tunnel, pursuit in progress. Approach with caution as the suspects are reportedly armed and dangerous.'

'I'll let you off with a warning this time madam, but please consult your Highway Code and observe the regulations in future. Now, you'd best be on your way.'

Candy sent a silent prayer to the sky and clicked the Porsche Cayenne into drive. A moment later, the police car raced past her with lights and sirens ablaze.

*****

D.I. Sharpe thumped Rossi's knee in jubilation.

'It's working, can't you see? Like rats into a blocked drain.'

'Awesome job Boss, we've got them.'

'For pity's sake will you stop calling me Boss?'

'Sorry Bo– Sir.'

Sharpe slowed as they drew up behind the line of stationary cars which now clogged the carriageway.

'Blue lights don't seem to count for much these days,' he said, as one by one, the cars lethargically edged aside and let them through. He pressed his palm firmly on the horn to speed them up. Meanwhile, the bikes weaved their way into the distance with relative ease.

'They've got nowhere to go,' he said. 'The closer they get to that tunnel, the closer we are to nailing this lot once and for all. They're doomed by their own stupidity. I can almost see a promotion on the horizon before my retirement, you wait and see.'

'Retirement?'

'Oh yes, not far off now. In fact, if the rest of today goes to plan it might just begin tomorrow.'

Sharpe failed to suppress his grin.

*****

One, two, three, four, the bikes made it into the southbound tunnel, slower than Scott had anticipated but still a reasonable distance ahead of their pursuers.

After rounding the second bend, he checked his mirror to see a complete absence of blue flashing lights. Perfect.

One by one, they edged to the right-hand side and bumped up onto the narrow pavement, then nudged through the emergency exit. They dismounted once inside the corridor and ran.

Ten yards later, they burst out onto the northbound carriageway.

In contrast to the stationary southbound lanes, cars flashed past at speeds up to seventy miles per hour.

'Where the hell is your girlfriend?' he looked to Jay, who shrugged.

'Where is she?' he repeated, but the answer was just a more exaggerated shrug.

'Back to the bikes,' Scott said. But just as they were about to push back through the emergency doors the Porsche screeched to a halt beside them.

Within five seconds they were moving again, pulling off their helmets. The car smelled of untouched leather and Barry Manilow played gently from the radio. The ping of a seat belt chime filled the air.

'You'd better have a damned good reason for leaving us hanging there,' Scott said from the passenger seat after pulling his helmet off.

'Can you put your seat belt on, that noise is really annoying.'

Scott bashed his fist into the centre console, startling her.

'Okay, cool it. I got pulled over by the police.'

At the end of the tunnel the windscreen wipers jumped to a furious pace as the sheets of rain pounded the windscreen.

'What did you tell them?'

'Nothing, he ran off to chase you lot almost as soon as it happened, so don't worry.'

'Let me be the judge of that.'

They drove in silence for another mile, but the tension ramped up as the interior filled with sporadic blue light. Candy floored the accelerator.

'Lift off, now.' Scott said, but she ignored him, continuing to accelerate. He grabbed her thigh and squeezed hard.

'Ouch! What are you doing?'

'Slow down and let them pass. They have no idea we're in this car but you're giving them a pretty big clue.'

She eased off, indicated, and pulled into the left-hand lane. The police car raced past and continued into the distance, pulling off at the next junction to loop back around to the southbound carriageway.

'Thank you. Next time do exactly what I say, when I say it. We've been through this multiple times, so just do your job, clear?'

She stared out of the windscreen, not saying a word, George Michael now coming out of the speakers.

'Am I crystal... fucking... clear?'

She nodded, chastened.

'And you can turn that crap off.'

He stabbed a finger at the screen to mute the careless whisper. After three miles, the rain eased. She turned down a series of wooded lanes which led to a small clearing. It was empty with the exception of a glossy black Range Rover with darkened windows.

The usual procedure followed and they left the scene in less than a minute. Scott was now at the wheel. He turned to Jay in the passenger seat.

'So how did you guys do?'

'Tick, tick, tick,' he replied, rocking his head side to side. And then the boom from the Cayenne's fuel tank exploding filled the car.

29

Scott took mostly motorway, but routinely left to take the parallel A roads just to break the continual CCTV surveillance on all of the main roads. The scenery morphed from fields to towns and back again through Hampshire and Surrey, then Kent and finally Essex. The boat from Harwich took them to the Hook of Holland, and then the smooth European roads led them to the quaint streets of Bruges. There had been little conversation between them, but now their final destination loomed they all became animated once again.

With the Range Rover secured in a nearby underground car park, they entered the plate glass doors of the Merino Hotel. It felt modern, neat and expensive.

'What is this?' Scott asked the receptionist.

'The cards for your rooms sir, is there a problem?'

'Yes, there's a problem, I booked first floor.'

'I apologise sir, we only have fourth floor.'

'I specifically booked first floor.'

'Like I said, we only have fourth.'

'Unacceptable.'

'That'll be okay, I'm sure the view will be better.' Candy interrupted.

'No, it won't. Go and wait over there,' he gestured to the bar.

'Jeez, you're so uptight.' She turned and walked away.

'I want first floor, or a refund, please.'

'Okay, give me a second. Maybe I can move some things around. Perfect. How does one-ten and one-twelve sound?'

'Are they first floor?'

'Yes.'

'Then they sound like music to my ears. Thank you.'

In the lift, Scott felt Candy's eyes burning into him.

'She was only doing her job,' she said.

'And I'm only doing mine. If a SWAT team comes calling at two o'clock tomorrow morning, would you rather jump out of a fourth-floor window to certain death, or a first-floor window onto the roof of a car that might have enough give to save your life?'

*****

Scott sat in Terry's room for over an hour in silence. He occasionally pushed his fingers through his hair as the fence meticulously measured and weighed each piece.

'Tell me Scott, what are you expecting?'

'You tell me.'

'You'd be lucky to score two hundred grand for this lot, but call me generous and I'll give you two fifty.'

'It's from several high-class jewellers, so don't give me that.'

'Two fifty, tops.

'Three hundred?'

'Two twenty-five if you want to haggle.'

'Okay, okay, two fifty.'

'Done.'

'Half cash and the rest to your Swiss account?'

'Sounds good. So, are you still seeing Zara?'

'Funny you should mention that, she's downstairs having a massage. Proved herself to be something of an asset. Knows as many people in the game as I do so I think I'll be keeping her on for a bit.'

'Result. She got a sister?'

'I take it you've not found a new fiancé yet then?'

'Piss off Terry, that's not funny.'

'Well I thought it was,' he said and then let out a chuckle.

Scott stuffed the rucksacks with cash and then stood. He made his way along the corridor to room one-ten. He entered, threw the rucksacks onto the bed, and then looked at his crew.

'Okay guys, we have the funds to get to China. Ramirez, have you sorted things to get us onto the build?'

'Well you, me and Jay are cool as they're unbelievably short of qualified welders, but Pascal's the problem because there's a ton of carpenters on the waiting list.'

'So get him on the welder's list.' Scott said as he walked to the bathroom and ran the taps.

'What do you mean?'

'If there's a shortage of welders and an abundance of carpenters,' Scott soaked a flannel and wiped it over his face, 'get him on the welder's list. He'll just have to bluff through until we need him.'

'But he's not got a coding certificate?'

'I'll scan mine and change the name and picture. Just get him on the job, will you? We can sort the rest out when we get there.' Scott came out of the bathroom, rubbing his face with a towel.

'I got ya.'

'Thank you. Right, dinner in one hour, meet in the downstairs lounge.'

*****

Showered and fresh, Candy waited in the hotel lobby. She loved the modern look of dark walnut and chrome, offset by red cloth cushions. The dark grey carpet that wore a speckled pattern of red, white and blood orange dots brought further contrast. It reminded her of a Lichtenstein. Zara was next to emerge from the lift.

'Somewhat unusual for girls to be the first,' she said, her Essex accent clear.

'Indeed, I'm Candy.' She extended a hand which Zara took.

'So, being the new girl on the block, how are you finding it?'

'Okay so far, you been here long?'

'Long enough to know the game,' Zara said.

'And the game is?'

'Complicated. Let's get a drink and play the get to know you in two minutes game.' She gestured to the bar in an adjacent room. After being served, they sat in deep armchairs at a low table next to the window.

'So how did you end up with this lot?' Zara said.

'Not sure really, ironic as my aim was to be on the other side of the law.'

'What d'ya mean by that?' Zara sat up sharply.

'Don't worry. My dad owned a farm in Norfolk when I was younger. There were droughts, then a flood. The crop was ruined two years running and he borrowed too much money from the wrong people. I'd just turned twenty-three and we all worked the fields.'

'Quite a jump to be here then,' Zara said, stirring her gin and tonic.

'Tell me about it. One morning Dad was found with a fractured skull. They said he'd tripped and fallen on rocks, but we knew what had really happened.'

Candy had her full attention.

'Mum sold the farm for virtually nothing a year later so we went to my aunt in Feltham after that, near the young offender's prison.'

'Nice.'

'Don't judge, we had no choice.'

'No judgement here, just saying.'

'After a few years getting nowhere, one crap job leading to a worse one, I decided on law. Felt a duty to try and help those kids who ended up in the prison we lived next to, so they didn't turn out like the tossers who killed my dad.'

'You're a solicitor?' Zara said, neglecting to pronounce the 't's as her eyes widened.

'No, a law student. Well, a waitress for Pascal actually, as I've got to pay the bills. And now here I am doing something that could land me in the very place I was trying to keep the kids out of.'

The men arrived a few minutes later, enough time for her to feel she'd forged a connection with Zara, albeit a thin one, but something to build on.

The crew exited through tall glass doors, and then wandered into the cobbled market square to mingle with the tourists and opportunists. They explored the narrow streets and alleyways, in and out of quaint little shops. She admired the gothic architecture and history of their surroundings before Terry suggested a small French bistro for dinner.

Candy sat between Jay and Scott, yet her conversation with the former petered out early, so she favoured talking to Scott for most of the meal. The food was good, if expensive, and she certainly felt relieved when Scott picked up the tab.

'So glad we had a lovely evening together,' Jay said to her, snatching his jacket from the back of the chair as they stood to leave.

'You weren't exactly being Mr Conversational.'

'Yeah, well like I said. Nice.'

As they wandered into the square Candy threaded her arm around Jay's waist, but he shrugged it off.

'Grow up, will you?' she said.

Within half an hour, they were sampling many of the local and not-so-local brews in a bar called Cathedral Cubed.

'Hey Scott, how come you became the leader of this merry band?' she asked.

'We don't talk shop in public. Pass me the salt, would you?'

'It's not shop. Anyway, didn't have you down as the touchy type,' she replied, bumping shoulders with him.

'Drink your Tequila and smile, we're in public now.'

Jay drew up beside her and did his shot before anyone else had. He was still in a foul mood, so she turned her attention back to Scott. Did she just catch him ditching his shot in a planter? She couldn't be sure, but Jay interrupted before she could challenge him on it.

'C'mon I want a word outside,' he said.

'No, we're having fun, it'll wait.'

'I don't think so. C'mon, now.' He closed his fingers around her forearm in a way that left no doubt she'd upset him. He steered her through the ornate stone archway, out of the front doors and into the square.

'What do you think you're up to? You're making me look an idiot in front of everyone.'

'No Jay, you're doing it without any help from me. We're all having a laugh and you're the one wearing a long face. Just relax, will you, we're celebrating.'

'Flirting with Scott more like. What is it with you?'

Before she could answer, Pascal came through the doorway, cupping his hands around the end of a cigarette as the clink and a spark from his Zippo brought it to life. After a long exhale, he looked towards them.

'Hey guys, what's up?'

'Party's over, we're going back to the hotel.'

'Speak for yourself,' Candy said as she snatched her arm away.

'Bitch.'

'Guys, chill out, you're just a bit tipsy,' Pascal said.

'You side with her and I'll break your face,' Jay said. He turned and stomped across the square alone. Candy threw her eyes up and went back inside.

30

Nanjing, China.

Ramirez stepped forward to passport control. The official looked impassively through the glass as he slid his blue passport forward. The official's features tightened once he reached the visa section of his passport.

'You American journalist?'

'No, I'm here as a welder.'

The man turned a few more pages.

'Afghanistan, Iraq, Iran, Pakistan, Bosnia. You war journalist?'

'No,' trying to show as little emotion as possible, 'I went to those countries for welding. Some buildings have metal frameworks and I'm a specialist welder who repairs them,' he lied, conscious of the war-torn combat jacket in his overnight bag.

The official tapped at his computer before staring at the screen for almost a full minute. Finally, he stamped the passport and slid it back under the glass.

The four re-grouped outside the terminal and Scott hailed a cab. A fifty-minute ride took them through the neon facade of downtown Nanjing, along beautiful rivers and through neighbourhoods with buildings that looked to be hundreds of years old. Eventually, the cab arrived at a newly built apartment block overlooking a vast lake.

Ramirez pulled his slab of a backpack from the cab's boot and entered the building. They crossed the marble-floored entrance hall and waited for the glass lift. Scott pressed level five, as a first-floor apartment had proved impossible to find within the timeframe they needed. The lift scaled the outside face of the building and delivered them to the door of what would be their home for several months to come.

Ramirez walked straight to the large windows overlooking the water.

'Wow,' he said in his deep American baritone, 'I think I'm going to like it here.'

Scott checked the accommodation before he made an announcement.

'Okay, one double room and a further with two singles.'

'Don't worry. I'll get a sleeping bag tomorrow and use the lounge floor,' Ramirez said pre-empting any discussion of bed allocation.

'You sure?' Scott asked.

'Trust me, this five-star palace is heaven compared to where I've been.'

'Okay, lounge it is, you two in the twin.'

'Naah, can't sleep if Pascal snores. You bunk with him. I'm taking the double,' Jay said as he picked up his suitcase and headed towards the room.

'Jay, knock it off.'

He continued towards the room, showing a raised finger over his back with his free hand. Scott shot forward and grabbed his brother's shoulder, spinning him around.

'My operation, my rules. Don't test me. Now get in the twin and do as you're told.'

They glared at each other a moment before Jay grinned. 'Just checking you still had some balls.'

Ramirez shook his head, 'This is fucked up already.'

*****

'What's breakfast in this town?' Pascal said the following morning as he emerged from the bedroom wearing nothing but a short towel.

'You're out of luck if you were expecting room service,' Scott said. 'The cupboards are bare and the fridge likewise.

'We'll head into town and have a proper breakfast today,' he continued, 'but then find a supermarket and sort our provisions for the rest of the week. We need to keep an eye on expenditure, agreed?'

Jay shrugged, Ramirez nodded, and Pascal stared blankly.

They found a small café within walking distance and took a table in a courtyard at the rear.

'Okay,' Scott said, 'today we loaf around and generally take in our locale but tomorrow we need to be at the shipyard for our interviews at eight a.m., so enjoy the moment, just not too much.'

'What if I get the questions wrong and they realise I'm not really a coded welder?' Pascal said.

'Then they'll cut your head off with a Samurai sword.'

'I'm trying to be serious.'

'So am I.' Scott picked a menu up from the table.

'Do I get a proper answer?'

'Pascal, just keep your cool and it'll all work out fine. This interview is all about character, not skill. So smile, give it your best, and I'm sure you'll get through. If not, maybe I'm the one who'll be borrowing that Samurai sword.'

'Funny, so funny my side's splitting.'

'Just stay calm and it'll be fine.'

'Still not convincing me.'

'Plus,' Scott handed him the menu, 'we need to get to the headlight factory pretty soon, so we'd best organise that.

'Headlight factory?' he asked.

'Xenon headlight bulbs,' Scott replied, 'filled by Xenon gas cylinders that not only make the world's headlights ninety per cent brighter but also have the capacity to knock three thousand people to their backs if fed into the air conditioning system of a large ship.'

'Ahh, now I get you.'

31

Pascal dragged a heavy chain from the rear of the van, then crossed the concrete towards the steel doors, and the horizontal steel beam which held them fast. He heaved the chains around the beam and then threaded the ends through the towing eye of the rented van using a crowbar to lock the ends together. A couple of bangs on the rear door told Scott to ease forward.

The metal groaned as the forward-rolling van took up the strain, and the links began to stretch. Scott revved the engine higher to create enough pressure to burst the horizontal bar from the doors. Pascal stood by, hoping the plan would work at this first attempt. But the higher the revs, the more the wheels span on the damp concrete.

*****

At the apartment, Ramirez went into the compact kitchen to mix a protein shake. Jay muted the television and picked up his phone.

'Hello sweetie.' Candice said she was enjoying an evening at home on the sofa, nothing more strenuous than junk television and the warm comfort of a recently consumed roast. After a moment of I miss yous Jay got to the point.

'Do you think you can pull this off then?'

'Why couldn't I? All I've got to do is pretend to be a nice, well-mannered wife then help you stash the gems. Not much to it really.'

The whine of a blender filled the room as Ramirez stuffed spinach and carrots into it. Jay plugged his ear with a finger.

'Agreed, not much to the job itself,' his voice raised, 'but can you cope with your conscience after nicking all of those posh git's loot?'

'I think you've answered your own question. No guilt whatsoever, darling.'

'Just make sure you sweet talk that booking agent at Bright Star Line into reserving us the right cabins. Wouldn't want to hide the gas in one we can't get to.'

'I'll be sure to put on my best damsel in distress voice.'

Jay smiled, but the whine continued from the kitchen, so he pulled himself out of the armchair and headed to his room.

'Talking of sexy voices, let me hear yours. I'm missing you like crazy and need you to tell me exactly what you're going to do to me once I get back home.'

*****

The engine revved and smoke poured from the rear tyres before a bang punctuated the air. It echoed all around and elicited a yelp from Pascal.

The steel bar broke free of the factory door and clattered to the ground, skidding across the concrete towards the back of the halting van. Pascal jogged over as Scott emerged.

'You know what to do. I'll go in and find the gas cylinders.'

Scott ran into the building under the glare of flashing red lights and the pulsating scream of alarm sirens. Pascal freed the van of its chains and climbed inside the back. He emerged a moment later dragging a stolen trolley and raced into the factory with it.

'Scott,' he shouted over the racket, 'where are you?'

'Here, at the back, I've found them.'

He wasted no time, making his way down the aisles of production-line benches to find Scott a moment later. Fifty Xenon cylinders were stacked in a steel rack against the wall.

One by one, they drew the cylinders forward and laid them onto the trolley. It could only take four at a time. They dashed back through the factory and loaded them into the van.

After five subsequent trips, they were done.

'We're not going to get any more cylinders in the van.' It was loaded front to back, bed to ceiling. Scott checked his watch.

'Okay, four minutes down. Leave the trolley, evidence be damned.'

They swung the doors of the van shut and jumped into the cab. Scott pulled away just as the first police siren became audible.

'Must have only been up the road,' Pascal said.

They were out of the industrial estate and onto the dual carriageway heading north by the time the blue flashing lights appeared. The only problem being, it was the only road out of the estate, so obvious it had been them doing the robbery.

Scott had his foot to the floor but the van's heavy payload and slower engine reduced their chances of escape to almost zero. The police car flashed past in the opposite direction, but didn't take long to reach the roundabout and loop around to give chase.

'Here we go,' Scott said as the lights in the mirrors got larger by the second.

A bend in the road gave Scott all the opportunity he needed. With the police momentarily out of sight, he yanked the wheel and the van hurtled down a steep embankment and through some bushes. The gas bottles clanged together louder than church bells as the van bucked and twisted over the rough ground.

'Help!' Pascal screamed from the passenger seat, and he bent forward, bracing for impact. But Scott remained focused, dabbing the brakes or tweaking the wheel to guide them onto a rural farm track several metres below the carriageway. When the van finally settled, he slammed on the brakes and came to a rest behind a large barn. The police car raced by overhead, oblivious to their ruse.

Thirty minutes later, the van tipped down the ramp to the car park beneath the apartment. He maneuvered down to the lowest level, where it would be less likely to receive any attention.

He checked the van over. A few dents from their off-road excursion, but nothing serious. He then removed the stolen registration plates with a stubby screwdriver and replaced them with the correct hire-company ones. Then, the stolen ones went down a nearby drain.

The pair rode the smooth lift up to their apartment in silence and slipped into their respective rooms without the pleasantries of a good night.

32

The shipyard looked much like any other factory might, with the exception of the sheer scale of everything around them. Even the nuts and bolts had heads the size of a hand. Scott led them to the cafeteria on the fifth floor of the main building.

'Noodles and egg, seriously?' complained Pascal when he sat down at the breakfast table. Then he caught the look Scott gave him.

'Sorry,' he shrugged, 'it's too early.'

'So, I presume we all have yellow wristbands?' Scott asked. They nodded. 'Which means there are only certain places we can go on the ship without being stopped? Anyone got any ideas on how we can get more freedom?'

'I thought that after the briefing when I was talking to one of the Dutch guys,' Pascal said. 'He had a red band for electrics and seemed to think they were allowed anywhere that had wires, meaning everywhere I guess.'

'Great observation,' Jay snapped, 'maybe you should have mentioned it then so I could have swiped a load of red bands from the office?'

Pascal shrugged. His lack of sleep and the fog of jet lag were weighing him down at this early hour. He returned to his noodles.

'I noticed the Chinese have blue bands.' Ramirez said.

'Yeah, well that doesn't help us either,' Jay said.

'Whatever.'

After finishing their food, the crew stood, all wearing their new regulation boots, blue boiler suits and white hard-hats, each a facsimile of the other. Scott wandered over to the window and looked out at the dull, industrial shipyard but then had to re-focus his gaze.

'Guys, would you come and look at this?'

The others joined him, looking at the grey wall on the other side of the glass and slowly realising that it wasn't a wall after all, it was the steel hull of Titanic II.

'Now that's impressive.' Ramirez said.

'Understatement. I've never seen a ship out of the water before, it's so much… bigger,' Pascal said. Scott nodded as he turned to them.

'Once more unto the breach dear friends, once more,' but Shakespeare not being a strong point, it was lost on them. They got the sentiment, though and gave a rousing cheer before heading out to begin work.

Two hours later, the atmosphere inside the ship's hull was thick with the soot of ground metal and welding gas. It wasn't yet ten o'clock, and the temperature was already just bearable. Pascal worked with Scott in the forward portside section, Ramirez and Jay working a little further aft. A scrappy trail of molten steel was punctuated by Pascal hurling the welding torch at the hull plates with all his might.

'Sick of this.' he shouted, the outburst lost to all but himself and Scott as the roar of machinery dominated the ears of all in the shipyard.

'Cool it, will you?'

'No, I won't cool it. I've had enough of trying to learn this crap. I'm a chef with a carpentry habit, not a welder.'

'Just do as I told you and loosen up, you're all tight.' He grabbed Pascal's shoulders and squeezed them. 'Just let go of too much control and the weld will flow.'

'Like you're so good at letting go of control,' Pascal said, but the shriek of a grinder drowned out his voice.

Scott collected Pascal's torch from the floor and held it out for him to take. The Frenchman snatched it a moment later, but the frown remained. Scott gestured to the two slabs of steel in front of them and, after adjusting the settings on the torch, gave a brief mimed demonstration.

Pascal reluctantly took position when the mime was complete. Scott moved in behind his frustrated friend to slowly guide his actions into achieving a uniform bead of molten steel, which joined the two plates in perfect parallel.

Pascal's light-reactive mask cleared, and he was beaming. He *was* capable after all. He just needed to slow down and loosen up.

Suddenly aware of a third person nearby, Scott and Pascal turned to see Mr Li, the site foreman, shaking his head slowly at them.

'Show, now,' he demanded as he pointed at the remaining gap between the plates. Pascal's eyelids fluttered, and he reached his arm out to steady himself. He suddenly felt all at sea.

He took up the torch and glanced helplessly back towards Scott.

'Now,' Li implored, stabbing his index finger at the gap in the steelwork. Pascal flipped his mask down once more and drew a long, steady lungful of dirty air.

'No, not you, *you*,' Li clarified, stabbing his scrawny finger in Scott's direction. Pascal almost collapsed with relief when Scott responded immediately to deflect the heat from his partner.

'Weld this now,' Li demanded, stabbing his finger again at the open channel between the two steel sheets.

Scott looked to Pascal, set his torch, and then dropped his mask to feed a perfect bead of weld the entire two-metre length of the steel plates.

Once complete, Li scrutinised Scott's work as if looking for a blemish the size of a grain of sand, but nodded once he reached the end and left without further comment.

'Jeez, thought that was me on a plane home,' Pascal said.

'Likewise, but now Li has gone starboard-side, I'm gonna sneak upstairs and do some recon.'

*****

The Grand Staircase was nothing like it was in the film. For the moment, it was simply a vast square hole plunging from the Boat Deck down to E-Deck where Scott stood, looking up at where the ornate glass dome was due to go.

A scaffold staircase zig-zagged its way up the aft side of the opening. He climbed it to the top, then exited the enclosed part of the ship out onto the steel deck. It felt high, really high. A look over the side triggered his vertigo, and he stepped back. How many stories was this?

Five minutes of carefully walking between the wires, pipes and steels that littered the deck had him entering the body of the ship once more. Into what he estimated was the staff corridor leading to The Bridge. After a short walk along the corridor, he found just what he was looking for. A hatch, inside of which there were numerous pipes and electrical conduit. The one he was looking for, marked 'Air Conditioning Service Port-Bridge', was present. He took a picture with his phone and–

'You, what are you doing?'

How the hell did Li get up here so quickly?

33

Candy flicked the light on in her small but neat lounge. It wasn't particularly early, but the weather outside was gloomy. It would probably be raining again before mid-morning. She slumped onto the sofa and opened her laptop. She then scrolled through the Bright Star line website until she found the contact page. Then, picking her phone off the sofa, she dialed the number. After a series of recorded menus, she finally got through to a booking agent just as Chester leapt up onto her lap.

The conversation wasn't going to plan.

'But I really want that particular cabin. Surely you can do this tiny little thing for me?'

'I'm sorry Miss….'

'Jones, but please call me Candice.'

'Okay Miss Jones, as I said before, I can reserve you a class and put in a deck request, say B Deck or C Deck, but I don't have the ability to reserve you a specific cabin. Company policy I'm afraid.'

'What if I come over and see you personally, we could certainly have fun choosing.'

'I'm sorry Miss Jones, it's all allocated by computer so completely out of my control, whatever it is that you're offering.'

She ended the call, hissing expletives under her breath, and then reached from the sofa to the coffee table to pull a small packet of tissues from her bag. Then, tentatively, she made the next call.

'Mum, sorry I've not been to the hospital for a couple of days, I've been working really long hours to try and get as much money as I can for us, how's she doing?'

After a long moment of static, only broken by a weak sound of whimpering from the other end, Candy gently pushed.

'Mum?'

'It looks like your sister's pulling through, but you know she'll never walk properly again after what that brute did to her.'

She began to sob deeply now and Candy felt the warmth of fresh tears down her own cheeks. The shame of her boyfriend attempting to rape her sister felt unbearable.

'They thought she'd been attacked by a gang, not just your sadistic boyfriend,' her mother continued between sobs.

'Oh Mum, I'm so, so sorry. What about the police, any progress on arresting Christian?'

'Some kid in a uniform poked his head in yesterday for what good that'll do. Nobody can't find him anywhere. They think he might have gone into hiding after what he did to Becky. That and leaving your flat like that. You'd think a whirlwind went through it.'

'It's been a couple of months, Mum, the flat's fine now.'

'That bastard, how could you ever have seen anything in him? Christian! Couldn't think of any worse name for the gutless bully.'

'Oh Mum, what can we do? I feel so helpless,' she said, tears streaming.

'Help Becky recover the best she can. That's all any of us can do dear, just don't you dare go putting yourself in harm's way trying to find him or my heart will just give up, I swear it, Candice. Promise me you won't, please love.'

'Of course, Mum, you and Becky are all I have in the world. I'll always be there for you. We need to stay strong, stick together.'

34

Scott threw the dish back into the sink and left the washing-up half finished. The call from Candy informing them of the unresponsive booking agent was a blow that left him struggling for ideas.

'I need to get some air.'

'Me too,' Pascal said, 'think I'll join you.'

'No, that was the universal code for leave me alone until further notice. Go and get your own air somewhere else.'

Scott grabbed his windbreaker and headed down the corridor, noticing the clammy drizzle on the other side of the windows remained as oppressive as it had been for the past couple of days.

He entered the lift and pushed G, squeaked his way across the entrance hall, and then turned right out of the front doors to make his way along the main road. Cars flashed past with a shissshhing noise whilst their headlights left blotchy imprints of green and yellow across his retinas for several seconds after they'd passed.

Along the road, he saw neglected strips of patchy grass between featureless concrete buildings, yards cluttered with rusting steelwork, overflowing bins and abandoned machinery. Nobody seemed to care.

Before long, his torso was slick with pelting rain. The lack of ventilation in his windbreaker, mixed with the muggy heat, meant his t-shirt was almost as wet on the inside.

A gust came in off the lake and buffeted him. It brought a squall that slapped at his face, then came another. The weather was deteriorating, and water ran in tiny rivulets from his hair, down his forehead, and into his eyes. He ran his fingers through his hair to keep it back, but the gesture was futile.

In need of a better option, he turned down a narrow street for no reason other than the awnings over the shops offered better cover than the open road.

He continued past a mix of scruffy shops interspersed with apartment buildings and workshops before stopping outside a bar. The clientele was all Chinese, so far as Scott could tell through the lightly fogged window. And a small television fixed high on one wall showed a newsreader, his mouth moving incongruously fast for the demeanour his body language conveyed. The map behind him showed even more foul weather heading their way.

The bar was about as good as his options were going to get. So, he pulled the windbreaker over his head and shook it outside the door before entering.

A few noted his presence with casual glances, but most remained busy with their card games or huddled in low-level conversations. There was no music, and the lighting seemed more appropriate for a kitchen than a bar, with stark fluorescent tubes and a blue mosquito ring that glowed above a kitchen hatch.

Once at the counter, he noticed that the room was 'L' shaped. The television served only one part whilst the other side was less brightly lit.

He gestured to the barman for a Coke, and the short, cheery man placed a bottle of gently bubbling liquid onto the bar once he'd popped the cap using the handle of a spoon.

Scott turned and surveyed the room, decided on a small table near the television and drew a notebook from his back pocket before sitting on one of the two plain wooden chairs.

Problem, he wrote, before filling in as much detail as he could about the issue of not being able to control the choice of cabins aboard Titanic II.

He often did his thinking on paper, but the text was disappointingly short because he didn't have any idea what the solution might be.

He sat back in the chair and joined the locals in staring at the television but became bored a moment later when he found the term language barrier proved just that.

After a few adverts, the screen jumped to life with a pair of sports commentators in a stadium. They were presumably discussing an upcoming fight by the look of the brightly lit ring in the background. The number of people filing into the small café increased. They joined others on tables around him, and a silent jockeying for position began as some were left standing.

A man gestured to the seat opposite, and Scott nodded. The man gave a brisk bow then dragged it away. The pre-fight commentary was rounded up, and the screen swapped to the ring just before the referee signalled the start of the fight. It appeared to be a particularly brutal mix of wrestling and kickboxing. After a moment's interest, Scott returned his attention to the notepad on the table and, more importantly, a solution to their problem. But with each idea that came, a contrary argument destroyed its validity. And before long, he'd run out of solutions. He entertained the idea that the heist was doomed to failure and he'd lost the chance of ever winning Jasmine back. And that was unbearable. So there just had to be a solution.

The animated cheers and jeers from the televised crowd were mimicked by the patrons of the bar and blow by blow, and the locals grew bolder in support of their fighter. Five minutes into the match, Scott was not only finding it difficult to concentrate but also aware of a man standing nearby trying to gain his attention. He looked up from his notebook and took in the man's miming actions, which roughly translated into Scott swapping his place for another at the back of the room. After some initial confusion, he realised that his reward for the exchange was another drink, given the man's miming actions of downing a bottle.

He looked to the back and clocked the table in question, just around the elbow of the room and far enough away to make it difficult to watch the television. There was also a fresh bottle of Coke waiting for him.

Scott took the bait and headed towards the back of the room, but as he went to sit down, the penny dropped as to how this could solve his own dilemma.

He left the bottle where it was and headed straight for the door.

35

The greenhouse heat of May built relentlessly to a muggy June, a stifling July and a fierce fireball of an August. Working inside the hot steel hull had become almost unbearable. The ambient temperature had risen to over forty-two degrees, and with the humidity high enough to peel wallpaper, it had left them feeling exhausted. Scott carried a large bowl of chilli to the apartment dining table and then returned to the kitchenette for rice, bread and salad.

'Lunch is ready guys.'

They took their places and began to devour.

'Listen,' Scott said between mouthfuls, 'I know the past few weeks have been hard, but we're making real progress. The first cabin, E32, is well under way with regard to creating the first hide. And E34 is pretty much prepped for us to start our work on next week. We should start thinking about getting our gas cylinders in place sooner rather than later. We just need the finishing crew to start work installing the wooden wall panels and we're good to go.'

Ramirez nodded, Pascal, shrugged.

'So as progress on the hides has been good, and we have tomorrow off, I think a night on the town is long overdue.'

'Halleluiah,' Jay said. 'About time the tyrant let his slaves leave the oars for a while.'

'You can row back to England any time you like.'

Jay raised his finger, but Scott ignored him and continued.

'I've heard there's a lively group of bars in a place called the 1912 district, half an hour away. Apt don't you think?'

'Not following,' Pascal said.

'1912, the year the original Titanic sunk.'

'Best we go sink some brews there then,' Ramirez said.

They headed into the district by cab several hours later, and walked into the first Irish pub they'd seen since leaving England.

'Guinness all round,' Jay said to the barman in the dimly lit bar. But this prompted objections from both Ramirez and Pascal, who opted for the lighter Budweiser brew.

'Bugger me sideways,' Jay then said just a little too loudly. Scott followed his brother's gaze to a red-haired girl wearing a green Gingham shirt and black jeans, who stood with some friends at the other end of the room.

'Bugger you, I'd rather not,' Scott said. 'But her on the other hand...' He strode towards her, not pausing to slide his pint from the bar.

*****

'No chance with that one,' Jay said, 'he'll be back in four seconds flat, guaranteed.'

Ramirez looked to Pascal, who shrugged.

Jay's assessment was out to the tune of an hour and a half. At which point Scott returned to the group who now occupied a booth. He sat down with a smile on his face and a new contact in his phone.

'So come on then, what's she like?' Ramirez asked.

'Samantha is delightful, and working as a staff nurse at the shipyard.'

'I can suddenly feel a swelling coming on, I'd best pop in and see her Monday,' Jay said.

'Hands off, or you might be seeing one of her colleagues to get some splints for some broken fingers.'

'Chill out there, bruv,' Jay said after the conversation had stalled for a moment, 'just having a laugh.'

'Guys,' Ramirez interrupted, 'can you stop with the heavy shit and just enjoy a beer?'

Scott acquiesced, 'I guess as I've been vacant for a while and somebody seems to have downed my pint, it must be my turn to get the drinks?' They nodded, and he made his way to the bar.

'What was all that about, Jay?' Ramirez asked.

'Scott always gets a little protective when I talk to his girls, kind of a jealousy thing.'

'Why would that be?'

'He's careless. Has a habit of losing them.'

'You mean when you're around?'

'Well, let's just say he's disappointed when they ditch him for somebody with a little more of an idea about how it all works.'

'You mean you?'

'You could say that.' A smile grew across his face. 'Who could resist?' he ran his fingers down his body.

Ramirez shook his head, 'if I think anything's out of line between you two, I'll be listening to him first.'

'Thanks for the support, arsehole,' his demeanour became sour. 'He's a control freak. Too uptight, and the way he's running this operation is a joke.'

'You could do better?' Ramirez said.

'Too right, he thinks that just because he gets the run-around from women, he can take out his frustration by controlling us,' the glare in Jay's eyes now malicious. 'He lost Jasmine because he was careless, but now he thinks some big heist where he's the hero will make up for that. It's bollocks.'

'Sounds like classic over-compensation.' Ramirez said.

'That's what I'm saying.' Jay replied.

'I meant you.'

'Whatever, wait and see, I'll be the one in charge soon enough. Anyway, I need a piss.'

36

Scott thrust the apartment curtains open.

'Come on guys, wake up,'

'Seriously, just crawl away, will you?' Pascal groaned.

'It's gone ten so don't be such a weakling, it's not like we were out late or anything.'

'Screw you,' Jay said.

Scott was undeterred.

'I'll give you guys an hour, and then we go. There's so much to do here and so little free time so come on, let's get a real taste for this place.'

An hour and a half later, he served a noodle, pork and egg breakfast to the lethargic crew.

'I suggest that as we have the day to ourselves,' Scott said, 'we visit this.'

He threw a leaflet onto the table advertising an exhibition of Chinese cultural diversity between the working and ruling classes through the ages, at museum five miles away.

'Okay, if we have to,' Pascal said. The others merely grunted in resignation.

On the bus, Scott stared out of the window as the neglected pea-shingle tower blocks slid by with their decaying cars outside. These slowly blended into more modern buildings, the glass more abundant, the surrounding areas landscaped and the detritus conspicuously absent. When they approached the city wall, another change was apparent. This time history reversed once more, as a mix of smaller, simple dwellings slowly increased in density to give the feel of an ancient village. The homes were often wooden and either terraced or built with only the width of a pair of shoulders between them. They were dark and Grimm-like, painted in greens, greys or black. All had the glazed semi-circular tiled roofs with the traditional flared edge that was instantly recognisable to any tourist. The roads narrowed and became cloaked in shadow from the trees that lined them. Multiple rivers also snaked around these suburbs and teemed with boats ferrying tourists and locals with a volume and speed that rivalled a European motorway. The bus crossed into the central part of city, and arrived at their destination shortly after.

'The Nanjing Centre for Cultural Education,' Jay announced as he read the bilingual sign attached to the brutalist-styled concrete building in front of them. 'It's not exactly a challenge to London's Natural History Museum.'

The others ignored him as they approached the entrance of the grey ten-storey building.

Inside, they mooched from feudal age dioramas to scale models of modern society. As the years passed by, the architecture grew cleaner in design but less ornate, giving an overall impression of how the area had evolved and grown. But Scott found it no more informative than his observations from the bus had been

'What a load of rubbish,' Jay said. 'Thought we'd get to play with a couple of Samurai swords or Ninja stars.'

'That'll be the war museum, idiot,' Ramirez said.

Towards the end of the exhibition, they came across a series of tall French doors which led out to a courtyard. Filling most of this outside space was a high-hedged maze with the roof of a building just visible in the centre, with enough of it showing to pique Scott's interest.

The maze entrance split into two paths. At the head of these was an acrylic sign which explained, beneath the wealth of Chinese characters, that this was an example of an 18th century 'Mirror House'. The bushes of the maze walls were tall enough to prevent seeing what lay ahead, so they decided to split into pairs. Ramirez and Scott took one entrance, Jay and Pascal the other, a sense of competition implicit.

Five minutes later, Jay was on the phone to Scott.

'Beat you, ya slouches. Although I must say it wasn't really worth the effort, it's a bit crap really.'

'Right Jay, master of understatement, where are you? Ramirez and I are at the front door.'

'Yeah right, you're probably still wandering around the hedgerow because I'm stood at the front door with Pascal and you're nowhere in sight.'

'Of course you are. We're heading inside.' Scott ended the call and turned to see where Ramirez had wandered off to.

With no sign of him, Scott entered the ornately decorated entrance hall and felt almost lost for words at the detail surrounding him. Not only was the furniture intricately carved and mostly gold-leafed, but also the ceiling beams, door frames and banister rail that led up the gently winding staircase.

A vast chandelier fashioned from antlers and gold-coloured cables filled the airspace between the polished hardwood floor and the beamed ceiling twenty feet above. The room also enjoyed a strong natural illumination from a partly stained-glass window which looked to be fifteen feet in length and almost that in height.

He found Ramirez in a study, and they wandered through the rooms taking in the opulence of an obviously wealthy family's home. On the second floor, the luxury and attention to detail continued until they reached the end of a landing where out of a small doorway, Jay emerged with Pascal following.

'What the bloody hell's all this about? It's like a different house through there,' Jay gestured towards the door.

'Okay dude, we'll take the bait, what's behind the door?' Ramirez said.

'It's like I said, a different house. Like where you'd keep the slaves compared to this lot,' he gestured to the surroundings.

Ramirez looked to Scott, who nodded, and the pair entered the doorway from which Jay and Pascal had come. The change startled him. Gone was the pleasant natural light from large windows and high ceilings. Now the flickering glow of artificial candles lit conservatively sized rooms which just had basic, unpainted furniture inside.

This side of the house was smaller by almost fifty per cent. It wasn't quite working-class, but did lack the obvious signs of wealth. Downstairs, Scott noted a second dining room and reception room. Again, all plain and conservatively decorated but not quite poor, just muted. He went down a passageway and into the kitchen, then realised it was the only room shared by both sides. Interesting but odd, he thought, two houses with one area in the middle for staff to serve both sides.

A low wooden doorway led outside, and as he ducked through an archway in the hedge, he found himself in a courtyard. On the far side he saw a tea hut and gift shop.

He bought tea, an exhibition guide, and then took a seat at a nearby picnic table to try and make sense of the strange house.

'What's the deal with that place?' Pascal asked as he, Ramirez and Jay sat down.

'According to this guide, it's called a Mirror House, used in the 18th century and owned by wealthy men who'd have been vast landowners.

'The idea being, if the owner entertained somebody he wanted to impress, he would invite them to enter by the large ornate side of the building.

'If he wanted to appear humble and conservative, like to a tax collector or his local priest, he'd give them the address of the other side, therefore influencing the impression the visitor had of them.'

'Cool,' Ramirez said.

'Yeah, interesting,' Scott said as a thought began to form as to how he could use this information to his advantage. He then noticed a kid of around seven placing superheroes stickers in a cartoon magazine. 'Funny, isn't it? We're on the other side of the world but still the kids love their heroes and the publishers love selling them sticker books.'

'True that.'

37

The early morning shift came around way too quickly. Scott traipsed into the shipyard just after seven with the others close behind, and they filed up the stairs to the fifth-floor cafe to check their rota sheet and queue for breakfast.

They sat and munched through their chow, and once finished, Jay leaned back on his chair to look out of the fifth-floor window and the shipyard below.

'Smurfs,' he said, 'there they all go like Smurfs to work.'

'What are you talking about?' croaked Ramirez, nursing a bowl of broth and a sore throat.

'Look at them, the workers all running around down there in their blue overalls and white hard hats, carrying their lunchboxes and tools. It's like we're watching an episode of The Smurfs.'

The others looked down at the busy shipyard and laughed.

'Hey, that old guy,' Pascal pointed. He's Papa Smurf.'

'That dude's gotta be Lazy Smurf then,' Ramirez said, pointing to a guy hanging around near the door, smoking.

'And that,' Jay pointed to Mr Li striding across the shipyard 'is undoubtedly Arsehole Smurf.' They all cracked up, and continued sniggering on and off throughout the day. Maybe the heat really was getting to them.

That evening, back at the apartment, Scott took the pans out of the cupboard and prepared dinner almost as soon as they arrived, eager to eat quickly. As soon as the steak and veg had disappeared, he was up and in the shower. Ten minutes later, he crossed the living area with his rucksack over one shoulder.

'I'm out seeing Samantha for drinks in the city this evening so won't be back any time soon.'

'See you within the hour then, if your endurance is anything to go by.'

'Funny Jay, go tug yourself off.'

Scott left to jeers and taunts about his manhood, and then rode the lift down in contemplative silence.

He exited the building and headed along the lakefront, past the bars and shops that showed little signs of life on a Monday. He arrived at the taxi rank outside of the railway station ten minutes later. He stopped at the first car available in the rank, slung his rucksack onto the back seat and got in.

'Where to mister?'

'Jao-Tu shipyard, gate twelve.'

He slid his blue overalls from the rucksack and began pulling them on.

38

The August furnace mellowed throughout September, became tolerable in October and turned to slushy grey snow by the time December arrived.

Scott left the crew in the apartment most evenings and headed out on the pretence of seeing Samantha. Each workday just a dull, boring repetition of all the others they'd endured since day one. But on the morning of Monday 2nd of December, everything changed.

As Scott approached the shipyard, he noticed that their usual entrance had a large sign above it stating it was for Chinese staff only. An arrow pointed to a second gate about twenty metres further down the fence, which had a further sign stating it was for overseas contractors only.

'What's all this?' Jay said.

They approached the gate and joined the queue. A moment later, Scott had an infrared thermometer pointed at his head. The man nodded and thrust a surgical mask towards him.

'You wear all times.'

Scott nodded and entered.

'What's up with this?' Ramirez said.

'No idea, hopefully it's just a knee-jerk virus precaution and not another outbreak of something nasty. Best just do as we're told, can't afford to get thrown out now.'

'Brekkie time, I'm starving,' Jay said, but as they approached the staircase leading to the 5th-floor café, another sign read that it was off limits to all but Chinese staff. Overseas contractors now had to use the ground floor rec room.

'What the hell is going on?' Scott said.

They followed the signs to the rec room, where trestle tables and benches were laid out in rows.

'Like prison,' Jay said.

'Don't joke,' Scott said as they entered. But before they reached their table, there was yet another sign. Scott read it quickly, but SARS and compulsory masks were the stand-out message.

'Have you guys seen next week's roster?' Ramirez said.

'Don't tell me, more damned welding,' Pascal said.

'Yeah, but all yellow wristbands are being moved to the cargo hold. There's no way we can finish the hides from there, we'll get stopped at the first staircase.'

'Shit,' Scott said. 'We've got to get hold of whatever colour wristbands the workers on E Deck now have. Any ideas?'

There was silence.

'How the hell are we going to get around this?' Jay said.

'I could certainly do with a break,' Pascal said, 'let's see what the next couple of days are like and hope it changes back. You never know, luck might be on our side.'

'Luck is a fool's plan,' Scott said. 'However, in this case, a little patience may have some merit.

'In the meantime, assume this situation will continue, and we need to do something about it. I want everyone to keep working on a solution and see what we can come up with, okay?'

There was a mumble of agreement, but nobody looked convinced.

39

The Boat Deck was the highest point of the ship with passenger access. Only a few crew cabins would be above it for the Bridge officers on rota. Pascal sat on a stack of six-metre steel beams close to where lifeboat three would hang and took a sip of coffee from his flask to wash down the last of his sandwich. Next to him, Scott looked out over the vast Boat Deck of Titanic II. He pointed to a half-built structure a few yards away.

'That'll be where they fit the doors, which lead out onto deck from the forward staircase.'

'Oui.'

'It's the ones we'll use to drag the empty gas cylinders out after the raid is finished. They'll go overboard and then,' Scott pointed to some mechanical arms at the edge of the ship, 'we'll launch all of the lifeboats that'll be hanging from those davits spaced along the length of the ship.'

'Okay, but why?'

'To confuse the authorities. Hopefully they'll have no idea of what's happened until we're on a plane headed for London.'

'But the gems, you still haven't told us how they're getting off the ship.'

'All in good time. You ready to go? Li's probably releasing Satan's dogs to come find us.'

They stood and walked inside the main body of the ship. Scott paused to look again at the framework which was to hold the glass dome above the Grand Staircase.

'It's going to be an incredible experience, being here when it's all finished and us mere mortals rubbing shoulders with the billionaires.'

'Becoming one, more like.'

Scott laughed.

'Not quite billions, but certainly doing okay once we're done here.'

They descended the scaffold staircase to return to work in the hold. When they reached E deck, Scott gestured to a door.

'Let's see if we can get to the hides from here.' They pushed through the opening, but immediately on the other side, there was a sign stating wristbands for E Deck remained red for electricians or blue for Chinese welders. Not the yellow that they wore for overseas welders. Just beyond the sign, a security guard sat at a temporary desk, flicking through his phone.

'I guess that's out,' Pascal said.

'Yup.'

They returned to the staircase, and were both surprised to see Samantha making her way up.

'Hey, I recognise you,' she said with a curious smile. 'Scott, isn't it?'

'Yeah, funny, I know I haven't been in touch but....'

'What do you mean?' she said, and Pascal noticed the puzzled look on her face.

'Gotta run, see ya sometime soon,' Scott said and began down the stairs.

'What was that about?' Pascal said, jogging to catch up. 'She look like she hardly recognise you.'

'Just a bit annoyed that I've not been over for a couple of days, you know how women can be.'

'Yeah, suppose, but–'

'Pascal, that's all it was okay. Drop the subject?'

He shrugged, but as usual, he had the feeling there was more going on than he could grasp.

40

Three days later, they again entered the rec room for breakfast but were confronted by yet another sign. Due to health restrictions, all overseas workers are to have their contracts terminated on 31st December. And they wouldn't be renewed for the foreseeable future.

A retch rose from Scott's empty stomach, then another. They all took a place at the trestle table, but Scott had lost his appetite. He pulled out his notebook but could hardly articulate a question, let alone find an answer. Ramirez was the first to speak.

'The first hide is finished, right? The second is almost there too, so we should start getting as much of the gas on board as possible. Hide it in the cargo hold where we're working then two of us come back at night to move it to the hides.'

Scott nodded, but his mind still searched for a proper solution.

'Makes sense to me.' Pascal said.

'Even if we only get half of the bottles on then at least we can still pull off part of the raid.'

'It doesn't work like that,' Scott snapped. 'The gas will be too diluted with the air conditioning. It won't be strong enough to knock people out. We only have a couple of weeks and that isn't the answer.'

'Better than doing nothing,' Pascal said.

'Okay. Jay and Ramirez, you head back to the apartment. Rent another van and start ferrying the gas cylinders from the damaged van to us here on the ship. Pascal and I will spend this time creating a space to conceal the cylinders in the cargo hold. Be as quick as you can, we really don't have a second to waste.'

*****

'No, you no come in with more bottle, too many already,' the security guard told Jay as he attempted to roll the pair of Xenon gas cylinders up the gangplank using a welder's sack barrow in order to pass them off as welding gas.

'But we need them for the welding, mate. No gas, no work.'

'No new allowed, just one out, one in. See Mr Li if you no believe.'

'Oh, I believe he'd make my life awkward, don't you worry about that, mate.'

'You need letter from Mr Li to bring more in. Insurance rule, understand?'

'Whatever you say pal,' Jay rolled the sack barrow around and headed back to the van.

Ramirez was waiting behind the wheel, unsurprised at Jay's failure.

'Your silver tongue a little tarnished today?'

'Sod off Ramirez, Scott's definitely not going to be happy. Look, I'm done with this shit, let's call it off. We can cash in what's left of Terry's money and split it. Then I'll come up with a new job, one I'll be in charge of.'

'Oh, I can just see how well that's gonna go down. Shut up and put your safety belt on.'

41

They trudged out of the shipyard the following evening, dragging their feet with heads down. It had been a tough week.

'Listen guys,' Scott said. 'I just can't face cooking tonight, let's just grab something on our way home.'

'I'm up for that,' Jay said, 'need a little brain stimulation, like a menu to read.'

'Might be a challenge for you,' Ramirez said.

'Funny man, you should be on stage.'

'Cut it out you two,' Scott said, running his fingers through his hair.

They arrived at a pizza restaurant, took a seat outside and then ordered.

'Such, bliss,' Pascal said, 'not a noodle in sight.'

Ramirez pointed to a kid forking spaghetti into his mouth with one hand whilst his other peeled stickers from a sheet and stuck them into a comic book. His mother was checking herself in a compact, applying some powder.

'Yeah well, you know what I mean,' he shrugged.

Scott sat up straight, 'I've got the answer.'

'To what?' Jay said.

'Stickers, that sticker book.' he said, pointing at the child. 'One of them is wearing an all-blue superhero suit similar to Captain America's, and Smurfs, you said they looked like Smurfs.'

'Someone call a psychiatrist.'

Scott stood and ran along the street, entering a shop several doors down.

'Superhero books? You got superhero books, or Smurf ones?'

The shopkeeper stared at him uncomprehendingly, so he turned to look for himself. Two minutes later he found just what he was looking for, a shelf of magazines featuring the blue coloured superhero.

He gathered them up and took them to the counter, adding a pair of scissors and a roll of clear sticky tape. The shopkeeper eyed him suspiciously but scanned the items all the same.

'Seriously mate, have you had a bang on the head?' Jay said when he dumped the contents of his shopping bags onto the restaurant table.

Scott ignored him and tore the sticker sheets from the comics. Then he trimmed all colours from the decals except for the blue. Finally, he rolled the yellow Tyvek band on his left wrist inside out and began sticking the blue strips around it.

'Nice try,' Jay said. 'But have you forgotten they're for the Chinese welders?' He sat back with a smug look. But Scott hadn't finished.

He leaned down, retrieved his safety helmet from his rucksack, and put it on. He then pulled his surgical mask over his face and dipped his head slightly. With the mask pulled high it obscured his mouth and nose, and the helmet's peak pulled low it cast a dark shadow over his eyes.

'Should work,' Pascal said. And the others grabbed the stickers to modify their own wristbands.

'Not wishing to put a downer on things,' Ramirez said. 'But we still can't get the gas aboard.'

'One problem at a time my friend, but a good point nonetheless.' Scott said.

42

The Rec room was virtually empty that Monday for breakfast, as many of the workers had already taken an early end to their contract and flown home for Christmas. Scott and the crew sat at their usual trestle table at the far end of the room.

'The plan is simple,' Scott said. 'We're allowed here as overseas welders until the end of December. So, until then we carry on as planned, but with one exception.

'Two of us, myself and Pascal today, Pascal and Jay tomorrow, myself and Jay on Wednesday, etcetera, will roll their wristband inside-out after lunch, so the blue is showing. We then sneak to E Deck as a faux local to finish off the last few bits on the hides and then return to the cargo hold for the end of the day.

'Obviously this excludes the big man here because of his dark skin.'

Ramirez nodded. Scott then noticed Pascal as he pulled a thermos flask of coffee from his rucksack, unscrewed the lid and poured the steaming liquid into it.

'What?' Pascal said.

'Nothing.'

'You're staring.'

'Thinking, actually. The way a thermos flask is made of a steel outer part with a glass liner. The air gap keeps the heat in.'

'We have a physicist on board now do we?' Jay said.

'Shut up, I'm thinking.'

Jay slapped his own wrist.

'If we reverse the make-up of the thermos, put the glass on the outside of the steel, we can create a false shell.'

'Is anyone else following this?' Pascal said before he took a sip of his coffee.

'It's simple,' Scott said. 'The problem we have is only one bottle allowed off, before one bottle is allowed on. Gas bottle, that is. But if we mimic a Russian doll...'

'You've definitely had a bang on the head.' Jay said, but Scott's glare silenced him.

'Think about it. If we take a fibreglass mould of the outside of a gas bottle, albeit slightly oversized, we can then make a pair of hollow, dummy gas bottles out of fibreglass and use them to disguise the originals.'

'And why would we want to do that?' Jay said.

'Because then we can take a pair of welding gas bottles off of the ship using a sack barrow, slide the fibreglass dummies over the top, and then take them back on board. Two off, two on, just like they insist.'

'Don't see that being much help.'

'Christ Jay, just let me finish. We then strap the two hollow fibreglass shells back onto the sack barrow and pretend to be taking off another two bottles of welding gas. At the van, we slide two of the Xenon bottles inside the fibreglass dummies and are then able to take them aboard without question.'

'That's really kinda slick,' Ramirez said.

'Where are we going to get fibreglass from?' Jay said.

'What do you think most boats are made of?' Scott said.

'Metal?'

'No, fibreglass. Especially the yachts and smaller vessels that they're making on the south side of the shipyard. All we need to do is sneak in one evening and swipe some resin and matting.'

'You make it sound so easy,' Pascal said.

'It's hardly going to be high security, is it? It's just fibreglass. Anyway, you're supposed to be a thief, so nicking stuff is in the job description.'

'Suppose so,' he said with a shrug.

'We need to do a quick recce this afternoon, just to get the lay of the land. Then break in tomorrow night when they'll hopefully be nobody else around the yard. Agreed?'

They nodded.

'Any of you know anything about fibre-glassing?'

'I did some with Papa when I was about twelve, fixed the hull of my rowing boat but I wouldn't say I'm expert,' Pascal said.

'Well, that's more than anyone else here. You need to join me for the recce, make it three o'clock when they're breaking for afternoon tea.'

'Okay, but I don't know what you expect.'

'Not much, just be on time.'

43

After a successful raid the following night, Pascal unloaded a gas cylinder from the back of the damaged van in the subterranean car park. He carefully chopped and laminated the fibreglass to create an oversize shell around it. He'd studied several YouTube videos and thankfully found it an easier task than anticipated.

'Just like a Russian doll, indeed,' he said, reiterating Scott's comment.

It cured overnight and he broke the mould open just after dawn the following day. Finally, he was ready to begin making his first dummy cover for the Xenon cylinders.

It took him two days to complete the pair of them, and by the early hours of Friday morning, he was ready to trim the edges and add a coat of paint in the same colour as the welding gas cylinders. It took him all night.

A final wipe-over with an oily rag gave them an authentically dirty look, and by six o'clock the following morning, the dummies were ready.

'Great job,' Scott said. 'Now go get some sleep. Your pallor is greyer than those cylinders.' Pascal gave a thin smile and lumbered over to the lift.

*****

At the shipyard, Scott wanted to do the first run. He wheeled the sack barrow with his two welding cylinders out of the ship and down the gangplank to get a 'two cylinders out' chit from the guard in the gate hut. Then he made his way over to the new rental van and banged on the rear door. Ramirez swung it open and hopped out, and the pair of them released the chain which held the cylinders to the sack barrow. They then slid Pascal's slightly oversized fibreglass dummies over the originals. And with the chain re-tensioned and the chit in his top pocket, Scott made his way back into the shipyard with nothing but a cursory glance from the gate staff.

Ramirez was to remain a few paces behind, just in case, but everything seemed to be going smoothly. He went through the gate, but wasn't more than five paces into the shipyard when the guard called after him.

'You, English, stop now.' Scott froze, and the hair stiffened on the back of his neck. Slowly he turned to see what the guard wanted.

'Your boot, dangerous,' the guard motioned to Scott's feet. He looked down to see one of his laces untied. He nodded, smiled, and bent down to tie it.

*****

'The guard rota changes at four o'clock,' Scott said over lunch, 'so even though it's unlikely I'd be noticed changing more than one pair of cylinders in a day, it's probably best we take turns and vary the pattern.'

'Logical,' Ramirez said.

'Now that we have the dummy fibreglass covers on board,' he gestured to Ramirez, 'you can do the first inbound run. Use the sack barrow to take them off after the shift change at four, then head to the van and slide them over the Xenon cylinders. Then, bring them back to the hides on E deck where I'll be waiting to help conceal them. With a cycle of taking the dummies off and returning with Xenon, say, one run of each per day. And then add in the safety of a day's break here and there, it will take us around three weeks.'

'Man, did you forget today's the twentieth of December?' Ramirez said. 'We're only here for another ten days.'

'You're forgetting the couple of days we'll need to seal the hides properly, so as they withstand any inspection from Li and his crew,' Jay said.

Scott rolled his wristband over to show the blue side.

'Then we'll just have to go fully local for the last couple of weeks.'

Jay pointed to Ramirez.

'Except for our friend here, of course,' Scott said, 'who gets to fly home early.'

Ramirez put his hand up for a high five.

'Gotta love that.'

'Time for a celebratory beer, being a Friday an' all,' Jay said.

'Not me. When I told you I had a plan to get into these specific cabins once we set sail, I thought it best not to share some of the finer details.'

'What are they then?' Jay asked.

'To be discussed once I've worked a few things out. Go have a beer. I've got work to do.'

Scott held his nose and popped his ears. The cabin became instantly louder, a baby crying and the 'bing' of the seatbelt signs illuminating added to the whine of the aircraft. He looked out of the window and saw the sparking lights of the English towns a few thousand feet below. Like diamonds ready to scoop up and be pocketed. It had been a long flight, but had given him time to reflect on their progress and what needed to be done next to complete this audacious heist. It was going to become part of history. It would go down alongside the Antwerp Diamond Heist and the Great Train Robbery. But that was also the dangerous part. If any of the others decided it was more about their ego than the end result, things could get tricky. He had to keep a tight lead on Jay for sure, maybe Pascal as well.

An hour later, Candy met them in the arrivals area and couldn't contain her excitement.

'So, what you been up to since I went away, you sexy thing?' Jay said as he wrapped his arms around her.

'Just the usual, keeping Pascal's café afloat, amongst other things.'

'Merci beaucoup, I really appreciate it.'

'Plus studying all those legal cases for my degree.'

'Aren't you forgetting something?' Jay said

'Oh, and waiting for you to return home, honeybuns, obviously.'

'How poetic you English are,' Pascal said. 'Where's the car? I'm beat.'

'Patience, loser,' Jay said before giving Candy a deep kiss on the lips.

'I hope you've been looking after Chester properly all this time,' Scott said.

'Don't worry, two meals a day and tuna on Saturday. He'll be disappointed you're back.'

Scott grinned, bemused at his concern for the cute ball of fluff.

In the car and slowly edging down the congested ramps to the exit, Candy looked at Scott in the rear-view mirror.

'We all set then?'

'Not exactly. As things stand, we're about a hundred grand short of what we need to get on board.'

'You're kidding us, right?' Pascal said.

'Unfortunately, not. And that doesn't include the cash we'll need for the cruise tickets.

'I didn't want to tell you this whist we were focussing on another part of the job but now we're back in the U.K. we need to pull another robbery, and quick.'

Pascal groaned, and then a barrage of questions hit Scott as to how the shortfall had happened.

'Look, we got an unexpectedly low price for the stash from Terry due to the Guildford jewellers not being adequately re-stocked and that bloody woman locking herself in cost us time.

'Then there was the news that we can't secure specific cabins, so we'll have to book a pair of first class cabins for the voyage.

'Whoa tiger,' Jay said. 'What's with first class? I thought this was a job, not a jolly.'

'Yeah,' Pascal said. 'What's with it?'

'The system won't let us book specific cabins, right Candy?'

'That's what the man said.'

'So, the only way to ensure we have access to the ones we've worked so hard to get the Xenon gas inside, is to use good old-fashioned bribery. As soon as we're aboard, we need to get hold of an officer's uniform for Jay. He can then use his silver tongue to persuade the occupants in the two second class cabins we need to move before they have a chance to unpack.'

'Won't be easy,' Pascal said.

'He can tell them there's an elderly guest onboard whose parents died in their cabin on the original ship. She wants to stay in the cabin for sentimental reasons, so would they like a free upgrade to first class for the inconvenience.'

'That could work,' Pascal said.

'Surely there's a cheaper way?' Jay said.

'I've run through every angle and this is the most realistic without throwing innocent people overboard.'

'Now you're talking.'

'Shut up Jay. Unless anyone can think of a better option, this is what we'll work towards.'

'What about this other job?' Pascal said. 'What's involved that can be worked on at such short notice?'

'I was just getting around to that. We can't hit Guildford again for obvious reasons. They're probably bankrupt, and if they aren't, they'll be highly secure.

'There's nothing for miles that's as rural, which would also hold a similar value of stock. Our only option is to head nearer London, so Kingston or Richmond. The city we choose needs to be on the river for my plan to work.'

'The river, cool, do I get to go in a speedboat?'

He leaned over and cuffed Jay on the side of the head.

45

The following Friday, as the night was gently fading to dawn, Scott took a stroll onto Kingston bridge carrying a selection of foil party balloons. They bobbed and fluttered in the light breeze as though alive. When he reached the third pair of iron streetlights, he stopped, confident he was near the centre of the bridge, and directly above one of the pillars which plunged deep into the riverbed. He dropped to one knee, slid the heavy rucksack from his back to the floor, and then removed an aerosol. He then pulled out a nylon netting bag which contained several items, including two belts threaded with lead weights and three fisherman's torches, which he switched on. He then tied the balloons to the netting, double-knotted them just to be sure, and used duct tape to reinforce the nylon cord where it attached to the balloons. He stood, and then launched it over the side. It splashed into the water a few yards out and took the balloons down without much of a struggle.

He picked up the aerosol, shook it, and sprayed a bright pink smiley face on the pavement next to where the balloons had gone over. He then resumed his stroll into town, tossing the aerosol into a nearby bin, after wiping it down with a bleach-soaked rag.

46

At nine thirty-four that morning, Detective John Sharpe walked briskly from where he had left the car on Bruton Street and entered Berkeley Square from the northeast corner.

After checking his watch for the third time in ten minutes he confirmed that he was still twenty-six minutes early. He crossed the road and entered a small park in the centre of the square via a squealing iron gate.

He took a seat on one of the benches and sat back to gather his thoughts, but found it a struggle, so pulled a small leatherbound notebook from his inside pocket. He opened it to the list he'd made earlier titled Career, but it was no good, he couldn't concentrate. Again, his hand slipped inside his jacket, but this time he drew out a silver cigarette case. A deep circular dent near the hinge made it stiff to open, but when he'd done so, and withdrawn a cigarette, he began to feel a little better. He lit it, took a deep, delicious draw of nicotine into his lungs, and then finally began to relax.

He placed the notebook on the bench beside him and took a second delicious draw.

'Heaven.'

To the east he saw a Bentley showroom. Elegant lines and polished walnut were their stock-in-trade. Next along was Rolls Royce, where elegant lines and polished walnut were also their stock in trade. To the north he saw Porsche with yet more elegant lines, but this time accented with carbon-fibre in lieu of more recently deceased trees.

'A Climate Activist's nirvana,' he muttered, picturing the ragged splashes of orange paint, protest banners, and teenagers glued to the zebra crossing like a distortion of the Abbey Road album cover. Then, as he looked to the west, he spotted Annabelle's. The notorious nightclub frequented by celebrities and royalty just a cocktail's sip away from embarrassing themselves for the ever-present paparazzi outside.

Sharpe picked up his notebook, the cigarette having worked some magic, and found the page. The summary of his career looked disappointingly short, but there were a couple of high points. It had seemed so much more illustrious at the time, an adventure. But now on the stark, single page, it looked so inadequate.

'It's just a job interview, you've done it before.'

He said this under his breath, and then repeated it like a mantra, as the weak sun gently warmed him. His breathing sank into a regular rhythm, 'It's just an interview, you've done it before.' His muscles softened with each breath in and each breath out, and the sun felt good, really good. So good that he could have sat there all day.

He observed a couple of children playing hide and seek, and followed the little girl's progress as she searched for the boy. In and out of the bushes she dashed, but without luck. She ran around the park, looking everywhere for the little scoundrel whom Sharpe could see kept moving away from her.

Like cops and bloody robbers, a total waste of time. He closed his eyes and sank back further into the bench. So relaxing, so peaceful, he could just nod off.

The blast of a car horn shocked him from him back awake. A glance to his watch confirmed that he was now five minutes late.

'Bugger, bugger, bugger,' he cursed as he leapt to his feet and sprinted across the grass towards the exit.

'DI Sharpe to see Lady Astbury please, I have an appointment,' he panted into the intercom.

'Yes Mr Sharpe, she is expecting you, just pull the door when you hear the buzzer.'

'Thank you, Maria; it is Maria, isn't it?' but the racket of the catch releasing drowned out his voice. It wasn't until the lift began to rise that he realised he'd left his notebook on the bench.

'Oh, bugger it.'

The apartment door was open when the lift doors parted and Maria stood sentry.

'Lady Astbury is waiting for you in the lounge, please follow me.'

'Thank you,' he said as he dabbed the sweat from his brow, using a polka dotted handkerchief.

'Detective Inspector Sharpe, what a pleasure.'

'Lady Astbury, the pleasure is mine. Awfully sorry I'm late,' he replied, but then realised he was bowing, so straightened immediately. 'Please, call me John.'

'If you insist, John, and thank you for coming at such a vague invitation.'

Maria returned and slid a tray laden with tea and miniature cakes onto the coffee table. 'There's something of great importance to me that I wanted to discuss with you face to face, and would rather it here than at the police station, for reasons that will become evident.'

'I have the rest of the day off, so please, take your time.' Sharpe took his tea from the tray and blew the surface, his saucer hovering a few millimetres below.

'I gather from our last conversation that you might consider a move into the private sector after a long and unfulfilling career in the Met?'

'That's correct. Although I've yet to make any real enquiries. One slight correction, my most recent posting has been in Surrey.'

'I don't mind telling you, John, that I've felt increasingly vulnerable since the mugging downstairs, from which you kindly saved me. So, I have decided that a certain amount of protection might be prudent for some of the events and trips I take throughout the year. I know we touched upon this briefly last time, but I'm especially concerned when wearing something like this…'

She unbuttoned her cashmere cardigan to reveal a large, clear stone held in an intricate gold necklace. Around it sat a cluster of smaller sapphires and four more diamonds.

'If it's not rude, might I ask the value?'

'It was a gift from my late husband,' Sharpe took a mouthful of tea, 'but Christies in Geneva achieved fifty-five million for something similar in January of this year.' She turned her head slightly to the side, 'and that was without the matching earrings,'

Sharpe almost spat his tea over her but managed to disguise it, albeit not very convincingly, as a hacking cough which forced some of the Earl Grey up, and then out of, his nose.

'Correct me if I've misunderstood, but if you are wearing the equivalent of several country mansions around your neck, it's little wonder you feel vulnerable out on the streets of London.'

'Yes, something like that,' she smiled. 'You can see my concern. However, most ruffians would probably have no idea and just think it's an old grandma's trinket worth nothing. Show them a phone and an Am-Ex and they're happy, I would think.'

'Very true, thank goodness for the great unwashed.'

'I was impressed by your actions and calm demeanour during my mugging, so I had my grandson take a look into your background. I hope you don't mind?'

'No, of course not. After all, if a Detective Inspector isn't a pillar of society, then…' he shrugged.

'Quite so, and I was impressed that you spent several years in the firearms division before being plain-clothes in the armed Anti-Terrorism Task Force, both here and then New York for three years. And now, as you pointed out, you reside in leafy Surrey. Tell me, do you still carry a gun?'

'Not currently, but it's only a matter of renewing my paperwork. I would have to make a special application for a concealed weapon, but as I'm ex-ATTF I can probably butter my old Super up to approve it. Why do you ask?'

'Because I wish to employ you on a part-time basis but with a retainer sufficient that you can leave the force with no loss of income. In fact, I have no objection to you taking other ad-hoc work so long as you are available when I need you. It's mainly for dinner engagements, parties and other social events, holidays, that sort of thing.'

'I'm sorry Lady Astbury, I think you may have misread my situation. I'm happily married.'

At this, it was Lady Astbury's turn to almost choke on her tea.

'Oh John, you're so funny, It's not like that at all. I need your services as a bodyguard, not my gigolo. I've plenty of wealthy men wanting to woo me into their country estates without my having to pay for it. So don't worry, you'll be quite safe with me so long as I'm quite safe with you. In fact, now we've truly broken the ice I think we'll get on just fine.'

Sharpe relaxed back into the soft cushions and felt his shoulders soften once more.

'So, when can you start? I have a few days with friends in Monaco next week but after that I'd like you to begin. It's a simple enough job, there's some etiquette training I would like you to undertake and you'll need a new wardrobe. Gresham's on Saville Row will sort you out but be sure to take your gun and holster so they can tailor it into your suits. I have an account there and they know the sort of thing I expect. Then of course there's the period costume for a week on the Titanic to consider but that's catered for by Crutchlow and Harris.'

'I beg your pardon?'

'I forgot to mention, we're planning to sail on the maiden voyage to New York, how thrilling.' She touched his arm.

Sharpe eyed her with suspicion. Was she just a loony old bat with a piece of worthless paste around her neck, or was this the opportunity of a lifetime?

'John, you look concerned. Don't you like sailing?'

'Titanic. You said you were planning a voyage on the ship which sank over one hundred years ago. I can't help but think you're mistaken.'

Again, she roared with laughter, reinforcing Sharpe's concern over her mental health.

'But haven't you heard? My close friend Lucien Croft has built a life-size replica. It's due to sail the original route and I have a first class suite with a further provision for two of my staff in adjoining rooms.

'Maria,' she called out. 'Bring me that iPad thingy to show John.'

Maybe his ship really had sailed in after all.

47

At ten o'clock that morning, Jay occupied the passenger seat of a stolen Audi RS6, Ramirez sat behind the wheel. The car was overkill for the role it had to play, but Jay always liked to nick a decent motor just in case they needed the horsepower to escape. McDonald's, Next and Primark slid past the window, as they neared the town centre. Ramirez slowed the car to walking pace.

'This clobber's too tight,' Jay complained as he pulled the top away from his chest to let a cooling draft inside. Then he slowly released the air to make a farting sound. Ramirez didn't respond.

'E.T.A. seven seconds,' the ex-Marine said into his phone. He killed the call and slid it into a plastic Ziploc bag, then the inside pocket of his top.

They reached Kingston's pedestrian zone a second later, but Ramirez ignored the 'no entry' signs and bumped up the pavement, performed a three-point-turn and gently reversed down the pedestrianised high-street. The rear of the car eased into the melee of shoppers, parting them and drawing curses and frowns.

'Just call me Moses,' he said, and they both pulled their masks on.

They continued at a walking pace until a series of bollards blocked their way. It was as close as they were going to get. Jay got out and could see the bridge in the distance, but it looked a lot further away than he'd have liked.

Ramirez snapped his fingers.

'Wake up.'

He grabbed his sawn-off shotgun from the back seat and pulled on both his front and rear rucksacks. The pair of them then jogged the short distance to the jewellers.

'Everyone on the floor, right now!'

Moments later, they burst from the shop. Jay fired a shot into the air and the shoppers scattered for cover, leaving their path clear to the bridge.'

'Back at you, Moses.'

Ramirez began running, shaking his head as he made for the Bridge.

Everything had gone to plan, but then Jay saw a police van appear on the opposite side of the river, lights and sirens blaring. It wasn't far from the bridge, but thankfully fighting the heavy traffic. Damn those silent alarm buttons. The police must've had an alert before they'd even crossed the threshold.

After just thirty metres his breathing had become laboured. Ramirez was already ahead by several metres and continuing to pull away. Panic began to rise. The weight of the rucksack was getting too much for him, not just jewels inside either.

He could ditch the gun, that would help, as he wasn't stupid enough to shoot anybody. But then there was the evidence, his D.N.A. all over it. Keep running.

Ramirez glanced over his shoulder but did nothing to help. They'd both need their own rucksacks in a few moments. He did slow a little, though.

Second, by second, they reduced the amount of pavement between them and the bridge.

The police van made progress through the traffic, almost at the bridge now. Their distance closing, more sirens, coming from all around. They were being boxed in.

Just a few yards to go, across the road outside the John Lewis building and Ramirez was on the bridge at last. A police car appeared out of nowhere, this time from the right. They were out of options. Finally, Jay reached the bridge, closing in on Ramirez as a final burst of energy shot through him at the fear of getting caught.

Ramirez pulled himself up onto the balustrade near the mid-point where a bright pink smiley was spray-painted on the pavement.

Jay reached it as a police car screeched to a stop just five feet away. Ramirez put out a hand, helped him up, as a uniformed officer leapt from the car and sprinted towards them, just seconds in it. He leapt from the bridge, sailing through the air for way longer than expected and impacted the water with such violence that it emptied his lungs.

The blast of cold water was both shocking and disorienting. He froze in panic, but the urgent need for air prompted action. He followed the drill they'd rigorously practised the preceding week, pulling the small oxygen cylinder from the backpack and opening the valve. Next were the goggles he wore around his neck. He pulled them up to his face and cleared the lens by violently exhaling air from his nose into the mask, forcing the water out. It was easier than he'd anticipated, maybe he could be a Marine too. If he could be bothered, that is.

A quick scouring of the immediate vicinity gave little information other than a cold, murky and disgusting river with virtually no visibility. He couldn't even see the light from the fisherman's torches. Then, a hand suddenly grabbed his arm and pulled him to the left, it was Ramirez. He'd found the submerged balloons that Scott had thrown from the bridge, marking where the netting sack sat on the bed. The balloons had remained well below the surface of the water, and inside the bag they pulled two pairs of fins, a weight belt for each of them and a compass. Now they could make their escape, skimming the silt covered bed using a military spec self-circulating air system that left no trace of bubbles on the surface.

The oxygen canisters only had fifteen minutes of breathing time, but it was enough for them to make it to the river barge that Candy and Pascal were aboard. It was moored less than a quarter of a mile downriver by an outcrop of foliage which provided cover for them to climb aboard undetected.

Once they were inside, Pascal cast off, and the boat made its way gently down to Hampton Court, where Scott waited behind the wheel of a plain white van.

48

St. Malo is a picturesque medieval walled city on the coast of northern France, and outside a street café on Rue Jaques Cartier, Terry sat sipping his coffee.

The weather was mild for February, and he admired the women moving elegantly along the cobbled street in their expensive heels and designer overcoats. Scott dropped his rucksack down in the chair next to him.

'I do wish you'd meet me in England. This travel lark really doesn't agree with me.'

'Listen mate, you know I can't set foot in Blighty. I wouldn't make it out of the ferry terminal without my collar being warmed by the palm of England's finest. Besides, it's good for you to see a bit of the world, give you something to talk about when you're chatting a bird up.'

'Whatever Terry, it's still a pain. Surely these days they can just nab you here, so what difference does it make?'

'Because the old bill on the continent have got their own villains to catch, they couldn't give a toss about some old jailbird like me so long as I don't get too comfortable in one place. I'd favour Paris over Pentonville any day; only just mind, filthy shithole.'

'Anyway, let's head somewhere more discreet, I'm on a bit of a tight schedule to get that God awful ferry back tonight.'

'I was just finishing.'

They walked along the promenade as the waves made inroads towards them. It certainly was a beautiful part of the world, and he conceded Terry's point about seeing more of it. Fifteen minutes later he was still looking at the incoming tide, but from six floors higher up, in Terry's opulent hotel room. After the usual weighing and inspection of the haul, Terry totted up the numbers with his worn pencil.

'I make it eighty-nine, but I'll round it up to ninety as you're a regular customer.'

'Come on Terry, I need a hundred grand for the job, no less or we just can't do it.'

'Ninety.'

'Shit, let me think.' Scott moved away from the window and began to pace, desperate to come up with a solution.

'Got it,' he said, 'how about we make it the hundred and I'll knock, say, fifteen off the price you offer me for the job once it's done.'

'What if it goes wrong? You really don't want to be owing me money, I can assure you.'

'It won't, it can't go wrong,' Scott blurted.

'How about we approach this from a slightly different angle? I took a peek at your website earlier. You've got a white nine-eleven cabriolet, left hooker, up for thirty-five grand. How about I give you your hundred plus fifteen on top when you deliver me that sporty little number?'

'Done,' Scott replied without hesitation. 'I'll bring it over tomorrow morning on the first ferry.' Terry nodded gently as a smile grew across his stubbly chin, hand outstretched to shake on the deal.

49

Tread by tread, Candy emerged from Oxford Circus tube station with a sense of wonder at the spectacle surrounding her. She began south down Regent Street, past the enormous glass frontages of H&M, Apple and Kiko Milano. It was difficult, but she managed to resist a quick diversion to look into the window of Liberty, the quaintest department store in the world, because she knew she wouldn't resist the draw to go inside and then hours would be lost. She kept on heading down Regent Street until a childhood memory drew her to a standstill outside Hamleys toy shop. There, she did take a moment to cup her hands around her eyes, and peer back in time through the window of every child's dream.

After some searching on her maps app, she found Crutchlow and Harris one third of the way down Saville Row. Impressive, even amongst the other high-end tailors famously located along this quarter-mile stretch. She double-checked the A5 gold embossed appointment card, which she gripped just a little too tightly and took a bold step up the broad flagstones.

A brass bell clanged above the large varnished door and announced her arrival to a clutch of impeccably attired middle-aged men, their only uniform being a fabric tape measure strung around the sharp collars of their dour suits. They welcomed her inside.

'Hi, I'm err Candice Jones. I got this in the post, for the Titanic.'

'Welcome Miss Jones, is it okay for me to address you as Miss Jones?'

'Suppose so.'

'Lovely, if you would like to follow me, Mrs Stapleby will be taking care of you today. She's an absolute whizz on early twentieth century fashion and will have you looking simply spectacular for the voyage. Such a bold venture, don't you think Miss Jones?'

'Bold? Hadn't thought of it like that but yes, I suppose so,' he didn't know the half of how bold the venture truly was for her and the crew.

The man led her through a broad pair of hardwood doors, revealing a large, ornate room brimming with fabrics, dresses, coats, and hats.

To one side, a rack held at least twenty different umbrellas and parasols. Each one elegant and lacy in satin colours of peach and lemon, emerald and grey. The hat and bonnet shelves above had everything from pastel Easter bonnets to what looked like black funeral veils. A range of mannequins also lined the back wall resplendent in period outfits ranging from richly coloured evening wear and lighter daytime outfits, to a rather frumpy looking bathing suit.

'This really is a bit too overwhelming. I'm not sure I can do this. It'll be okay if I just wear my jeans, won't it?'

'Certainly not, madam,' came a gruff Aberdeenshire voice from behind a row of fabrics, 'Mr Croft insists that every passenger be in period clothing from boarding to disembarkation. It's a condition of sale, or sail, if you mind the pun.' A woman of around seventy hobbled out into the open, her posture stooped but eyes sharp enough to cut the fabric she worked.

'Come, my dear, let's get you in suitable shape for your trip. Will your husband be joining us?'

'Husband?'

'You're on my list as having a first class double cabin. That is correct, isn't it?'

'Yes, it's my boyfriend, Jay. I am travelling with him, but he's busy this morning so his appointment is later, about four o'clock, I think.'

'Shame, it would have been nice to do some pairing but not to worry, that can be Mr Harris junior's task once we have your outfits settled.

'Let's get on my dear. Do you have a preference for colour palette?'

'Pall, um, no not really, whatever you think is appropriate. Although I've been told to dress down a bit, more like second class, you know?'

Mrs Stapleby pulled the face of someone emptying a particularly pungent litter tray, and then busied herself amongst the greys and browns. She ignored the brighter colours reserved for the more extrovert of first class passengers.

A flurry of cream and white lace collared tops, deep red, emerald green and chocolate brown velvet skirts were all laid out on the vast cutting table. Then waistcoats, jackets, and frilly undergarments were added in a pile high enough to clothe several families.

'Right my dear, let's get you started. Put these on and hop onto the platform,' she said, and handed Candy a skirt and blouse, 'I need to get it pinned so as we show off the lower half of your ankles perfectly.'

*****

Two hours later, she returned to the main shop, where a man who appeared to be in his late fifties was signing for his order.

'So, would you know a place nearby for a decent cup of tea and a slice of something sweet?' John Sharpe finished scrawling his name and handed the paperwork back to the clerk.

'Well, sir, there is a lovely little Moroccan restaurant just behind us,' the assistant said. 'It's on Heddon Street, accessible via Regent Street.

'They do the most delightful pastries and mint tea, or a range of couscous dishes if you're yet to have lunch?'

'Dear God, no,' replied Sharpe, 'I was thinking Earl Grey and Victoria sponge, not that foreign muck.'

'My apologies sir, perhaps the Café Royal would better serve your taste? At the end of the row, turn left, then right on Regent Street. You can't miss it, sir.'

'Thank you.' Sharpe turned and looked somewhat taken aback to see Candy behind him.

'Good day, madam,' he smiled. Candy returned the gesture and took her place at the counter. Then, with a quick scrawl, she signed for the ridiculous quantity of outfits she would apparently need for the six-day crossing.

'That Moroccan sounded lovely. Could you let me know how to get there please?'

Fifteen minutes later she was sipping mint tea at a window table, lost in the distraction of people watching along the pedestrian zone of Heddon Street.

Smiling at this unexpected luxury, she slid her phone from her jeans, took a photo for Facebook, and then swiped to her phone book favourites.

'Hey Mum, just calling for an update on Becky.'

'Hi love, much the same, I'm afraid. Her kidneys seem to be working better and she's finally back on solid food. But her legs are still a mess. The doctors just seem at a loss.'

'Did you remember to ask them about a referral to that Swiss clinic I found online?'

'Candice, darling, I know you're thinking the best for your sister but it's just the NHS. They can't do things like that. We have to find the money ourselves. I've been spending a fortune on scratch cards to try and win it but it's hopeless.'

'Oh Mum, that's never–'

The shock of recognition, it couldn't be, could it? Seriously? Jay walked towards the restaurant, arm in arm with a tall brunette girl. He was laughing and teasing the way he always did with her.

'Candice, Candice, you still there?'

They paused outside the restaurant to read the menu. But deciding on somewhere else, they turned away.

'Mum, I've got to go.'

Candy slapped a ten-pound note on the table and grabbed her bag.

50

Sparks flew in a brilliant crescent from the angle grinder's disc as it skated over the welds of a steel table Scott was fabricating in the workshop. He tested the top once more, and finally, it slid into place, concealing the hidden compartment below and the hollow legs. His phone buzzed on the workbench, so he took a couple of strides to catch it before the caller hung up.

'Whoa, whoa, Candy, take a breath,' he put down the grinder and held the phone several inches from his ear. 'Get yourself together and meet me here at my workshop in twenty minutes. Can you do that?'

'I look a state.'

'I doubt it. See you soon,' he ended the call before she could respond. The last thing he needed right now was hysterics, let alone from a crucial team member.

Fifteen minutes later, he heard a banging on the roller shutter. That was quick.

'It's open,' he called from under the table, pausing a seam of weld mid-way. 'There's a coffee for you on the workbench.' He continued the bead of weld.

'Kind, but we not here for coffee.'

A jolt of pain shot through his leg as one of the Bulgarian thugs walloped him with a wrench. Before he could react, a large boot pressed down on his chest to keep him pinned to the floor. He flicked his welding mask up to see both men towering above him.

'You have choice today. Pay money or we break both legs.'

'I told you, it's taking some time, but I'll have it soon.'

The thug without a foot on his chest picked a hammer up off of the workbench.

'This one good, it do job,' he walked to the Mustang and smashed it down onto the front wing.

'Nooo!'

'What? You prefer Gregor do legs?'

'No, look, just give me a chance, I'll pay you.'

'Today? It's money today or break legs, then money next week or break arms. You decide. When we run out of bones…'

Scott's mind reeled with the pain and struggled to expand his options.

'Cars, take two of the cars I have in stock this week and I'll sort you some money for next week. How about that?'

The Bulgarian thought a moment, looked to Gregor holding the hammer, and then the Mustang. He nodded.

Scott's heart sank.

'Okay, but we take from showroom. This one has dent now. Fix dent and we might trade for broken legs next week. I like American car, it cool.'

'Okay, just give me a minute to find the keys for the two in the showroom.'

Fifteen minutes later Candy arrived. She plonked her bag onto the wing of his Mustang and Scott flinched.

'Please don't put your bag on her.'

'Her? It's buggered anyway so grow up. And I can't do this robbery thing, I'm out.'

'It's a matter of respect,' he walked over, picked up her bag and placed it on the workbench. 'And no, you're not out. We're all in this together, until the end. We all take the same risks and suffer the same consequences if things go wrong. Plus, I simply can't let you leave with what you know.'

He went to the side and flicked on the kettle.

'It's just a six-day crossing and then we go our separate ways until payday. I should have known better than to involve one of Jay's floozies but-'

The crack of Candy's hot palm striking Scott's face echoed around the workshop.

'I'm here by my own ability. You wouldn't have involved me if that wasn't the case, and you damn well know it. So don't demean me with that floozy crap, treat me with respect.'

'I don't respect quitters.'

'I'm not a quitter.'

'Then why are we having this conversation?'

Candy was silent. Her eyes welled up before she continued.

'I followed them for half an hour, not knowing how to interrupt. They looked so happy, cuddling, laughing and kissing. Eventually I couldn't take it anymore so I confronted them in a department store shopping for bedding for fuck's sake.'

'I'm not following?'

'Jay and one of his *floozies* as you so eloquently put it. But he denied even knowing me.'

She broke down, and Scott gave her time to get it out of her system before he replied.

'Jay's not a nice person. I looked up to him when we were kids. But we were constantly in foster care and I felt an obligation to look after him, even though he was a couple of years older than me. But he's proven over and over that he can't be trusted. He's, I don't know…'

'A tosser.'

'Yes, he is, but a useful tosser who also happens to be very good at his job. I only deal with him when I have to, and when I do, I take certain steps to ensure he can't screw me over.

'Nobody on my team ever knows more than what's needed to get the job done. That way nobody gets ripped off and we all walk away with an equal share.'

'What, so you're withholding information that might be important? That's not fair. I need to know everything before this goes any further.'

'I thought you quit.'

'I thought I wasn't allowed.'

'Now that's cleared up, let's find a solution to you and Jay. For appearances you will have to stay in the same cabin as arranged, but obviously the second class one now.' Candy shuddered.

'I can't, not after what he's done. I trusted him, believed it when he said he loved me. What an idiot I've been.' She shook her head. 'But it's over. You'll have to stay in the cabin with him.'

'What have I told you? My job, my rules.'

'Screw your rules. I can't share a bed with that snake.'

'Lucky for you the second class cabins I chose have a sofa in the room.'

Candy's eyes closed, and with the glint of a tear in the corners. She nodded slowly.

'For Becky.'

51

It was like having the guts torn slowly from his abdomen. A cramp which began behind his eyes and went right through him, down to his numb feet as they stood, shoulder width apart, on the forecourt of his almost empty showroom. The last he saw of the white Mustang which meant so much to him, was a casual wave from the new owner as he rounded the bend towards Esher. The loss represented more than just the feeling of redemption that the restoration of both his own body and another more tangible object had given him. It represented hope. Hope that he could rebuild more than just himself after being so broken. Hope that he could create the sort of life that would win Jasmine back. Yes, what he saw in the distance was his dwindling hope of her ever coming back to him. And then it was gone.

Before he'd had time to dry his eyes, a beaten-up old Audi banged onto the forecourt and parked diagonally over the space where two cars had been the previous day.

'Stock's looking a bit thin mate,' Jay said when he'd got out. 'Been having a two-for-one sale?'

'Bulgarians. Taken all but the Range Rover in the showroom. Apparently they're too easy to nick these days.'

'You let them take the Mustang?'

'No, I managed to sell it just in time. But they think they're coming back for it tomorrow afternoon, so I don't want to be anywhere near this place when they do.'

'Good plan. What did you get for it?'

'Eighty-five grand. Cheap, but better than the Bulgarians taking it. Talking of which, make yourself useful. I need to get all of the windows on this showroom covered in plywood before they come back. And you can help me, as they tend to get a little clumsy around glass when they're upset.'

'Righto boss. I'll stick the kettle on.'

Scott raised his eyes to the clouds, asked for strength, and they made their way around to the back of the building. Propped against the wall near the back door was a 'for sale' sign. Jay pointed to it and raised his eyebrows.

'The money we need for the cruise has to come from somewhere, I just didn't want the sign on display until I'm ready to evacuate.' Scott said, then pointed to the back of the Range Rover. Not an inch was left without one of Scott's possessions in. Even Chester was waiting patiently in a cat basket on the front passenger seat.

'I'll get the car out, you start bringing the sheets of wood around the front.'

'Righto, do you want sugar in your tea?'

52

Finally, the tenth of April arrived. Not only the departure date for the original Titanic in nineteen-twelve, but also for its namesake well over one hundred years later. Even their arrival was other-worldly with the steam train's laboured chuffs becoming more widely spaced as it reduced speed. A wheezing whistle blow announced their arrival under the shelter of Southampton Portside, a station and rail link built exclusively for the berth of Titanic II.

Candy looked out at the ornate ironwork, and curved glass roof, which she'd read mimicked the drawing offices of Harland and Wolff in Belfast, where the original Titanic had been sketched, refined and built. A charge of electricity enveloped her, and she squeezed her silk gloved hands together in her lap.

The closed carriage containing Scott, Ramirez, Jay and herself had remained awkwardly silent for much of the journey. Not only because of the tension between her and that vile serpent Jay, but additionally, the fifth seat of their six-seater carriage held a bowler-hatted stranger with a facial twitch and frequent sneeze.

The satin of Candy's dress rustled when she uncrossed her legs and then shifted in her seat directly opposite Scott. She hated the outfit already and resented that she was obliged to wear it, even if it did make her look striking in the royal blue with light grey accents she'd chosen.

The change of outfit also suited Scott. A starched collar turned down at the corners, and a vivid blue tie went well with his charcoal suit and matching pocket square. Silver cufflinks, a pocket watch chain and a light grey waistcoat gave him a dapper but understated look. It was the first time she'd noticed why he had chosen the vivid blue. It matched the twin gas-ring intensity of his stare almost perfectly.

Jay had gone against Scott's instruction to dress down, in preparation for the move from first to second class. He wore a white shirt and sunflower yellow tie under a purple waistcoat. His jacket and trousers were a slightly darker purple with a faint silver check. Since she'd last seen him on Heddon Street, he'd grown a handlebar moustache, but his attempts to curl the ends didn't quite work, as it just wasn't long enough. He, of course, had a top hat in the luggage rack above his head. The idiot looked more like the Joker.

Ramirez stared out of the window, a brown tweed suit with an open, rounded collar and bowler hat. A deeply tanned Dr Watson, I presume.

She stepped out of the carriage with more apprehension than strictly necessary.

'First class to the right, sir, second to the left,' a tall man announced as they neared the platform's end. The gent was also made taller by the addition of a black felt top hat.

He wore a knee-length jacket sporting three vertical rows of brass buttons, glinting in the light. Grey pinstripe trousers softly covered the top of his lacquer-polished shoes, and the large handlebar moustache which graced his top lip protruded three inches beyond his cheeks. It made Jay's look pathetic.

'First class to the right, sir, second to the left,' he repeated. His bellowing enough to cause arrhythmia.

They made their way to the right-hand corridor marked 'First', and Candy felt her shoulders soften when their sneezing companion took a left.

She thought of Pascal, already aboard and no doubt preparing cutlery for the first sitting of lunch. Even with the cash from the Kingston-upon-Thames job, there hadn't been the funds for everyone to get a paid ticket, so somebody got to enjoy the full experience of ship's life by working in the dining and entertainments section. That somebody was Pascal, he'd drawn the short straw.

She felt guilty but also thankful that he hadn't noticed that the draw had been rigged. Scott had too much to do, Jay was too lazy, she was too distinctive, and Ramirez simply refused. She hoped things weren't too rough for him, but the thought evaporated as soon as she entered the first class check-in lounge.

It was more like The Ritz than the airport-style desk she'd expected. A hostess escorted them to a table. Tea and biscuits were served shortly after, and then a clerk came to each group, in turn, to run through everything from dietary requirements to preferred hours of service for their personal maid or butler.

If this is just the check-in, what on earth have we gotten ourselves into?

A familiar voice brought her back to the present, and she turned to look over her shoulder. She gave a small wave to the man sitting a couple of tables along, with what she presumed was his wife. Then felt the wrench in her guts when she realised what she'd just done without thinking.

'Friend of yours?' Jay said before pulling a large grin. He turned to look. But then it was her turn to smile, as Jay looked just as shocked to see the A-list actor and another awfully familiar face just a few feet away.

She took in the rest of the room. It was like being at the zoo as a child, gazing into what she thought was an empty tank in the reptile house only to see it full of camouflaged snakes when her focus changed. Like the reptile house, she suddenly saw celebrity after celebrity when the camouflage of their Georgian era costumes evaporated. Musicians, actors, politicians, tech millionaires, and billionaires were all around them.

She felt so out of place that a rising panic became increasingly difficult to ignore.

'Scott, I... err... I think we need to re-think this.'

'Please be quiet, we're just here to enjoy a lovely voyage.'

'But...' his look silenced her.

*****

'Here, Scott.' Jay said, pointing. 'You'll never guess who's over there.'

He looked away from Candy and focused on his brother.

'What are you going on about?' but he knew even before he'd turned his head.

'This just isn't acceptable,' Jasmine said in a high-pitched voice as one of the wait staff worked feverishly to mop up some spilled tea. 'Jacob, Jacob, do something. He's making a mess of the entire table.'

The actor Jacob Del Toro stood slowly and took Jasmine's hand.

'Now darling, he's doing his best. Let's just–'

'Jasmine!' Scott said. 'What are you doing…?' but he didn't have the power to finish the question. Of course she was here, everyone who is anyone was here, in this room. And Del Toro was way more than just anyone in Hollywood.

An awkward silence fell over the room as faces turned in their direction. She reddened and threw a serviette at the waiter.

'I should be asking the same of you? I didn't know they stooped so low as to let used car dealers in here. Or are you working as a busboy now?'

Rage filled him at her unexpected shift from perfect fiancé, carefully balanced on that gold plated pedestal, to self-entitled, stuck-up bitch. Could he actually be hearing things?

But then flashes of their argument on Brighton pier filled his head. Her being unreasonable to the wait-staff. Then the hotel, her complaining about the air conditioning, the shower, the soap even. She'd been totally unreasonable. It hit him like a thunderbolt. What on earth had he ever seen in her?

'Come along Jacob, we need to be moved. I can't be seen with such a,' she looked down her nose at him, 'lower specimen of society. I thought I'd got rid of you, but clearly not.' As she passed Candy, she paused. 'Get out now, or he'll suck your ambition and will to thrive like a vacuum.'

Del Toro stood close to Jasmine and puffed out his already well-developed chest, silently daring Scott to utter another noun.

Then a ripple went around the room and most heads turned away, towards a second entrance. The one for those who were VIPs even above this crowd.

'Oh my God,' said Candy. 'I think that's Harry and Meghan. We have to call this off, we can't nick the crown bloody jewels.'

*****

'Good morning, my name is Maggie and I'll be your boarding host. Please follow me to the gangway.'

'Just so long as we don't have to walk it mid-cruise,' Jay said.

The boarding host smiled politely. 'It's a trans-Atlantic crossing on today's schedule, sir. Cruise season is from the fourth of June onwards.'

Candy stood, as did the others, her skin prickled and her mind raced in anticipation of what it might be like inside. Ramirez gave her a smile, and the group walked through a broad arch. Ahead of them lay a wide, deeply piled red carpet. Gleaming gold posts holding swags of red velvet rope lined their way and kept the paparazzi at a safe distance. It was like arriving at The Oscars, all this attention, just on her.

'It's more of a runway than a gangway,' Scott observed when they exited the building. The sheer number of white-light flashes from the cameras was a sure test for epilepsy, and they began down the carpet.

Streamers filled the sky, a marching band played on the quayside fifty feet below them, and thousands of well-wishers had come to see them off. Scott had been right, they really were part of a truly historic event.

The horse-drawn carts, vintage motor cars and cloth-capped lads running up planks with sack barrows topped with provisions was a spectacle to rival any Hollywood set. Candy stopped and gasped in awe at the sight of the great ship before them.

'You never told me it was so….'

'Jeez, that is simply incredible,' Scott said. Jay was speechless, his smart mouth hanging open an inch. Ramirez nodded his approval.

'It's as tall as a hotel,' Candy said.'

'That, Miss Jones, is because it is a hotel. The most luxurious floating hotel in the world,' replied Maggie. 'Now let's get you inside and settled in your cabins.'

They stepped from the gangway to an ornate hallway, with wooden trimmings in limed oak accenting the crisp white walls. All around them, the ship's corridors looked as sumptuously untrodden as the gangway.

'This carpet's so deep it'll keep my shoes nicely shined. Save me doing it,' Jay said.

A waiter offered each of them a glass of champagne from a silver tray, and then a handshake from Captain Roberts in front of a Titanic II life ring was captured for social media by one of the ship's photographers. Scott looked decidedly nervous about this but had little choice.

'You're two floors up, on B Deck, so follow me to the lifts and I'll show you the way,' Maggie said.

'Could we take the staircase?' she asked, 'I've been dying to run up it since watching the film.'

'All in good time, you'll have a week to discover the rest of the ship, so don't worry.'

The sound of a string quartet caught her attention, and she wandered from the group to find them. Ever since she was small, she'd loved the sensation through her jaw as she'd drawn her frayed bow over the taut strings. But that had been so long ago that it felt like a dream.

'Oi, Candy,' Jay said just a little too loudly. 'This way, my love.'

He, Ramirez and Scott had already begun down the almost never-ending corridor of cabins. She hurried to join them in silence, taking in their environment and absorbing the wealth and privilege like the kids in Wonka's chocolate factory.

'It all smells so new. The paint, the varnish, the waxed wood, everything. It's simply wonderful.' The rest ignored her and carried on walking, except for Scott, who dropped back to have a discreet word.

'Knock off the Walter Mitty act. We're here to do a job, so get focused or get off before we depart. Clear?'

'I was only thinking out loud. Why don't you go talk to your amazing brother over there and leave me alone.'

'Thinking aloud is a dangerous pastime in our profession, so stop it immediately.'

His tone took her aback.

Midway down the corridor, they arrived at an opening to a large atrium that housed the famed Grand Staircase and a bank of three lifts. Candy hurried to the bottom of the staircase and looked up. She gasped at the spectacle of the levels above, crowned by the most amazing ornate glass dome. It was all she could do to stop herself from shrieking with excitement.

'Candy,' Jay snapped as the steel concertinaed gate withdrew to reveal a small wood-panelled lift with a uniformed bellboy at the controls.

'Right,' Maggie announced as she opened a cabin door on B Deck by sliding a large key into the brass door handle. It gave a click without being turned.

'This is you two.'

Scott and Ramirez stepped inside. Twin beds sat in a decent-sized room, and two rectangular portholes around a metre high dominated one wall. Whitewashed panelling to waist height continued all round, the upper half being gold embossed floral patterns on dark green wallpaper. The centrepiece of the cabin was an intricately patterned, black enamel fireplace on the far wall. A single gold and opaque glass inverted half-dome hung from a ceiling rose on three chains. It wasn't that powerful but still had the strength to cast a few shadows.

'It's all a bit unbelievable, the detail's amazing,' commented Candy.

'It's correct for the period. Every cabin on the original ship is believed to have been much the same as they are decorated today. They didn't have The White Company back in 1912, but they did have the White Star Company. Hence the reason for the décor.'

'Oh, is mine going to be so lovely?' Candy asked with a hint of hope. Jay shook his head, and she immediately realised the folly of her question.

'If the pair of you follow me, we'll get you sorted as well. There's a telephone system for cabin-to-cabin calls so just dial the number of the cabin you wish to converse with. In your case it's B139, and this room here is B127.'

Candy and Jay left Scott and Ramirez behind, but her wonder turned to dread as soon as she realised, she'd be spending the next six nights in a confined space with this vile, arrogant man.

She didn't have to wait long, he started just as soon as the host had shown them the finer details of their cabin and left them to it.

'Stop being a div and wait here in case Pascal actually turns up with my officer's uniform. I'm going to head down to the restaurant to see if I can find the useless git.'

Candy threw a pillow at the door as it closed behind him and barely suppressed a scream.

*****

The kitchens of Titanic II stretched out forever. Bright stainless steel work surfaces and copper pans filled the vast space as cooks and prep lads worked at their stations preparing the first lunch service in the ship's history. A cacophony of bangs, tings and chop, chop, chopping filled the air. It mixed and swirled with the heady scent of roasting meats, seared fish and boiled cabbage as it carried in the billowing steam.

'Come on, you could easily get another sack on that barrow lad. Those arms of yours full of air?'

Pascal grunted with the strain and then looked to his new boss, Mr Healey.

'It's too heavy to push up the gangway as it is,' he complained, his shirt clung to his back almost as tightly as the barbed wire he could feel around his struggling lungs.

He wasn't used to manual labour. Maybe a spatula, a whisk, or a wood saw, but this was going to kill him. He pulled off the stupid flat-cap and wiped his brow with the prickly surface.

'I'm a waiter, not a kitchen porter, sir.'

'Don't you sir me lad, and it's Mr Healey, nothing else. You hear me?'

'Yes Mr Healey.'

'We all muck in on my ship, so pull your weight. Don't let me catch you slacking or you'll find yourself shut in the cold store for a couple of hours to think about it.'

Pascal continued unloading the sacks of vegetables, checking the time on his phone after Healey had gone to scrutinise another recruit. Merde! Twenty minutes late already, and not a chance in hell of slipping away.

He scanned the area for anyone who might be able to take his place, even for just half an hour. No such luck. The frenzied loading, sorting, mixing and stacking proved everyone had far too much to do themselves. He hated the job already and was only five hours in. Another call to Jay, the tenth in as many minutes, but the same beep, beep, beep of no service filled his ear. How could it be going so wrong already?

*****

Candy looked at the steamer trunks sat on luggage horses and smiled. For just a moment, she could imagine she really was a fortunate young lady who could afford such luxury without thinking. Her reverie was broken by the captain's voice, causing her to jump. He wasn't in the room in the truest sense, but his image filled the dressing table mirror as it transformed into an interactive tablet.

'Welcome aboard, Mr Jason Rainey and Miss Candice Jones. I hope you enjoy an incredible voyage with us here on board the jewel of The Bright Star Line's fleet, Titanic II.

'This is a recording, so you can use the touch-screen mirror to guide your experience. It works in much the same way as a phone or tablet, both of which are banned from use during our voyage, and an electronic blocker will be activated for the duration.

'But fear not, each user has a thirty-minute timed session each day using this interactive mirror to access emails, web, face-time calls, etcetera. Just log in using your email, date of birth and then answer the security question you gave during check-in.

'Being first class passengers, you will be dining in the Queen's Grill, and I will have the pleasure of your company at my table for one meal throughout the voyage. This is currently set for Tuesday's evening dinner service. If this is not convenient, please message the Maître-d's office by clicking here,' the captain pointed to the bottom of the mirror where a small email icon appeared. 'And you can access the menu here.' He then pointed to a small menu icon next to the email.

'As is traditional aboard Bright Star's fleet, all the tables in the ship's restaurants are circular eight seaters, so you will be getting to know some of your fellow passengers even better than you may have expected.

'Breakfast is between six-thirty and ten-thirty, lunch at twelve-thirty sharp and dinner at seven-thirty. Please be punctual for these latter two services, or you may miss something exceptional.' Captain Roberts continued to run through the wealth of information, but her mind had begun to drift. How were they to communicate if there was no phone signal? The timing of the job relied on her calling everyone to let them know when the deck doors were locked so that they could commence the raid. Without comms, they would be flying blind. Could they rely purely on physical timing? She doubted Scott had even considered this, much yet planned for it. He wasn't going to be happy.

53

Jay waited for Scott to answer the cabin door as he glanced up and down the corridor, hoping to chance upon a maid. He was surprised when it was, in fact, a maid that opened Scott's door.

'Good morning my lovely, I was hoping my friends would be inside.'

'Who may I ask is calling please sir?'

'Lord Rainey, dignitary of the Wessex estates. I've come to collect taxes.' She looked bemused. Her first day on the job, and she gets a smartarse like him, poor girl. Taking advantage of her confusion, he stumbled forward, bumping into her and causing her to take a couple of steps backwards.

'Roll of the sea, I'm sorry my love, please forgive me.'

'But we haven't left port yet sir.'

'Practicing for later, be a poppet and let the captain know I called.'

'Excuse me sir I'm not following. This isn't the captain's quarters. He's probably on the bridge.'

'My mistake, better go. Good day to you, madam.'

'No, wait, I'm confused.'

'That's the idea.' He tipped his top hat before strolling back down the corridor. After several metres he opened his hand to reveal the maid's master key. It looked like a traditional key, but instead of a row of jagged teeth on the blade, it was rectangular with a sim-card chip set into it. He slipped it into his waistcoat pocket. Next job, find an officer's uniform. Now where was that laundry room?

*****

'Good morning, Mr ...'

'Shiller, Conrad Shiller, how can I help you, officer?' Jay stood taller in his uniform, unsure of what precisely the cuff and epaulette braids signified. For all he knew, he could be playing chief sanitation officer.

'Might I ask sir, are you travelling with your partner today?'

'Yes, my wife Elise. She's just unpacking.'

'I have great news for you, sir. The cabin you are currently occupying belonged to a relative of one of the passengers on the original Titanic, and she was unable to select this cabin specifically when booking her trip so purchased a first class ticket instead.'

'Okay.' He said cautiously, 'how's that relevant to us?'

'I'm here to offer you a free upgrade to a beautiful, top of the line first class suite, simply so we can let this poor lady travel in this cabin that has such a strong emotional connection for her, I'm sure she will be extremely grateful.'

Mr Shiller's eyes pinched at the corners as a broad smile crept across his face. Then Scott and Ramirez arrived in porter's uniforms to do the heavy lifting.

Pleased, Jay moved to the adjacent cabin and rapped on the door. But after waiting a few moments, there was still no answer.

He knocked a second time, and this time, it swung open.

'Good morning Mrs....'

'Gratton, Mrs Gratton. What do you want?' her sour tone had even Jay's charms on the ropes in seconds. 'What do you want? I'm in the middle of unpacking.'

Jay began the pitch once more, laying it on even heavier for this miserable specimen, but Mrs Gratton was having none of it.

'I'm sure I can arrange a complimentary bottle of champagne with every evening meal,' Jay offered as a last-ditch attempt at bribery. He'd noticed the ruddy complexion and reddened eyes of someone who likes their booze just a little too much.

'Every meal,' she replied. Jay's heart sank, but never one to give in, he countered, 'I would love to, and I'll see what I can do. But I'm only authorised to allow evening meals. Let's get your bags moved upstairs, and I'll see if I can work my magic on the purser to get you a champagne breakfast in your room on, say, day two to give you time to settle in?'

'Done.' She didn't even smile but turned around and bellowed, 'TONY, get them bags packed back up. we're first class passengers now.'

54

The hot stench hit Pascal like a battlefield in the height of summer, the muscles in his guts clenched once his cabin door had fully opened.

'Can you guys turn the air-con on or something?' a ripple of laughter was followed by the slapping cheeks of a loud, wet fart.

'I'm Gordo,' an overweight Scotsman announced from a top bunk, 'there's your air-con mate. Welcome to the party.'

He edged inside and noticed a rota sheet attached to one wall, so he checked it immediately.

'Twenty minutes, you've got to be kidding me? I've only just come down from loading the cold store,' he threw his bag onto the only available bunk.

'No, that's all we get,' said the second of the men in the tight cabin. He lay on the lower bunk next to Pascal's. 'I'm Jakub, we will be working same table and same shifts so you better like it, I'm not carrying your arse for you.'

'So nice to meet you too.'

Gordo released some more pollution and laughed. 'So, as I'm number three chef in the Britannia restaurant you'll both be my bitches too. Hilarious, I'll take a wee tipple to that.' He cracked the lid of a bottle full of amber liquid and took a couple of gulps, 'Anyone else for apple juice?'

*****

Jay was back twenty minutes later with a thumbs up and a grin on his face.

'All good my lover, let's go settle in.'

'I'm not your lover,' Candy said. 'And would appreciate it if you kept that in mind over the next few days.'

Jay mocked being shot through the heart. Once recovered, he grabbed one end of Candy's steamer trunk, struggling and straining as he pretended it was too heavy to lift, flexing his muscles like a Vaudeville bodybuilder but failing to shift it a millimetre. Candy struggled to suppress a smile, despite her animosity towards him. She turned and stomped into the bathroom, but not before her face had betrayed her.

55

Candy's unpacking paused as the silence was broken.

'Let's go and see the spectacle as we set off, shall we?' Jay said. He pulled himself from the small sofa in their now second class cabin. 'I'll go and rouse the others.'

Candy nodded, dreading the prospect of spending more time with Jay, but also excited at the chance to explore some new parts of the ship.

They entered the next-door cabin, an exact mirror of theirs, and she saw Scott crouched, checking the panels that concealed their hides for any sign of tampering.

'Is everything okay with them?' she asked.

'All seems to be in order. Let's head upstairs.'

They took the stairs from E Deck up to the Boat Deck, the highest part of the ship the public could reach, where a black waist-coated lad of around twenty held the door open for them with his white-gloved hand.

As Candy stepped from the interior out onto the wooden deck, the breath stalled in her throat. She slowed a moment to take it all in.

A thirty-strong military marching band moved in unison along the quay. The soldiers, immaculately presented in their formal navy uniforms and white pith helmets. White-gloved hands gripped polished brass instruments or drumsticks as they played a series of rousing tunes, and they were so far down they looked like toy soldiers. The civilian onlookers also took part, as they spun wooden football rattles and squeezed the rubber bulbs of brass horns to cause a cacophony as the sounds mixed with the whistles, cheers and shouts of good luck from what must have been over a thousand well-wishers.

A screech followed by a thunderous roar dominated the air as the Red Arrows performed an aerial fly-by so low that the deck rumbled under her feet.

'Pinch me someone, I really can't believe what's happening around us.'

Jay didn't need a second invitation.

'Christ Jay, it was a figure of speech,' but her objection was lost to the thunderous roar of two dozen cannons firing a haze of paper streamers high into the air and over the decks. Gently and in her own graceful way, the ship began to move, and the distance grew steadily wider between them and the quayside.

Despite being taken with all that was happening, Candy slowly edged away from the group. She jumped with surprise when the unmistakable sensation of Jay's arm came snaking its way around her waist.

'Going somewhere, my love?'

'Yes, and it's none of your business.'

She shrugged him off but bumped into Scott. He turned to see what the disturbance was. Jay crossed his arms over his chest and looked back to the crowds on the dock, a counterfeit smile frozen on his face. Sensing an opportunity, she slipped back into the mass of people, eager to get away and explore the ship in peace.

Down the Grand Staircase, one delightful tread at a time. She ran her hand over the freshly waxed balustrade and a tingling sensation amplified with each step she took closer to adventure.

She crossed a vast lounge that spanned the ship's width on A Deck before pushing her way through a heavily bevel-etched and polished set of rotating glass doors.

Before her was a seemingly unpopulated room, probably first class by the expensive-looking décor, but it wasn't easy to tell with the whole ship being so opulent.

Midway down, next to the vast row of windows, she noticed the back of a man's head poking from a leather Chesterfield chair.

Plumes of grey smoke rose around him and danced in the air before being sucked ceiling-ward by an extraction system. Candy approached at a three-quarters angle so as not to startle the tweed suited man, but found it was she who was surprised at the sight of a familiar face.

'You. I really don't think you should be smoking in here.'

'Do I know you?'

'From London, you were in the tailors on Saville Row and seemed particular about your choice of tea.'

'Ahh yes, I should have remembered a face like yours, must be slipping.'

'But you still shouldn't be smoking.'

'I beg to differ. This is the first class smoking lounge, and there's no law forbidding it indoors in international waters, even if it will turn this tub into a floating tinder box. But I might ask what you're doing here. Are you travelling first class?'

'No, I mean yes,' flustered now. 'Well, it's yes and no. I was before but now I'm not.'

'That certainly clears things up. Are you sure you're indecisive or still thinking about it?'

'I'm sure, I think,' she fanned herself with her hand. 'My, it's warm in here.'

'Not really. I'm John,' he extended his hand to take hers, steadying it before giving a formal shake.

'And yours is?'

'And mine is what?'

'I can tell you're new to this conversation thing,' a brief smile. 'Let's start again. My name is John, and yours is?' He raised his eyebrows.

'Oh, silly, it's this boat and all the new stuff around us. I'm not really used to it.'

'A kindred spirit at last.'

'But you're in first class?'

'Not by choice. I'm working here as a personal aide to Lady Astbury, and thought it wise to get a few puffs in before the toffs descend.'

She smiled as Sharpe continued.

'Then, as Southampton fades from sight, they'll be in here polluting the air with their self-congratulating bull manure and expensive cigars. You won't be able to breathe.'

'But they might be lovely people,' she said.

'Call me old fashioned, but I doubt it.'

'Ahh, there you are, darling,' Jay said, close enough behind her to make her jump. 'Come along, my dearest, time to prepare oneself for a marvellous luncheon.'

Her face dropped, and she turned toward him. 'Coming.'

56

The maître-d' led Scott, Ramirez, Jay and Candy around a two-metre-high statue of atlas balancing the world on his back, just inside the stained-glass double doors of the bustling Britannia restaurant.

When they arrived at their table, Scott was irked to see it was an eight-seater with four places already taken. He'd hoped to discuss certain logistical matters over meals, but this was clearly not possible. He wanted to request a smaller table but held his tongue upon realising every one in the restaurant was the same. A headache wasn't far away.

Once seated, a flock of immaculately turned out wait-staff in stiffly starched grey jackets over white waistcoats drew equally starched napkins over their laps.

A sommelier arrived for the drinks order, and Candy opted for a cocktail which only served to increase the tension between Scott's temples.

'...and soup of the day is vichyssoise,' the waiter said, ending the list of specials. Scott wondered if an interpreter was available for each meal.

'I'm confused,' whispered Candy. 'So do we choose one of those or several?'

'One for each of the five courses,' Scott replied. 'But wait 'till we get to dinner. There's supposedly even more for that.

'It might just be easier to stick to the main menu. At least we can look up the ingredients on our phones. And by the way, you're not meant to be drinking.'

'You haven't noticed yet? There's no phone signal.'

'I'm sure there will be soon, they don't seem to have had any restraint on budget for anything else on board so they'll probably just flick a switch to engage a signal booster once we're out of Southampton Water. Until then we'll just have to ask the staff what on earth half this stuff is.'

'Seriously Scott, didn't you know? There was a welcome message from the captain when I went to the cabin earlier and it said there's a blocker on all mobile signals. The only way around it is we get access to email and internet for just half an hour per day in the cabin. Other than that, we're out of luck.'

'Shit.' Scott's response caused a ripple of attention around their table. 'So how are we supposed to communicate?' he ran his fingers through his hair. Why hadn't there been anything about this on the booking forms? or on the website?

'It's a kind of interactive screen on the dressing table mirror. I had a little play with it before getting ready for lunch and it seems like a really simplified iPad with just information about the ship, then email and internet access once you log in.'

'That's it?'

'So far as I can see,' she replied. The tension between Scott's temples ratcheted tighter.

'As nobody is going to do the introductions, maybe I should begin,' offered the man sitting directly opposite Candy, his face had the texture and colour of a large sultana. 'My name is Hanbal Hassan, and this is my beautiful wife, Lapis.' He beamed towards the woman to his left. Her face was indeed beautiful, but the rest of her proportions resembled that of a tortoise. She gave a small laugh, and fanned her reddening face with a frilly fan.

'We are in the sand business,' Hanbal continued. 'Or, more accurately, we have an ancient farm that my forefathers have handed down for fifteen generations. Each had worked the land with goats and cattle, unaware of the fortune they were standing on.

'Oil?' said Jay.

'No, like I said, sand. Can any of you guess where I send my precious granules?'

A slim, bespectacled man who made up the last two seats at the table with his runway model girlfriend was first to reply. 'You probably send it to my factory near Cairo,' his Southern California accent softer than a chinchilla cardigan. The Egyptian looked so startled that it almost smoothed his wrinkles.

'Curious,' Hanbal said once composed. 'Please, go on.'

'I'm Seth Emslow, founder of S.E.E. Technology and we have a processing plant there for our silicon chips. Am I close?'

'My goodness Mr Emslow, how astonishing we should meet in this way. Your company was something of a lifeline to my family over ten years ago and we have been supplying you ever since. We provide you with the extremely rare red sand you find so valuable for your chips.'

'Yes,' Emslow replied, placing his business card in front of the Egyptian. 'Valuable is certainly the word given the sudden spike in your prices two years ago.'

'Well,' the Egyptian shrugged, 'it's just supply and demand. I'm sure you would have sourced a new supplier if you could have.'

Emslow returned his attention to the menu without further comment.

'So,' Jay said, breaking the ensuing silence, 'now the elephant's in the room and sat on the table, let's finish up with the introductions.' He was openly leering at Emslow's girlfriend.

'Eloquently put. Let me introduce Kyla,' Emslow said, straightening the salt and pepper shakers in front of him and checking they were centred between his cutlery. 'We met at a tech convention where she was doing a little promotional work, but I made her a better offer, and she was working for me soon afterwards. We fell in love, became inseparable, and the rest, to use a cliché, is history.' Kyla held the large diamond ring up for all to see, not realising it was now on Scott's shopping list.

After the third course, Scott excused himself from the table. He scoured the room for Pascal and was relieved to find him stationed nearby.

'Where were you earlier?' he asked, 'You were supposed to get us the officer and porter's uniforms for the room swap.'

'You've got no idea what it's like here. I've only had ten minutes to myself since five this morning.'

'No excuse, we need to stick to the plan.'

'I'm not exaggerating, they treat us like dogs out of public view.'

'I get it, but listen. You're not here to wait tables or make friends. You'll be a multi-millionaire once we're finished with this place, so don't baulk at upsetting a few people. Are you listening?'

'Table twenty-three,' Jakub interrupted. 'Clear damned soup bowls, now.'

'See what I mean? And he's my serving partner, not even my boss.'

'Listen,' Scott repeated, 'due to this morning's cock up you need to get a bottle of champagne to the Queen's Grill every dinner time for the whole trip. It's the first class restaurant, Mrs Gratton's table.'

'No way, I just won't have time.'

'Make time. The last thing we need is for her to go to the purser asking where her free champagne is and have him looking into why she's in the wrong cabin.'

'But they have different uniforms in the first class dining rooms.'

'So nick one, you're a thief aren't you?'

Pascal drew a breath to protest further when Jakub grabbed his shoulder.

'Soup bowls, asshole,' then shoved him in the direction of table twenty-three.

When Scott returned from the gents, he paid particular attention to the conversation between Ramirez and Emslow, the Californian seeming to like the sound of his own voice, which suited Scott just fine.

'It's a multi-faceted company specialising in advanced technology.

'Primarily, we have the S.E.E.3-D system. Which, as the name might suggest, is a three-dimensional mapping software that acts in the same way as traditional radar but creates a virtual world on-screen, similar to how a modern computer game does.

'The 'world' the operator sees replicates what is around the vehicle or vessel they are travelling in. Therefore, no windows or cameras are required to 'see' where you are going.

'This has clear applications for navigating a ship through an ice field in heavy fog or operating a tank through a complex battle scenario where there will undoubtedly be diminished visibility.

'We are the leading developers of AI and drone technology in the U.S. and have made massive leaps forward by combining all of these technologies to make our world a safer place. We are currently developing a system for remote guidance using these combined systems.'

'You mean it lets the commanders play a modern version of the board game Battleships. But everyone gets to die in the end except the precious commander, sat comfortably in his underground bunker.' Jay said.

Emslow regarded him in a way he no doubt reserved for waiters who laid up dirty cutlery.

'Quite the contrary, Mr …'

'Rainey, Jay Rainey. We're all friends here so Jay'll do.'

'The technology is saving lives, not costing them. This ship we are all aboard represents the first of many private companies to introduce this technology. It increases safety whilst decreasing the margin for human error.

'The original Titanic sank because the lookouts didn't have binoculars so couldn't see what was ahead of them. The ship was effectively blind and travelling too fast for the conditions.'

'I thought it was flat as a millpond, with clear visibility the night it sank?' Hassan said.

'Correct. Which is why the lookouts didn't see the iceberg until it was too late.'

'That doesn't make sense.'

'Oh, but it does. If there had been a swell, small breakers would be visible at the point where the ice met the water.'

Emslow began buttering every millimetre of his roll as he continued in his soft voice.

'Lives were also lost due to a lack of communication with nearby vessels that were a mere ten miles away.

'If this ship were presented with the same scenario, then the S.E.E.3-D would identify the threat fifty miles before it was even visible. It would plot the likely course of the iceberg using live data, captured every thousandth of a second, and then devise a safe path around it.

'The man at the helm would be informed by a computer-generated 'movie', for want of a better word, of how various courses of action would play out so he could select the most appropriate. Even if the entire crew were asleep, the software kicks in and corrects the course.

'I'm in the saving lives business Mr Rainey, not the taking of them. And this is the safest ship on the ocean today.'

'I think they used that line in the sales brochure for the original Titanic, didn't they?' Jay said, raising a snigger from Emslow's fiancé, but he quashed it immediately with a stern look.

'I've used this system before, a couple of years ago, quite impressive,' Ramirez said.

'No, I don't think you have,' Emslow said.

'Yeah, I recognise the logo on your business card, from the start-up screen.'

'You've been in combat with Special Forces?' Emslow said incredulously.

Ramirez realised his error and remained quiet. Again, the deep creases in Hassan's tanned face smoothed with his look of surprise.

'Sorry, I didn't catch your name,' Emslow persisted.

'Just call me Ramirez. And I must be mistaken, unless you also make computer games.'

'No Mr Ramirez, our technology whilst virtual is still rooted firmly in the real world, not killing zombies. Pass me the water would you.'

'So this communication technology of yours,' Scott said, 'I presume it works despite there being a phone signal blocker on board?'

'My communication systems don't work in the same way a traditional phone signal does, it's completely secure and uses my patented bi-wave technology. This blocker is just a simple gimmick I installed at the owner of this ship Lucien Croft's request, child's play really.'

'So, you could unblock it?'

'I could, but that wouldn't be cool. The whole idea is for people to have an immersive experience of the original ship's grace and beauty, and that wouldn't be possible with everyone's face entranced by a screen like the real world.'

'True, and I get that. But in an emergency how would you unblock the signal?'

'Nice try Mr …'

'Scott Rainey, pleased to meet you.'

'Mr Rainey…'

'Scott, please.'

'Scott, be assured there are emergency protocols in place and trying to reinstate a mobile phone signal in that kind of situation is as futile as trying to look for a match to send a smoke signal compared to the S.E.E.-Hear system the crew have on board.'

'So, all the crew carry radios that work even though there's a blocker in place?'

'No, they rely on the quaint system of being where they're supposed to be at the time they're supposed to be there. Although, in the spirit of not breaking the illusion, the one or two high-ranking officers who are in communication use lapel mikes and earpieces, not physical radios.'

'So how many officers would that be?'

'Questions, questions. So, are you two related? Or is it coincidental you share the same surname?'

57

For the rest of the day, Scott had insisted on performing timed drills. How long did it take to get from the cabin to the Bridge? First by lift, then by stairs. Then by another set of stairs and then yet another. How long from the Infirmary to the deck, the deck to the cabin, the cabin to the deck via the Purser's office? It felt so unnecessary, but Candy supposed he knew best.

Exhausted, she made her way along the corridor that evening towards their cabins, but turned to Scott as they walked.

'Isn't it funny, everyone taking their shoes off and leaving them outside their cabins? Like being at home when Mum insists on it before going into the lounge.

'It's the overnight shoe polishing service, you div,' Jay said before Scott could answer.

She knew her cheeks had flushed crimson from the heat they instantly generated. Maybe she should just keep her mouth shut.

'Goodnight,' Scott and Ramirez chimed in unison to her and Jay once they reached their adjoining cabins. Candy smiled, her attention mostly directed towards Scott, for whom she felt a growing warmth. Jay gave an exaggerated bow, top hat in hand, and produced their room key with a flourish.

Once inside, Candy rushed to the bathroom and closed the door. She took a steadying breath and noticed that the swaying of the ship had become more pronounced, or was it the champagne? It grated having to spend time alone with him after catching him with that slut in London. It made her shudder to think she had ever been taken in by him.

But then, like the devil's advocate was whispering to her from the mirror, she thought back to that flourish to produce the room key a moment ago, and the way he dealt with Pascal not turning up with the uniforms so calmly. Could it be she was being too harsh on him?

A rap of knuckles on the door startled her.

'You going to be hours? Captain Pinky's bursting to let his bladder free.'

She stifled a giggle and replied, 'One moment, Lady Pink has her requirements too you know.'

She flushed the loo, checked her face and opened the door.

*****

The impact on the side of Pascal's head was brutal and unexpected. He dropped his handful of cutlery to the floor of the closed restaurant and immediately put a palm to his throbbing temple.

'You leave during service again, I kill you,' said Jakub, cradling the fist he had just used to thump Pascal.

'I've got the shits, had to go before an accident.'

'Bullshit. You go for rest as you're lazy Frenchman. Come to Czech Republic and we teach you about work, not cry baby like you.'

'Seriously, I'm not used to this food,' Pascal said, 'I've got a sensitive stomach, and with the waves it sent me right over.'

'I throw you right over side if you do it again.'

If he's getting this upset after the first time I go upstairs to serve that cow her complimentary champagne, how will I get away with doing it every night? Pascal bent down to collect the cutlery from the floor as Mr Healey walked up.

'I hope you're not going to put that anywhere near linen, now it's been on the floor. Get back to the kitchen and clean it thoroughly before I see it anywhere near one of my tables. And mark my words, I've been watching you lad, and I'm not impressed. We've got an hour before those doors are back open to the public so get your arse in gear.'

'Sorry sir, I mean Mr Healey, won't happen again,' he replied to the man's back. Healey strode in the direction of the midnight buffet tables that the other staff members were setting up.

'See,' Jakub said, 'even arrogant English hate lazy French. And this is what I have to deal with. You are my shit on shoe.'

'I think you'll find that's, *'the shit on my shoe.'* I wouldn't want you to show your ignorance by insulting me incorrectly.'

'You have spirit, lazy French, I like that.' Jakub smiled, 'Something for me to break.'

*****

Candy lay in her bed and listened to him emptying his bladder. The movement of the ship sent her rolling back and forth like an excited child, and she wondered what the hell all these emotions were doing swimming around inside her? She was supposed to be furious with him. But then, he could be so charming. And the opulent surroundings were just as intoxicating. How many cocktails had it been? Three? Or was it four? Maybe she should be a little more forgiving.

'Ta. Daaa!' he flung open the bathroom door wearing nothing but the top hat over his genitals. 'And welcome ladies and gentlemen to the main event of the evening.'

He moved the hat forwards and backwards to give her a tantalising view of what was on offer, but his immaturity had broken the spell.

'Jay, seriously, I'm tired and need to go to bed.'

'Exactly my point dear, you're already there. And in just a mo–'

'Hold it right there, I'm really not up for this, so just make yourself comfy on that sofa and I'll see you for breakfast.'

Jay's palms thumped against his chest. He collapsed to the floor and writhed in apparent agony,

'My heart, my heart. Call for the ship's doctor, I think it's broken.'

Candy smiled but turned the lights out and settled down to her first night aboard Titanic II feeling better than she had done in a very long time.

58

The door out onto A Deck was stiff to open, but once outside, Scott noted it was the automatic closer causing the friction and not wind, as there was only a light breeze on deck.

He walked to the aft section and looked to the Poop Deck, a level below where a group of young girls were having fun playing shuffleboard near the outside swimming pool. After a moment, Ramirez appeared next to him at the rail.

'Take away the option of staring into a phone screen and ping,' Scott clicked his fingers, 'they become normal children playing the same games kids have enjoyed for centuries.'

'I'm sure it's been a long twenty-four hours for those parents. More snap-back than Snapchat,' countered Ramirez, his deep South American accent more pronounced away from prying ears.

'Indeed. Still, there's more fun and games to be had in a moment.'

'Lifeboat drill?' asked Ramirez, holding his lifejacket aloft.

'Lifeboat drill,' confirmed Scott, doing likewise. 'We'd better get to our muster station by lifeboat twelve, pronto. I want to make sure I'm at the front of the crowd and get direct access to the davit operator.'

'Before we go,' Ramirez said, pulling the lifejacket to his shoulder, 'I hear you've challenged Jay to a game of squash tomorrow morning. I know everything's in place for the raid but do you really think that's wise on the eve of the job, what with his overly inflated sense of competition?'

'He'll be okay, I'm sure he knows he's beaten before he starts.'

'Wouldn't count on that.'

'No, me neither,' they climbed the iron stairs to the Boat Deck just as a deafening roar of seven short and one long blasts on the ship's whistle indicated that the lifeboat drill had commenced.

There was a sense of confusion and mild panic from a few passengers at the sight of bright orange lifejackets over traditional tweeds and herringbone as passengers began to pour from every exit.

'I guess some people missed the front page of The Bright Star this morning,' Ramirez said.

'The Bright Star?'

'The on-board newspaper, it came under our door.'

'Oh right, I did see it,' pulling the lifejacket over his head whilst they walked, 'just didn't clock the name of it.'

Once at lifeboat twelve, Scott searched the crowd for Jay and Candy.

'Where are the others?'

Ramirez shrugged.

'How the hell are they going to know how to lower the lifeboats if they aren't here?'

Ramirez shrugged again.

'Come along, all gather in tightly so you can hear,' the uniformed seaman instructed. 'In the unlikely event of a real emergency–'

'Bet they said that on the first Titanic,' heckled a man from the back. The seaman took a second to smile before repeating, 'In the unlikely event of a real emergency, you will all muster here in preparation for boarding the lifeboats. There will be two Bright Star Line staff members present to operate the lowering of the lifeboat from its davits.' He gestured to the iron arms holding the boats in place. 'And a third who will join you in the boat to start the engine and take you to any ships in the vicinity.'

'So how do we operate the davits in the absence of a crew member, given it might be an emergency situation?' Scott asked.

'Rest assured there will be adequate staff to perform the tasks needed to get you to safety sir.'

'Answer my question please.'

'Sir, there's really no need, I can assure you–'

'Answer my damned question. How do we operate the lifeboats if there's no member of staff present?'

'Sir, I really can't foresee a situation that a crew member–'

'Yeah,' the heckler shouted from the back, Scott now recognising Jay's slightly disguised voice, 'like your predecessors didn't foresee an iceberg coming.'

The seaman began to stutter his words as a red hue flooded his face. Scott thought he might even buy this familiar heckler a drink.

'Please, young man,' a feminine voice came from over his shoulder. 'Please show us how it works, or I'll be unable to sleep with the anxiety of not knowing how to save myself.'

Candy pushed her way forward and wrapped an arm around the young Bright Star employee. His face flushed to a deep scarlet.

'Um… okay, look, I'm not supposed to be telling you this, but…'

Scott and Ramirez paid close attention to the sailor's words for the next few minutes.

*****

Pascal opened the door to his cabin, but all hopes of a peaceful afternoon nap evaporated as the rancid smell hit him. Gordo lay on his back, dead? But then a grunting sound came from his carcass to prove that he was unfortunately still breathing.

'Listen, Jakub, I'm sorry about yesterday, it's all so new to me and I don't know where to start,' he shrugged.

'Save your bitching for when talk to your ugly mother.'

'I'll get better, honestly, I just need some time. I'm a chef, not a waiter, and your ignoring me isn't going to help either of us.'

Jakub rolled over to face the wall, their conversation over.

He glanced to Sinjin in the top bunk, the fourth crew member in their cabin. Yes, he really was moving his bedclothes in an undeniably suspicious manner.

'Seriously Sinjin, do you have to?'

'My wife send me saucy picture before we leave port, only just had time to look,' he grinned, 'I'll be done in jiffy.'

Pascal dropped his head and rolled onto his lower bunk.

Once Sinjin's rhythmic movements had reached an intensified peak, then slowed to a silence, Pascal thought it safe to pose his question.

'So, Sinjin–'

'Can you pass Kleenex please?' Pascal cringed and checked his immediate surroundings for a box of tissues. In the absence of anything more appropriate, he decided on one of Gordo's t-shirts.

'If you're finished, I need to ask you a quick question please, my friend.'

'Oh,' Sinjin replied, 'if you're saying 'my friend' I assume you're wanting favour?'

'Well, you being technical with computers and stuff I thought you'd be able to tell me how to switch that phone signal jammer off.'

Sinjin roared with laughter, 'My friend, there isn't just a big red switch on the wall you can flick, it's all part of ship's communication software that controls not only phone signal but everything from lighting and music to the radio sets in passenger cabin. It's incredibly complex, not something you can just switch on and off at will. Why? Is that naked selfie you're waiting for from someone really that special?'

'Oui, kind of like that. So, is it something you can do or not?'

'I could, but it would take time, and as each user has a unique log-in code I would get caught pretty easy, so as I really need this job, the only way I'd compromise my position would be to charge a large fortune, so unfortunately unless you're offering a million bucks I'm not interested.'

'Is that price negotiable?'

Sinjin again burst into laughter, which caused Gordo to stir. The sound of a wildebeest in its death throes eventually morphed into deep snoring.

Pascal pressed his head into his thin pillow and closed his eyes. How had he ever agreed to this part of the deal?

*****

When the drill had finished, Candy heard Scott persuade the seaman to run through the navigation system on the lifeboats. She glanced around for Jay, but he was nowhere to be seen. Surely, he should be here listening to this?

'The magnetic catch releases once the lifeboat hits the water, right?'

'Yes, sir, it works on a small electrical circuit that detects when the ropes go slack after contact with the water and releases them. The propulsion also starts automatically after one minute to take you safely away. Once clear of the ship, the navigation system heads for the ship's original destination unless otherwise programmed.'

'Okay,' Scott countered, 'how do I override the system? Select a different destination?'

Candy had heard all she would need to for her role in the heist, so she walked the length of the Boat Deck searching for Jay, but to no avail. She returned just as Scott thanked the sailor for his help, whilst slipping a banknote into his palm.

'Have you got all of that Candy?' Scott said.

'Yes, I think so.'

'Think so isn't good enough. Do you know what to do, yes or no?'

'Yes, but what about Jay? He needs to know all of this but I think he may have gone back to the cabin to rest. He can't have got much sleep on the sofa last night.'

'He'll be fine,' Scott said, 'I'm going to run through this whole system again when we meet in my cabin for a briefing later today. In the meantime, I'm going to test a few scenarios with Ramirez. We'll then take another look around the first class accommodation and check access to the bridge. Why don't you have a little time out and meet us at my cabin at four o'clock?'

'Four o'clock it is.'

'And if you see Pascal in your travels, make sure to remind him about it, thanks.'

59

Candy took the opportunity to explore the magnificent ship further, perusing the shops, theatre and ballroom before returning outside for some air. She walked towards the stern on A Deck and saw several cabin stewards walking a range of dogs, from tiny handbag pooches to Alsatians and Great Danes. Upon rounding a corner, she almost stepped on a sausage dog.

'Oh, I'm terribly sorry, slightly below my radar.'

The owner, a short man wearing a terracotta suit cursed in German, tugged the lead and then walked on. Candy laughed when further down the deck, he shuffled sideways in a little jig, losing his balance with the ship's sway. The height of the waves had been relentlessly building since breakfast.

'He's probably upset at that,' commented John Sharpe from a few feet along the railing. He gestured towards two young boys sitting on a bench, chewing their way through ketchup smeared hot dogs. 'Seeing all his doggy's relatives rolled up in a bun must be absolute torture.'

'Oh stop,' she suppressed a smile. 'I am starving, though. I couldn't face a full sit-down lunch after that ten-course dinner and a cooked breakfast, especially now that the ship has begun to act like a roller coaster. How do people do it day after day?'

'Easy,' Sharpe replied. 'They become obese, too lazy to walk their own dogs and then die of heart disease.'

Her cheeks tightened as a smile spread across them, she was beginning to get his dry humour. 'Yes, I suppose the only time they see the gym is when they walk past it on their way to the restaurant.'

'Indeed, and talking of unhealthy habits,' Sharpe pulled a tatty cigarette case from his pocket and offered her one of its contents.

'No, thank you. I'd rather die unexpectedly.'

It was Sharpe's turn to smile. He lit one for himself, took a few deep drags and gazed out to the horizon.

Two levels below, the Poop Deck stretched out to the rearmost point. On it was a few souls brave enough to crowd around the aft swimming pool. Uninviting, even if it did give off a haze of smoky steam.

'Bit of a waste heating the swimming pool at this time of year,' Candy said.

'Not really, I was going to go skinny dipping once I've finished this. Will you be joining me?'

She smiled, 'Yeah, sure.'

'You know it's not actually a waste. It's heated by the water that cools the engines, and would only be dumped into the sea. Almost like the way the heater works in your car.'

'But Mr Sharpe, we don't have heaters in our cars, it's 1912.'

'Maybe I should wire my office to patent the idea. I could make a few shillings out of it. Maybe sell it to that Ford chap.'

He glanced back towards the boys and their hot dogs.

'I'm famished,' he continued, 'but don't really fancy Labrador in a roll, even if we will be in its namesake in a day or so.'

'Namesake?'

'The Labrador current, it's a shipping lane we'll use to take us to New York. Ships don't just run in a straight line across the ocean you know, they follow specific routes and then branch off when nearer the coast to their chosen port. It's something to do with currents and so there's usually another ship close by to lend a hand in the event of us meeting an iceberg.'

'My, you do have a way of putting a girl's mind at rest. And talking of currants, I think they'll be serving afternoon tea in the Café Parisien soon. Would you join me?'

'I'd love to,' he replied, tossing his cigarette overboard, inadvertently giving Candy a flash of what he had concealed inside his jacket.

'My God, is that a gun?'

Sharpe smiled.

'The name's Sharpe, John Sharpe, agent 009 at your service.'

Candy's stomach dropped to F deck. Noticing her unease, he placed a palm on her forearm.

'Nothing to worry about, I'm just on personal protection duty for a nice old lady with more money than Bill Gates.'

'But why the gun?'

'Your guess is as good as mine. She insisted on it, said she had a bad feeling about the crossing, but went on to say she wouldn't miss it for the world.'

'I know the feeling.'

'Quite.'

They strolled along the deck past the Palm Court and the gymnasium, then down to A Deck and eventually the double doors of the café.

'Here we are,' Sharpe held the door open for Candy to enter the French-themed establishment. 'We could almost be in Paris.'

'Well, in Seine I'd say given the sway of the ship.'

'And it's predecessor's history,' Sharpe said.

A white starched waiter greeted them and showed them to a table near a large window.

'So, Mr Sharpe–'

'John, please.'

'John, how is it you're allowed to carry a gun on board if you're just a personal security guard?'

'Just?'

'Sorry, that was rude of me to–'

'Don't worry, only teasing. I was in the Anti-Terrorist Task Force for several years but then eased off and moved to Surrey. Retired when I was offered this position, and I must say it suits me quite well.'

'Wow, must have been interesting on the terrorist team?'

'Not really, lots of kicking down doors and shouting. Nobody ever got a round off for fear of the mountain of paperwork that would follow. Plus, I'm a bit clumsy, so not the ideal trait with live rounds rolling around.'

'Probably not, no.'

'Being a detective is far more satisfying. Picking out clues, analysing the forensic data, chasing the suspects down and putting them behind bars. It was much more me than booting the door of a council flat down in Peckham with a bunch of armed grunts.'

'The detective side sounds interesting, but do you have an arch-nemesis like in the films?'

He flinched, paused a moment, and then replied. 'I never quite finished my last case, and it continues to eat away at me.'

'Tell me more.'

'A crew of jewel thieves who specialised in making my team look like a bunch of buffoons. Hitting Guildford, Kingston and Chelsea in quick succession with escape and evade tactics like roaring off on motorcycles or a dip in the Thames. Bloody infuriating, but I'll track them down eventually, even on my own time.'

The bang of Sharpe's fist on the small table made both of them jump.

'Sorry, I get so worked up sometimes. Hey, are you alright? You look a bit pale.'

'It must be the sea,' Candy mumbled as she thrust her chair back and then rushed towards the door.

60

Captain Kelly Roberts looked from the bridge to the ominous grey waters ahead. Waves repeatedly struck the ship's bow and exploded in a fine white spray over the Fore Deck.

'You wouldn't catch Kate Winslet waving her arms around out there in that,' the Helmsman said.

After taking a sip of tea, the captain turned to his right and asked First Officer Nakagami for a report.

'Intermittent pack ice and bergs, twenty-five degrees north-west sir. About one hundred and twenty miles out. Wind at force four currently but looking to increase to a six or more by this evening. Swell is moderate but also set to increase if hurricane Lara continues to creep up from the south. Expect things to escalate if we remain on our present course, sir.'

'Thank you, Nakagami. Take a few hours off. I'll be here until at least eight so get your head down, you look shattered.'

'Very good, sir. Before I go, given the shipping forecast, should I tell Nav to initiate the S.E.E.3-D system and set a course further north to reduce the risk of running into the storm?'

'That won't be required.'

'But sir–'

'Mr Nakagami, I have been at the helm of more ships over the past thirty years than you will ever be. Not only that, but I have weathered the most treacherous of seas. And in that time, not once have I felt the need for gadgets or gimmicks to avoid storms or icebergs, so please do not presume you have the experience to outthink me. Now, you are dismissed until eight.'

'Apologies, sir,' Nakagami pulled a quick salute before leaving the bridge.

Captain Roberts looked out, the darkness closing in as relentlessly as the weather.

*****

'Excuse me, sir, sir,' the Japanese officer called after Ramirez and Scott, 'what are you doing here? It is clearly marked staff only.'

'Apologies,' Scott said after cursing under his breath, 'my friend and I wondered if we would be able to take a quick look at the bridge. After all, it's such an iconic vessel for us humble shipping enthusiasts to travel aboard, so it would really be a treat.'

'Quite out of the question. It's out of bounds to all but authorised crew members, so if you wouldn't mind,' he gestured back down the corridor, 'I will have to escort you back to a public area.'

'Don't tell me,' Scott said, 'it's more than your job's worth.'

'Please, sirs, this way.' He turned and gestured once more, but a door ahead of them opened, and a familiar face looked out from the Marconi room.

'Thought I recognised that voice,' their dining partner Seth Emslow said. 'Don't worry, Officer Nakagami, I'll see they find their way back to civilisation.'

'As you wish, sir, but I will have to make entry into ship's log of the security breach.'

'But they're here as my guests, so I'm sure that won't be necessary.'

The officer looked dubiously at the pair, raised his eyebrows, and continued along the corridor alone.

'They can be such sticklers these ex-Navy types,' then noticing Ramirez's frown, 'present company excepted, of course.'

'Did I say I was Navy?'

'You didn't have to. Your knowledge gave you away at the dining table last night. Special Forces, I presume?'

Ramirez looked at Emslow with a neutral expression.

'As I thought,' he continued in his soft Southern Californian voice. 'So now you're here, I may as well give you a tour of the communications and navigation room which the owners quaintly named the Marconi Room.'

'And the bridge?' Scott said.

'Unfortunately, not. Even though it's just through an adjoining door to where my company's equipment is installed, they wouldn't even let me show my fiancé. So, Mr Nakagami was right on that point.'

'Let's begin the tour, I'm fascinated,' Scott said.

Emslow led them down the freshly painted corridor and into the room, spouting his well-rehearsed patter on how the systems were second to none and the technology unsurpassed. Barely listening, Scott scanned the walls for the access hatch Candy would need in just over twenty-four hours.

61

Candy snatched the brass concertina gate of the lift open. She was too impatient to wait for the bellboy to take action. She ran to the cabin, but found it empty. She had to warn Jay that there was a detective on their trail, but where the hell was he?

She ran the length of E Deck on both sides after also finding Scott's cabin empty, but still no sign of him. She tried D Deck next, and was hurrying along a corridor when she caught the flash of a familiar purple suit jacket in one of the laundry rooms.

'Jay, there you are. What the hell are you doing?'

The girl straightened her dress before hurrying out of the room, her head bowed low.

'Seriously, Jay?'

'Babes, you know you're the only one for me, I was only trying to get a pass key.'

'How could I have been so stupid? I believed you. You told me you'd changed.' She slammed the door, but it bounced back open again. Exasperated, she stomped back up the corridor.

'It was nothing,' he called after her, 'come back and let me explain.'

Suddenly the corridor lurched deeply to the left, and she staggered into the wall. This was starting to get scary. And then the ship let out an ominous rumble.

*****

'Christ, I hate ships,' Scott groaned as he lay in his bunk. The curtain above his head swayed out from the wall and then back with every roll of the creaking ship.

'Go to the infirmary, they'll give you a shot to sort your yellow ass out,' Ramirez said.

'What do you mean a shot? Anyway, I can't. We have our team briefing at four. Just over an hour in case you'd forgotten?'

'Phenergan, it's an injection to quell you landlubbers' fragile stomachs. You won't be much good to us if you puke in your gas mask and pass out after taking it off.'

'Pascal said he could only slip away for twenty minutes maximum. He won't wait if I'm not here.'

'Just go,' Ramirez said, 'I'll keep him here even if I have to sit on him.'

Scott glanced at his pocket watch once more, gave a resigned nod, and drew himself up from his bunk.

Scott pushed open the door to the infirmary and stopped dead. Could he be seeing things?

'Take a seat over there and I'll get to you in as soon as I can. Please fill in a registration card, you'll find them on the desk.'

The young doctor paused to curl an elasticated band around her red ponytail. She hadn't recognised him.

His instincts screamed at him to leave, but the churning in his stomach was so violent that he simply had to get it sorted before the big night tomorrow. Resigned, he took his place beside a gent whose pallor mirrored the bottle-green suit and waistcoat he wore.

'Next, please,' the doctor said after a girl of around ten or twelve, wearing a cream dress over a black undershirt, emerged from her clinic. The man in the bottle-green suit stood and walked hesitantly towards the door. The pattern repeated a few minutes later, and Scott made his way to the consulting room.

'So, Mr …' she checked his form, 'Rainey. What can I do for you?' She looked up and tilted her head to the side, squinting. 'Have we met before?'

'Samantha?'

'Yes, but…'

'Scott, from China, when you were there on the build.'

'The build? Ahh yes, the ship build. Sorry, I remember now, we met in that bar.'

'Yeah,' Scott said, regretting already that he'd brought China up. 'So how come you're here?'

'Natural progression, I guess. Croft wanted some of his regular staff in China to keep an eye on the workers.'

'Croft?'

'Lucien Croft, the owner.'

'Ahh yes, sorry, I'm with you now.'

'He's paranoid about scandal and didn't want anyone claiming over-exhaustion from slave-like conditions. The company had me out there for almost a year.

'So how about you? I doubt a workman's salary would run to a weekend in Marbella, let alone a trip on this gin palace. What are you doing here?'

'Nothing,' a little too aggressively, 'I'm, err…' think, think, 'here as a consultant.'

She eyed him sceptically.

'As you say, Croft is paranoid about scandal so I'm here to keep an eye on all of the welds in the hull. I spend my days traipsing up and down the engine room looking for cracks and stress marks in the steel. The last thing this tub needs is a front-page headline claiming it's sprung a leak.'

'So why aren't you in an engineer's uniform?'

'So many questions, you're not related to Jeremy Paxman, are you?'

'Nope,' she smiled. 'So, what can I help you with?'

'Well, I'm a great welder but an awful sailor. Apparently, there's an injection to stop the sea-sickness?'

'I thought you looked a little greener than when we last met. Drop your trousers and bend forwards over the bed please.'

'Be gentle.'

62

Scott heard the dull boom of Jay shouting from the end of the corridor. A smashing sound had him run the final few yards to their cabin.

He yanked the door but found it locked, then rapped with his fist hard enough to draw a stare from a passenger further along the corridor.

'Piss off,' the muffled voice from inside.

'It's Scott, open up.'

After a few indecipherable sounds and several moments, Jay opened the door a crack.

'We're busy.'

Scott pushed the door, but Jay's foot prevented it from moving more than a couple of inches.

'Like I said, we're busy. Come back later.'

'Get next door now, we've got a meeting, if you'd forgotten.'

'Be there in a tick, just putting on some lip gloss.'

Jay shut the door in his face.

Scott returned to his cabin, cursing his brother. Thankfully Pascal and Ramirez were there as arranged. Jay entered a few minutes later, Candy several after that, her face flushed red and her gaze lowered to the carpet.

'Right, now we're all here let's get on with it. Pascal, have you remembered to get a bottle of champagne to that awkward cow Mrs Gratton for the dinner service?'

'Did yesterday but it's really difficult. Surely, she won't kick off if I don't bother? She got a free upgrade, didn't she?'

'Keep the long game in mind. You'll be the one with the last laugh when we're cashing out with Terry in Monaco.'

'Doesn't help me now though,' he shrugged.

'Moving on,' Scott said. 'There have been some slight changes to the plan so pay attention. It's all set for tomorrow. Pascal, are you still scheduled to work the captain's cocktail party?'

'Oui.'

'Good, make sure you get all your sleeping pills crushed to powder and into as many of the champagne flutes as possible. Use a rolling pin or something. We'll do likewise, but be as subtle about it as possible. If you see an unattended glass, put a sprinkle in.'

'Okay, if that's me done I'll bid you adieu.'

'No Pascal, that's not you done. Stay put and pay attention.'

'But I've got to get back to work.'

'Well, by all means leave,' that tension growing between his temples again, 'and then you can spend the rest of your life working shit manual service jobs like the one you're currently enjoying, while we sail our private yachts around the Bahamas.'

Pascal shook his head but took a seat on the bed next to Ramirez.

'I know we've been over this repeatedly, but this is our last chance to make sure we are all crystal clear on the drill for tomorrow night.

'Ramirez, what's stage one?'

'At two forty-five in the a.m., Candy and I will head to the Boat Deck. We'll open the access hatch to the air conditioning duct for the bridge and Marconi Room. I connect a small cylinder of Xenon gas, and then I hide until the crew in those areas are unconscious.'

'At which point….' Scott gestured to Candy. No answer, her frame wilted and her eyes still down. 'Wake up, Candy. What's next?'

'I head back here to let you know the connection was successful so you can turn on the gas for the rest of the boat. As there's no phone signal, obviously,' she mumbled.

'And then…?' Scott said.

Silence.

'Whatever's going on here, I need you to snap out of it and focus. And I mean all of your attention, right now.' He clicked his fingers, and a murmur of agreement followed.

'So, what comes next? Jay?'

'I hide in a closet, then nick everything.'

'Congratulations,' Scott's tone sarcastic. 'You head to A Deck and find the maid's laundry cupboard, which will be….'

'We've been through this loads,' Jay said as his glare burned into the side of Candy's head.

'So, you should know the answer.'

'Fine, Grand Staircase, turn left, third door. Happy?'

'Wasn't so difficult, was it? And you forgot the bit about putting your gas mask on.'

'Whatever.'

'Ramirez?' Scott said.

'Time is tight and I need to lock down the outside deck doors from the remote switch on the bridge by three a.m. I'll also check the S.E.E.3-D system is activated.'

'Good. By quarter-past three, the gas should have filled the entire ship and knocked everyone unconscious, both in their cabins and any public area.

'I will place two laundry carts outside of this cabin so you have a visual reference. It'll save you counting cabin numbers along this eternal corridor.

'Any questions so far?'

'How will I know when to put my mask on?' Pascal asked, 'as I'm going to be in the staff quarters.'

'Three a.m. no sooner, no later. Just don't fall asleep beforehand.'

'Okay, can I go now?'

'No. Shut up and listen will you, this is important. Jay, Jay, are you even listening?'

'Yeah, mask on, A Deck, hide in the laundry room,' he said apathetically.

'Christ,' Scott said. 'Once the public is out cold phase two begins. Everyone needs to find a maid's laundry cart on A Deck, a master key and a swipe card from an unconscious staff member, and then get on with the raid.

'Follow the hierarchy of value. First class suites take priority, then second etcetera. Work your way down the ship until your cart is pretty full. Then head back here to exchange it for an empty one. The gas cylinders should take around twelve minutes to empty, so if there's one in the laundry cart outside here you take it to the Boat Deck for disposal later. Understood?'

Silence.

'Can I get a little feedback so I know you're not all actually dead?'

'Affirmative,' Ramirez said.

Jay gave a slow clap, Pascal nodded and Candy mumbled something indecipherable. Scott ran his fingers through his hair before continuing the briefing. Five minutes later, he'd almost finished when Pascal interrupted.

'I need to go.'

'In a moment. The final step is to head inside and pass out with all the other guests in case a blood toxicity test is done in New York.'

'I really need to be in the restaurant, sorry.'

'Oh, for Christ's sake. If clearing plates is really more important than two hundred million pounds worth of diamonds then yes, by all means go. But remember, three o'clock tomorrow, gas mask on.'

'Got it,' he winked.

Scott took a deep breath.

'Right, I've also got some personal business to attend to, so if you'll all excuse me,' he looked to Jay and Candy, who still hadn't broken their funk. 'And sort your shit out, you two. This has to go smoothly for everyone's sake.'

Jay turned his silent scowl towards Scott, who ignored it and left the cabin.

63

Scott pushed the library door open and stepped inside, past the 'Closed for private meeting' sign pinned to a slim lectern. A dim glow from wall and table lamps lit the wood-panelled room. Armchairs sat in three concentric semicircles in front of an ornate fireplace nearly two metres in length. From it, tongues of fire flickered and danced on the hearth, creating a pattern of animated shadows along the rows of bookshelves. It was as if he'd stepped into a scene from Sherlock Holmes.

He took a seat in the middle row next to a bearded man he thought vaguely familiar, but it was difficult to tell in the poor light. Only after a brief hello, did he recognise the voice and the radio celebrity who owned it. The man tried to distract him with small talk, but Scott's focus centred on how to keep the plan and its players from crumbling around him.

Over the next fifteen minutes, the chairs filled, and as the mantelpiece clock finished striking five-thirty, the host made himself known. He asked them all to rise for a rendition of every recovering addict's anthem.

'God grant me the serenity to accept the things I cannot change,

'Courage to change things I can,

'And wisdom to know the difference.

'Be seated.'

Silence hung in the air for a moment, just the creaking of the vessel beneath them, before he spoke again.

'Welcome everyone, to what is the most surreal meeting I have ever hosted, given our attire and the surroundings. But no matter, we are a mixed bag this evening. For some of us, the temptation comes from a bottle. Others a needle, or some powder. Others still, the promise of flesh or the spin of a roulette wheel. But we're all here together. '

He was interrupted by the sound of a latecomer. The group turned to see Candy take a seat in the outermost row. Scott was baffled. What was she doing here? Had she followed him?

'As I was saying,' the host continued. 'We're all together in support of one another aboard this merry carousel of devilish temptation. So, we must remain strong in support of one another.'

His speech ran on for a few moments before asking if anyone was willing to share.

'My name's Candice and it's been one year, three months and sixteen days since I last used.'

A flutter of applause filled the room, but the sound of her voice hit Scott like a fist to the chest. He did the maths to discover that it would have been around the time she had joined his crew.

'I was in a bad place. A string of abusive relationships and dead-end jobs had me struggling for answers. I tried overdosing twice but couldn't even get that right. My boyfriend found me both times and took me to the hospital just in time. Then sent me right back again with the beatings he gave me once I'd been discharged.

'I finally snapped out of it with the shock that he had tried to rape my sister one afternoon when I was at college. She'd only come to my flat to drop off some shopping she'd done for me.

'She put up a good fight but he threw her down the stairs and broke her pelvis and legs so badly she hasn't walked since. That's when I knew I had to do something to stop the nightmare.'

Scott was immediately on edge. Was she actually going to divulge their plan here in front of everyone? Was that what all the tension between her and Jay was about earlier? Muscles tense, hands taut, itching to smother her mouth. Was she about to ruin everything?

'I know it's not my job to live my sister's life,' she continued, 'but I do need to act, so as to get her the medical help she needs. So she has some chance of returning to a normal life. And that takes a lot of money and the right surgeon.' One slip, and he would spring from his seat. His leg jittered in anticipation of the strike. 'That's what this is all about. It's why I'm here today.'

Candy sat back down, and her sleeved arm came up to wipe the tears from her face. The flood of relief that washed through him was way more intoxicating than any drug. He applauded just a little too loudly, and stood in support of her.

'Thank you, Candice,' the host said. 'And you, sir, would you like to share?'

Scott realised too late that he was the only one on his feet, and the question had been directed at him. The sinking feeling returned but now it had nothing to do with the rise and fall of the ship. He paused for a few seconds.

'I suppose so. My name's Scott, and I'm an alcoholic. It's been one year, five months and seven days since my last drink.'

The flutter of applause again, 'I'm not sure why I drink. It's a form of release, I suppose.

'A particularly bad day or stressful event is my usual trigger. So here, being on this magnificent ship, I can control it with ease. There's something about luxury that chases the urge away. But living out there,' he pointed through the vast black windows to the ocean, 'that's not so easy. Back in the real world, I mean.'

He ran through his life and addiction for the next few minutes and finished to another flutter of applause. He needed a drink more than ever. But he daren't go there, to his dark place. It would consume him for the next two days, possibly longer. Blow the whole job just for the bliss of a few hours of abandon. The depths of a depression he might never recover from would follow if he let this opportunity slip through his fingers.

Then the demons came. Why should he even care about this heist? Without Jasmine, what was the point? It was clear she'd found her equal in Del Toro. Her next rung to climb the ladder and what was he? Just a step down. And a pretty big one at that.

He remained in his chair for the rest of the meeting, oblivious to anything else said. He was dangerously close to the edge, sitting there, staring at his feet.

'Come on daydreamer, everyone's left.' It was Candy, and then the realisation they were alone in the flickering light.

'Sorry, I was miles away. I had no idea you'd be here.'

'Well, it is called anonymous for a reason.'

Scott smiled, 'I suppose so. I'd suggest we go for a drink but I think that might be frowned upon.'

'No kidding. Anyway, we need to get ready for dinner as it's formal tonight. I'm looking forward to seeing you dressed as a penguin.'

'Don't remind me. I look awkward in a normal suit, let alone black tie.'

'That's not how I'd put it, but hey, let's go and get all dressed up and find out.'

Scott stood and shuffled his way along the row of chairs.

'For a moment there I thought you were going to say something about why we're really on board this ship.'

'For a moment, so did I.'

That stopped him dead.

'After all,' she continued, 'these meetings are all about honesty.'

'Some honesty we can keep to ourselves.'

'I get that. It's just difficult to draw the line sometimes.'

'Well, if you feel the urge to be overly honest again, make sure it's only me in the room with you.'

'Yes, Boss,' she saluted. 'Now if I'm not mistaken, we only have thirty minutes to get to our table. So come on, let's get out of here.'

*****

Jay heard the cabin door open, so he walked out of the bathroom to see Candy entering.

'That looked nice and cosy.'

'What are you talking about?'

'Your little rendezvous with Scott in front of the fire.'

'You're following me now? Actually, forget I even asked. I've not got long to get ready, so if you've finished with the bathroom…'

He blocked her path and replied, 'All those chairs in a circle, what was it, a séance for the drowned passengers a few miles beneath us?'

'Yes Jay, that's exactly what it was. Now, if you don't mind.'

'Oh, but I do. I mind a great deal as it goes,' he leaned forward with his face an inch from hers. 'Or don't you think I care if I see you carrying on with someone else? My brother of all people. I thought you'd have higher standards than that.'

'After you Jay, a crazy tramp would be a few rungs higher.'

He grabbed the front of her dress and shook her fiercely.

'You're the only tramp I know of. Need a bit of common sense shaken into that thick head of yours? Allow me.'

'Jay, leave me alone.' she pulled away, breaking his grip. 'Just let me get on with my life, and you can do what the hell you want with yours. Three more days, and you won't see me again until spring, so do us both a favour and stop acting like a hormonal teenager.'

He retreated and gave her a look which he hoped conveyed sincerity. 'It's because I still love you, I always have. I can't stand it.'

'Save it for Jerry Springer.'

'No babe, seriously, you're the best thing that's ever happened to me. Without you I'm lost, I really am, can't you see it in my eyes?' even he was surprised at the stir of tears welling up.

'Maybe you should have thought of that before you started screwing that woman I saw you with in London.'

'Babes I know that was a mistake, if you'd just–'

'Don't Babes me. And if it was such a mistake, how come I found you trying to screw the maid a couple of hours ago?

He realised that the slight hesitation had given him away.

'For the job, I needed a pass key like Scott said at the meeting.'

'Nice try. But I caught you before the meeting, and we get the pass keys from the unconscious staff, not whilst... Oh forget it.'

'Yeah, well Scott had mentioned it to me before and–'

'Save it, seriously, let me get in that bathroom or we'll miss dinner. And you need to be in formal dress so I suggest you stop bleating and put it on.'

She pushed past him into the bathroom and he heard the lock slide home.

He walloped his fist into the door in lieu of having the last word. It was mahogany, so really hurt.

*****

She waited until she heard the cabin door slam before unlocking the bathroom and gingerly stepping out. She crossed the cabin, took a seat at the dressing table with its ornately framed mirror and worked quickly.

A dusting of powder to the cheeks, a couple of cherry-coloured lines on the lips and a little mascara were all she had time for.

Her dress had been laid out to air by the cabin steward, and her corset thankfully had the modern wonder of a zip instead of having to endure the tedium of threading long laces. Once dressed, she picked up the hand mirror for a quick check. But in raising it, she dusted her chest and face with the lines of white powder he'd left on it.

She could kill him.

64

Captain Roberts speared the last of his halibut and brought it to his mouth. Despite spending his life on the sea, he'd never been particularly keen on the taste of its inhabitants, but the fish course was a staple on Bright Star menus.

He sat at a large table in The Queen's Grill, an opulent boutique restaurant reserved for first class passengers, and surveyed the room. It was full of people he had no desire to talk to.

As the waiters cleared the bone china plates, he noticed an additional one approaching their table clutching a bottle of champagne by the neck. Not on a tray as per regulation. The man also wore the grey jacket assigned to second class staff and not the white waistcoat and jacket of first class. A rather harried looking seaman entered behind this waiter and Roberts didn't know which of them to challenge first.

The decision was made for him as the seaman overtook the waiter and headed straight for him, whereas the waiter stopped short on the opposing side of the table where that insufferable Mrs Gratton was holding court.

'Sorry to disturb your dinner, sir, but First Officer Nakagami has asked me to relay some urgent information.'

'Go on.'

'He requests permission to activate the S.E.E.3-D navigation system, sir.'

'Permission denied. He's well aware of my opinion on untested technology. My ship is not going to be the guinea pig.'

'But sir, he says the storm is now force ten and closing rapidly. And if we head north there's a risk of running into ice fields.'

Roberts grabbed the seaman's jumper and pulled him down to eye level before calmly and deliberately replying to the man in a volume only he would hear.

'If you ever, ever mention ice fields aboard this ship again I will personally see you relieved of duty and barred from ever working aboard a passenger vessel again. Is that clear?'

The man paled.

'Yes, Captain Roberts, I'm sorry.'

'Do you want to start a panic?'

'Captain,' Mrs Gratton shrilled, 'was that an iceberg warning I just heard you trying to hush up? You're so naughty, really you are. Do we need to abandon ship?'

She chuckled and wrapped her palm over the hand of the passenger sat beside her. 'You'll save me, kind sir, won't you?'

A murmur of unease spread rapidly throughout the restaurant and several diners even stood to leave.

'Now look what you've started, you damned fool.'

He needed to make a short speech to allay concerns, but before he'd even pushed his chair back, that damned waiter in the grey jacket came to his attention. As the cork popped, the champagne bottle slid through the man's fingers and hit the floor. An eruption of foam and fizzy spray burst upward from the bottle and rebounded off the ceiling to shower several nearby diners.

'God give me strength,' the captain muttered as he got to his feet.

*****

Scott scoured the dining room. Where had Candy got to? It was a sea of black dinner jackets and white bow ties nestled beneath collars as stiff as the occupant's upper lips. Women in brightly coloured gowns featured feathers of every colour possible, accessorised by fans or strings of beads and pearls which hung in deep curves below necklines. But no Candy.

The light clatter of flatware on bone china joined the soft melody of a Steinway Grand in the centre of the room. The pianist rolled his fingers along the keys with the practised fluidity of an old pro.

He was about to ask Jay, when he spied Candy rush through the dining room, almost colliding with a passenger.

'Sorry,' she shouted over her shoulder before then almost colliding with a heavily laden waiter. She slowed to a stroll as she neared the table.

'So glad you could make it, love,' Jay said.

'Sorry everyone,' she sat clumsily as a waiter pushed the chair in for her and draped a napkin across her lap. 'But Jay left a bit of a mess on the hand mirror, had to clean up before the maid saw.'

This raised a few chuckles, but conversation resumed as the waiter thrust their menus upon them.

'Gee,' commented Emslow, 'I thought the six courses we had last night were a bit much. But ten, this is obscene.'

'If I might point out, sir,' the waiter said. 'The first and last evening of travel are what we call informal evenings, so only six courses are served.'

'Just the six, how shocking, where's the refund desk?' Jay said. Nobody laughed.

'But all other evenings are formal,' the waiter continued, 'in both attire and menu. So yes, ten courses are normal for the days spent at sea.'

'You'll be alright, Candy,' Jay said, 'you can turn into a lazy obese slag with ease, blend right in when we get to New York.'

'Less of the language,' Scott said. 'What's got into you?'

'Sorry, would you rather we all held hands and took turns confessing our sins?'

'Enough,' Ramirez said. And surprisingly, Jay complied.

'So, Mr Emslow,' Ramirez continued.

'Seth, please.'

'Seth, thanks for showing us around earlier, fascinating stuff.'

'You're welcome, although I must apologise that none of it was active for a full demonstration. I just do the concept design and my staff arrange the tech side of it. I couldn't re-wire a toaster.'

'With all the communication hardware in that room,' Ramirez said, 'does that mean the navigation side of it is in there too?'

'I really couldn't say, I signed a non-disclosure before the project began so my hands are tied.'

At that, his fiancé's face reddened, and she let out a little giggle. Emslow frowned before continuing.

'My company designs the software and the chip manufacturing is done in Cairo where our friend over there sends all his precious sand.'

The Egyptian smiled as Emslow continued.

'And then the circuits and component parts are outsourced to a plant in the Far East. The manufacturers even supply three operators on a twelve-month contract to run the system with every order I place. I really am just a salesman.'

'It's not specifics, I'm asking in general terms,' Ramirez pressed. 'I'm just curious what the procedure might be if an unexpected hazard appeared, another ship for argument's sake. How would the S.E.E.3-D navigation system operator communicate with the comms engineer if one is on the bridge and the other in the Marconi Room?'

'I didn't say they were in different rooms, now did I?'

'No, but our tour earlier didn't include the bridge, and I didn't see any navigational screens in the areas we toured.'

'Very observant of you, Ramirez, if I didn't know better, I might suspect you of fishing for a little industrial espionage. What was it you said you did for a living?'

'Import and export of fine arts,' he said just a bit too quickly. 'For selected European buyers,' he continued in a softer tone. 'I don't hold stock, just acquire precious items to order.'

'An art thief,' Emslow teased.

'With the commission I charge, yes, but I have an uncanny ability of acquiring pieces that are not usually for sale so that's how I justify my fees. It's only theft if someone loses out, isn't it?'

'I suppose so. But I don't get what this has to do with your work.'

'I didn't say my interest in systems was anything to do with my work, did I?'

'Touché. Shall we order some wine?'

*****

Pascal hurried down the staff corridor, through the double-hinged door and into the Britannia Restaurant. He saw the aggression in Jakub's features from twenty yards but continued towards their workstation.

'Sorry mate, I can't help–'

'I don't care your excuse, leave again and it is being this.'

Pascal felt an uncomfortable sensation. He looked down to see Jakub's hand pressing a paring knife into his groin.

Jakub lightly slapped his cheek with his other hand.

'Do as I tell you and you keep balls.'

Pascal shoved him away. He staggered a couple of steps but caught his hip on a dessert trolley. It teetered but thankfully didn't go over, although a seven-layered cake did slide from its stand and splatter onto the pristine carpet.

With horror, Pascal saw the ruddy scowl of Mr Healey as he thundered towards them. He grabbed them by their lapels and yanked them towards each other with such force they almost banged heads.

'What the hell are you two playing at?' he admonished in as calm a voice as he seemed capable. 'Bickering mid-service is unforgivable. Get into the kitchen, now.' He pulled away, the purple skin on his face ripe enough to burst.

Healey surveyed the immediate scene, clicked his fingers to attract the attention of two nearby waiters and made a circling motion to one of the tables on which Jakub had been clearing before the incident. The incoming waiters sprang into action without need for further explanation.

Before leaving, Jakub took a moment to glare at Pascal, lifting the knife he still held to point it at Pascal's throat.

'You fucking dead.'

Pascal replied with his middle finger before following Mr Healey to the kitchen for their dressing down away from the delicate eyes and ears of the paying passengers.

65

Captain Roberts walked onto the bridge, prying a strawberry seed from between his teeth as he entered.

'Status report please, Mr Nakagami.'

'Much the same as Seaman Brooks gave you thirty minutes ago, sir, only I took the decision in your absence to change our heading by twelve degrees to starboard for the next thirty miles, which should buy us some calmer water for the next few hours. But given the propensity of ice–'

'Save your breath Mr Nakagami. I'm not going to authorise the use of those new toys you seem so keen on trusting your life in, not to mention mine and all of the passengers.

'Tell the lads to keep a keen eye on the regular radar screens and change the heading back five degrees to port as soon as we've got some distance from the storm. The last thing we need is mountains of ice floating past the portholes for passengers to scream at.'

'Yes, sir.'

'I'll be in the Queen's Room. The cabaret looks pretty good this evening. Should anything change up here, let me know immediately.'

'Will do, sir, enjoy the show.'

Captain Roberts left the bridge and headed for C Deck. He had a nagging feeling that the first officer would ignore his orders and try the 3-D hardware he seemed so keen on before the band below decks had even tuned their instruments.

'Like a child on Christmas Eve, desperate for the latest gadget.'

He shook his head and pushed the call button for the lift to take him down.

*****

The wooden planks of the dance floor flexed with the thirty or so couples swinging to the beat of a formal looking six-piece.

Candy crossed the Queen's Room, an enormous ballroom at the heart of the ship, and found Scott in conversation with Ramirez and Jay around a low table. He looked to be using hand gestures to punctuate his points because the roar of the music was making it hard to be understood.

She drew up a chair just as the music died away, and the evening's host stepped up to the microphone to introduce the first act.

Candy buzzed with excitement at this unexpected addition to the voyage, and the hairs on her forearms stiffened.

The band struck up once more but with a slow, seductive number and four girls in sequin and tassel laced leotards appeared from each side of the stage, feather boas and a large peacock feather pointed upward from each of the girl's headdresses. They danced and twirled, performing a well-choreographed act for several moments before the lighting dimmed and a woman of Middle Eastern appearance emerged from the shadows to take a spotlight in the centre of the dance floor.

She also danced and twirled, and it took a moment before Candy gasped at the realisation that the boa around her neck was not feather but a real one. The snake wound its way around the performer's neck and down her arms. It even appeared to be curling and slithering in time with the music.

'Best make sure we avoid her cabin on our little job tomorrow,' said Jay over the music. This got a smile from both Ramirez and Scott.

'I'm sure I can handle it,' Candy said. 'After all, I'm sharing my cabin with a viper.'

Snake lady performed another two numbers, continuing to use the reptile as a prop, but the act quickly wore thin.

'Bet they have a juggler next,' again, it was Jay, but this time they ignored him. 'Or a clown, everyone loves a clown, eh Candy?'

'No Jay, they don't.'

'Look who drank a large glass of bitter venom with their evening meal, next you'll be accusing me of hitting on the captain.'

'It's very tiring this whole un-funny comedy act. Maybe you should just leave it to the professionals.'

She gestured to the stage, then turned her back on him, determined to enjoy the rest of the show.'

'And now, to marvel you with feats of incredible mind reading and magic, hypnosis and predictions of the future, please give a warm, absolutely Titanic welcome to the one, the only Mr Paul Berglass.'

Candy's hands sprang from her sides, and she clapped until they tingled. It was like being in a different world, a dream. But it wouldn't be long before the dream was over. Just a few more days until New York and their flight back home, to reality once more.

If only Becky could see all this, she'd absolutely love it. I wonder how she is? Must call Mum the minute we dock.

A couple of hours passed, maybe more, before she turned back to see just Scott and Ramirez sitting there.

'Where's Jay?'

'Left half an hour ago. Said he was going to the bar but never came back,' Scott said.

'My lucky night.'

Scott smiled at this, which surprised her. She'd expected a grilling as to why she and Jay weren't playing happy families. But then again, he'd probably asked Jay earlier. The boys stuck together, just like always.

'I'm going to head down to the cabin,' she said over the music.

'Likewise,' Ramirez said.

'I need to get a good night's sleep ahead of tomorrow's all important squash match,' Scott agreed. 'Reputations are at stake, after all. A stroll around the deck and a breath of sea air before heading down should do the trick. See you both tomorrow.'

A waiter appeared with a drinks chit for him to sign, and then he was gone. Candy downed the remains of her drink and stood.

'Shall we?' she said, holding her elbow out for Ramirez to escort her.

When they stepped out of the lift and into the long corridor of E Deck, Candy felt herself sway to one side. Maybe that last drink hadn't been a great idea after all. Scott would have certainly disapproved if he'd realised that she'd had vodka in her orange juice. But to her, this was a holiday until their work began at the cocktail party.

'This is me,' Ramirez said, stopping one door short of Candy's cabin.

'Okay, I can make it alone from here. If I'm never seen again, remember to send out a search party.'

Ramirez smiled and slipped his key into the door. Candy took the few paces further to her own cabin, but noticed a muffled banging noise coming through the wall. Engineers working at this late hour?

She slid her key into the slot. As the door clicked and opened, the bang, bang, bang sounds became more urgent.

'Baby, oh baby that's right, harder baby, harder.'

She took a second to process the scene. The maid from earlier had her hands on the headboard, straddling Jay, who lay on his back. Her dress pulled down to her waist, her bra was gone, and her hair a tangled mess. Jay appeared naked apart from his socks and thrust into her from beneath. Her head bounced up and down in rhythm with his actions.

'Hold up, we've got company,' Jay said to the maid. 'Joining us for a little threesome, love?'

'For fuck's sake Jay,' she shouted. 'And on my bed as well. How dare you.'

She ran at them and grabbed the flustered maid by the hair, dragging her off. She thumped to the floor but didn't pause before grabbing the rest of her clothes and hurrying out.

'You utter lowlife. How could I have ever been so stupid? Get out, now. Actually, don't bother.'

She slapped him hard across the face, a nail leaving a livid slice across one cheek. She then turned and ran from the cabin, vision blurred by tears.

Her legs weak and her entire body shaking, she shouldered the walls of the corridor left then right back towards the lifts. She needed to get as far from that vile man as possible. She needed air. But, more importantly, she needed this to be over soon so she could free herself of his poison once and for all.

She jabbed the lift call once, twice and then a third time. Two seconds later she thought better of it and took the stairs.

Up the Grand Staircase, one flight at a time, until she finally reached the uppermost deck. She dashed across the foyer and burst through the outer door.

*****

'Woah, cool it,' cried Scott, taken aback when he opened the door only to have Candy barge straight into him.

'Jeez, you nearly knocked me off my feet. Hey, what's up? What happened?'

'It's that bastard. Christ, he makes my blood boil. Caught him screwing the maid, of all people.'

She leaned into his chest before wrapping her arms around him. Unsure of how to respond, he tentatively returned the gesture.

'It's okay,' he reassured. 'Jay's a bit of a bastard, he can't be trusted. Just be glad you didn't get too deep before you realised. I know it's hard but you're better off without him, trust me. I wish I could be.'

'A bit of a bastard, don't dress it up too much.'

'Look, I'm trying to keep this team together and feel like I'm swimming out of my depth. Everything's going to hell and I can't seem to stop it.'

'You've got Ramirez and me,' she said, pulling away. 'We don't need your brother.'

'For this to be successful we need to work together, all of us, not be locked together in a war of egos. Think what this means for your sister, the end game.'

Candy sniffed and gave an involuntary shudder. 'Let's walk. I need to get things straight in my head.'

They went the length of the Boat Deck arm in arm and passed the Palm Court before arriving at the iron staircase.

'I want to look out from the back of the ship,' she said, 'where the churning water leaves us behind.'

He didn't quite get what she meant but complied. They went down another two levels and across the length of the aft Well Deck before taking the steps back up onto the rearmost Poop Deck.

'Wouldn't it be incredible?' Candy said, 'to just strip off and dive in.'

'I think you've been watching too much of that film. Because suicidal is the term you're looking for.'

'Killjoy, when are you going to relax and live a little?'

'Jumping from a mid-Atlantic ship isn't living, it's the opposite.'

'Living, dying, whatever, you're so uptight all of the time. Everything has to be controlled, your emotions to your actions. Why can't you relax just a little?'

'Definitely not, and nor should you. We're here to do a job, then disappear. That's it. So don't give me that 'live a little' speech.'

'The fact you brought it up means you're aware that you probably should.'

'You brought it up, not me. I'm just fine.'

'Really? You hide it so well.'

They'd reached the railing at the stern and looked out, a moment of relative silence between them, just the rumble of the engines and churning of water.

'It's strange isn't it, standing here and although it's cold out we're cloaked in a pocket of warm air. Can you feel it?' she asked. 'It's as if the slipstream is taking all the heat from the inside of the ship and channelling it back here, right where we're standing.

'And the taste,' she continued. 'It's all salty on my lips. What about yours? Can you taste it?'

He looked down. Her lips were deep, red and waiting. They edged closer, then closer still. Their faces just a centimetre apart. It would be so easy to just lean in a little more, bow to the irrepressible urge building inside of him.

'No,' he said, 'not now, not before the job. I can't risk any complications.' He pulled back.

'All work and no play makes Scott a dull boy,' she teased, stepping back and unbuttoning her top.

'What are you doing?'

'After my second heartless rejection of the evening, I might take a swim after all,' she said, stepping out of her dress.

He grabbed her arm, but she shrugged him off and scampered away.

She pulled off one shoe, ran a few feet further and then pulled off the other. Now just in her underwear, she did a pirouette, and Scott grabbed for her once more.

She snaked out of his grasp again, and he started after her, but his leather-soled shoes found little purchase on the cold, wet deck. He slipped, collided with a deck chair and went down.

There was a scream, a splash, and then silence.

Scott got to his feet and looked towards the railing. His heart sank at what might have just happened. What the hell had got into her?

Laughter came from behind him, and he swung around.

'Aren't you going to join me? I dare you,' she called from the swimming pool sunk into the ship's rear deck. 'It's lovely and warm.'

Relief flooded his body. He felt like dropping to a lounger, spent. But he shook his head and made his way over to the pool-side to crouch down.

'Christ you gave me a scare. Don't ever do that again.'

She splashed him with the water and he was surprised at its warmth.

'Let me help you out,' he stretched his hand forward. She swam over and took it with both of hers. But then she shoved backwards, using her legs to push away from the side. It took him by surprise and launched him into the water on top of her. They both went under, surfaced, and she wrapped her legs around him, locking them together.

'Those legs of yours are trouble.'

'You don't know the half of it,' she pulled him closer. They looked at each other's lips once more but only as a brief prelude.

He slid his fingers around the back of her head, pulled her towards him, and they met with a passion that surprised him, nerve endings tingling like the fizz of champagne bubbles.

66

At eight twenty-five, Scott rounded the base of the staircase and made his way past the glowing stained-glass doors of the Turkish bath before continuing along a narrow corridor to the squash court. Thankfully the pitch and roll had reduced from the previous day. He'd have called it off if it hadn't.

'What kept you? Get lost or something?' Jay asked when Scott entered the court to the *whakak* sound of him warming up.

'It's unlike you to be early. Fall out of bed?'

'Off the sofa, you mean. Unless you've forgotten I'm a third class citizen in my second class room.'

'Cabin.'

'Whatever. Anyway, you ready to be beaten?' Jay continued whacking the ball against the wall.

'You've got no chance. I could beat you blindfolded,' Scott said.

'Hundred quid says otherwise.'

'Okay, one hundred pounds on the first game.'

'Done.' Jay continued his warm-up whilst Scott dropped his bag in the corner and pulled out a racquet.

'Can't believe they make you wear this crap. I mean who wears long trousers and a tie to play a bloody game of squash?' Jay said.

'Well let's hope it doesn't get bloody, I'd hate to turn your whites into pinks.'

'Got a coin? You'd better do the honours, being a tosser n' all.'

'Hilarious Jay, it's a racquet spin for squash. Call.'

Scott spun his racquet but lost.

'On a losing streak already?'

'Just serve.'

Jay fired the ball at the wall before Scott had even taken position.

'One to me,' he smiled. Scott conceded the point but prepared himself for the next one as they crossed positions.

He returned the second serve easily, and Scott enjoyed the to and fro of a vigorous rally. The next point went his way, but then Jay won the next. And so, it continued up until the final point of the game at ten-all.

'We're playing sudden death, yeah? Not two points clear?' Jay said.

'Sudden death suits me.'

'Good. I'll remind you of that someday. And as we're talking winners, let's make it double or quits for our little wager.'

'You can't quit as we're at match point on an existing bet, so double or existing stake would be more accurate.'

'Whatever, if you're being picky then let's make it two grand on the outcome.'

'You already owe me twelve grand.'

'If your plan is so good it'll just be a chip off the iceberg for you.'

'Just questioning your motivation,'

'My motivation is to be number one. You can't put a figure on that now, can you?'

'Evidently you just have,' Scott said. 'But you've always been second best, ever since you were filling your nappy with what's now coming out of your mouth. So, let's raise the stakes a little higher than kindergarten, shall we? Say, one hundred grand?'

'One hundred large it is.'

Scott walloped the ball as hard as he could, the thwack louder than any that had preceded it. But the effort was in vain as Jay returned with a neat backhand which had Scott reeling in the opposite quarter. Jay had hammered his point home.

'Game one to the king.'

'No need to look so smug, it was only a point,' Scott said.

'Best of three then, not five as we don't have the court for long.'

'Best of three it is. And let's double the stakes as it's your serve.'

'May as well round it up to two-fifty,' Jay said. But the ball went low, below the line.

'Not the best start. You sure you're up for this?'

Jay collected the rolling ball from the floor. He threw it in Scott's direction, low enough to make him lunge.

'I'm up for it, how about you? Not going to run off and empty your stomach any time soon?'

'No Jay, I commanded the sea to be calm this morning and what do you know, looks like if you're the king then I'm the God.'

'Just the calm before the storm.'

Scott hammered the ball, sending it into the corner before ricocheting off the wall and beyond Jay's reach. It bounced twice as he scrambled to reach it.

The following serve went straight to Jay's position, allowing him to return with a spin on the ball, which dropped it too low for Scott to return. The rest of the game went back and forth, to a heated climax after two aggressive rallies.

'A comprehensive victory,' Scott said. 'Care to go double once more?'

'Is that all you've got? You seem to be a one trick pony.'

'I thought that was you, one trick of taking what's not yours, story of your life, isn't it?'

'Talking of taking what's not yours I'm surprised your shoes aren't squelching this morning, or did you leave them out for your valet to dry?'

Scott paused for a moment.

'Five hundred grand for game set and match,' Jay said, and then smiled.

'Five hundred grand, and sets are for tennis. We're playing squash if you hadn't noticed.'

He served the ball hard with a light spin. Jay reacted well but lost the point.

'One-nil Jay, you need to win this as I don't see you having the means to pay without everything going smoothly tonight.'

'Thought you'd planned it properly?' he fired the ball back after Scott's next serve.

'It's the execution I'm concerned about,' Scott said. The ball danced around the upper edges of the court, then dropped too close to the back wall for him to get a return shot in.

'Didn't know you'd worked an execution into the plan, but not such a bad idea given the revelations I've had this voyage.'

'Find God, did you, Jay?'

'Could say that,' he paused for breath before taking his stance. 'Aries being the one of choice. God of war and vengeance,' he served, hard.

Scott returned the shot, only to have it go low enough to hit the tin.

'Let's hope the plan's better than your game,' Jay said as he took position for his next serve. 'Three one by my count,' he turned his head to glare. Scott had never seen such a demonic look in his eyes before.

'We can always count on you, Jay.'

He won the next serve and went on to take the following two points.

'Three-all, then,' Jay said. 'Now we're level, how about raising the stakes?'

'More than half a million?'

'If your plan's so fool-proof, then half a mill's pocket money compared to the take. In fact, why not raise things further? Let's say we bet a quarter of your share. That should spice this dull little game up a touch.'

'Dull little game, what's got into you?'

'It's not what's got into me Scott, it's who you've gotten into.'

'What the hell do you mean by that?'

'Catch,' Jay said, tossing the ball. 'Your serve, isn't it?'

Scott fired the ball to the wall once more, but again it went low.

'Temper, temper. I believe that's my serve now. Four three.'

He threw the ball to Jay's feet. It went past him but gently bounced with the ship's roll to the centre of the court.

'You really should control that sulky side of your character. It'll get you in trouble one day.'

'Get on with the game.'

'Fuck the game,' Jay was up in his face now, 'you might be in charge of this job but you're not in charge of me. So, once we're done here, maybe you'd better watch out.'

'Is that a threat?'

'Threat, warning, good advice, take it how you like.'

Scott glared at him, a throb in his temples, a tremble in his hands, fury barely contained as an explosion inside him fought to get out.

'We'd better make it count then. Half your share of the take on the outcome of this game, therefore the match.'

'To making it count,' Jay said and he mimed the raising of a glass. 'What happened to the set?'

'Fuck the set, your serve.'

Jay adopted the stance, and from then on, Scott fought each point with increasing aggression until it was ten-nine in his favour. Match point.

He served a clever shot that had the ball bounce close to the side wall near Jay, but he returned it.

Scott darted back and swiped, but a slight error in timing had the ball float to the wall.

'Damn.'

Jay hit the ball softly once more, requiring Scott to dash from the back of the court to avoid a double bounce and lose the point, prolonging the game.

He lunged forward, shoes squeaking on the hard floor and racquet outstretched for the final yard to the ball. But without warning, Jay side-stepped in front of him, they collided and crashed to the floor.

'That was obstruction. I win, no argument.'

'You ran into me. I don't have eyes in the back of my head.'

'Bullshit, that was blatant obstruction and you know it. Accept defeat, or aren't you man enough?' He grabbed Jay by the collar and yanked him backwards, they grappled for a moment, and both went down. Scott moved first, and his knee pinned Jay's neck to the floor.

'You're a tosser Jay, you seem to be doing everything to rile me on this job and I won't stand for it. Sort your shit out or I'll sort you out once and for all.'

After a pause long enough to reinforce his authority, he eased the pressure on Jay's neck and stood up.

'It's ten-ten, match point.'

'If you want to make this personal,' Jay said as he rose to his feet, 'let's wager our entire share of the haul on this final point. Winner wins, and loser loses. Sudden death.'

'Done. I've just about had enough of this shit from you. Serve.'

67

Captain Roberts was disturbed from his novel by rapping on his private cabin door. He pulled himself from his armchair and cursed.

'Officer Nakagami, what can I do for you?'

'May I come in, sir?'

'Nothing urgent I hope?'

He stepped aside to let the officer in and closed the door behind him.

'Could this not have waited until ten when I'm due back on the bridge?'

'Possibly, but I thought it best to ask for instruction sooner rather than later.'

'Very well, get on with it.' Roberts glanced to his wall clock and tutted.

'It's the weather, sir. The storm has grown to gale proportions, and is tearing up the east coast at an alarming rate. It's due to reach us in around ten hours on our current heading. Might I–'

'Suggest we head even further north?' Roberts interrupted. 'And risk taking us into the ice fields we've been avoiding at all costs?'

'It would make sense, now that we have the technology to scan what's ahead with the 3-D system.'

'That we should finally switch it on so you can play with your new toys. Am I right?'

'It's a matter of passenger safety, sir.'

'It's a matter of passenger panic taking hold,' Roberts returned aggressively. 'One tiny ice cube in the water and we'll have hysteria on our hands. More people are likely to get hurt in the melee that would ensue than a little pitch and roll from a few hours of bad weather. Hopefully it'll keep them in their cabins and I can cancel the damned cocktail party this evening, can't stand those things anyway.'

'Sir, the way I see it, we only have two options. We either head south to face it head on, even though it will likely be at its peak, batten the hatches and hope for the best. Or as I previously suggested, head north and hope it will die down a little for when we need to head into it closer to land.'

Roberts thought a moment, so Nakagami continued. 'I hope you don't mind, but I took the liberty of getting a weather printout from the Marconi room on my way here.'

'Well, hand it over.'

The officer produced the rolled sheets of paper he'd been holding behind his back.

'Oh,' the captain's eyes widened, 'I see.'

68

Jay liked the bustle of The Midships Bar, he relaxed into the soft padding of the armchair and gazed out to sea through one of the large windows. After a moment, he saw reflected in its glass, his waiter approaching with another ice bucket.

'Your champagne, sir, shall I pour?'

'Sounds like a fabulous idea,' a slight slur. Surely, he hadn't had that much?

The waiter gestured to the couple who were sharing his table. Jay gave the nod.

'Cheers, good health, and may the only ice we encounter be in our Martinis.'

'Cheers,' the man, Tobias, said. 'I think we must be somewhere over the site where the original ship went down. After all, it's the third night and we've made similar if not better progress.'

'Wasn't it the fourth night it went down?' the yellow sequin-dressed Penelope said, 'they're having some sort of memorial service on deck tomorrow evening, so presumably that would be over the grave site.'

'Who cares?' Jay said. 'A toast to frozen, stuffy stiffs, it is then?' He raised his glass but was alone in doing so.

'I say,' Tobias replied, 'bit poor in taste, don't you think?'

'Get over it. Give the boy a bow tie and he's the high and mighty lord of the ocean.'

'Unlike you?' Penelope said after she stood up. 'Come along Tobias, we can't have the captain's cocktail party starting without us.'

'Go on Tobias, good boy, good doggy, follow the boss, there's a good boy.'

He sat alone, but it was only a moment before the seat opposite became occupied once more.

'What the hell are you playing at? You're supposed to be in position.'

'Oh, if it isn't the ship's squash pro, got any tips for my backhand or do you save that stroke for your compliments?'

'How much have you had to drink?'

'Not nearly enough, look.' He stood and balanced on one leg with arms outstretched, but his display of sobriety failed and he fell sideways into one of the empty chairs.

'Roll of the ship, gets me every time.'

Scott got to his feet, yanked Jay up by the lapels of his dinner jacket and glared at him.

'Go to the gents and splash some water on your face, then straighten that bow tie. We've got work to do.'

'You've got work to do you mean, make sure you count all my money carefully, wouldn't want any mistakes.'

'What are you talking about?'

'The share you stole off me by cheating this morning.'

'I won that game fair and square and you know it. Sober up and do your job.'

'No point my lovely, caring brother. I've got no gain in helping you now so why should I risk getting caught just to bolster your bank account?'

'Keep your voice down. You have a moral obligation to the rest of the crew.'

'Moral obligation?' his pulse quickened. 'Where was your moral obligation last night then?'

'What are you talking about?'

'Sod it,' he sat back down and clasped his flute. 'I'm staying here, I'll find it quite entertaining, watching you lot running around trying to pull this off without me.'

Scott lashed out, swiping the glass from Jay's hand to send it tumbling onto the freshly laid carpet.

'Now look what you've done, put an ugly mark not only on our relationship but also this lovely new ship. You've got a knack for ruining things today, don't you? Maybe if you get away with your little heist, you can offer to replace the flooring, but some things can't be bought.'

'Let's test your theory, shall we? Twenty-five percent of my cut should be enough to motivate you out of that chair.'

'Thirty or I stay put.'

'Twenty-five is generous.'

'Said the robber to the thief. Thirty.'

'I'll split the difference if you get up right now and do your job properly. One slip-up and I'm cancelling this agreement.'

'No slips, scout's honour.'

'Just get up will you. Did you remember the crushed sleeping pills?'

Jay stood, patted his pocket, and winked. Maybe Scott was right, he did feel a little worse for wear. He pushed past his brother and walked across the room in search of the gents, noticing how much more pronounced the roll of the ship had become since he'd taken up residence in the bar just an hour before. The sea wasn't helping, but couldn't be entirely to blame for him shouldering the wall several times on his way down the corridor. Maybe a quick toot of Uncle Charles would sort him out. Yes, that should do it.

*****

John Sharpe stood in line with Lady Astbury, inching closer to the entrance of The Queen's Room. Captain Roberts shook the hand of every passenger as they entered, to the flash of magnesium from a wooden box camera mounted upon a tripod. The photographer called 'smile' to each before the flash, and the couple were momentarily blinded. The line was swaying like a thin Mexican wave at the increased rock of the ship, and a repeated creaking noise had become quite pronounced with every pitch and yaw the vessel made. The string quartet was also doing little for his mood.

His tight-fitting dinner jacket was already becoming a chore, the shoulder holster digging into his ribs after Her Ladyship's insistence that he keep it on him and buttoned up out of sight at all times.

Fat chance of that after dinner.

'Enough to give you a migraine. I feel sorry for the captain having to endure both Blackpool illuminations every few seconds and paying lip service to these dullards one after the other.'

'Now John, I'm not going to have you complaining and showing me up, am I?'

'Sorry Lady Astbury, I forgot my place for a moment, won't happen again.'

'See it doesn't, I shouldn't have to keep reminding you so please make an effort. I've got a number of important people to meet this evening and I don't need a miserable chaperone to put them off. Put a sparkle in your eye and play the part you've been employed to.'

He bristled at being spoken to in the same manner he had once adopted with the fresh recruits at Hendon. But the thought of that flamboyant Italian Rossi, still eating his lukewarm focaccias in an unmarked squad car whilst staring out at a grey, wet England warmed him as his glass of chilled champagne edged ever closer. He'd certainly need a few of those to survive the evening.

*****

'Where do you think you're going?' Mr Healey's voice boomed above the raucous noise of the staff corridor which led from the kitchen to the cocktail party. Pascal was only a couple of metres from the entrance to The Queen's Room, and beyond that, the table which held dozens of trays of brimmed Champagne flutes. His stomach lurched, and he took a second to formulate a reply.

'Desperate for the toilet again, this swell's really not agreeing with me.'

'Forget your stomach, what's happened to your face?'

He touched his swollen left eye, 'My serving partner Jakub lost his temper in the cabin last night.'

'You're not going out into public service looking like you've done three rounds with Frank Bruno, you're barred from all public spaces from this second on.'

'But Mr Healey, I'll be as unobtrusive as I can.'

'Out of the question, you've notched up far too many black marks this voyage. I'll not have you on one of my ships again. Report to the kitchen and help the lads prepping veg.'

'Yes, Mr Healey, of course.'

How was he to doctor the champagne now? But as soon as the thought had formed, a solution followed. He hurried to the staff lifts, pressed the down button and prayed Mr Healey didn't appear before it arrived.

The stainless door slid open, and he stepped inside. His shoulders relaxed an inch or two, and then he punched the button for D-Deck. A few moments later, he slipped through a staff door into a public corridor and was on his way back up the Grand Staircase to C-Deck.

69

Jay stared into the mirror above the row of sinks. The reflection wasn't kind. Before him, on the counter, sat two clear Ziploc bags. Both containing white powder. He opened one and sniffed the acrid contents, and almost gagged before opening the second and repeating the process. No idea, they were both different. But which was his coke and which held the crushed sleeping pills was anyone's guess.

'Eanie, meanie, miney, mo, snort some Charlie, watch me go.' His finger landed on the bag to his left.

'Okeydokey, the winner is…' he pulled a credit card from his wallet and poured himself a heavy line on the marble worktop. A few chops, a scrape, and a sniff, had him gagging again. But once settled, he shook his head and smiled. As a precaution, he placed this bag in his left pocket and the other in his right.

'Charlie left, snoozy right, well hopefully. Let's find a quick breath of fresh air, then get this party started.'

*****

Scott and Ramirez mingled amongst the guests of the captain's cocktail party.

'Let's circulate for fifteen minutes,' Scott said. 'Let people get through their first glass or two, then they'll be less likely to notice the taste of the powder.'

'Cool.'

'Have you seen Jay or Candy yet? Come to think of it, where's Pascal?'

Candy appeared from the other side of the room, gliding across the dance floor towards them.

'Wow.'

'Wow indeed,' Ramirez said. 'She certainly scrubs up good.'

Scott couldn't contain his smile, but it dropped when she planted her lips squarely on his and reached around his waist. He pushed her away.

'Behave, the last thing I want to do is provoke Jay again.'

'Again?' Ramirez said.

'Don't ask.'

'Yeah, what are you talking about?' Candy said.

'It's nothing. He's just a little off the rails at the moment.'

'Scott, full disclosure please, I'm not putting myself at risk without knowing the truth.' Candy said. Ramirez agreed.

'Okay,' Scott sighed, 'first Ramirez needs to know about last night…'

*****

'And then, of course, the Duke of Devonshire invited me to join him in Fez for the weekend, so…' Lady Astbury nodded appreciatively, a thin social smile fixed in the direction of the ruddy-faced clot doing his best to impress her.

'Just popping to the gents, won't be a tick,' Sharpe whispered in her ear and slipped away before she could respond.

He took the stairs two at a time, quite an achievement given the size of the treads, and exited onto the Promenade Deck. Immediately he withdrew the silver cigarette case from his inside pocket and fumbled to free one of its contents, only pausing to light it once he was clear of the sheltered stretch of the deck.

'Ahh, bliss,' he exclaimed after his first inhalation. He then drew a second deep pull before continuing towards the aft at a more sedate pace.

A man stood there alone, also wearing formal attire. He clutched the rear-facing rail with both hands spread wide as the wind buffeted him from all directions. Sharpe drew up alongside, and after a moment's observation, decided to strike up a conversation.

'I know you, don't I?'

The man ignored him, possibly hadn't even heard him over the wind, so Sharpe repeated the question with more gusto.

'Doubt it,' the man said.

'Yes, you were with that lady on the first day, Candy, as we left Southampton. You came into the smoking lounge and whisked her away.' The wind had lulled halfway through, and he found himself shouting unnecessarily.

'What of it?'

'Nothing, just trying to make polite conversation and obviously failing. So shall we be terribly British and talk about the weather?'

'No.'

'It's certainly cutting up a bit choppy. Stormy night ahead, if you want my opinion. Do I take it you're feeling a little seasick?'

'No, and I wasn't looking for your opinion.' Jay yawned deeply.

'Ahh, keeping you up, I see. Got young kids, have we?'

'No, I bloody haven't,' a gust caught Sharpe's dinner jacket and snatched it open. He managed to get a hold and pull it closed, but not quickly enough.

'What's that?' Jay demanded. Sharpe shrugged. 'I saw something metal under your Jacket.'

'Oh, you mean this? It's my lucky cigarette case.' Sharpe produced the case and carefully buttoned his jacket. Maybe the old bat did have a point. 'I say it's lucky because it belonged to my grandfather in the war.' Sharpe showed Jay a circular dent in the face of it.

'Saved his life, did it?'

'Not quite, it caused the bullet to ricochet upwards, through his jaw and into his brain. Killed him instantly.'

'That's lucky?' Jay threw his cigarette butt over the side and stifled another yawn.

'Relatively speaking. Could have been an agonisingly slow death from a simple puncture wound. Would have probably got infected, could have hung on for days, delirious with pain.'

'Lucky bloke. Does it run in the family?'

'Well, I've not been shot yet, so don't wish to test it. But I suppose I've been fairly lucky so far.'

'Long may it continue. I'm off,' Jay pushed away from the railing to fight the wind and perpetually rolling deck, back towards the door.

Sharpe looked out to the rising and falling horizon, a faint spread of indigo in the dark. He had to admit, it was certainly getting rough out there.

He lifted his hand to take another drag on his cigarette, surprised to see the strong wind had caused it to burn down to almost nothing. He lit another. To hell with Lady Astbury for a few more minutes.

*****

Pascal entered the cocktail party through the revolving door next to the Grand Staircase lobby on C Deck. He scoured the room to ensure that Mr Healey hadn't emerged from the staff corridor at the far side whilst he was gone. The string quartet was still in full swing.

He edged his way around the outside of the room towards the area where several trays of filled flutes were laid out for the serving girls to exchange for their empty ones.

It was a massive risk, doctoring the drinks in front of all of the guests, officers and his fellow wait staff, but with Healey blocking his access to where the glasses were filled behind the scenes, it was his only chance.

He drew the clear plastic bag from his stiff grey jacket and pulled the Ziploc open.

'What are you doing here?'

He jumped, spilling some of the bag's contents on a tray of glasses, and then glanced around to see one of the waitresses behind him.

'Just lending a hand, looks like you need it with everyone here like this,' he replied.

He swapped her empty tray for a filled one and shooed her away before she had a chance to see the spilt powder. He bent, gave the table a blow, and carefully doctored the remaining trays.

Two minutes later, he was done. Best get out of here.

He crossed the room, pushed his way into the revolving door, and then glanced over his shoulder to scour the room one final time. Horrified, he saw Scott, the plastic bag held low in his left hand, approaching the same table of Champagne flutes he'd just done.

Panicked, he shoved the glass pane in front of him harder and did an entire circuit of the revolving door. But it ejected him back into the Queen's Room faster than he'd expected.

*****

Captain Roberts excused himself from the intolerably dull conversation with an American retail tycoon and an Icelandic tech entrepreneur. It had been about flowers, of all things. The sudden increase in pitch and roll of the ship could mean only one thing, and he needed to take immediate action.

He made his way as efficiently as possible towards the nearest exit, but became ensnared by passenger after passenger with every step he took. He supposed it was to be expected in a room where everyone was vying for his undivided attention.

After seven long minutes, he finally made it to the entrance. He was just about to exit through the revolving door when a harried-looking waiter was spat from it, almost barging him off of his feet.

'What the blazes are you doing man? I could have been a passenger.'

'Sorry sir, I…'

'You again. You're wait staff, so you shouldn't have been on that side of the door in the first place. More to the point, what are you doing in a public space with a clearly visible bruise in your eye socket?

'I'll be having words with Mr Healey about this for sure. Give me your name and then get out of my sight this instant.'

'My name is… Jakub.'

*****

'So how are you doing with all of this free-flowing alcohol?' Candy said.

'As most of it should be laced with narcotics, I could ask you the same question,' Scott replied. 'Where's your boyfriend?' he continued.

'Ex, and you know it. Anyway, what about last night? Was that the beginning or the end of something?'

'Can we focus on the job at hand please?'

'Talking of hands,' she tried to slip hers into his, but he pulled away, sliding it into his jacket pocket.

'Killjoy,' she said. 'I've sprinkled all of my fairy dust, so what more is there to do but have polite conversation?'

Scott drew his hand from his pocket and pressed another bag of powder into hers. She squeezed back and held his gaze.

'Go work your magic, please.'

'You old romantic,' she kissed him fully on the lips and then slipped back into the crowd. He watched her with such a raw longing his chest ached.

'Oh, look at you two getting all cosy,' Jay said as he drew up alongside.

'Have you done your job yet?'

Jay tapped the pocket of his dinner jacket and winked.

'Just get on with it will you, we're running out of time.'

*****

'Weather report please Mr Nakagami,' Captain Roberts asked as he entered the bridge.

'Force ten, closing faster than expected from the southwest, should hit us in less than an hour. When it does, wind speed will be averaging seventy-five knots, swell thirty-five to forty feet. It looks to have decreased from a force twelve over the past hour but it's heading straight for us.'

The captain looked out at the dark rolling sea for several moments, searching for clues.

'How much further north can we go to lessen the impact before we run into an ice field?'

'There is scope for running, sir, maybe twenty miles. It might have dropped to a force seven by the time we're in it.'

'It can't be much off that now.'

'Six currently sir, but we're right at the northern edge of the shipping lane so we'll be effectively on our own with regard to ice updates and I doubt any other vessels will follow us.'

'Okay, have it your way. Turn on your S.E.E. toys and plot a course to that effect. But keep her steady, no dramatic course changes. And I want to be informed if there are any developments.

'Let's pray those toys of yours do their job. A repeat of history would be just unthinkable.'

'As you wish,' Nakagami saluted, and then left for the navigation room.

70

Jay bumped and barged his way through the cocktail party, spilling champagne and earning frowns of disapproval. How could he be feeling this off his face? He'd only done a few lines since The Midships Bar toilet. It usually gave him focus, not this fuzzy, hammered feeling.

He spied a waitress with a tray full of flutes emerging from behind a screen, so he headed towards it. It must be a re-stocking station.

He closed in. Twenty feet, ten feet, then a man emerged, making him jump.

'Christ Ramirez, you nearly gave me a heart attack.'

'Dude, the trays are right behind this partition. I've laced the ones on the left but run out of powder so you do the ones on the right.'

'Yeah, sure, got some lovely powder for 'em.'

'Are you okay? You don't look so good?'

'All good mate, all goo….' Jay yawned.

'You need to sharpen up, right now.' Ramirez walked away.

'Charming. Right, let's get you little beauties topped up.' He slipped behind the screen to find several trays of drinks. He tapped his pockets, cokey leftie and snoozy rightie? No, that didn't sound right. Maybe it was loosey snoozy leftie, tighty cokey rightie?

'Bollocks, can't remember,' nor could he remember which side Ramirez had already dusted. He opted to sprinkle the middle glasses from the bag of powder that had the most in it.

'Done, you certainly have been, ladies and gentlemen.'

*****

Candy closed in on the partitioned wall obscuring the staff corridor as Ramirez emerged. She smiled as they passed but couldn't help but sense a warning in his expression. As she rounded the partition, her heart sank.

'Oh look, if it isn't the ship's slut come to pay me a visit.'

'Are you done?'

'Are *we* done? That's the question I've been asking, love.'

'You know damned well. Get out of my way and let me do my job.'

'Didn't think screwing my brother was in your job description, or did I miss that part of the contract?'

'Seriously Jay, move aside and let me get on with this.'

'Move aside, just move aside so that dictatri… dic..tcotor… dick ta torr…eee…aa' he gave up. 'Bully, can steal you from me? You expect me to just watch that happen, eh?'

Her body tensed with a burst of adrenalin, but she willed herself to stay calm. Jay's right eye twitched, and his eyeballs darted everywhere. He was losing it, that was clear. How long would he last before he imploded?

'Well?' he snapped his fingers in her face.

'Well, what? It's over. It has been for a long time. And no, I'm not screwing your boss.'

'Don't you ever call him my boss. I work for my own ends, not his.'

'Selfish as always. Now are you going to let me do my job? Or–'

'Good evening, madam, might I ask is this gentleman harassing you?'

An officer in a gold-braided uniform approached from the staff corridor.

'No, no it's fine. We were just returning to the party, weren't we, darling?'

Jay scowled and pushed past her into The Queen's Room. The officer accompanied him, allowing Candy a moment to do her work. She then returned to the party, discarding the empty Ziploc in a nearby planter.

Ahead, she saw Jay apologising to a couple after nudging the lady's arm. A waiter hurried over with cloths to clean the champagne from the dance floor. It wasn't only Jay who was tottering, she noticed a marked escalation in the sway of all passengers.

Plant pots also looked precarious, some sliding a few millimetres left then right in time with the guests. She hurried back to Scott for an update. He was talking to Emslow's girlfriend.

'Scott, can I have a word?' he held up a finger, waiting for Kyla to finish. Anger shot through her. Hopefully, there'd be the chance to grind a heel into that woman's plastic chest once the gas worked its magic.

'Sorry Candy, Kyla was just telling me about living with a workaholic.'

'Sounds riveting. We need to talk,' turning to Kyla, 'Would you excuse us?' she took his arm and drew him away, through the crowd and over to an alcove near the revolving door.

'What's so urgent?' he said.

'It's not me you need to worry about, have you seen Jay? He's losing it big time.'

'Just focus on your job and let me handle him. Now go and mingle politely.'

'So how am I supposed to do that? I'm so out of my depth here I can't even look them in the eye without going red with embarrassment. All these famous, successful people and I'm just a phoney from Feltham.'

'Listen,' he took her hands, 'you're way more than that. And they're just regular people like you and me.'

'I can't do it, sorry.'

'Yes, you can,' he paused in thought for a couple of seconds. 'Try pretending that you're a journalist looking for a story, and the juiciest one wins. Go and talk to them as if it's your job and they need the publicity.'

'That will really work?'

'Of course, they'll want to talk to you. Who wouldn't?'

'Now you're just trying to flatter me.'

'I don't need to.' She saw the sincerity in his eyes. 'Just treat it like it's a game, then we all win in the end.' He leaned in to kiss her but broke off after a second.

'Go.'

*****

Jay's head swam, everyone in the room moving back and forth in rhythm with the music, the floor rising and falling beneath him. His head hurt, vision blurred, and fatigue had really taken a hold. He'd be having strong words with his dealer once he got back home, even break a couple of fingers.

Everything around him seemed to be moving in slow motion. But next to the window he spotted an unoccupied table. He made a beeline for it and flopped into one of the chairs. Adjacent was a table of two couples he didn't recognise, each with almost empty drinks. A waitress approached and replaced their glasses, then handed one to Jay.

He downed the drink in a single gulp, closed his eyes and sat back on the cushions. A deep yawn and a stretch conspired to send him off within a few seconds.

He jolted awake, not knowing how long he'd been out. It was different, he felt far less tired, but now a rush hit him, like coming up on an E. The people beside him had also transformed, animatedly talking way too fast. They interrupted each other at the slightest chance. In fact, everyone in his immediate vicinity seemed to be on fast forward, like they'd all done a load of coke. Then the realisation dawned. 'Bollocks,' he groaned.

He stood, staggered, and caught his balance. His head swam, and walking really was a challenge now, let alone in anything like a straight line. But the more momentum he had, the better. He decided to head towards the dance floor, but barged into a couple, and then tripped over his own feet to take two further couples down with him.

Champagne and canapés flew as a waiter's tray smashed to the ground. Another man slipped on the mess, and as he flung his arm out for balance, he caught the side of a lady's chin with the back of his hand.

The fracas between her husband and another male passenger quickly descended into a fistfight.

In minutes The Queen's Room emptied at the urging of the staff. Some passengers made for their respective dining rooms, but most took the staircase down to their cabins.

'Nice one, Jay,' Ramirez said, yanking him by his collar to his feet. 'First useful thing you've done all trip. Hopefully they'll stay down there like good green sailors and have a nice, deep sleep. Go clean yourself up and grab a couple of sobering hours shut-eye. We've got a long night ahead of us.'

71

Confusion and a muffled voice crept into Jay's awareness as he began to return from a deeply unconscious state. Startled by a rush of cold water hitting his face, he flinched and gripped the bed covers tighter.

'What the…' his throat tight.

'Wake up sleepyhead, just a glass of water.' It was Candy. 'Two thirty, time to move. I'll be next door with the others so I suggest you take a quick shower and get yourself into gear.'

He looked up in time to see the cabin door close. A savage thirst and a need for painkillers dominated his thoughts. He headed to the small bathroom and gulped several mouthfuls of water from the tap.

After five minutes under a red-hot shower and a mouthful of headache pills, he felt better. Not brilliant, but at least able to function. He went to the cabin next door, where he found Scott and Ramirez laying the kit out on the bed, whilst Candy passed it to them from the open hide.

There were gas masks, a small gas bottle, tools, duct tape, several military-style knives and two sets of overalls.

'Looks like a bondage party, when do the girls show up?'

Scott threw a mask, hitting him in the chest.

'Why don't you put that on now to save one of us punching you before we even begin.'

Jay sat down in the second class cabin's sole chair and crossed his arms.

'Final recap,' Scott handed Candy a set of overalls. 'You and Ramirez put the small gas bottle in a laundry cart which you'll find in the maid's storage room along the corridor on the left, then get to the bridge. I timed the journey again yesterday, and it takes eleven minutes to get there using the lifts at the forward Grand Staircase.

'Ramirez, you gas the bridge, then lock down all of the outside doors. Candy heads back here whilst you ensure the ship's autopilot system is activated.

'Once she's here, I'll connect the first of the full-sized gas bottles to the ship's main air-con system at the back of this hide.

'From then it's masks on until we meet on the Boat Deck at the end of the job to release the lifeboats and dump the empty gas cylinders overboard.'

He handed out A4 sized rectangular chalkboards with a cord attached in a loop to hang around their necks. Jay ignored his.

'For communication. Once the gas is on, do not remove your mask for any reason until we're out on deck.

'Remember, I'll place a couple of laundry carts outside this cabin to give everyone a visual reference. You won't need to look at cabin numbers. All clear?' they nodded. 'Let's get to it then.'

Ramirez and Candy left. Scott leaned into the hide to connect the first gas cylinder but left the valve closed. He slid Jay's chalkboard into a leather shoulder bag and held it out to him.

'Put your mask in that and get up to first class. Make sure you're near the maid's storage room precisely twenty-five minutes from now, then sneak inside it.

'Hide for ten minutes with your mask on to allow the gas to make its way around the ship and then get to work. If anyone's still conscious they'll be too out of it to trouble you.'

He stared at Scott, his arms still folded across his chest, and held eye contact for a moment. Then he snatched the bag, and slunk out.

*****

John Sharpe hadn't been in his cabin more than a couple of minutes when the longing for nicotine overcame him. He'd been stuck playing cards with a bunch of loud-mouthed snobs for hours at the behest of his employer. He'd lost almost every hand, but thankful they'd only been playing for matchsticks.

The Smoking Lounge was out of the question, he'd just about had his fill of vapid conversation for the evening. Christ, was there really still three more days of this to endure? The solitude of the open deck was his only choice, even if it was a bit blustery out there.

He removed his shoes and tiptoed from his room, across the reception area of Lady Astbury's suite, and opened the main cabin door. Once in the corridor, he felt a sense of relief and bent to slip his patent evening shoes back on. Then cursed, as he'd forgotten his overcoat.

A short walk from B12 was the exit door that would take him out on deck. But as he heaved it open, he was confronted by one of his competitors from the card table heading back inside.

'Thank you, old chap. Out for a sneaky smoke before bed, are we?' the man was obese, and like Sharpe, still in white tie and tails. His heavily bearded face was scarlet, and his full head of bright orange hair had been thrown into ragged disarray by the wind.

'Something like that, yes.'

'I'm heading to the bar for a cheeky nightcap, will you join me?'

'Love to,' he lied, 'but I'm a bit tired actually, so probably see you for one tomorrow.'

The man winked, muttered something about stamina and swayed along the corridor towards The Midships Bar like an intoxicated orangutan.

It was blustery on deck, even in the sheltered area. He paused for a few seconds to look out at the menacing ocean. It rose and fell like the chest of an enormous beast, waiting to devour them.

With the roar of the wind and the relentless churning sound of the engines, he was surprised to hear a distinctive but short buzzing from the door through which he'd just passed. He gave it no more thought and walked towards the aft of B Deck, where the shelter ended, and smoking was permitted. He drew a cigarette from his silver case and lit it as he walked.

*****

Pascal lay in his bunk facing the wall, sick of the unending conversation between Jakub and Gordo. Surely it must be time to go soon?

'What are you doing there, Laddie?' it was Gordo. 'Crying into your pillow at not being allowed oot-a-tha the kitchen?

Pascal curled up tighter on his side, making every effort to disguise the gas mask he held just under the covers.

'Cannot believe Healey took Pascal from service and gave to you in kitchen.' Jakub added, 'But then, you deserve such useless fool, he no use anyway. That right Frenchie?'

Pascal ignored him, counting the seconds until he could get to work. He slid his head beneath the covers and pulled on his mask.

*****

Candy led the way as Ramirez pushed the laundry cart close behind. They were nearing the bridge and passed the officer's lounge just as the door swung open and a Japanese man emerged.

'It late for maintenance, I think.' he said.

'Oh hi,' she replied, 'we've been called up here on the captain's orders to sort an urgent plumbing issue.'

The man looked at her skeptically.

'This is not correct. Please show passes.'

'Well officer...' Candy looked to the man's name badge, 'Nakagami, I don't think I–'

A flash of movement startled her, Ramirez struck using an open-palm chop to the man's throat, and he dropped to the floor like a sack of flour.

'Jesus Ramirez was that really necessary? Is he dead?'

'Unconscious, we don't have time for delays. Take this and get on with your job,' he shoved the cart towards her. She caught it and was several paces down the corridor before she glanced back.

Ramirez had dragged the inanimate officer into the staff galley next to the lounge. He caught back up with her a couple of seconds later.

'Here,' he said, pointing at the access hatch in the wall between the Marconi room and the bridge. He pulled a screwdriver from his pocket and turned the catch, revealing a service port for re-gassing the air conditioning system. He lifted the gas bottle from the laundry cart into the cupboard and connected the valve, switching on the xenon gas before closing the hatch.

'Five minutes should do it. I'm going to hide in the galley with our new friend, you need to head back downstairs and tell Scott to get the main gas started.'

*****

Scott set the timer on gas bottle one to zero and then went to the nearby maid's storeroom to retrieve two carts. He took them, one by one, back to the cabin as markers for his team. Then he went back inside to wait for Candy. Five minutes later, there was the rap of fingernails at the door.

'Who is it?'

'Your friendly neighbourhood hottie, come to light up your evening, sir.'

He rushed over and pulled the door open.

'When this is over,' he began, but she pulled him towards her, and they sank into a long, deep kiss. He broke away after several seconds.

'Come on, we don't have long. Get yourself up to first class on the opposite side of the ship and hide with your mask on until it's time, then get to work. You've got nine minutes to get there, go.'

She pulled him back in for another kiss but he pushed her away.

'Meanie.'

He pecked her on the cheek and pushed her towards the door.

'Later, I promise. We'll have all the time in the world. Here,' he flung the chalkboard at her, 'remember to use this for messages.'

She blew him a kiss, scrawled a heart on it, and then held it to her chest before disappearing out the door. Ten minutes later, he pulled on his gas mask and opened the valve. After five minutes, the magic should have worked. So, he grabbed a screwdriver from the hide, went back out into the corridor, and began unscrewing the cabin number. If everything went to plan, nobody would be any the wiser.

If it didn't, well, all bets were off.

*****

In the dim light of the maid's storeroom on A Deck, Jay reached into his waistcoat pocket and pulled out his watch. It was difficult to read with his mask on, and anyway, was it ten past or twenty past he was supposed to start nicking on?

Start at quarter past, as a compromise.

He needed to cut down on the coke, it had started to rot his brain. And if it was that obvious to him, then it must be getting really bad.

But then, with all the cash from this job, he wouldn't have to worry about anything for a very long time. Maybe a brain rotted from coke wasn't too high a price to pay for sipping cocktails on a beach in Miami for the rest of his days. Candy might even see sense and give him a second chance, or was it a third?

Whatever.

But Scott, that thieving bastard, he'd stolen her. And most of his cut too. They'd see about that when it came down to it. Yeah, Scott had it coming to him, one way or another.

He noticed a metallic tang from breathing inside the rubber mask and felt the urge to spit, but that really wasn't a good idea.

He glanced at the time once more, almost a quarter past.

Maybe he should leave it a bit longer.

He closed his eyes and leaned back onto a shelf packed with duvets and pillows, still groggy from the sleeping pills. It was soft and inviting. Comfortable. So comfortable that he felt himself sinking right into it and closing his eyes for a just moment, maybe another moment, and then… just drifting off a little.

*****

Ramirez swiped the screen vigorously. It just didn't make sense.

No matter what he did or which menu he found on the complex touch-screen display, he couldn't convert the Chinese characters into English or anything close.

He rolled the unconscious operator onto his back, also Chinese.

'Damn.'

It hadn't occurred to him, or Scott evidently, that when Emslow had said the system was designed in California but manufactured in the Far East and came complete with its own operators, that it would be in anything other than English.

Ramirez continued to swipe at the large display, desperately trying to activate the autopilot system which, unbeknownst to him, was already on. Icons appeared and disappeared, menus and confirmation boxes flashed up and vanished but still no clue as to what they actually meant.

He was getting nowhere, and his hollow sense of dread deepened when a warning flashed onto the screen, accompanied by a buzzer and what appeared to be a countdown.

Five seconds later, the screen went black and the autopilot shut down.

72

Pascal noted the silence and checked his watch, nearly quarter-past. He took a deep breath and then pulled his mask away from his face.

'Gordo?'

The room was silent.

'Jakub?'

Still silent, it was time.

He swung his legs from the covers and rolled out of his bunk. Then he tightened the straps over his head to ensure a good seal and slid into his trousers, jacket and shoes.

Before leaving, he went to Jakub's bunk and shook him by the shoulder. Nothing. He was out cold.

Smiling, Pascal looked up onto Gordo's bunk and spotted his bottle of apple juice. He removed the cap, lifted his mask for a second and took a sip.

'Apple juice my arse,' he said, pouring the single malt over the Scotsman's groin and bedsheets.

Then it was Jakub's treat. He took the bottle by the neck and walloped the bridge of the Czech's nose with enough force to elicit both a satisfying crunch and a river of blood streaming down his chin. Not wanting to be responsible for murder, he rolled the man onto his side and propped his head up on a pillow.

'Payback's a bitch, eh ladies?'

Satisfied, he made his way along the maze of monochrome staff corridors and then out into the contrasting elegance of the public areas. He bounded up the aft second class staircase and then along E Deck as far as he could go but hit a dead end. Strange, he must have taken a wrong turn somewhere.

He retraced his steps to the staircase and tried once more. This time he used a different corridor. Once again, he got to the end, but now the stairs led only down.

He tried yet another but now couldn't even find the second class staircase he'd come up in the first place. Even worse, this increased effort was causing his mask to fog.

With frustration building, he decided to take the next door he came across to see what options lay on the other side of it.

*****

A thud on the door startled Jay from his dose. Was it someone trying to get in? He checked his pocket watch.

'Shit.' He jumped from his soft perch and pushed the door, but it only opened a couple of inches before stopping. He shoved it harder, but it held firm. Peering through the crack, he could see the body of an obese man lying against it.

'Oh, for Christ's sake.'

He retreated, grabbed the maid's cart, and rammed the door. Over and over, he slammed into it, but the body wouldn't budge. It was useless. All he'd achieved in several attempts was to buckle one of the cart's front wheels and open the door another inch.

*****

The howling wind buffeted John Sharpe left and right as he walked the length of B Deck, checking every door. First the port side and then starboard, but none would open.

Maybe it was just a deck thing. He ascended the stern staircase and tried his luck along the A Deck promenade. There was a marked drop in temperature with just a dozen feet of increased altitude, so he rubbed his hands as he walked forward, checking every door, but still no luck.

Obscured or stained glass filled most of the windows along the promenades to protect the passengers' privacy whilst in their cabins. But he happened upon the first class library and looked enviously at the open fire still roaring in an otherwise dimmed room. He cupped his hands and breathed into them, then stifled a sneeze. He knew it would come back. They always did.

Then, in the flickering shadows, he saw what appeared to be a body on the floor.

Suddenly alert, he banged on the window to rouse the man. Unsuccessful, he ran further towards the front of the ship, trying to raise the alarm banging on every window he came to, opaque or not.

The horror hit him when he reached the foyer for the forward Grand Staircase. Several bodies scattered about, both men and women seemingly dropped to the floor in mid-stride. Panic rose inside him, and his last chance was to head up to the Boat Deck where he could hop the barriers and get to the bridge, alert the captain.

A movement then caught his eye, and from one of the corridors emerged a figure wearing a gas mask and pushing a trolley. They stopped at every passenger to remove jewellery, watches, and wallets instead of offering assistance.

'It's a bloody heist.'

He couldn't believe it, watching the efficient way the thief operated. Then the tickle he'd been ignoring in his nose came back with a vengeance. He sneezed, and although the sound couldn't have travelled through the window, his sudden movement caught the eye of the thief, who shot a glance in his direction.

He dropped to the deck, lay arrow straight, and rolled up to the wall, unsure if he'd been seen. He held his breath.

The figure's shadow loomed large in the light that projected onto the deck. He could feel the thud of his heart, it pounded with such ferocity that he feared it might actually fracture a rib.

*****

Ramirez cursed and gave up trying to restart the navigation console. His time would be better spent elsewhere. He stormed back into the corridor and yanked the pass key from Nakagami's jacket, and a swipe-card from his wallet. Then he went down a deck to the first class cabins of A Deck to begin looting.

It was a simple system. Gain access, check the bedside tables and dressing table for jewellery, then open the safe using his officer's swipe-card to override the lock.

Finally, check trousers and handbags for cash, and then the occupants for what gems they might be wearing. Chuck it all in the laundry cart and move on to the next cabin.

He was astounded at the number of jewels lying around, diamonds and sapphires, emeralds and gold were all just left on bedside tables and desks. It was unbelievable, as were the owners.

He'd never seen so many famous people in one day, heck, in his whole life. But each time he went from cabin to cabin, he noticed a banging sound that at first had seemed muffled but now was louder.

He paused a moment to listen. It was coming from further down the corridor. Someone was lying unconscious but rocking ever so slightly with each banging noise.

Intrigued but cautious, he went closer.

*****

Pascal found himself back in the staff corridor on E deck, commonly known as Scotland Road, but still struggled to find his way to the upper decks. Then he came upon the short passage leading to the kitchen lifts, which would bring him to the staff area behind the Queen's Room on C Deck.

For the first time in half an hour, he knew where he was going. He ran along the corridor, but his humour evaporated as he turned the corner. Water ran along the floor and sloshed into a drain. It was coming from under the doors to the second class kitchens.

'Merde, merde, merde!' he stepped into the corridor, but what should he do? Crack the doors open a little to see how bad it was? With horror, he realised the lifts were on the other side of them. He had no choice.

But he'd seen the film, and he knew what happened next.

*****

Ramirez got to the man on the floor and saw he was blocking the door to the laundry room. He bent, and dragged the body free. But no sooner had he done this, the door flew open and a laundry cart hit him square in the shoulder. It knocked him hard into the opposite wall and momentarily dazed him. A gas-masked man followed, also banging into him and winding him further.

'Christ, you idiot, what are you doing?' he gasped, but it was inaudible to Jay and just reverberated around the inside of his mask. Once on their feet, he scratched out a message on the chalkboard around his neck.

WTF R U doing?

Jay shrugged, so Ramirez rubbed off the message and tried again.

Take my cart & finish filling. I'll take empty one & keep going.

Jay nodded and grabbed the cart whilst Ramirez righted the other and began down the corridor, only to find the wheel buckled.

He abandoned the damaged cart and ran back to Jay, startling him due to the reduced vision inside the mask.

Push your own fuckup, he wrote on Jay's chalkboard, and snatched the good cart away.

*****

Jay couldn't believe this crew. First Candy, then Scott and now Ramirez. All acting like tossers. The sooner he was out of this game, the better. But with time ticking, he'd better get nicking.

The first few cabins held ancient duffers, eighty years old at least. But then he was taken aback to see the face of one Sacha Jameson on the pillow of the fifth cabin he entered. No, surely it couldn't be, could it? Sacha Jameson, the runway model and reality television star. Tipped to be the next big thing. Could it be?

He went closer, the temptation too overpowering.

'Oh Sacha, where have you been all my life?'

*****

Pascal splashed towards the steel doors with trepidation, water running over his shoes as soon as he stopped. What to do? Could there be another way around to the lift? He couldn't think of one, and he was seriously late already.

He grasped the handle. Cold. Merde, was there a wall of water behind it waiting to be released? He paused a moment. Could he do it? Open the floodgates?

*****

Candy withdrew from the window. Maybe it was just a shadow she'd seen out on deck. There didn't seem to be anything out there now. Get on with the task. She pushed the cart down one of the corridors and stopped to retrieve a pass key and card from an unconscious cabin steward.

The first class cabin she entered was similar to the one she was momentarily in on the first day before Scott made them switch. It was wood-panelled and quite dark in décor. But she wasn't here as a design consultant, she was here to clean it out of any valuables.

She found the safe in the back of a cupboard, just like her cabin, and swiped the steward's card through the slot. A click sounded, a green light shone, and the door swung open.

Inside she saw layer upon layer of jewel boxes from Tiffany, Chanel, DeBeers and many others. With haste, she emptied each box into the cotton liner of the cart as an electric fizz of adrenalin shot through her so strongly, she felt giddy.

The next cabin was much the same, boxes and boxes of jewels, bricks of cash and even a bag of loose diamonds, probably fifty of them inside. It was incredible, like winning the lottery on a double rollover week.

After fifteen minutes, her cart was almost full, and it wouldn't be long before she had to go and do a swap over for a fresh one. Two more cabins, then head back.

*****

After a few agonising seconds, the shadowy figure had retreated. But Sharpe thought it prudent to wait a full two minutes before moving. Slowly and carefully, he slid along the wall. Ten yards later, he was clear of the foyer and stood.

The coast was clear. Relieved, Sharpe wasted no time in finding the nearest staircase. He bounded up the wet steps but slipped and lost his footing. He crashed to his knees but thankfully received nothing more than a small cut to his palm.

Up he continued to the Boat Deck, sprinted towards the front of the ship, and then clambered over the waist-high class dividing barriers as he went. The last one he came to had a Crew Only sign fixed to it. He was almost there.

Confident, he vaulted it in one great stride, memories of the school hundred metres' hurdles somewhere in his mind. But much like his last sports day at Saint Sebastian's, he failed to clear the final hurdle and caught his leading foot on the handrail. It sent him tumbling over the barrier, and with nothing to break his fall, his face was first to smack into the wet deck.

73

Pascal took a deep breath and turned the handle. A clunk sounded as the mechanism released the door, and it opened. He wasn't swept off of his feet or taken away by a torrent of water. But he stood looking at three kitchen porters slumped over industrial-sized sinks brimmed with washing-up. The water flooded onto the floor from the fast-running taps. He stepped through the doorway, shut the water off, and then jogged to the staff lift further along the corridor.

*****

'Behave yourself and get on with the job.' Jay chided before taking things further, even though his primal circuitry was doing its best to overrule that thought.

He cleaned out the safe and bedside drawers, then her handbag. He took a final look at the half-covered Sacha Jameson, closed the cabin door and moved further down the corridor.

The cart's buckled wheel caused it to act like a cat on crack. Also not helped by the floor tilting forty-five degrees to the left, then back to flat before rolling forty-five degrees to the right. It was impossible to make progress, and the steady increase in frustration was taunting his wrath. It was half-full. Time to ditch it.

He skipped the last few cabins and arrived at the aft Grand Staircase. He pressed the call button, and moments later, a lift arrived.

He drew the concertina doors open to find an unconscious lad inside. He dragged the bellboy out by the arms, wheeled the cart inside and punched the button for E Deck.

No sooner had it begun moving did the inherent instability of the lift become obvious. It swayed in the shaft to such a degree it banged into the walls on either side.

Too late, it was on its way down.

*****

Pascal arrived at the cabins denoted by the two laundry carts. He entered the first and took a quick look around. No sign of Scott. But someone had done some serious tidying since the last time he was here. It looked un-lived in. He went out into the corridor and took a look in the second cabin but still no Scott. He was walking back out into the passageway when Scott appeared from a couple of doors along.

Where were you? Scribbled Pascal on his chalkboard, but Scott just spun his fingers in a 'get a move on' gesture.

Pascal was taken aback at Scott's apparent anger, but then it hit him, he'd got confused whilst lost. He wasn't supposed to come to this cabin until he'd been up to first class and filled a laundry cart with gems. Idiot.

*****

Jay stepped out of the lift and swerved down the corridor, aiming for the two laundry carts marking their cabins. He parked the one with the buckled wheel and activated the wheel lock before swapping it for one of the empty ones. Surely there should be an empty gas cylinder in one of these carts by now? But no, they were empty. Typical Scott, can't keep up.

He left the damaged cart behind and headed back to the lifts, happy with the compliance of his new charge.

He was slightly apprehensive, drawing the lift concertina closed once more. The ride down had been pretty scary, but... Sacha Jameson. The thought of her was driving him to distraction. He shook his head, 'once in a lifetime opportunity,' he said aloud, 'get rich thieving, and the beautiful women will follow forevermore.'

*****

Ramirez worked with a practised efficiency honed from his many special ops missions to quickly fill his cart. He returned to E Deck and pushed it towards the two serving as markers ahead, a gas bottle protruding from one of them. He swapped carts and banged on the door to alert Scott of his presence. It swung open, and Scott poked his head out. Ramirez scrawled a message on his chalkboard.

S.E.E. system down, no navigation, DANGER!

Scott scrawled a reply.

Carry on, no problem yet.

Ramirez countered.

Going off course, rudderless.

Scott pointed to his previous message and then closed the door.

'Asshole,' Ramirez cussed inside his mask.

He made his way up to the Boat Deck and unloaded the empty gas cylinder in the closest foyer that had a deck exit.

He tried to balance the bottle upright, but it tottered, with a fall imminent. The sea had cut up pretty bad, and waves were now crashing over the Fore Deck. Scott. The fool, didn't he didn't realise how serious things were getting?

He laid the bottle down and wedged it between two armchairs.

Once secure, he went to the glass and looked out, trying to get a bearing from the moon, but the cloud cover was too dense. He was a confident sailor and had weathered many storms but didn't like how the boat was behaving. He'd seen it before, and things could go wrong quickly at sea. And the consequences were often fatal.

*****

Candy was next for a swap-over. She arrived at the cabin just as Scott hauled another empty gas cylinder into one of the laundry carts. He took the jewel filled sack from Candy's cart, but she reached out to hold his arm, capturing his attention.

Don't like this, stealing V personal stuff. She scrawled on her chalkboard. He shrugged, but a shot of anger flashed through her.

Insured, they get paid. He countered.

Can't insure a memory.

Can't steal 1 either. Don't have time for this.

It's wrong. Not just stuff, precious to people.

Tell that 2 yr sister. It's Y you're here, isn't it?

He held her arm so she couldn't scrawl any further objections.

She conceded that he had a point, then hauled the cart with the empty gas bottle down the corridor and made for the Boat Deck.

*****

Pascal had made reasonable progress, he thought. He was halfway through his second run in first class when he got to cabin B12 and noticed a plaque stating 'The Molly Brown suite'. The door opened after a swipe. Similar to the other cabins in this part of the ship, it had a sitting room and two bedrooms.

He scoured the living room with little success, then tried his luck in the first bedroom. Although occupied, it was currently empty. Maybe the lucky sod was in someone else's bed. Still, there were slim pickings so far as valuables go, but one thing jolted his attention. A police ID card in the top drawer of the bedside table.

Despite a red stamp across it saying RETIRED, it gave him the creeps. He backed out of the room quickly and decided to abandon this cabin for fear of who he might find in the adjoining bedroom.

But as soon as he was in the living room, he heard a muffled scream followed by a sharp pain on the back of his neck.

He shot around, ready to defend himself and came face to face with an old lady pounding him with a walking stick. He raised his arms in defence and thought that maybe the gas had run out early and the policeman wouldn't be far behind. Then, he noticed the oxygen tank on wheels next to her and the small clear mask she was wearing.

The pensioner was relentless. He'd be black and blue in the morning. He ducked down and then lunged forward to grab her oxygen tank. He ripped the tube from it and hurled the tank away. It hit the wall valve-first and dislodged the top. A burst of gas, a snarling hiss, and it spun around rapidly on the floor.

The stunned woman's actions slowed. Her sharp hits faded to light taps as the severed tube dangled uselessly from her mask.

The xenon did its work, and she wilted to the carpet.

*****

John Sharpe came around to the sting of hailstones drilling into the left side of his face. He peeled his right cheek from the deck, crawled to his feet, and stumbled forward in search of cover.

There was none apparent, so he clambered back over the barrier to the public side and continued along the Boat Deck, trying every door.

Finally, one opened. Halleluiah. But it was just a broom cupboard stacked with cleaning equipment and some deck games.

'Bugger.'

He climbed inside, teeth chattering, and pulled the door shut with an unsteady hand. After a few moments of controlled breathing, he took stock of his situation.

He could squint at an angle through a louvered ventilation panel in the cupboard door, with the inside of the ship just visible. Every few minutes, one of the masked men would appear to dump tall cylinders near the foyer entrance, presumably waiting for the doors to be released and get them outside.

Was this part of their getaway plan? He couldn't think how, so his only option was to wait it out and see what happened next.

*****

Candy dumped her empty cylinder next to the others in the Boat Deck foyer and then returned to B Deck and into the first cabin of her next run. She used her swipe card to enter but was shocked to see a bloated man sprawled on the bed with his anorexic teen girlfriend. The man was nearing his sixties, and the sight repulsed her. Maybe some of these people didn't deserve what they had after all.

She went through his pockets, drawers, and cupboards. Finally, she opened the safe. But before leaving, she also rinsed the girl's handbag of anything that remotely sparkled. Her conscience was clear with people like that, and also the likes of Jerry Fame, the talk show host who enjoyed humiliating his guests on live television. She found him passed out in the arms of another man in the next cabin along.

Her system evolved from cabin to cabin, judging marks purely on appearance. If they looked like they could afford it, as most did, then she took almost everything. No heirlooms or intimate possessions, she told herself. But modern sparklies, yup, they all went in the cart.

The following twenty cabins were a blur. In and out, next one along, then in and out again.

But when she least expected it, she was taken aback a second time. Not in disgust but a heart-breaking sight in one of the smallest first class cabins.

No bathroom, just a simple basin and wardrobe. The light thrown from a delicate Tiffany lamp exposed a frail lady surrounded by her faded monochrome life. The small silver photo frames spread around the room, a couple on the bedside table, a few along the sill, and several on the floor with their glass broken. The tilt and pitch of the ship had been too much for these fragile frames to stand.

Her twig-like arms clung to a threadbare teddy that looked as old as she was. Candy went back out to the cart, found a roll of hundred-dollar bills and tucked it into the lady's suitcase.

Before long, the cart was heavy, and she climbed into the lift for another swap-over.

*****

Scott had lost count of the number of runs the crew had done, but with only three cylinders and thirty minutes left. He knew the job had gone incredibly well. His body ached with the work he'd done man-handling the cylinders and cosying away the filled laundry sacks. He could feel the sweat, damp on his back and beads trickling down his neck and under his collar.

Things were going to plan, but he knew everything could change in a heartbeat. No sooner had he thought it, the reality came. Instead of the usual knock to signal a changeover, Ramirez appeared in the doorway. He scribbled frantically on his chalkboard.

ABORT NOW.

No. Nearly done, keep going. Scott countered.

Ramirez underlined his message three times. Scott shook his head and mimed thirty minutes by pointing at an imaginary watch face on his wrist. Exasperated, Ramirez rubbed out his demand and scrawled *ICEBERGS,* then jabbed a finger towards the porthole.

It took a second for Scott to process the information, and then he rushed to look outside. The hair on his neck bristled, and his nausea returned in a rush. He looked to Ramirez and slowly nodded.

I kill gas, U release outside doors.

Ramirez gave a thumbs up and left the room.

Scott grabbed a screwdriver and began sealing the hide with the gems inside. Once done, he checked the corridor and then moved the empty laundry cart two doors along.

This was the cabin where the last few gas cylinders remained in the hide. He had almost finished sealing it when Candy arrived. She pointed to what he was doing and shrugged.

Time 2 quit, whilst ahead. He scribbled.

Her relief was evident as she did a little dance before miming for Scott to raise his mask. He shook his head vigorously, but against his instruction, she leaned in towards him. She pulled both her and Scott's masks up simultaneously to plant her lips on his for a deep kiss.

A sudden impact on his hip, and Scott hit the floor. Hard. Fists pounded his face, and he reflexively put his arms over his head. Aware of the gas, he groped for his mask, but it was impossible as the attacker continued to pummel him.

He felt weak, dazed and confused. Beaten already, without returning a single blow. He needed his mask, and quickly, just for a fighting chance.

Through the fog of semi-consciousness, he could just make out the figure above him. He was wearing a mask. Could it really be Jay?

Then the violence stopped as suddenly as it had begun. His attacker slumped forward as Candy stood above them, bedside lamp in hand. Its shaft now bent from its impact on the side of Jay's head.

She threw the lamp and bent down to push the mask back onto Scott's face. Ecstasy as he took his first full breath for what seemed like an hour. After a moment's composure, Scott read what Candy had scrawled.

Must'v watched us.

Scott nodded, and then replied.

Take last cylinder, he pointed to the corridor, *outside doors open soon.*

She nodded and looked about to leave when Pascal entered the cabin. He did a double-take at Jay laid out on the floor.

WTF?

Scott grabbed one of Jay's arms and gestured for Pascal to do likewise. He shrugged, took the other arm, and they dragged him into the corridor.

Candy followed them out as Jay began to stir. He clutched his head and looked to be slowly regaining consciousness.

Finish 2nd hide, I go & release lifeboats, Scott scrawled on his board to Pascal. He cleaned his slate and turned it to Candy.

Cylinder upstairs, then start on lifeboats.

She left immediately. He waited until she reached the end of the corridor and had disappeared into the foyer with the lifts. Then he checked Jay was still out cold, confident he would remain oblivious to Scott's next move.

74

Ramirez trusted his instincts over Scott's instructions, so went straight to the ship's infirmary. After his surprise at seeing Scott's ex-girlfriend Samantha sprawled out, he rifled through the supplies to find what he needed.

If the ship collided with an iceberg, then Scott's plan was for nothing. He couldn't allow all of their hard work to end up on the ocean floor like this ship's predecessor.

If being on a special ops team had taught him anything, it was to prepare for every eventuality and always have an exit strategy. Scott's exit strategy wasn't looking so hot right now.

He found what he needed, left the infirmary and headed to the lift. He cursed at the time it took to rise, but once inside, he was on his way to the Boat Deck without any stops.

Research had told him that Xenon gas worked partly on lowering blood pressure whilst also reducing the breathing rate, so the antidote had got to be a reversal of these:

Pure adrenalin.

On The Bridge, he knelt over the inanimate S.E.E.3-D operator and drew a syringe from the inside pocket of his jacket. Carefully he screwed the needle in place and inserted it into the operative's arm. The theatrics of plunging the sharp end through this man's ribcage was pure Hollywood overkill.

With the syringe empty, he left the man to rouse on his own and headed to the control panel which released the outside doors. Next, he began opening the windows on The Bridge, staggering back as the wind roared in.

He left through a side door and out onto the rain-soaked deck for the final stage of the raid.

*****

Jay's head hurt like hell. That bitch had clouted him a good one. Those two were certainly going to pay for it now.

He struggled to his feet and took stock of his surroundings. There was a single cart left but no gas cylinder in it. That meant the raid was over and they were all up on deck. He tried the first cabin door but found it locked, so went to the second and found it open. Inside, Pascal worked away to get everything sealed up.

It was time to confront Scott and that bitch. He left the Frenchman to it and staggered towards the lifts.

*****

A loud buzzing took Sharpe's attention, and almost immediately, one of the masked figures came from the ship out onto the deck. They dragged one of the large cylinders awkwardly, obviously having trouble with it.

Pathetic, he thought, can't even handle something like that. But he decided to wait until all of the thieves were present before revealing himself for the arrest. He slid a hand inside his jacket, just for reassurance. The gun was still there and ready for action. But he gasped when the raider removed her mask to reveal she was the woman he'd had his eye on the whole voyage. Candy.

'Well, I'll be buggered.'

*****

Ramirez reached the foyer on Boat Deck as Scott heaved an empty cylinder through the open doors. He grabbed a cylinder and followed. Outside, the pelting rain stung. He ripped off his mask and took a great lungful of fresh air. Scott did likewise once his cylinder was at the railing.

'God, this air feels great.'

'Indeed, it does,' Scott said. 'Just a half-dozen cylinders to go.'

'Followed by financial freedom.'

'I'll sleep to that. You start releasing the lifeboats further aft with Candy and I'll ditch the rest of the cylinders. When you're done, meet back here.'

'Roger that.'

Candy was a few yards down the deck, so he jogged towards her to help with the boats.

*****

Soaked through but far from cold with the effort, Scott gathered the cylinders around lifeboat number three. He unfastened the railing which cordoned the boat from the deck and swung it back to get a clear run to the edge.

He peered over the side at the horrifying drop and then shakily rolled the first cylinder to the edge. He grasped a nearby rope and wound it around his arm, not wishing to join the gas cylinders as they rolled overboard. He shoved the cylinder with his foot and it fell, seemingly forever, and then splashed into the ocean below like a pathetic firework.

Within three minutes, the last one went overboard, plummeting to the depths. He paused to recover and then set about releasing the nearest lifeboat.

He found the button, pressed it hard, and the boat swung out on its davits. It lowered away. He watched the slow progress impatiently as the hail and spray drilled into his face.

The boat banged and clattered as it hit the side of the swaying ship, acting like a pendulum as it hung over the side. A loud crackle filled the air, and a fork of lightning illuminated the sky, then struck the water just the other side of another wave that resembled the Berlin Wall.

He scarcely had time to count to two before the deafening bass of thunder filled his chest and reverberated through his entire body. He heard the bang of a door and turned to see Jay out on deck.

*****

Sharpe was lucid enough to know he'd had a blow to the head but struggled to believe what his eyes were showing him.

Candice had been a shock, but then the next to reveal himself was that Rainey character. Yes, the car dealer he'd questioned after the first Guildford heist. So, he could have had him with that engagement ring after all, but hadn't been confident of the connection at the time. Stupid, stupid, stupid.

They must have been behind all of the jewellery shop heists. It had to be. Why had he dismissed Rainey as too small-time? Even with the ring as a clue. But Guildford was nothing compared to this.

Oh, the look on his former Superintendent's face was going to be priceless.

He clutched his gun and was about to burst from the cupboard when yet another masked man appeared from the ship's interior. How many of them were there? Surely there couldn't be more than these four.

Wait a moment longer. After all, two of them had walked out of sight and the remaining two now appeared to be arguing. He didn't feel there was any urgency.

Hail clattered on the roof, and the ship tossed around like a child's toy. This alone might have been a concern, but as his eyes changed focus, something really took his attention. Icebergs. Up to sixty feet high, for as far as he could see.

*****

Pascal finished the hide and made his way back out to the corridor. Jay was gone, and the floor lurched and tilted at such worrying angles he continually steadied himself against the walls as he moved.

There was only a single laundry cart left in the corridor, so he grabbed hold to push it back to the maid's storeroom. He hoped it would steady his balance, but the opposite became quickly evident. Whenever he heaved it forward, the thing just shuddered and swerved.

'Devil of a thing, move!' he shouted, fogging his mask.

He crouched to check the brake was off. It was, but the damned thing continued to misbehave. Again, he checked but now noticed that one of the wheels had a buckle. His solution was just to shove it harder.

'Come on, stupid bastard thing.'

Then, a severe lurch from the ship caused him clout the wall. He lost control and the cart upended, spilling Jay's first run of jewels into the corridor.

'What the...?'

He scooped everything back into the linen sack, removed it and retraced his steps to re-open the hide and stash it with the haul. But without a laundry cart to mark the cabin, he struggled to remember.

'Think, think, what was the number?'

Then it came to him.

'Magnifique, E34.'

Inside, he drew out his screwdriver, and after an agonising few moments to remove enough screws to bend the panel back, he finally had a gap big enough to squeeze the laundry sack inside. Finished, he looked around. The room was a mess. How did that happen?

*****

John Sharpe crossed himself and shoved the louvered door open.

'Get your hands up immediately,' he shouted. The two thieves ignored him, continuing their heated argument. Maybe they hadn't heard him with the roar of the storm? He repeated himself with more authority.

Still no reaction. A warning shot over their heads, that should do it. He set his aim slightly high, but the tumbling ship caused him to stagger forward just as he pressured the trigger. With the crack of gunfire, one man ducked, but the other spun and hit the deck.

The haze of blood hung in the air a second longer than the victim had.

'Oh Christ, that's all I need.'

Shocked and feeling unsteady, he backed away in need of support. But he kept the gun trained on the other man, who now held his hands in the air. What now? Where had the rest of them gone?

He really should have thought this through.

*****

Jay lay face down, the pelting hail almost soothing on his back as the fire he felt in his left shoulder eased ever so slightly. Maybe it was going numb.

He rolled onto his back and sat up, tentatively checking the fresh wound.

'You shot me, you absolute tosser,' he shouted to the pale-faced man now leaning against the foyer wall. Scott knelt beside him, arms still raised, and inspected the injury.

'Just nicked your shoulder, mate. Couple of stitches and you'll be okay.'

'Can't believe he shot me,' Jay said and then winced with pain. 'And you're no mate of mine, so piss off, get out of my sight.'

*****

Pascal again sealed the hide, fretting that he was now late for the winding up of the raid. He hurried up the corridor unencumbered and entered the lift. When he punched the button for Boat Deck, a sense of relief washed over him. The lift shuddered into life and began its journey upwards.

Moments later, despite the bangs and scrapes of the cage swaying in its shaft, Pascal bolted from the lift with a real sense of urgency.

He looked around to see that all the gas bottles were gone. How late was he? He ran across the room with the added momentum of the floor tilting in his direction and shoulder-barged the deck door open.

*****

Sharpe's elbow was resting on the handle when the door exploded out. A man in a waiter's outfit immediately followed. The impact forced Sharpe's arm violently forward. He lost grip of the pistol and sent it skittering across the deck to within inches of the man he'd just shot.

'Typical.'

He exhaled, and then slowly raised his hands above his head.

*****

'Take it easy, Jay,' Scott said. But his brother's demeanour reversed as soon as the gun was in his hand. Gone was the wounded victim, now only bitter revenge filled his eyes. The pair slowly rose but Jay kept the weapon trained on Sharpe.

'Think it's funny, do you? Shooting people without warning?'

'No, no, I did try but–' Jay pulled the trigger. Sharpe hit the deck clutching his knee, writhing like an eel.

'Hilarious, isn't it?' He shot again, this time hitting Sharpe's chest. 'Where's your lucky cigarette case now, eh?'

'Enough,' Scott shouted, but he was ignored.

Three shots gone, three to go. The alarm in Sharpe's features was obvious as he gasped and choked, struggling to fill his lungs.

'I said enough,' he slowly placed a hand on Jay's outstretched forearm.

Jay threw him off, and then kicked out with his right leg. It caught Scott on the thigh and knocked him back several yards.

When he regained his composure, he saw the gun now trained at his forehead.

'What are you doing? This is madness. Get him down to the infirmary, or you're in for a murder charge.'

'Should have minded his own business, been inside like all the other obedient mugs, not out here threatening to destroy everything I've worked for.'

'You mean we, Jay, everything *we've* worked for. We're still a team so just put the gun down and–'

'Shut up! This is my operation now,' he turned to look at Sharpe, still showing signs of life but only convulsive shudders.

'Say hello to Satan for me.' He pulled the trigger, and a red mist exploded between Sharpe's frantic eyes.

The gun was quickly back on Scott, who had begun to take a step forward.

'Uh, ahh, no creeping up on me. And that includes you, Pascal.' He said, glancing to where he'd last seen the pathetic waiter.

Jay backed away from Scott as another bolt of lightning shot from the sky. It plunged into the water uncomfortably close to the ship, and the reverberation of heavy thunder instantly followed.

The eye of the storm was upon them. Scott staggered left, then right. The ship's movements now so violent it was difficult to stand upright. Surging sheets of hail pounded them and then escalated to an almost solid downpour of ice. Their clothes, soaked through, hung heavily and reduced their movements to a slow motion.

'Jesus Christ, Jay, take a look around you. We're in the storm from hell and surrounded by icebergs the size of buildings. We're on the verge of greatness, of completing the biggest robbery the world has ever seen, and you choose now to have a cock waving match. Are you utterly insane?' he held his hands out pleadingly. 'Throw the gun overboard with that guy's corpse, and let's finish the plan.'

'Finish the plan, Scott and his precious plan,' Jay took a second to laugh. 'No,' he shook his head, serious again. 'Still pretending you're the one in-charge, even when I'm pointing this in your face.'

'Give it up, Jay. Where's this going to end, everyone dead?'

'No, just you,' Jay replied, and then pulled the trigger. But as he did so, a sudden lightning strike exploded off one of the railings. He flinched and his shot went wide.

Five shots gone, just one to go. How could he provoke Jay into wasting his last bullet? Think, think.

'Look out,' he shouted, pointing to the side. The ruse fell flat and Jay grinned. But a furnace was burning again.

'Pathetic, just like your ability to keep women.'

Fury shot through him at the sour memory of Jasmine's betrayal, brought back as raw as if it was yesterday. He lunged forward, but held back when Jay raised the gun to his forehead once again.

'Yes, I enjoyed Jasmine,' Jay shouted, oblivious of the pounding hailstones. 'Not the greatest shag, though. Too easily pleased,' he laughed. 'So perfect for you, I guess.'

'You?' Scott struggled to grasp what Jay was saying. 'What are you talking about, it was Del Toro?'

Jay roared with laughter, but the furnace quickly returned to his eyes.

'He just conveniently turned up after I'd finished with her. Whilst poor little Scott lay crying into his Kleenex in the hospital. You're pathetic.'

'It almost destroyed me.'

'So that's what Candy's about, is it? Petty revenge 'cos I screwed your fiancé?'

'I had no idea.'

'Bullshit. Or maybe you're more naïve than I thought. But you need to walk away from Candy. Tell her you hate her. Then I might let you live.'

'Fuck you. For the first time in years, I've found happiness. You're just some sleaze who can't control himself. It backfires on you every time,' his fear was turning to rage. 'You're delusional if you think she'd ever have you back. She hates you, and what I've done was as easy as taking Candy from a baby. So, man up and put the gun–'

The muzzle flash was brilliant in the night air. An instant, shattering pain wracked his body as it threw him backwards, stumbling, clutching the wound, feet catching on a rope from the lifeboat davit, and then he was falling, over the un-railed edge of the ship, tumbling head over heels as the brightly lit portholes raced past.

He felt no impact as the blackness had already engulfed him.

75

Candy sat on the bed with her knees drawn up under her chin, her arms wrapped around them. She stared unblinkingly out of the porthole as the famous green lady slipped by. The numbness and grief which had penetrated her entire being since learning of Scott's demise flared momentarily to anger, and then frustration. It faded back to a blank, vacant apathy before the statue had even passed from sight. Someone gently knocked on the door.

'It's open.'

Ramirez stepped into the cabin. The corridor outside teeming with people.

'We'll be arriving in a short while. Got everything ready?'

'I was really looking forward to this,' tears welled up from eyes so sore they felt bruised. 'Our arrival, this was supposed to be so special. A new start, everything getting better. But now what? I feel so lost.'

Ramirez came and leaned in, enveloping her in his massive arms. She shook and sobbed for what felt like a week.

'It's going to be okay. You'll be fine.'

'But what about the diamonds, the gold? Scott's bloody rule of not telling anyone the whole story means we're stuck. How are we going to get them off without being caught?'

'We don't.'

Candy broke down again, 'so this was all for nothing? We just leave it all here?'

'No, no. Jay and I have been talking. Between us we've pieced quite a bit of Scott's plan together. We just have a few details to think about. We'll get off the ship like nothing's happened and then run through everything back in England. For now, you just need to focus on getting through immigration.'

'But what about Scott? Surely, they'll notice he's not gone through passport control?'

'Don't worry. Like I said, Jay and I have most of it worked out. Just wait here until he comes to get you.'

A shudder ran through her as warm rivulets of tears streaked down her cheeks anew.

'I haven't left the cabin yet. What's it like out there?'

'Crowds of passengers in angry mobs demanding answers from the crew. It's mayhem. But also, a great distraction, so we'll disembark without a problem so long as we blend in and do a little complaining ourselves.

*****

Jay relaxed back into the armchair and surveyed the first class arrivals lounge. The occupants may have returned to their regular clothes, but the room was just as opulent as the one back in Southampton. Only a sombre mood hung heavily from the crystal chandeliers.

'I'd keep that grin under control,' Ramirez said. 'Don't want to go attracting attention.'

'Don't you worry big man. I'll have to act miserable when the time comes just to keep in character.'

'Talking of which, you seem to be taking the death of your brother a bit lightly.'

'I'm sure everyone will get over it. No point in putting off 'till tomorrow what you can start today, an' all that.'

Before Ramirez could answer, an arrivals host drew up to them.

'Good afternoon gentlemen. I'm Salwa and I'm here to escort you through immigration. Have you completed your visa declarations?'

They handed the woman their cards and followed her to the row of desks at the far end of the room. As they walked, Ramirez leaned in closer.

'Did you remember to tell the Grattons and the Schillers they had to go through second class arrivals?'

'Yeah, although that stupid cow Mrs Gratton was quite prickly about it. Told her she'd get thirty percent off her next trip as compensation if she complied. Bloody woman.'

'She believe you?'

'Of course, mate. It's all in the silver tongue.'

'Well, best warm it up again,' he nodded towards the six officials sitting at their individual tables, and the wall of New York cops standing behind them, primed like sprinters on the start line, just itching to make the headline-grabbing arrest.

Jay set his face and took a seat. The man staring back at him looked more like one of the cops than a customs official. But hey, everyone wants to feel important in America. The man reviewed his paperwork for several seconds and then looked up.

'Mr Scott Rainey, is this your first time in America?'

'Yup.'

'Is that a yes Mr Rainey?'

'Yup,' Jay said and glanced over his shoulder to throw his eyes up at a stony-faced Ramirez. Jay returned his attention to the official with a grin plastered across his face.

'Please answer my questions correctly. As you are aware, there has been some alleged criminal activity during your voyage, and the men behind me have authorisation to hold anyone for up to seventy-two hours who I find to be acting in a suspicious manner. So, once again Mr Rainey, is this your first time in America?'

Two minutes later, his passport was slid back across the table. The customs official then turned slightly in his seat and gave a single, curt, nod to one of the cops.

'Mr...?' the cop said.

'Rainey.'

'Mr Rainey, please would you come with me. We have some questions we'd like to ask regarding this crossing.' The cop wrapped his considerable hand around Jay's upper arm and guided him towards a door at the back of the room.

Two hours later Jay traipsed into the main arrivals foyer. Porters waiting with polished brass carts stacked high with steamer trunks and designer suitcases were everywhere and he struggled to see a familiar face in the mass of people. He plucked his phone from the pocket of his grey chinos, but before he could make the call, Pascal appeared out of the crowd with Ramirez just behind him.

'Hurry,' the Frenchman said, 'don't want to be missed. Healey is on the rampage like a bull.'

'Chill mate, I'll be back in two shakes of a bunny girl's bum.'

Pascal handed him his staff swipe card and a set of whites.

'Through the staff door, down the corridor and take gangway number five. It should bring you out near the kitchen lifts which run up to The Queen's Room. You'll know the way back to your cabin from there. Hurry, please.'

Jay gave him a wink and was about to head towards the staff entrance when Ramirez clutched his arm.

'Remember to change your shirt and hair. And maybe act less like a jerk to the customs guy this time.'

'No shit.'

'And go easy on Candy, she's fragile.'

Jay snatched his arm away, gave a crocodile smile, and then started towards the door.

76

Two months later

Jay slouched on his sofa in track-suit bottoms and a stained t-shirt. His rented flat was so littered with the detritus of takeaway packaging and empty bottles, there was hardly the room to put down a beer can.

A sixty-inch flat-screen dominated one wall, spouting news of another war, another famine and another sailing of Titanic II. He sat forward and focussed.

'We cross now to Derek O'Halloran in New York where the owner of Bright Star Line, Lucien Croft, is holding a press conference on the re-launch of Titanic II.'

Croft stood at a branded lectern and spoke with the gravitas of a presidential candidate.

'Ladies and gentlemen, the events of Titanic II's maiden voyage have been covered widely in the press, so I feel no need to go over old ground.

'The minor damage sustained by its collision with multiple icebergs is now fully repaired and stands as a testament to the integrity of this ship that it was able to reach New York despite suffering a similar challenge to that which defeated its predecessor.'

A flutter of applause quickly petered out before he continued.

'But not wishing to tempt fate, we have suspended all sailings via the Far North Atlantic Route indefinitely.

'There is now a revised timetable. After a short tour of the Bahamas, we will return to England via the Southern Route to begin our European cruise season. It will commence four weeks from today, and tickets are now on sale.

'But this slight delay does mean that there have been some minor changes to the advertised schedule. Madeira has been temporarily removed in favour of Tangier due to a shortage of berths on the revised dates.'

'But Mr Croft, what about the robbery?' enquired O'Halloran.

'Former police inspector John Sharpe is still at large. But, as not all of the loosed lifeboats have been recovered it remains unclear at the current time as to where the manhunt should begin.'

'There's talk of over half a billion pounds worth of diamonds alone being stolen. Can you comment?'

'As you say,' Croft smiled, 'it's just talk, nothing more. I believe The Commissioner can answer any questions relating to the alleged theft of one or two items of passengers' jewellery. Now, if anyone has a more constructive question?'

Jay killed the sound and began looking for his car keys. Ten minutes later, he was in his Audi, praying it would start. It didn't.

'Scott you bastard, where's your Mustang money stashed?' he yelled at the roof lining before punching it.

Another try of the key had the fifteen-year-old car splutter into life. He threw it into gear and pulled out onto the main road.

They were so close to finishing this job, but with all avenues for cash exhausted, it seemed they were no further forward than square one. What good was a haul of hundreds of millions if it remained just out of reach?

He could ask for an advance off Terry the Fence. Actually, sod that. Way too risky. The consequences would be brutal if anything went wrong. Bollocks, it's got to be another job. Something big enough to do in one hit but small enough not to draw too much attention, but what?

He reached the end of Cobham High Street and turned right onto the Portsmouth Road towards Esher. A mile later, he reached Scott's old showroom, which had been for sale when they boarded Titanic II. The sale of it had been their plan A to fund this second stage. But today, a Sold sign was nailed over the For Sale one.

'Think it's time to call the agent,' he said with a smile. Maybe things are looking up after all.

He pulled onto the forecourt and made his way around the back to the workshop entrance. Leaving the car running, he hopped out to peer in through a grubby side window. He rubbed an area clean with the heel of his hand and then wiped it on his track-suit.

The workshop looked empty except for a few tools and the table and chairs Scott had been making before the voyage. Over the next three seconds, all of the pieces fell into place. He pulled out his phone.

'Pascal, meet me at Scott's showroom tonight, eleven o'clock. Bring Ramirez, we'll need some muscle.'

*****

At ten fifty-nine, Pascal pulled a stolen van into the yard behind Scott's workshop.

'I'm guessing you trust Jay about as much as I do,' he said to his passenger.

'Nope,' Ramirez said, 'probably a whole lot less.'

Jay banged on the side window.

'Bung it over there,' he pointed, 'turn them lights off.'

Pascal complied, and they all gathered at the roller-shutter door.

'Need to jimmy the bugger up,' Jay said.

'The side door would be easier,' Ramirez said, crowbar in hand.

'Whatever.'

Ramirez went to the side, popped the crowbar through the window and leaned in to turn the door catch. There was no alarm.

A moment later, they were inside.

'That table and chairs has to be something to do with Scott's plan,' Jay said.

'Oui, I made removable tops to all of them using concealed catches, like a Chinese puzzle box.'

'And you didn't think to mention it earlier?'

Pascal shrugged.

'Right, show me how it works then.'

Pascal went to the table, crouched down, and released six catches around the circumference. The top lifted off, and underneath were hundreds of nuts and bolts.

'To test the strength,' Pascal said before tipping it over and sending a wash of metal over the workshop floor. He tipped it up, and yet more came out of the legs. Finally, a notebook skittered across the floor.

Jay picked it up and rifled through the pages.

'Looks like we've found Scott's evacuation plan,' he said, as a smile grew across his face.

77

Detective Lorenzo Rossi stuffed the last of his Iberian ham and goats cheese Panini into his mouth as he strode towards the Chief Inspector's office. He rapped his knuckles on the door and entered before hearing a reply.

'Rossi, good of you to come.'

'Sir.'

'I know it's somewhat outside of our patch, but head office has been leaning on me with regard to your former superior D.I. Sharpe and this robbery he's been implicated in. I've appointed you as head of the investigation.'

'I heard, sir but,' he shrugged, 'what use can I be?'

'You knew Sharpe, his habits and foibles. Maybe there were some clues left behind that those who hadn't been so intimate with him have missed.'

'Foibles?'

'Quirks, eccentricities, that sort of thing, Sharpe had plenty from what I remember.

'We've also picked up some inconsistencies with regard to passenger behaviour on that original sailing. People in cabins not assigned to them, some passengers reporting large amounts of personal possessions going missing yet others in the next-door cabin not reporting a thing. It doesn't quite add up. There's very limited CCTV footage, and only of the public areas of the ship. In this clip,' he rotated the monitor around for Rossi to see, 'one of the thieves appears to be wearing a staff uniform. Of course, that could just be to throw us off.'

He scrolled through more footage and found a sequence on the Boat Deck at the end of the raid.

'Unfortunately, the severity of the hailstorm sent the cameras haywire, so we can't quite make out what happened. This is as enhanced as they can get it.

The screen resembled the snow of an out-of-tune television from the 1960s.

'We believe it was five people in total, but only Sharpe is missing from the passenger and staff list according to U.S. border control. Therefore, the others remained aboard whilst Sharpe made off with the haul in one of the lifeboats. The rest either trust him implicitly, or had some kind of leverage. Find out if anyone could have been blackmailing him.'

'Okay, sir, anything else?'

'Yes, interestingly, our only eyewitness is Sharpe's former employee, Lady Astbury, who had her own source of oxygen during the gas ingress. I need to know if it was coincidence, or was she warned? Sift through what footage you can, run through the passenger list and then interview anyone you feel relevant to the case. I want this solved, and fast.'

'I'll do my best, sir.'

'Oh, and before you go, I also want you to get aboard for the first Mediterranean cruise to see what else you can unearth. Probably best to travel incognito, under a false identity, so as to not arouse any suspicion now the media plastered your face everywhere. See Taylor downstairs once you leave here for ideas on how to become invisible, blend in, different passport etcetera.'

'But sir, I was just leaving for the day, got a five-aside this evening and it's a league semi-final.'

'Very well, just don't do yourself a mischief. I need you in tip-top shape for this.'

*****

Candy entered the park and walked toward the children's play area. The sun's orange glow had gradually sunk behind the trees, but the day's warmth remained. The only people left were a small group of teenagers passing a spliff between them, and three familiar faces a little further on.

Jay sat on the swing, gently moving back and forth whilst the others stood a few feet in front.

'So, what's the way forward?' said Ramirez.

'Difficult,' Jay said. 'I spoke to the agent but he pulled that data protection crap, bereaved brother or not. Said the sale of the showroom had completed and finances settled but couldn't tell me anything else. Even after I'd threatened to break his children's legs.'

Candy felt pure revulsion as Jay continued. 'I guess he either doesn't have kids or takes his job very seriously.'

'You're sick, get some help,' she said.

'Thanks for that constructive input, Miss Slut. Got anything else to help us achieve our goal?'

She scowled.

'The showroom's a dead end so forget it,' Jay said. 'We need to raise at least two hundred grand to get the first class suites for the cruise, and then bribe the passengers in E34 and E36 like last time. Who has any ideas?'

'That Michael Caine film,' Pascal said, 'Diamond Kings or something, about the Hatton Garden robbery, we could do that.'

Jay threw his eyes up.

'Firstly, it's a film, so therefore not on this real planet of ours. Secondly, it's been done, hence the film. Thirdly, they got caught.'

'No,' Candy said, 'he's got a point.'

'Shut up, what do you know about robberies?'

'Jesus Jay, what did I ever see in you?'

'Ambition, looks and charisma, I'd guess.'

'Look, I think Pascal is onto something,' she continued. 'Hatton Garden is the UK's centre for not only precious stones but also precious metals so it makes sense to focus our attention there.'

'Okay Miss Slut, so how we going to do that?'

'You call her that once more and you'll be breathing through a tube.' Ramirez said.

'Thank you,' she said. 'I don't know yet, obviously, as I've only just thought of it myself. What about you guys?'

She turned to Pascal and Ramirez.

'I'm all for that, seems the obvious job to me,' Ramirez said.

'Yeah, why not,' Pascal said.

'We need a plan though. Any ideas?' she said.

A distant buzzing sound became gradually louder, and then a headlight appeared at the park gate. A moped entered and rode along the path to where the spliff-smokers sat.

The rider dismounted and slid a couple of pizza boxes from the top box at the rear.

'I don't believe it,' Candy said. 'Ask the right question and the answer rolls right up, law of attraction at its finest.'

'Have you had a bang on the head, love?'

'No Jay, and I'm not your love, so cut it out. It's given me an idea. We watch the jewellers during the daytime to see if there's a pattern to the food they order in for lunch. If a shop favours a local Pizza restaurant or McD's, or whatever, we can use that information to get inside whilst disguised as one of those food delivery riders.'

'What are you on about?' Jay said.

'If someone in the jewellers regularly orders, say Domino's Pizza, then one of us dresses as a Domino's rider and presses the entry buzzer slightly earlier than the time the usual guy turns up. That way someone will buzz them in even wearing a helmet and face mask, therefore disguised. The shotgun can even be inside the pizza box. We hit two or three shops at once, all at lunchtime.'

'I like it,' Ramirez said. 'And the clothing will also help our exit strategy as there are so many food delivery guys in London it'll be impossible to chase us. We'll just blend right in.'

'I love it,' Pascal said.

'Whatever,' Jay said, his feet swinging him gently back and forth, 'someone give me a push.'

*****

Detective Rossi sprinted along the edge of the pitch, careful to remain on-side. He hung back a moment, allowing his opposite player to get within a few yards but not close enough to challenge. He was into the last quarter and waiting for the ball, perfectly positioned.

Bradley appeared from behind him, far sided and tapping the ball fluidly, swerving around one defender after another.

'Cross,' Rossi called. Bradley glanced over but continued.

Two midfielders were converging on Bradley from behind, the goalie advancing head-on. Rossi sprinted forward, centring himself in front of the goal.

'Cross,' he shouted again. This time Bradley reversed, went back two paces to throw off his attackers and booted the ball through the air, high towards him.

It landed short. Rossi sprinted. The overhead floodlights left marks on his retinas, but the ball was his, and the goal defenceless.

It bounced lightly, his left foot placed perfectly beside it and his right thundering down to strike it into the goal.

A perfect shot, but then the impact of a sliding tackle hit Rossi from the side with full force.

He heard the crack of cartilage as his knee dislocated, and he went down hard. Pain like a burst of flames engulfed his whole leg. He rolled, screamed and clutched his knee, but nothing abated the agony until he was on the stretcher, taking deep gulps of gas and air. Oh, the irony of it.

78

Candy made her way along the familiar route to the first class departure lounge. She was sad at the prospect of losing the luxury of their first class cabin, but she reminded herself that if all went to plan, she could go first class for the rest of her life.

'All aboard for Titanic, first class to the right, second class to the left.'

When she reached the lounge, it just felt hollow without Scott beside her.

The gloss stripped not only from her memory of that maiden voyage, but also the fact that the room was no longer filled with A-list celebrities, just overpaid company directors and the occasional C-lister taking their leave from a soap or Netflix series. It dawned on her that although fame might be fleeting, the ability for mere mortals to grasp onto its coattails is even more so.

They were called to board, but whilst the host showed them to their suites, Candy recognised the same music piped through the speakers and the parrot fashion spiel turned out by their host. It was like returning to Disneyland as an employee after visiting as a child. The magic gone, and she was just here for the money.

After being shown to their first class suites, Jay thankfully left her alone and went to tempt the passengers of E34 and E36 to a free upgrade. But unlike previously, he returned half an hour later with the dismal news.

'The people in E34 won't change, they're adamant and don't care about a first class suite.'

'If that's the case Jay, maybe you should respect that.'

'Pull yourself together. Their stubbornness is costing us a fortune, literally.'

'Well, I'm sure Scott would have had an answer, but–'

He slapped her hard. 'Go to hell.'

She ran for the door and burst into the corridor. It was she who was in hell, having to tolerate him for another week.

By the time she had reached the Boat Deck, she'd calmed enough to appreciate the benefit of them remaining in their first class berth. And on reflection, felt relieved that with two bedrooms in the suite, the question of who took the sofa was not going to arise this time.

She walked towards the doors which led out on deck, there was a smear on the glass, and dust had gathered in the corner. How quickly things slip.

She pushed through the door, devoid of a bellboy now, and out onto the deck. There was a noticeable drop in temperature. Not the Med, she thought, but still pretty good for Southampton.

Outside she saw they had not only begun to move but were also quite a distance from the quayside, which this time had offered no marching bands, no streamers and no fanfare.

But despite, or maybe because of, the anticlimactic send-off, she felt more at ease. Free from the constraints of not only the role she had to play for the upcoming week but of her life in general. Becky had shown signs of improvement, and her mum had grown accustomed to the regular hospital visits.

She crossed herself before offering up a quick prayer that everything would work out and she'd soon have the money Becky needed for her many operations. Slowly, the last sights of seafront England slid past, and they headed out to sea once more.

*****

Pascal sat, and the waiter pushed his chair in to meet the table. God, it felt good to be on the other end of the silver salver.

'Can we have the wine list please? And don't hold back on the bread and olives. Balsamic and extra virgin I should hope.'

The waiter retreated with a nod.

'Seriously Pascal?' Ramirez said, 'knock off the lord of the manor act.'

'Can't help it, the shit passengers gave me when I was doing this.'

'So you of all people should have some empathy.'

'Suppose. Anyway, have you noticed that man over there in all white? I saw him coming out of the cabin next to ours earlier.'

Ramirez subtly looked to where Pascal had gestured. He nodded.

'Yeah, I saw him earlier too. A priest, I think. Uses an ebony cane to help him along. What of it?'

'Nothing really, just thought it odd with everyone in all this dower 1900s stuff and him in white, that was all.'

'I guess it's period, just white instead of black. And being a man of the cloth, he's probably descended from some missionary. Although that would probably be in the tropics, back in the day.'

'Trust you to say back in the day. Anyway, this is a Mediterranean cruise not a tropical one, explain that.'

Ramirez shrugged and drew the large menu up from the table.

'Man, I could eat an elephant.'

79

Bubbles rose from the priest's mouth, past his nose and over his panicked eyes—Underwater, desperate to escape. The rope bound tightly around his limbs pulled him down, further into the depths. Cold, so bitterly cold, it's unbearable. The pain drew its teeth once more and sunk them into his skin, all the way to the bone.

Then, a jerk upward, rising quickly. Then air, glorious air. It filled his lungs with a burning relief like never before.

A gasp of breath and the sudden realisation he had woken was enough to unsettle him in his single, dry bunk. He drew the covers to his shoulder and waited a moment before sliding from the sheets and crossing the cabin to the sink. Another nightmare.

He studied his reflection in the mirror. The allergic reaction he'd had to the false beard gave him an angry red stain around his jaw and top lip. It was sore but not a concern. Thankfully the wig of long white hair hadn't had the same effect, and his cropped head remained clear of the itchy rash.

He changed his focus towards the porthole, and through it, the sea was a gently rolling carpet. Just miles of water to the horizon as the ship ploughed its way to the Mediterranean.

A knock at the door.

'Come in.'

A steward clutching a tray entered and slid it onto the dressing table.

The priest's suit jacket swung gently on the hanger, and he retrieved his wallet to pull out a note and offer it to the steward.

'That's okay, Father, just a good word for me upstairs'll suffice.'

He felt guilty but thought he might carry out the request anyway. What was the harm? Surely his word was as good as a real priest's.

Today, he was a free agent. After all, they wouldn't be up to anything just yet. But the ship would be the other side of the Bay of Biscay in twenty-four hours. So soon, the solid ground of Vigo would be beneath his feet.

That's when things would start happening, when he'd really have to start paying them close attention. But subtlety was key. If he got caught, it would all be for nothing.

*****

Shouts and the rumble of heavy dockside machinery alerted Jay to the fact they had arrived at their first port. He yawned and rose from the large bed on which he had enjoyed a decent night. That bitch was insisting on separate rooms, which in hindsight, suited him fine.

The breakfast trolley was already in the lounge, and a couple of fingers to the coffee pot told him it'd been there for quite some time. He poured a cold cup, inspected the fatty bacon and opted for a couple of slices of buttered toast with apricot jam.

Showered and shaved, he made his way to the promenade section of A Deck to observe the procedure dockside.

Where had the others got to? The deck was virtually empty, and a glance over the railing showed that most passengers were already on the quayside or disembarking along the many gangways to dry land.

From his high vantage point, he first picked out the distinctive image of the priest who had been the subject of conversation between them all the previous evening. Ramirez thought there was something not quite right, and it might be wise to keep an eye out when he was nearby. This proved wise, as it appeared that the holy man was now following the trio of Ramirez, Candy and Pascal from a discreet distance.

He hurried back inside the ship and pressed all of the call buttons for the lifts, taking the first one down to E Deck.

'Hey, wait your turn like the rest of us,' a passenger shouted. But Jay barged past the queue and into the changing rooms. He dodged through men in various states of undress, morphing from Edwardian gentlemen into modern tourists before setting foot in Vigo. He didn't pause at his locker to change clothes.

Halfway down the gangway, he realised he couldn't see where the others had gone. He tapped his pockets only to find them empty, his phone and wallet still in his disembarkation locker.

'Shit.'

He turned and barged his way back against the flow, drawing more objections as he shouldered several people out of his way.

*****

The priest pulled his collar away from his throat for the fifth time in as many minutes. The gentle sea breeze was now gone, and the oppressive city heat consumed him as he limped on, leaning heavily on his cane. He had to keep within range of Pascal, Candy and Ramirez through the city's streets.

They were heading towards the old town, which meant narrow alleyways and dark streets. The gothic grey, soot-stained buildings and their iron-railed balconies encroached overhead to cast deep shadows with only the upper halves lit by the intense sunlight. His wig had also begun to itch.

The situation was far from ideal. He had to remain undetected, so kept as far back as possible without losing touch. But the concertina effect of following the group had him rushing to catch up with every turn of a corner. He then let the distance grow once they were in clear sight, but it was causing havoc with his injury.

He stopped in a doorway to swallow more painkillers, almost choking as he didn't have any water to wash them down.

Ahead, they paused, and Ramirez answered his phone. He then looked around as if searching for a street name, indicating that the others do likewise.

What exactly did they have planned? Were they meeting someone? And why was it just the three of them?

The answer came five minutes later when Jay emerged from a side turning slightly ahead of the group, where the street opened out to a large square filled with bars and restaurants.

After a quick conversation, the group started looking around, concern evident on their faces. Had he been made already?

He slipped into the doorway of a cookware shop and used the reflection of a gift shop opposite to monitor the group. Use a little more caution going forward. He couldn't blow this. He needed to know their plan.

In the square, they took an outside table in front of Café Dani for tapas and beers. He couldn't remain in the shop much longer, but cover was scarce. He took a chance when they were busy with the arrival of their drinks and hobbled across the street to a better vantage point.

It was over an hour before a call on Jay's phone prompted their action. They rose, left some Euros on the plate and made their way across the open square directly towards him.

Again, the dread of being caught, but he had nowhere to go. He felt cornered.

Pushing back, he flattened himself into a small shadowed recess and remained unnoticed as they passed by.

After waiting a few beats, he exhaled and then followed.

Could this be an arranged meeting? The final set-up which allowed them to retrieve the gems? What was their plan?

Their destination was only three streets away, the Cathedral de Santa Maria.

The building was plain from the outside. A continuation of the surrounding grey stone, with two unremarkable bell towers protruding from the roof.

But once inside, the contrast was stark. A wealth of light flooded in from the many stained-glass windows set high into the walls. And whilst the height of the building wasn't notable from the outside amongst the four or five-storey residences surrounding it, the vast, airy space felt coolly welcoming once over the threshold. It had an intricately painted baby blue and gold leaf-embellished ceiling almost twenty metres above the milling tourists and an occasional local kneeling away their sins. But no sooner had he entered, he knew his mistake.

A crowd of waist-high school children swarmed around him loudly, asking questions in a language he couldn't grasp, other than the one repeated word Padre.

Any hope of entering this sacred space with subtlety was gone. He looked around, but the four were nowhere to be seen.

If this had been a ploy to shake him off, it had certainly worked. He stood centre stage for all to see whilst his quarries melted away. He felt a damned fool.

80

With Madeira struck from the itinerary, Tangier was their next port, so what options were left? Getting caught in the cathedral wearing a priest's collar was an amateur mistake, and he chided himself for being drawn into such an obvious trap. Maybe he'd underestimated them? Then again, it's only ever about the outcome, so maybe not so much. They clearly had to return to the ship, so he'd been there waiting for them.

Two days later, they docked at the northern-most port of Africa an hour ahead of schedule. Five-thirty, just as the sun began its climb from the horizon into the open sky. And whilst a few quayside stalls had been erected before dawn, many were yet to be readied for the first of the disembarking passengers when the ship's doors opened at eight o'clock.

He sipped coffee from a bone china cup and sank back into his deck chair situated on A Deck, waiting.

*****

Terry the Fence looked to his brother Mikey,

'Will you grab the other end of this gazebo thing before I thump you? It ain't easy doing this on your own you know.'

'I'm finishing my pitta. Hold steady a moment will you?'

'How on earth I agreed to you coming along I'll never know. Just don't cock anything up.'

'You're all heart, must tell Mum when I'm back, she'll be so pleased.'

'Shut up you runt. Pull your weight or I'll slap you.'

They got the freestanding shelter up easily once the two of them worked together. Within half an hour their quayside market stall was starting to take shape.

'No, don't sit down on the first piece of furniture you've unloaded, cop hold of this will you?'

Terry slid a substantial iron-framed table from the back of the rental van until it was on the edge of the vehicle. Mikey pulled himself out of the chair and grabbed the end of the table. Both of them lowering it to the ground once inside the portable gazebo.

'Remember, don't under any circumstances sell this, or the matching chair set, to anyone but Jay or Ramirez. In fact, don't sell anything to anyone without asking me first, that way you won't cock it up.'

'I'm not a complete idiot.'

'I wouldn't quite agree with that, now help me with this lounger will you?'

*****

He had to exercise more caution this time, so ensured he was first in line for disembarkation. The tap, tap, tap of his cane reminded him how conspicuous he was, as he made his way down the gangway and onto the quayside. His head felt raw under the damned wig.

'Morning, Father,' an officer greeted, handing him a boarding card for his return. He smiled and pocketed it, eager to gain a little distance from the ship and find a concealed spot to observe from.

But his haste did not mean that he missed a clue so obvious it practically shouted at him.

There, not twenty yards from the gangway, was a Luton van sporting the livery of a South London rental firm. He shook his head at such a basic oversight on behalf of Terry's brother and concluded the way things would play out without the need to watch it happen. A glance at the wares being unloaded from the back of the van gave him all the information he would need for his next move.

He changed his plan for the day and headed straight for the terminal building.

Once through to the other side, an assault on his senses commenced as the pungent, dusty mayhem of a Moroccan morning hit him. He glanced around to get his bearings, politely refused the help of several locals wanting to show him the city, for a small fee of course, and went in search of fresh pastries and a well-brewed pot of mint tea.

He returned three hours later refreshed and relaxed. And once back on the quayside, he gave the pair of Englishmen's stall a wide berth as fresh eyes may yet reveal his true identity.

Instead, he made his way to the ship's loading area, where one of the porters was organising and labelling the goods passengers had purchased that were due to go in the hold.

'Young man,' he began, pulling a fifty-pound note from his wallet and pushing it into the top pocket of the lad's waistcoat, 'my friends in cabin E34 have bought some furniture, and being very religious have asked me to bless it for good luck.'

The lad looked sceptical, but the red banknote was helping his belief in the pastor's yarn.

'I wonder if you could let me know the location in the hold where it might be?'

'Oh that's easy father. Each passenger's stuff they've bought goes onto a pallet and their cabin number is stamped on it. Once inside, each row represents a passenger deck and then they're put in number order. So A Deck is the first row, and the stuff for cabin A1 is at the front with each number getting higher the further back it goes. So E34 is fourth row, and about a third of the way back.'

'Bless you my child, you've been very informative.'

'But you can't go in there, its crew only I'm afraid.'

'Oh not to worry, I'm sure now I know the location I can send it my prayers from afar.'

He tipped his hat and made his way back towards the gangway, leaning heavily on his cane as his lower body had begun screaming with the pain over an hour before. He reached into his white blazer for the reassuring feel of the boarding card and the knowledge that this charade was finally near its climax.

81

There was a gentle knock on the door.

'Oui, open,' Pascal said. Jay and Ramirez walked in.

'Moment of truth, which one of you losers would like the glory of revealing our beautiful treasure, me hearties?'

'Grow up Jay, seriously?' Candy said.

She went over to the porthole and looked out to the grey glow of the moonlit Mediterranean. Dawn was only a couple of hours away, Monaco shortly after that.

Jay glared at Pascal as he set to work with a screwdriver on the hide. Three minutes later, there was a staccato groan as the woodwork gave way to reveal the cavity.

'What the…?' Ramirez said as he'd peered inside.

'It's empty,' Pascal said. 'Weren't there supposed to be laundry sacks full of loot in here?'

'Get out of the way you idiots,' Jay said, shouldering his way past them to check for himself. Their report had been accurate, just two of the unused gas cylinders inside.

He reeled at the thought of a mistake, but the hide really was empty. Well, almost. There was just a handwritten envelope addressed to him. He snatched it up from the dusty floor and tore it open.

If you're reading this, I was correct in assuming that you'd double-cross me. By now, you know I put my plan B into operation from the beginning, way back in China, when you started throwing your ego around, telling everyone you were going to be number one. Well guess again.

So, during the raid, whilst everyone was busy delivering their loot to the cabin marked out by the two laundry carts, I had correctly presumed that none of you would actually check the cabin number. Because the carts were sat outside a completely different one.

Think of the Mirror house, such a simple deception, but it gave me the idea. So, by all means, Jay, take apart every cabin on E Deck and eventually you might find your reward. But I think you'll make so much noise doing it, you'll be in a long-term prison cell before you hit pay dirt.

If you hadn't double-crossed me, you'd know the correct cabin number before you boarded for the Mediterranean cruise. Your mistake, but I always have a plan B, and here it is.

Have fun searching, but there really is no point. You'll never find it.

His world was collapsing, senses numb except for the tension of his guts churning in shock and anger.

'Concentrate,' he chided, but his head swam, eyes running over the page for alternate meaning, reading it twice, three times before the full impact exhausted his fuse and his aggression couldn't be contained.

'Fucker, absolute motherfucker!' he roared, punching the wall and then ripping the lampshade from its socket and hurling it across the room.

'What about next door, the other hide?' Pascal said.

'We could check, but probably just as empty.' Candy said, the resignation in her voice evident. 'Plus, it still has passengers inside.'

'Sod it,' slightly calmer. 'Yeah, let's go,' Jay said. He looked inside the hide once more, where he found a few of their old tools and a roll of duct tape. 'Tape the bastards up. Let's get on with it.'

'Really?' Ramirez said. 'It's pretty unlikely there's anything there given Scott's note.'

'Forget Scott, this is my operation now.'

'And it's going so well…'

'Fuck you, Ramirez.'

'No, fuck you Jay, this has all gone to hell because of you. I don't need much more of a reason to snap your neck.'

'Yeah well, big man. If I want your opinion, I'll give it to you.'

'You are this close.' Ramirez held two fingers a centimetre apart in Jay's face.

'Whatever.'

'I agree,' Candy said. 'Although it's occupied, we've got nothing to lose now.'

Ramirez snatched the duct tape from Jay. 'C'mon Pascal, let's get this done.'

*****

The priest listened intently. Although muffled through the wall, it sounded like a South American voice, so had to be Ramirez.

'As I thought, a laundry sack that isn't even half-full and now we've added assault to the rap sheet with those guys on the bed. Or are you going to kill them too?'

Jay shrugged.

'That's the sack I found after the raid was over,' Pascal said. 'In the wobbly cart.'

The priest leaned against the wall as best he could, glass pressed to his ear, hip feeling like it was on fire.

'I'm done, done with you, done with your petty jealousy and lousy planning. I'll take my handful and I'm gone,' Ramirez said to Jay. 'I'm heading to the bar to douse the flames that might engulf you if I have to spend another second in your company. Pascal, you coming?'

He didn't hear a reply, but the sound of multiple footsteps past his door confirmed that it was only Jay and Candy who remained in the cabin.

At first, it was just shouting, mostly Jay, but the argument became more animated.

When to intervene? That was the question. But when a scream penetrated the air, followed by another, he decided it was time. He grabbed his cane and headed out.

'Leave her alone,' he shouted once their door had given way under his shoulder.

Jay crouched above Candy's fallen body, his fist drawn back, and a look of panic clear in her eyes.

'Hit her again, and I'll kill you,' he said, charging into the room.

'I'm an atheist, do your worst.' But Jay held back at the shock of who the man was.

'No, it can't be.'

Without his wig, or false beard, the ruse was over. Taking advantage of Jay's shock, he launched an attack with angry fists. Back and forth the blows went, a left hook from Jay crunching a tooth loose and freeing some blood into his mouth. He spat it in Jay's face before wrapping his hands around the man's throat. They went down, rolling back and forth on the cabin floor until Scott managed to pin Jay down.

'Didn't you know. Ghosts always come back in white?'

'You're dead, I shot you,' Jay rasped as Scott's hands closed tighter, pressing Jay's head deeper into the carpet.

'Like usual, Jay, you didn't do it properly. You shot me in the hip, you idiot.'

'But how the–' a flash of movement startled Scott, followed by a loud crunch. The moderate heel of Candy's shoe pierced Jay's eyeball and the sole smacked into his cheek. He convulsed, writhed around and then his animation faded to nothing.

Scott looked up. The shock evident on Candy's face at what she'd done. He rose to his feet and drew his arms gently around her.

'Have I killed him?'

'I hope so. Cockroach.'

She sobbed into his shoulder, muted at first, but then deeper heaves of emotional relief.

It took a moment for Scott to register what he was looking at over her shoulder. An elderly man and woman were tied up on the bed, eyes wide with fear and mouths sealed with duct tape. He winked, and they visibly relaxed.

After a few moments, Candy's sobbing eased. She pulled back to look at him, and drew a breath through her congested nose.

'How? How are you still alive?'

'When I went overboard, the lifeboat I'd been lowering away was only halfway down. I landed on it. I guess it got lowered fully sometime later. I don't know who by.

'I was picked up three days later by a trawler, and taken to a small monastery in Greenland. They got the bullet out and nursed me back to health.

'I managed to get to Newfoundland on another boat, and then stowed away on a container ship headed for Liverpool.'

'But everything else, how did you–'

Scott noticed the vigorous head shaking of the bound man a moment too late. He turned and just caught sight of Jay, pouncing up from the floor. A demented scream filled the room, and then a dazzling flash of light shot through his brain as something hard impacted his head. He went down on one knee, everything blurry, and then felt himself keel over as consciousness left him.

*****

Jay walloped Candy on the side of the head with the same weighty lamp straight after Scott went down. She crumpled to the floor and lay next to him in a mess of limbs.

'I suggest you two keep quiet.' He said, pointing the lamp at the elderly couple. They nodded enthusiastically.

He checked his face in the mirror. Probably not the best idea, as the sight revolted him. His right eye was mostly missing, just a cavity with some whitish sludge at the bottom of the socket. It oozed a clear liquid mixed with blood which ran down his cheek.

Strangely, he felt very little pain. And with just his left eye, he looked at his pink-stained skull through the empty socket with fascination. He pressed his index finger inside and rubbed the bone. He then tasted the liquid oozing from the wound. Sweet but metallic. He turned to the horrified couple.

'Now don't go wandering off, I'll be back soon. Pinkie promise.'

He balled up some toilet roll, pressed it into the socket, and then drew one of the man's knotted ties around his head to hold it in place.

Outside, the corridor was empty. Not that he cared, but he made his way to the aft staircase anyway as it was usually less busy.

Once there, he looked at the directory to locate the infirmary. F Deck, one floor down.

'Perfect. Should have just the kind of drugs and wheels I'm looking for.'

82

Scott slowly came around. The throbbing in his head felt like chilli sauce had replaced the blood in his veins.

Everything was fuzzy, a mild concussion, but the thought of Candy at Jay's mercy brought him unsteadily to his feet.

A note on the floor. It was the one he'd written to Jay, but it now had something scribbled on the back.

Call me with the location of the loot, or she dies. You have until midday.

He tossed it aside and looked towards the two still tied and gagged on the bed.

'Sorry, this isn't going to be pleasant.' He ripped the tape from the man's mouth and then his wife's. They both yelped but nothing more.

'How long ago did they leave?'

'Just minutes, he injected her with something and put her in a wheelchair.' The woman said. Scott slit the tape binding the man's wrists and left the cabin.

He made straight for the disembarkation gangway, and from it, he spotted Jay in the distance. His brother looked unsteady and pushed a wheelchair erratically along the quayside with no regard for anyone in his path. Presumably, it was Candy slumped in the seat, and one of her arms hung over the side.

Scott forced his way down the ramp and set about catching the cockroach as fast as his damaged hip, and supportive cane, would allow.

Jay had a fifty-metre advantage but was unaware of Scott's pursuit, so he didn't appear to be in a hurry.

By contrast, Scott charged along the quayside, desperate to make up ground. But with twenty metres to go, Jay glanced over his shoulder. His one-eyed face gave a burst of surprise, and he upped his pace.

The gap grew to thirty metres, then forty. Scott pounded his cane into the ground as forcefully as he could, his hip screaming with pain, but Jay steadily edged away, taking Candy with him.

At the end of the quay, the road forked into two. The right led down to a square lined with cafes and bars, the left into a tunnel which bored into the hillside. Jay chose left and entered the tunnel.

'One bad decision after another,' Scott said under his breath, the gap now closing again.

The pavement section of the tunnel disappeared almost immediately, forcing both of them onto the main road.

Horns blared as Ferraris and Bentleys swerved around them. Stranded, they continued into the oncoming traffic at the pace of a lame but furious mule.

The tunnel grew darker, lit only by the flashes of passing headlights, and Scott feared he might lose them with his decreased pace. The pain was almost unbearable, his body screamed for mercy. But then, a light glowed from around the next bend, and gave him hope.

When he rounded the curve, a large multi-storey car park came into view. A dead-end, and Jay had no escape.

Scott continued up the road, leaning on his cane, and saw his brother standing by a wall near the car park entrance. He glanced furtively back at the tunnel whilst he jabbed the wall. It wasn't until Jay pushed the wheelchair into the wall that Scott realised it was actually a lift cut into the rock face.

'Nooo.'

He arrived several moments later, and it was then his turn to repeatedly push the button.

After an agonising wait, the torture continued as a group of chatty Japanese tourists slowly exited. Thankfully there was only one option. He pressed the button.

He exited onto Avenue Saint-Martin. Jay had stretched out a fifty-metre advantage. But he now appeared to be having difficulty pushing the wheelchair. He swerved left and right in his bid to escape, scattering tourists. Scott put it down to the increase in altitude. Candy's heel must have damaged Jay's sinuses.

They were high above the Med now and passed the entrance to Monaco's prison. The view over the ocean was breathtaking, but the building sent a shiver down Scott's spine.

Ahead, Jay took a left into the Gardens Saint-Martin, a clifftop sanctuary of footpaths that threaded along the rock face overlooking Port Hercule.

Suddenly he faltered, upending the wheelchair.

*****

Sod this, thought Jay. It was all about getting away now, fight to see another day 'n all that.

He left her where she lay and tried to run. But within two steps, he knew something was seriously wrong.

No balance. Maybe losing that eye had an effect, or could it be a concussion? Whatever, the wheelchair had given him stability, so best use it.

He went back and righted it, leaving Candy unconscious on the ground. With a shove, he continued pushing the empty chair up the hill. His head felt as dizzy as hell, but he chanced a look over his shoulder.

That brother was still gaining on him.

*****

Scott took a few vital seconds to stop and check she was okay. Then a more primal urge forced him on. He was almost within striking distance, ten metres at most.

Keep the pressure up, even though the pain in his hip had become almost intolerable. Close Jay down one metre at a time, the shrinking distance giving all the incentive he needed.

Nine, eight, seven. Almost close enough to grasp.

They left the gardens as the path opened out onto the battlements of the palace, even higher now, over one hundred and fifty metres above the marina with old cannons facing over the cliff edge as a warning to potential invaders.

Jay tripped, stumbled and went down. It was all the incentive Scott needed. He pounced, punching and thrashing his brother in a fury of fists. But almost as quickly as it had started, his power diminished and the adrenaline gave way to exhaustion.

Jay gained the upper hand and grabbed Scott's cane. He drew it back and began to beat him with it, but the tables quickly turned when Scott got a hold of it. He wrenched it from Jay's grasp, pressed the concealed button to release the handle, and drew from it a long steel spike. He pulled it up and then thrust it at Jay's heart. Shockingly, it bounced off and out of his hands, skittering down a gulley and out of reach.

'That copper's lucky cigarette case,' Jay said as a smile crossed his face. Scott raged with fury, punching and grappling with his brother. He had to eliminate this parasite.

Then, a punch landed on Jay's belt buckle. Pain exploded right through his hand, but the flash of an idea came with it. He reached back down, unbuckled it, and quickly drew it through the loops until clear. He then whipped it up and around Jay's neck in a lightning-fast move. Then the tongue went back through the buckle and he drew it tight, really tight before Jay could react. The leather cut into his windpipe and his eyes bulged. His hands shot to his neck in a vain attempt to loosen it.

'You couldn't stick to my plan, could you?' Scott said as Jay kicked and bucked. His face becoming swollen and purple. 'Even though I spelled it out clearly enough in that notebook I left you to find.' He re-gripped the leather. 'Well, I did. I followed the plan,' he pulled the belt tighter still. 'I went to the hold last night and put all our lovely loot inside the table and chairs you pretended to buy from Terry the Fence. You must know it Jay, it's the set sitting on the dock right now with your name on it. I stuck to the plan, Jay, because I knew you wouldn't. And look where it's got you.'

Scott drew himself up and dragged his panicking brother across the flagstones towards the battlements. There, he hauled him up by the throat and then tossed him over the edge. But he kept a very tight hold of the belt. His knuckles whitened at the strain of holding his brother up, but he braced his shoulder against the battlement wall.

'If you'd stuck to my plan, you'd be made now. But you thought you knew better. Now you'll hang like the traitor you are. You even look like a bloody pirate with that eye patch.'

He hauled a few inches of leather up and then bashed one of the belt holes onto an iron spike set vertically into the battlement wall. After a second to regain his breath, he stood and looked over. Below him Jay hanged, mostly inanimate now, choking to death with his trousers around his ankles.

83

At four o'clock, Pascal left the kitchen and stood amongst the tables and chairs outside his café, taking a deep breath of Parisian air.

He looked up to see the familiar silhouette of the Gare du Nord and the shadow it cast, then down the avenue to the bicycles chained to railings and the wooden tobacconist's huts.

Autumn had arrived, and the trees were looking sparse. But at least the sky was clear.

He placed his tray onto an outside table and cleared the plate, cutlery and cup. His girlfriend Simone had served whoever had sat there, but now they had gone, just an English copy of The Times remained. Poking out of the first page was a scribbled note on a gold-edged napkin.

Be at Hotel George V, midday tomorrow, room 223.

Okay, what's this? A set-up? An opportunity?

There was only one way to find out.

*****

Ramirez finished his ride. Thirty-seven miles of hills and countryside, yet he'd hardly broken a sweat. Well, maybe up that hill towards Petworth.

He unclipped as he eased up to his pickup and lifted the carbon-fibre triathlon bike into the bed. His helmet followed, and then he was inside the cab, taking a long shot of VitaPro from his water bottle.

There was a ticket under his windshield wiper. A parking ticket? He got out and pulled it from under the wiper.

Be at Hotel George V, Paris, midday tomorrow. Room 223.

A job? A girlfriend? A set up?

One way to find out.

*****

Detective Rossi, glad you're finally back on duty,' the Chief Inspector said.

'And as you've been off for a couple of months, we've gone a little cold on the Sharpe case. Go and see Travers on the fourth floor, get up to speed with this social media fraud thing and report back to me next week.

'Well done by the way on the winning goal, for what it's worth.'

'Thanks, Boss.'

'And don't call me Boss, ever. Is that clear?'

84

Ramirez approached the imposing building, fronted with three arched entrances that rose fifteen feet high, each decorated with elegant black and gold scrolled ironwork. The name George V was picked out in gold, circled in the centre arch.

A doorman in a greatcoat tipped his top hat with a grey gloved hand as Ramirez entered. Inside, his footsteps echoed off of the marble entrance hall, and he took a second to take in his surroundings. There was a reception desk, a courtyard boasting a pink and white marble floor, a couple of elevators and flowers everywhere—even some palm trees. He went to the stairs and jogged up.

Room 223, as expected, was unlocked. He pushed the door and entered the suite. Its décor, a mix of whites, yellows and pistachio, wouldn't have looked out of place in Hampton Court Palace.

He'd barely had time to check behind the curtains when there was a noise behind him.

'Pascal,' he said as the door opened and the Frenchman walked in, 'what are you doing here?'

'I receive a note, you?'

'Same.'

'What's this all about?' he shrugged.

'I don't know, but I'm liking it a whole lot less right now. You armed?'

'Non.'

'Shit. Help me check things out. I've not looked around fully yet.'

Pascal walked into the suite fully now and headed towards the bedroom.

There was another noise at the door. Pascal stopped walking and turned around.

*****

Terry the Fence relaxed at a small table in L'Orangerie, a beautiful courtyard filled with pink and white floral bouquets, iron tables and chairs, which weren't the most comfortable, mind, but did have a perfect view of the hotel's entrance lobby.

He had a copy of The Times clasped in his outstretched hands, and an empty coffee cup sat on the table. He glanced over the top of the paper to see the Marine arrive first, then the pasty Frenchman a few minutes later. The latter took the lift to the second floor, lazy bastard.

He finished his coffee, folded his paper, and then rose from his chair. After tucking more than a few Euros under the saucer, he crossed the foyer to the staircase.

On the second floor, he paused to look out of the large window at the city around him. He was growing fonder of it, but he'd still say it was a shithole if you asked.

Along the corridor, and then he was at number 223. It was time. He reached inside his jacket, took a breath, and pushed the door open.

*****

Ramirez turned towards the door. He was unarmed, vulnerable and suddenly feeling very stupid.

'You.'

'Yes son, me,' Terry said. 'Have you looked in the bedroom?'

'No,' Pascal and Ramirez said in unison.

'Well, maybe you should have. By the way,' Terry drew his hand from inside his jacket, 'these are for you.'

Ramirez tensed. But relaxed when Terry held out two envelopes. One addressed to Pascal, the other him.

'Okay, what next?' Ramirez asked.

'Go take a look in the bedroom. I'm done, can't wait to get some clean air, so I'll leave the pair of you to it.'

Ramirez held out his hand. Terry took it but pulled him in for a hug. He did the same with Pascal and then left without further word.

The two accomplices went to the bedroom. Inside, on the king-sized bed, were two large bags.

Pascal's eyes widened, but Ramirez showed more caution.

'This could go both ways you know, loose ends 'n all.'

'You only live once,' Pascal said.

'So why didn't Terry hang around?'

Pascal shrugged, 'Busy?'

'Let's just be a little cautious.'

Ramirez walked over to the bed and probed the zip for some kind of trigger. Pascal came alongside, shouted, 'Vive le France!' and ripped the zip open.

An explosion of notes as hundred-dollar bills burst out over the bed, flooding onto the floor with Ziploc bags full of diamonds and small ingots of gold.

*****

The glossy black Lamborghini Urus SUV sat idling outside a tall, glass building. Its frontage was set back just sixty metres from Lake Geneva. A security guard wearing a crested cap and a Smith and Wesson continued to look alert four hours into his shift, which was more of a comfort than an obstacle. Scott turned to Candy.

'Are you ready for this?'

'Of course, I'm always ready.'

'I'm being serious.'

'So am I.'

Scott checked his old Rolex.

'Nearly time. Remember, go easy, and don't show too much emotion. It'll be difficult, but I've got faith in you.'

'I know, enough of the lecture,' she smiled. Scott's phone chimed. He glanced down to look at it just as the large glass door behind the security guard opened.

'You're on,' Scott said, glancing up again, 'take your time.'

He looked down to read the message properly as Candy opened the car door and climbed out.

'Who's the text from?' she asked.

'Terry. Parcels and invitations delivered. Says he's had an idea for the perfect job. LA, of all places.'

'Great,' she said. 'Mum could do with a holiday,' and then rushed across the car park to where her sister Becky was shakily pulling herself out of her wheelchair.

If you've had fun, visit me at:
alanhartwell.com

From the author.

Thank you for taking the time to read Buoyant. It has been quite some journey to write, so I hope you've enjoyed coming along. The original voyage of Titanic in 1912 is such a powerful story and has touched so many lives that it would be a disservice to not acknowledge the enormous loss left in its wake. No other crossing has fuelled so much speculation, interest and analysis. Books, both fiction and non-fiction, films, stage plays and large-scale exhibitions have all come from the tragedy. And I have watched, read, travelled to and absorbed myself in each one of these mediums for over seven years in order to bring you the most accurate backdrop possible for the successor to the most famous ship in history.

This novel was inspired by the announcement of Australian billionaire Clive Palmer, that he intends to build a full-size fully functional replica of Titanic and put her into service.

'How do I get a ticket?' was my first thought.

'Imagine the calibre of people an event like this would attract,' was my second.

'Imagine George Clooney and Brad Pitt dusting off their Ocean's Eleven characters to perform the slickest heist in history on that maiden voyage,' and the story was born.

I have endeavoured to keep the details of the ship as close as possible to the original. However, there have been some exceptions in the name of credible fiction. One such example is the cabin services. Titanic buffs the world over no doubt rolled their eyes at me placing these inside the wall cavities as they would have most likely come up through the floor on the original ship. Also, the second class cabins would have had bunk beds as opposed to a double bed and the couch which Jay found himself relegated to. This layout would have been reserved for first class on the original, but made for a better story to have him sulking in the soft furnishings.

Another notable deviation from the original ship was the elevators which accompanied the Grand Staircase. These only went as high as A Deck, not the Boat Deck as they have been described here. The likely cause is the mechanics to operate them would have been in the area above the shaft in 1912, so there wasn't the room for it to reach the top deck without the workings being above the ship's roof Line, and therefore draw a scowl from Mr Andrews. For Scott's team to get the gas cylinders overboard with this restriction, they would have needed to haul them either to the rear of the ship or up a flight of stairs. Neither option being particularly good for story pace so an extra level on the lift shaft solved the problem. If there are any other technical errors in the design of my fictional ship, (like the fully enclosed Bridge…) they are there for similar plot reasons.

I, like the fictional Scott, studied the blueprints of the original long and hard to come up with not only a credible plan, but also an idea of the time it would take to perform such a heist. Therefore, I apologise in advance to Clive Palmer, if this gives someone a little less scrupulous than myself the blueprint to their next heist. Sorry about that.

Writing a novel seems like an incredibly lonely thing to do, yet this story would be half as rich if it wasn't for those who have helped me along the way. So, a massive thank you must go to my early readers; James Lowe, Mandy Stevens, Karla Fetrow, Christine Lawrence, Clare Campbell and Jackie Green.

Also, a special thanks to Matt Wingett for his support, and James Cameron for creating the best research tool I could have ever dreamed of. I must have watched the film on frame-by-frame twenty times to gather the wealth of information and ambience it contains. Thanks also to the extremely helpful staff at Titanic Belfast, especially Rob the tour guide who tolerated my endless questions with patience and grace. Thanks to Tim Maltins for his tenacious research, Ken Marschall for the incredibly detailed pictures depicting the interior layout of the original ship in his book 'Inside the Titanic' which was invaluable in my plotting of the heist. Thanks also to Joanna Penn for her insights into the whole publishing process, and Xavier Comas for his help in designing a cover that really pops.

Finally, thank you to you, the reader, because without you I couldn't share these crazy ideas in my head without being taken off somewhere soft and quiet for a nice pacifying injection…

If you've had fun, visit me at:
alanhartwell.com